The
Shiloh
Collection

Books by Phyllis Reynolds Naylor

Witch's Sister
Witch Water
The Witch Herself
Walking Through the Dark
How I Came to Be a Writer
How Lazy Can You Get?
Eddie, Incorporated
All Because I'm Older
Shadows on the Wall
Faces in the Water
Footprints at the Window
The Boy with the Helium Head
A String of Chances
The Solomon System
Bernie Magruder and the Case of the Big Stink
Night Cry
Old Sadie and the Christmas Bear
The Dark of the Tunnel
The Agony of Alice
The Keeper
Bernie Magruder and the Disappearing Bodies
The Year of the Gopher
Beetles, Lightly Toasted
Maudie in the Middle
One of the Third Grade Thonkers
Alice in Rapture, Sort Of
Keeping a Christmas Secret
Bernie Magruder and the Haunted Hotel
Send No Blessings
Reluctantly Alice
King of the Playground
Shiloh
All but Alice
Josie's Troubles
The Grand Escape
Alice in April

The
Shiloh
Collection

Three novels by
Phyllis Reynolds Naylor

Shiloh

Shiloh Season

Saving Shiloh

ATHENEUM BOOKS FOR YOUNG READERS

New York London Toronto Sydney

Shiloh copyright © 1991 by Phyllis Reynolds Naylor
Shiloh Season copyright © 1996 by Phyllis Reynolds Naylor
Saving Shiloh copyright © 1997 by Phyllis Reynolds Naylor
This edition specially printed for Borders Books by Simon & Schuster, Inc.

2004 Borders Books
Book design by Daniel Roode
The text for this book is set in Goudy.
Manufactured in the United States of America
First Edition
03 04 05 06 07 08 MC 9 8 7 6 5 4 3 2 1
ISBN 0-689-87393-X
These titles were originally published individually by Atheneum Books for Young Readers.

The Shiloh
Collection

SHILOH

SHILOH

by Phyllis Reynolds Naylor

Atheneum Books for Young Readers

Atheneum Books for Young Readers
An imprint of Simon & Schuster Children's Publishing Division
1230 Avenue of the Americas
New York, New York 10020

Book design by Eliza Green
Printed in the United States of America

22 24 26 28 30 29 27 25 23

Library of Congress Cataloging-in-Publication Data
Naylor, Phyllis Reynolds.
Shiloh / by Phyllis Reynolds Naylor.—1st ed.   p.   cm.
Summary: When he finds a lost beagle in the hills behind his West Virginia
home, Marty tries to hide it from his family and the dog's real owner, a
mean-spirited man known to shoot deer out of season and to mistreat his
dogs.
ISBN 0-689-31614-3
[1. Dogs—Fiction.   2. Animals—Treatment—Fiction.   3. West
Virginia—Fiction.]   I. Title.   PZ7.N24Sq   1991
[Fic]—dc20   90-603

To Frank and Trudy Madden
and a dog named Clover

SHILOH

CHAPTER 1

The day Shiloh come, we're having us a big Sunday dinner. Dara Lynn's dipping bread in her glass of cold tea, the way she likes, and Becky pushes her beans up over the edge of her plate in her rush to get 'em down.

Ma gives us her scolding look. "Just once in my life," she says, "I'd like to see a bite of food go direct from the dish into somebody's mouth without a detour of any kind."

She's looking at me when she says it, though. It isn't that I don't like fried rabbit. Like it fine. I just don't want to bite down on buckshot, is all, and I'm checking each piece.

"I looked that rabbit over good, Marty, and you won't find any buckshot in that thigh," Dad says, buttering his bread. "I shot him in the neck."

Somehow I wish he hadn't said that. I push the meat from one side of my plate to the other, through the sweet potatoes and back again.

"Did it die right off?" I ask, knowing I can't eat at all unless it had.

"Soon enough."

"You shoot its head clean off?" Dara Lynn asks. She's like that.

Dad chews real slow before he answers. "Not quite," he says, and goes on eating.

Which is when I leave the table.

The best thing about Sundays is we eat our big meal at noon. Once you get your belly full, you can walk all over West Virginia before you're hungry again. Any other day, you start out after dinner, you've got to come back when it's dark.

I take the .22 rifle Dad had given me in March on my eleventh birthday and set out up the road to see what I can shoot. Like to find me an apple hanging way out on a branch, see if I can bring it down. Line up a few cans on a rail fence and shoot 'em off. Never shoot at anything moving, though. Never had the slightest wish.

We live high up in the hills above Friendly, but hardly anybody knows where that is. Friendly's near Sistersville, which is halfway between Wheeling and Parkersburg. Used to be, my daddy told me, Sistersville was one of the best places you could live in the whole state. You ask *me* the best place to live, I'd say right where we are, a little four-room house with hills on three sides.

Afternoon is my second-best time to go up in

the hills, though; morning's the best, especially in summer. Early, *early* morning. On one morning I saw three kinds of animals, not counting cats, dogs, frogs, cows, and horses. Saw a groundhog, saw a doe with two fawns, and saw a gray fox with a reddish head. Bet his daddy was a gray fox and his ma was a red one.

My favorite place to walk is just across this rattly bridge where the road curves by the old Shiloh schoolhouse and follows the river. River to one side, trees the other—sometimes a house or two.

And this particular afternoon, I'm about half-way up the road along the river when I see something out of the corner of my eye. Something moves. I look, and about fifteen yards off, there's this shorthaired dog—white with brown and black spots—not making any kind of noise, just slinking along with his head down, watching me, tail between his legs like he's hardly got the right to breathe. A beagle, maybe a year or two old.

I stop and the dog stops. Looks like he's been caught doing something awful, when I can tell all he really wants is to follow along beside me.

"Here, boy," I say, slapping my thigh.

Dog goes down on his stomach, groveling about in the grass. I laugh and start over toward him. He's got an old worn-out collar on, probably older than he

13

is. Bet it belonged to another dog before him. "C'mon, boy," I say, putting out my hand.

The dog gets up and backs off. He don't even whimper, like he's lost his bark.

Something really hurts inside you when you see a dog cringe like that. You know somebody's been kicking at him. Beating on him, maybe.

"It's okay, boy," I say, coming a little closer, but still he backs off.

So I just take my gun and follow the river. Every so often I look over my shoulder and there he is, the beagle. I stop; he stops. I can see his ribs—not real bad—but he isn't plumped out or anything.

There's a broken branch hanging from a limb out over the water, and I'm wondering if I can bring it down with one shot. I raise my gun, and then I think how the sound might scare the dog off. I decide I don't want to shoot my gun much that day.

It's a slow river. You walk beside it, you figure it's not even moving. If you stop, though, you can see leaves and things going along. Now and then a fish jumps—big fish. Bass, I think. Dog's still trailing me, tail tucked in. Funny how he don't make a sound.

Finally I sit on a log, put my gun at my feet, and wait. Back down the road, the dog sits, too. Sits right in the middle of it, head on his paws.

"Here, boy!" I say again, and pat my knee.

He wiggles just a little, but he don't come.

Maybe it's a she-dog.

"Here, girl!" I say. Dog still don't come.

I decide to wait the dog out, but after three or four minutes on the log, it gets boring and I start off again. So does the beagle.

Don't know where you'd end up if you followed the river all the way. Heard somebody say it curves about, comes back on itself, but if it didn't and I got home after dark, I'd get a good whopping. So I always go as far as the ford, where the river spills across the path, and then I head back.

When I turn around and the dog sees me coming, he goes off into the woods. I figure that's the last I'll see of the beagle, and I get halfway down the road again before I look back. There he is. I stop. He stops. I go. He goes.

And then, hardly thinking on it, I whistle.

It's like pressing a magic button. The beagle comes barreling toward me, legs going lickety-split, long ears flopping, tail sticking up like a flagpole. This time, when I put out my hand, he licks all my fingers and jumps up against my leg, making little yelps in his throat. He can't get enough of me, like I'd been saying no all along and now I'd said yes, he could come. It's a he-dog, like I'd thought.

"Hey, boy! You're really somethin' now, ain't

you?" I'm laughing as the beagle makes circles around me. I squat down and the dog licks my face, my neck. Where'd he learn to come if you whistled, to hang back if you didn't?

I'm so busy watching the dog I don't even notice it's started to rain. Don't bother me. Don't bother the dog, neither. I'm looking for the place I first saw him. Does he live here? I wonder. Or the house on up the road? Each place we pass I figure he'll stop—somebody come out and whistle, maybe. But nobody comes out and the dog don't stop. Keeps coming even after we get to the old Shiloh schoolhouse. Even starts across the bridge, tail going like a propeller. He licks my hand every so often to make sure I'm still there—mouth open like he's smiling. He *is* smiling.

Once he follows me across the bridge, though, and on past the gristmill, I start to worry. Looks like he's fixing to follow me all the way to our house. I'm in trouble enough coming home with my clothes wet. My ma's mama died of pneumonia, and we don't ever get the chance to forget it. And now I got a dog with me, and we were never allowed to have pets.

If you can't afford to feed 'em and take 'em to the vet when they're sick, you've no right taking 'em in, Ma says, which is true enough.

I don't say a word to the beagle the rest of the way home, hoping he'll turn at some point and go back. The dog keeps coming.

I get to the front stoop and say, "Go home, boy." And then I feel my heart squeeze up the way he stops smiling, sticks his tail between his legs again, and slinks off. He goes as far as the sycamore tree, lies down in the wet grass, head on his paws.

"Whose dog is that?" Ma asks when I come in.

I shrug. "Just followed me, is all."

"Where'd it pick up with you?" Dad asks.

"Up in Shiloh, across the bridge," I say.

"On the road by the river? Bet that's Judd Travers's beagle," says Dad. "He got himself another hunting dog a few weeks back."

"Judd got him a hunting dog, how come he don't treat him right?" I ask.

"How you know he don't?"

"Way the dog acts. Scared to pee, almost," I say.

Ma gives me a look.

"Don't seem to me he's got any marks on him," Dad says, studying him from our window.

Don't have to mark a dog to hurt him, I'm thinking.

"Just don't pay him any attention and he'll go away," Dad says.

"And get out of those wet clothes," Ma tells me. "You want to follow your grandma Slater to the grave?"

I change clothes, then sit down and turn on the TV, which only has two channels. On Sunday after-

17

noons, it's preaching and baseball. I watch baseball for an hour. Then I get up and sneak to the window. Ma knows what I'm about.

"That Shiloh dog still out there?" she asks.

I nod. He's looking at me. He sees me there at the window and his tail starts to thump. I name him Shiloh.

CHAPTER 2

Sunday-night supper is whatever's left from noon. If nothing's left over, Ma takes cold cornmeal mush, fries up big slabs, and we eat it with Karo syrup. But this night there's still rabbit. I don't want any, but I know Shiloh does.

I wonder how long I can keep pushing that piece of rabbit around my plate. Not very long, I discover.

"You going to eat that meat, or you just playing with it?" Dad asks. "If you don't want it, I'll take it for lunch tomorrow."

"I'll eat it," I say.

"Don't you be giving it to that dog," says Ma.

I take a tiny bite.

"What's the doggy going to *eat,* then?" asks Becky. She's three, which is four years younger than Dara Lynn.

"Nothing here, that's what," says Ma.

Becky and Dara Lynn look at Dad. Now I had *them* feeling sorry for the beagle, too. Sometimes girl-children get what they want easier than I do. But not this time.

19

"Dog's going right back across the river when we get through eating," says Dad. "If that's Judd's new dog, he probably don't have sense enough yet to find his way home again. We'll put him in the Jeep and drive him over."

Don't know what else I figured Dad to say. Do I really think he's going to tell me to wait till morning, and if the beagle's still here, we can keep him? I try all kinds of ways to figure how I could get that rabbit meat off my plate and into my pocket, but Ma's watching every move I make.

So I excuse myself and go outside and over to the chicken coop. It's off toward the back where Ma can't see. We keep three hens, and I take one of the two eggs that was in a nest and carry it out behind the bushes.

I whistle softly. Shiloh comes loping toward me. I crack the egg and empty it out in my hands. Hold my hands down low and Shiloh eats the egg, licking my hands clean afterward, then curling his tongue down between my fingers to get every little bit.

"Good boy, Shiloh," I whisper, and stroke him all over.

I hear the back screen slam, and Dad comes out on the stoop. "Marty?"

"Yeah?" I go around, Shiloh at my heels.

"Let's take that dog home now." Dad goes over

20

and opens the door of the Jeep. Shiloh puts his tail between his legs and just stands there, so I go around to the other side, get in, and whistle. Shiloh leaps up onto my lap, but he don't look too happy about it.

For the first time I have my arms around him. He feels warm, and when I stroke him, I can feel places on his body where he has ticks.

"Dog has ticks," I tell my dad.

"Judd'll take 'em off," Dad says.

"What if he don't?"

"It's his concern, Marty, not yours. It's not your dog. You keep to your own business."

I press myself against the back of the seat as we start down our bumpy dirt driveway toward the road. "I want to be a vet someday," I tell my dad.

"Hmm," he says.

"I want to be a traveling vet. The kind that has his office in a van and goes around to people's homes, don't make folks come to him. Read about it in a magazine at school."

"You know what you have to do to be a vet?" Dad asks.

"Got to go to school, I know that."

"You've got to have college training. Like a doctor, almost. Takes a lot of money to go to veterinary school."

My dream sort of leaks out like water in a paper

bag. "I could be a veterinarian's helper," I suggest, my second choice.

"You maybe could," says Dad, and points the Jeep up the road into the hills.

Dusk is settling in now. Still warm, though. A warm July night. Trees look dark against the red sky; lights coming on in a house here, another one there. I'm thinking how in any one of these houses there's probably somebody who would take better care of Shiloh than Judd Travers would. How come this dog had to be his?

The reason I don't like Judd Travers is a whole lot of reasons, not the least is that I was in the corner store once down in Friendly and saw Judd cheat Mr. Wallace at the cash register. Judd gives the man a ten and gets him to talking, then—when Mr. Wallace gives him change—says he give him a twenty.

I blink, like I can't believe Judd done that, and old Mr. Wallace is all confused. So I say, "No, I think he give you a ten."

Judd glares at me, whips out his wallet, and waves a twenty-dollar bill in front of my eye. "Whose picture's on this bill, boy?" he says.

"I don't know."

He gives me a look says, I thought so. "That's Andrew Jackson," he says. "I had two of 'em in my wallet when I walked in here, and now I only got one.

This here man's got the other, and I want my change."

Mr. Wallace, he's so flustered he just digs in his money drawer and gives Judd change for a twenty, and afterward I thought what did Andrew Jackson have to do with it? Judd's so fast-talking he can get away with anything. Don't know anybody who likes him much, but around here folks keep to their own business, like Dad says. In Tyler County that's important. Way it's always been, anyhow.

Another reason I don't like Judd Travers is he spits tobacco out the corner of his mouth, and if he don't like you—and he sure don't like me—he sees just how close he can spit to where you're standing. Third reason I don't like him is because he was at the fairgrounds last year same day we were, and seemed like everyplace I was, he was in front of me, blocking my view. Standin' in front of me at the mud bog, sittin' in front of me at the tractor pull, and risin' right up out of his seat at the Jorden Globe of Death Motorcycle Act so's I missed the best part.

Fourth reason I don't like him is because he kills deer out of season. He says he don't, but I seen him once just about dusk with a young buck strapped over the hood of his truck. He tells me the buck run in front of him on the road and he accidentally run over it, but I saw the bullet hole myself. If he got caught, he'd have to pay two hundred dollars, more than he's got in the bank, I'll bet.

We're in Shiloh now. Dad's crossing the bridge by the old abandoned gristmill, turning at the boarded-up school, and for the first time I can feel Shiloh's body begin to shake. He's trembling all over. I swallow. Try to say something to my dad and have to swallow again.

"How do you go about reporting someone who don't take care of his dog right?" I ask finally.

"Who you fixing to report, Marty?"

"Judd."

"If this dog's mistreated, he's only about one out of fifty thousand animals that is," Dad says. "Folks even bring 'em up here in the hills and let 'em out, figure they can live on rats and rabbits. Wouldn't be the first dog that wasn't treated right."

"But this one come to me to help him!" I insist. *"Knew* that's why he was following me. I got hooked on him, Dad, and I want to know he's treated right."

For the first time I can tell Dad's getting impatient with me. "Now you get that out of your head right now. If it's Travers's dog, it's no mind of ours *how* he treats it."

"What if it was a child?" I ask him, getting too smart for my own good. "If some kid was shaking like this dog is shaking, you wouldn't feel no pull for keeping an eye on him?"

"Marty," Dad says, and now his voice is just plumb tired. "This here's a dog, not a child, and it's not our dog. I want you to quit going on about it. Hear?"

I shut up then. Let my hands run over Shiloh's body like maybe everywhere I touch I can protect him somehow. We're getting closer to the trailer where Judd lives with his other dogs, and already they're barking up a storm, hearing Dad's Jeep come up the road.

Dad pulls over. "You want to let him out?" he says.

I shake my head hard. "I'm not lettin' him out here till I know for sure he belongs to Judd." I'm asking for a slap in the face, but Dad don't say anything, just gets out and goes up the boards Judd has laid out in place of a sidewalk.

Judd's at the door of his trailer already, in his undershirt, peering out.

"Looks like Ray Preston," he says, through the screen.

"How you doin', Judd?"

Judd comes out on the little porch he's built at the side of his trailer, and they stand there and talk awhile. Up here in the hills you hardly ever get down to business right off. First you say your howdys and then you talk about anything else but what you come for, and finally, when the mosquitoes start to bite, you say what's on your mind. But you always edge into it, not to offend.

I can hear little bits and pieces floating out over the yard. The rain . . . the truck . . . the tomatoes . . . the price of gasoline . . . and all the while Shiloh lays low in my lap, tail between his legs, shaking like a window blind in a breeze.

And then, the awful words: "Say, Judd, my boy was up here along the river this afternoon, and a beagle followed him home. Don't have any tags on his collar, but I'm remembering you got yourself another hunting dog, and wondered if he might be yours."

I'm thinking this is a bad mistake. Maybe it isn't Judd's at all, and he's such a liar he'd say it was, just to get himself still another animal to be mean to.

Judd hardly lets him finish; starts off across the muddy yard in his boots. "Sure as hell bet it is," he says. "Can't keep that coon dog home to save my soul. Every time I take him hunting, he runs off before I'm through. I been out all day with the dogs, and they all come back but him."

I can hear Judd's heavy footsteps coming around the side of the Jeep, and I can smell his chewing tobacco, strong as coffee.

"Yep," he says, thrusting his face in the open window. "That's him, all right." He opens the door. *"Git* on down here!" he says, and before I can even

26

give the dog one last pat, Shiloh leaps off my lap onto the ground and connects with Judd's right foot. He yelps and runs off behind the trailer, tail tucked down, belly to the ground. All Judd's dogs chained out back bark like crazy.

I jump out of the Jeep, too. "Please don't kick him like that," I say. "Some dogs just like to run."

"He runs all over creation," Judd says. I can tell he's studying me in the dark, trying to figure what's it to me.

"I'll keep an eye out for him," I say. "Anytime I see him away from home, I'll bring him back. I promise. Just don't kick him."

Judd only growls. "He could be a fine huntin' dog, but he tries my patience. I'll leave him be tonight, but he wanders off again, I'll whup the daylights out of him. Guarantee you that."

I swallow and swallow, and all the way home I can't speak a word, trying to hold the tears back.

CHAPTER 3

I don't sleep more than a couple hours that night. When I do, I dream of Shiloh. When I don't, I'm thinking about him out in the rain all afternoon, head on his paws, watching our door. Thinking how I'd disappointed him, whistling like I meant something that first time, gettin' him to come to me, then taking him on back to Judd Travers to be kicked all over again.

By five o'clock, when it's growing light, I know pretty much what I have to do: I have to buy that dog from Judd Travers.

I don't let my mind go any further; don't dwell on what Judd would want for Shiloh, or even whether he'd sell. Especially don't ask myself how I'm supposed to get the money. All I know is that I can think of only one way to get that dog away from Judd, and that's what I'm going to have to do.

My bed is the couch in the living room, so when Dad comes in to fix his breakfast, I pull on my jeans and go out to sit across from him in the kitchen.

First he makes himself a lunch to carry to work. He drives his Jeep to the post office in Sistersville, where he cases mail for around two hundred families and delivers it, then comes back to the Friendly post office where he cases mail for two hundred more. Delivers that, too. Route takes him 'bout eighty-five miles on roads you can hardly git by on in winter.

" 'Mornin'," he says to me as he stuffs a sandwich in a sack, then starts in on his breakfast, which is Wheat Chex and any fruit he can get from our peach tree. He makes himself coffee and eats the cornbread or biscuits Ma saves for him from our meal the night before.

"Can you think of a way I could earn myself some money?" I ask him, with this froggy kind of voice that shows you aren't woke up yet.

Dad takes another bite of cornbread, looks at me for a moment, then goes on studying his cereal. Says exactly what I figure he'd say: "Collect some bottles, take 'em in for deposit. Pick up some aluminum cans, maybe, for the recycling place."

"I mean real money. Got to have it faster than that."

"How fast?"

I try to think. Wish I could earn it in a week, but know I can't. Have to go out every day for a whole

29

summer collecting cans and bottles to have much of anything at all.

"A month, maybe," I tell him.

"I'll ask along my mail route, but don't know many folks with money to spare," he says. Which is what I thought.

After Dad's gone off, Becky gets up before Ma, and I fix her a bowl of Cheerios, put her sneakers on so she won't stub her toes, and brush the snarls from her hair.

Read once in a book about how some kids earned money baby-sitting. Boy, if *I* ever got paid even a nickel for every time I've taken care of Becky—Dara Lynn, too—I'd have a lot of dollars. I do a whole bunch of jobs that other kids, other places, get paid to do, but it wouldn't ever occur to me to ask for pay. If I asked Dad, he'd say, "You live in this house, boy?" And when I'd say yes, he'd say, "Then you do your share like the rest of us."

Which is why I never asked.

"More Cheerios," says Becky, and all the while I'm making her breakfast, I'm thinking the best route to take to find aluminum cans. By the time Dara Lynn gets up, wearing one of Dad's old T-shirts for her nightgown, I'd figured how I could double my can count. But when Ma gets up a few minutes later, she takes one look at me and guesses what I'm thinking.

"You got that dog on your mind," she says, lifting the big iron skillet to the stove top and laying some bacon in it.

"Thinking don't cost nothing," I tell her.

She just gives me a little smile then and sets about making my bacon crisp, the way I like it, and we don't say any more about Judd's dog.

Must walk five miles that morning, and all I find is seven cans and one bottle. When Dad comes home about four, he hasn't found anybody looking for help, either, but he says, "The Sears fall catalog come in this afternoon, Marty. You got nothing better to do tomorrow, you could ride my route with me, help deliver 'em."

I say yes to that. Know I won't get nothing more out of it than a soft drink at the gas station, but I like going around in the Jeep, riding over back roads like Rippentuck and Cow House Run Road with Dad. Can take a bag with me just in case, pick up any cans or bottles I happen to see.

That night Dad and I sit out on the porch. Ma's in the swing behind us shelling lima beans for next day, and Becky and Dara Lynn's in the grass catching lightning bugs and putting 'em in a jar. Dad laughs at the way Becky squeals when she gits a bug in her hand. But seeing those bugs in a jar reminds me of Shiloh all chained up at Judd's, a prisoner as sure as those bugs. Truth is, about everything reminds me of Shiloh. You once get a dog to look at you the way Shiloh looked at me, you don't forget it.

"Got seventeen!" Dara Lynn shouts. "Aren't they pretty, Ma?"

"Almost could turn off the electricity and let 'em light the kitchen," Ma says.

"You going to let 'em go?" I ask.

Dara Lynn shrugs.

"They'll die if you keep 'em in a jar," I tell her.

Becky, she comes over and crawls onto my lap. "We'll let 'em go, Marty," she says, and kisses me on the neck. A butterfly kiss, she calls it. Bats her eyelashes against my skin, feels like a moth's wings. She laughs and I laugh.

Then far off I hear a dog. Leastwise I think it's a dog. Might could be a fox cub, but I think, Shiloh.

"You hear that?" I ask Dad.

"Just a hound complaining," is all he says.

Next morning Dad gives me a nudge when he comes through to the kitchen, and I'm up like a shot. We ride to Sistersville and I haul all those catalogs out to the Jeep while Dad cases mail. Not everybody gets a catalog, of course, but anyone who places an order with Sears during the year gets one, so there's lots to load up.

By quarter of nine, we're on the route; Dad pulls

the Jeep up close to the mailboxes and I stuff the mail in, turn up the little red flag on the side, if there is one. Some folks even wait down at the box, and then you feel real bad if you don't have anything for them.

Dad knows everybody's name, though, and he always takes time to say a little somethin'.

" 'Mornin', Bill," he says to an old man whose face lights up like Christmas when we stop. "How's the wife doing?"

" 'Bout the same," the man says, "but this catalog sure going to cheer her." And he sets off for his house, mail tucked under his arm.

People even leave somethin' in their boxes once in a while for Dad. Mrs. Ellison always leaves a little loaf of banana bread or a cinnamon roll, and Dad saves it to eat with his lunch.

After we finish Sistersville, we do the Friendly route, but as the Jeep gets up near Shiloh, my heart starts to pound. I'm thinking of closing my eyes tight in case the dog's around. If I see his eyes looking at me, they'll just drive me crazy. I can hear dogs barking when we're a half mile off from Judd Travers's trailer; dogs can pick up the sound of a Jeep that quick.

I get Judd's mail ready for him. He hasn't got any catalog coming, but he's got two other magazines that'll probably warm his heart—*Guns and*

Ammo and *Shooting Times.* Why don't he take a magazine about dogs, I'm thinking—teach him how to be kind?

All the dogs is chained when we get to his place, so none's waiting for us at the box. But Judd is. He's got a big old sickle; is cutting weeds along his side of the road.

" 'Mornin'," Dad says as the Jeep pulls up.

Judd straightens his back. His shirt's all soaked with sweat, and he wears this brown handkerchief tied around his forehead to keep the sweat from running in his eyes.

"How you doin', Ray?" he says, and comes over to the Jeep with his hand out. I give him his mail, and he even stinks like sweat. I know everybody sweats and everybody's sweat stinks, but seems to me Judd's sweat stinks worse than anyone's. Mean sweat.

"How come you aren't at work?" Dad says.

"You think this ain't work?" Judd answers, then laughs. "Got me a week of vacation coming, so I take a day now and then. This Friday I'm going hunting again. Take the dogs up on the ridge and see if I can get me some rabbit. Possum, maybe. Haven't had me a possum dinner for some time."

"Dogs okay?" Dad asks, and I know he's asking for me.

"Lean and mean," says Judd. "Keep 'em half starved, they'll hunt better."

"Got to keep 'em healthy, though, or you won't have 'em long," Dad says. I know he's saying that for me, too.

"Lose one, I'll buy another," Judd tells him.

I can't help myself. I lean out the window where I can see his face real good—big, round face, whiskers on his cheeks and chin where he hasn't shaved his face for five days—tight little eyes looking down on me beneath his bushy brows.

"That dog that followed me home the other day," I say. "He okay?"

"He's learnin'," Judd says. "Didn't give him a ounce of supper that night. Just put him where he could watch the others eat. Teach him not to wander off. Got him back in the shed, right now."

My stomach hurts for Shiloh. "That dog," I say again. "What's his name?"

Judd just laughs, and his teeth's dark where the tobacco juice oozes through. "Hasn't got a name. Never name any of my dogs. Dogs one, two, three, and four is all. When I want 'em, I whistle; when I don't, I give 'em a kick. 'Git,' 'Scram,' 'Out,' and 'Dammit'; *that's* my dogs' names." And he laughs, making the fat on his belly shake.

I'm so mad I can't see. I know I should shut

35

my mouth, but it goes on talking. "His name's Shiloh," I say.

Judd looks down at me and spits sideways. Studies me a good long time, then shrugs as the Jeep moves forward again and on along the river.

CHAPTER 4

"**M**arty," Dad says when we're around the bend, "sometimes you haven't got the sense to shut up. You can't go tellin' a man what to call his dog."

But I'm mad, too. "Better than callin' him 'Git' or 'Scram.'"

"Judd Travers has the right to name his dog anything he likes or nothing at all. And you've got to get it through your head that it's *his* dog, not yours, and put your mind to other things."

The Jeep bounces along for a good long mile before I speak again. "I can't, Dad," I say finally.

And this time his voice is gentle: "Well, son, you got to try."

I eat my peanut-butter-and-soda-cracker sandwiches with Dad at noon, plus the zucchini bread Mrs. Ellison had left in her mailbox for him, and after all the Sears catalogs and mail is delivered, we head back to the Sistersville post office. I get my Coca-Cola at the gas station while Dad finishes up, and we start home. I forget all about looking for cans

37

and bottles. The can I'm holding is the only one I got.

"Judd Travers goes hunting near every weekend, don't he?" I ask Dad.

"I suppose he does."

"You can shoot at just about anything that moves?"

"Of course not. You can only shoot at what's in season."

I'm thinking how, 'bout a year ago, I was fooling around up on the ridge and come across a dead dog. A dead beagle, with a hole in its head. Never said anything because what was there to say? Somebody out hunting got a dog by mistake, I figured. It happens. But the more I think on it now, I wonder if it wasn't Judd Travers shooting a dog on purpose— shooting one of his own dogs that didn't please him.

Dad's still talking: "We've got a new game warden in the county, and I hear he's plenty tough. Used to be a man could kill a deer on his own property anytime if that deer was eating his garden; warden would look the other way. But they tell me the new warden will fine you good. Well, that's the way it ought to be, I guess."

"What if a man shoots a dog?" I ask.

Dad looks over at me. "Dogs aren't ever in season, Marty. Now you know that."

"But what if a man shoots one, anyway?"

"That would be up to the sheriff to decide what to do, I guess."

The next day I start early and set out on the main road to Friendly with a plastic bag. Get me eleven aluminum cans, but that's all. Could walk my legs off for a year and not even have enough to buy half a dog.

The questions I'd tried not to think about before come back to me now. Would Judd Travers want to sell Shiloh at all? And how much would he want for him if he did? And even if I got Shiloh for my very own, how was I supposed to feed him?

There aren't many leftover scraps of anything in our house. Every extra bite of pork chop or boiled potato or spoonful of peas gets made into soup. If we'd had enough money for me to have a dog and buy its food and pay the vet and everything, I would have had one by now. Dara Lynn's been begging for a cat for over a year. It isn't that we're rock-poor; trouble is that Grandma Preston's got real feeble, and she's being cared for by Dad's sister over in Clarksburg. Have to have nurses anytime Aunt Hettie goes out, and every spare cent we got goes to pay for Grandma's care. Nothing left over to feed a dog. But I figure to get to that problem later on.

I wonder if maybe, in time, if I never see Shiloh again, I'll forget about him. But then I'm lying on the couch that night after everyone else has gone to bed, and I hear this far-off sound again, like a dog crying. Not barking, not howling, not whining even. Crying. And I get this awful ache in my chest. I wonder if it *is* a dog. If it's Shiloh.

"I know you want a dog, Marty," Ma says to me on Thursday. She's sitting at the kitchen table with cardboard boxes all around her, folding a stack of letters and putting them in envelopes. Ma gets work to do here at home anytime she can. "I wish we had the money so every one of you kids could have a pet. But with Grandma seeming to need more care, we just don't, and that's that."

I nod. Ma knows me better'n I know myself sometimes, but she don't have this straight. I don't want just any dog. I want Shiloh, because he needs me. Needs me bad.

It's Friday morning when I hear the sound. Dad's off on his mail route, Dara Lynn and Becky's watching cartoons on TV, Ma's out on the back porch washing clothes in the old washing machine that don't work—only the wringer part works if you turn it by hand. I'm sitting at the table eating a piece of bread spread with lard and jam when I hear the noise I know is Shiloh. Only the softest kind of noise—and right close.

I fold the bread up, jelly to the inside, stick it in

my pocket, and go out the front door. Shiloh's under the sycamore, head on his paws, just like the day he followed me home in the rain. Soon as I see him, I know two things: (1) Judd Travers has taken his dogs out hunting, like he said, and Shiloh's run away from the pack, and (2) I'm not going to take him back. Not now, not ever.

I don't have time to think how I had promised Judd if I ever saw Shiloh loose again, I'd bring him back. Don't even think what I'm going to tell Dad. All I know right then is that I have to get Shiloh away from the house, where none of the family will see him. I run barefoot down the front steps and over to where Shiloh's lying, his tail just thumping like crazy in the grass.

"Shiloh!" I whisper, and gather him up in my arms. His body is shaking all over, but he don't try to get away, don't creep off from me the way he did that first day. I hold him as close and careful as I carry Becky when she's asleep, and I start off up the far hill into the woods, carrying my dog. I know that if I was to see Judd Travers that very minute with his rifle, I'd tell him he'd have to shoot me before I'd ever let him near Shiloh again.

There are burrs and stickers on the path up the hill, and usually I wouldn't take it without sneakers, but if there's burrs and stickers in my feet, I hardly feel 'em. Know Judd Travers and his hounds won't be over here, 'cause this hill belongs to my dad. Get me as far as the shadbush next to the pine, and then I sit down and hug Shiloh.

First time I really have him to myself—first time I can hug him, nobody looking, just squeeze his thin body, pat his head, stroke his ears.

"Shiloh," I tell him, as though he knows it's his name, "Judd Travers isn't never going to kick you again."

And the way his eyes look at me then, the way he reaches up and licks my face, it's like it seals the promise. I'd made a promise to Judd Travers I wasn't going to keep, Jesus help me. But I'm making one to Shiloh that I *will*, God strike me dead.

I set him down at last and go over to the creek for a drink of water. Shiloh follows along beside me. I cup my hands and drink, and Shiloh helps himself, lapping it up. Now what? I ask myself. The problem is looking me square in the face.

I got to keep Shiloh a secret. That much I know. But I'm not going to keep him chained. Only thing I can think of is to make him a pen. Don't like the idea of it, but I'll be with him as much as I can.

I take him back to the shadbush and Shiloh lays down.

"Shiloh," I say, patting his head. "Stay!"

He thumps his tail. I start to walk away, looking back. Shiloh gets up. "Stay!" I say again, louder, and point to the ground.

He lays back down, but I know he's like to follow, anyways. So I pull him over to a pine tree, take the belt off my jeans, loop it through the raggedy old collar Shiloh's wearing, and fasten the belt to the tree. Shiloh don't like it much, but he's quiet. I go down the path and every so often I turn around. Shiloh is looking at me like he won't never see me again, but he don't bark. Strangest thing I ever see in a dog, to be that still.

Ma's still on the back porch. When she washes, it takes her near all day. Dara Lynn and Becky's stuck to the TV. So I go to the shed by the side of the house and I take the extra fencing Dad used when we had us more chickens. I take me a piece of wire, too, and go back up the hill.

Shiloh's still there, and he don't try to get up while I set to work. I string the fencing around the trunks of three small trees, for corner posts, and then back to the pine tree again where I fasten it with wire. Pen measures about six by eight feet.

I go back down to the shed again, and this time I get the old rotten planks Dad took out of the back steps when he put in the new. Pick me up an old pie tin, too. I take the planks up to Shiloh's pen and

43

make him a lean-to at one end, to protect him from rain. Fill the pie tin with water so's he'll have something to drink.

Last of all, I take the lard bread from my pocket and feed it to Shiloh in little pieces, letting him lick my fingers after every bite. I wrap my arms around him, pat him, run my hands over his ears, even kiss his nose. I tell him about a million times I love him as much as I love my ma.

The worry part is whether or not he'll stay quiet. I'm hoping he will, 'cause he was a silent dog to begin with, but all the way back down the hill to the house, I put my finger to my lips and turn back.

"Shhh!" I say.

Shiloh, he don't make a sound. Like he had the bark beat out of him when he was a pup and it just never come back.

I'm tense as a cricket that night. Tense when Dad drives up in his Jeep, afraid the dog will bark. Tense when Dara Lynn and Becky are out in the yard playing after dinner, squealin' and yellin', afraid that Shiloh will want to get in on the fun and maybe dig a hole under the fence. He never comes.

I manage to take a piece of potato and some cornbread up to him before it gets dark. I sit down in his pen with him, and he crawls all over me, licking my face. If he'd been a cat, he would have purred, he was that glad to see me.

Tell him I'm coming back tomorrow with some kind of leash for him. Tell him we're going to run all over that hill, him and me, every day. Tell him he's my dog now, and I'm not never going to let anybody hurt him again ever, and then I leave, wiring that fence good. I go home and sleep a full night, first time in a long while.

CHAPTER 5

I got to take one problem at a time, I tell myself.

Problem number one: where to keep Shiloh hid. Solved.

Problem number two: Would Shiloh be quiet? Yes, he would.

Problem number three: How am I going to get food out of the house, enough to feed Shiloh twice a day, without Ma noticing?

The next morning before breakfast, as soon as Dad's gone, I take a biscuit from the kitchen and a rope from the shed outside, and run up the far hill before Ma and Dara Lynn and Becky get out of bed.

This time Shiloh's on his feet waiting for me, tail going like a windshield wiper, fast speed. A soft yip of pure joy cuts off quick when I say "Shhh!" but as soon as I'm in the pen, Shiloh's leaping up almost shoulder high to lick my cheek, nuzzling my hands, my thighs. He gulps down the biscuit I give him. Wants more, I can tell, but he don't bark. Seems to know he's safe only as long as he's quiet. I tie the rope to his collar.

"Shiloh, boy, we're goin' for a run," I tell him.

To get in and out of Shiloh's pen, I got to unfasten the piece of wire that holds the fencing against the trunk of the pine, then move the fencing aside long enough to slip out. Shiloh lets me go through first, he follows, and then we're both together, like a six-legged animal, pounding along up the path, legs bumping, Shiloh leaping up to lick my hand. I let go of the rope and let Shiloh run free for a while. If he goes ahead even a few steps, he stops and looks back to see if I'm coming; if he stops to sniff at a tree or bush and I go on by, his feet pound double time to catch up.

Just out of the woods on the other side of the hill, there's a meadow, and I slump down in the grass to rest. Shiloh's all over me, licking my face sloppy wet. I giggle and roll over on my stomach, covering my head and neck with my arms. Shiloh whines and nudges his nose under my shoulder, working to roll me over. I laugh and turn on my back, pulling Shiloh down onto my chest, and for a while we both lay there, panting, enjoying the sunshine, belonging to each other.

"What'd you do today, Marty?" Dad asks as he gets out of his Jeep late that evening.

"Oh, looked for ground hogs up on the hill. Fooled around," I tell him.

"How's the can collecting coming?"

"Found some a couple days ago."

"Saw some bottles in the ditch down near Doc Murphy's," Dad says.

"I'll go take a look," I tell him, and set out with my bag. I have to keep on collecting cans, enough to cover some money for meat and bones from the grocer down in Friendly. The bigger Shiloh grows, the more he'll eat.

When I get back home, supper's on the table, and I slip into my chair just as Dad asks the blessing: "Dear Lord, we thank you for the food you've provided for our table. Bless it to nourish the good within us. Amen."

Ma picks up the meat loaf and passes it around, and the meal begins.

I eat about half my supper, then say, "I been getting this sort of full feeling at dinner, Ma, and then I'm hungry again before I go to bed."

Ma don't even look up. "Well, don't eat so much at dinner, then, and eat again before bedtime."

"Food'll be all gone by then."

"There's always cornflakes or something."

"But I get hungry for meat and potatoes later."

"Save some back, then."

"Dara Lynn'll eat it."

"For goodness' sake, Marty!" says Ma.

"Who wants cold meat loaf?" Dara Lynn says.

Forks continue clinking on the table; Becky keeps on digging her fork in her boiled potato. No one looks up. No one pauses. No one even questions. Easy as falling off a log.

I get up from the table finally and put some of my meat loaf and half a potato on a saucer.

"I'm puttin' this in the fridge, Dara Lynn," I say. "Don't you go pickin' at it."

"I *won't,* I told you!" she says.

I go into the other room and sit down on the sofa. So far, so good.

"You seem restless, Marty," Ma calls.

"Me? Heck, no. I got lots to do."

"Where's David Howard this summer? Haven't seen him around."

"Think he went to Tennessee to visit his uncle."

"Fred? Michael?"

"Haven't seen Fred. Michael's gone to some kind of camp."

"You're not lonely?"

"How can I be lonely with the whole outdoors to play in?" I answer. Wish they'd get off my back.

"You can ride along to work with me again anytime you want," says Dad.

I pick up the comic book I bought a few weeks back. "I want to go, I'll let you know," I tell him.

Gradually the kitchen clatter dies down. Dad

belches and goes out on the back porch to look at the sky, same as he always does. Becky's fooling with her food, and Ma sends her away from the table. Dara Lynn giggles at Becky and gets asked to clear the dishes.

I wait until everyone is out of the kitchen and sitting around on the back porch to catch the breeze. As usual Becky and Dara Lynn whoop and tumble around in the grass, glad for an audience, and after I sit a respectable amount of time, I say, "Think I'll take my .22 and go up the far hill awhile."

"What you figure on shooting this time of evening?" Dad asks.

"Just workin' on my aim," I tell him. "See how good I can hit when the light's dim."

"Don't you ever, never, aim your gun toward this house or yard," Ma says.

"I'll point it dead away," I promise. I go back inside for my gun, slip the leftover food from the saucer into a little plastic sack, and set off up the hill, the sounds of my sisters' shouts and giggles behind me.

Again, as I get near the pen, I hear soft, happy yips. But soon as I say, "Shhh!" the noise stops. The only sound you can hear is the swishing of Shiloh's tail, hitting the fence, the soft pad of his paws as he leaps up in the air in sheer, pure happiness; the sloppy slap of his jowls together as he gobbles down the supper I've brought him and then he commences to slobber love all over me as well.

I unhook the wire, push the fence open, and lead Shiloh to the stream for a drink, filling the pie pan with fresh water. When I lead him back to the pen again, I can tell he's disappointed, wanted to go for a run, but I give him enough hugging and squeezing and petting to last the night, with the promise of another run through the meadow the next day.

I'm halfway down the hill when I remember I haven't fired my gun once, and wonder if Dad will say anything. By the time I reach the back porch, though, the whole family's facing down the driveway, 'cause there's the sound of a truck motor growing louder and louder.

I stop in my tracks, fingers tightening around my gun.

Dad, sitting on the edge of the porch, leans forward so he can see. "Looks like Judd Travers's pickup," he says.

My chest feels tight, like I'm having trouble breathing.

The truck pulls up by the side of the house, and the door swings open.

" Evenin'!" Dad calls out as Judd, wearing his old western-style boots with the sharp heel, gets out and comes over.

" Evenin'," he says.

"You had dinner?" Ma asks. "I got some left-overs I could heat up real quick."

"Had me some ribs already," he says. "Ain't looking for a meal, Mrs. Preston, I'm looking for a dog." He sure don't waste any time getting to the point. Now my heart's really pounding.

"That new dog of yours run off again?" Dad asks him.

"I swear to God I find him this time, I'm goin' to break his legs," Judd says, and spits.

"Oh, come on, Judd. A dog with four broke legs ain't no dog to you at all."

"He's no dog to me at all the way he keeps runnin' off. It's the fourth time he's left the pack when I had him out huntin'. I got to teach him a lesson. Whup him good and starve him lean. Wondered if you'd seen him."

"I sure didn't see him on my route today, and you know if I had, I'd have put him in the Jeep and brought him to you straight away," says Dad.

"What about that boy of yours? Think he's seen him?"

Dad had heard me coming back from the hill, and he turns around. "Marty?"

I stand rooted to the ground at the side of the house. "What?"

"Come on around here. Judd's dog's missing again, and he wants to know have you seen him."

"H-his dog? Here in this yard? Haven't seen any dog of any kind in our yard all day," I say, coming a few steps closer.

Judd is sure studying me hard. So is Dad.

"Well, how about when you went out looking for bottles?" Dad asks. "You see him then?"

"Nope." My voice is stronger now. "Saw that big German shepherd of Baker's that gets loose sometimes, and saw a little old gray dog, but sure didn't see that beagle."

"Well, you keep an eye out sharp," Judd says, "and if you see him, you throw a rope around him, drag him over. Hear?"

I only look at him. Can't speak. Can't even nod my head. I wouldn't never promise him that.

"You hear what he asked you, Marty?" says Dad.

I nod my head. Yes, I heard, all right.

"Okay, then," Judd says, and gets back in his pickup.

"Have any luck hunting yesterday?" Dad calls after him.

"A rabbit. Saw a groundhog but didn't get it. That new dog hadn't run off, he would've got it for me. He wasn't such a good hunting dog, I would have shot him by now."

"Sheriff would get on you if you do somethin' like that, Judd."

"Law never told me before what I could do with my dogs, won't be tellin' me now," Judd says. He laughs, waves his hand, starts the engine, and the pickup pulls away.

CHAPTER 6

Night in West Virginia is as dark as black can be. No car lights sweepin' across my walls or ceiling like when I stay overnight with David Howard down in Friendly. No street lamps shinin' in the windows, no lights from next-door houses. Where I live, there ain't no street lamps at all, no house close enough to see from our windows.

My eyes are open, anyway. I stare up into the darkness of the living room and the darkness stares back.

I'm remembering how once, several years ago, when Ma bought milk chocolate rabbits one Easter for me and Dara Lynn, I'd finished eating mine, but Dara Lynn took only a nibble of hers every day or so, keeping it up on her dresser in its pink and yellow tinfoil, driving me nuts. And one day I just crept in there and ate off one of that rabbit's ears. Dara Lynn, of course, threw a fit, and when Ma asked me if I'd done it, I said no. I could feel my cheeks and neck burning red.

"You *sure,* Marty?" she asked. I'd only nodded and left the room. It was one of the worst days of my life.

About an hour later she come out on the porch where I was pushing myself slow in the swing and sat down beside me.

"You know, Marty," she said, "Dara Lynn don't know who ate the ear off her candy rabbit and I don't know who did it, but Jesus knows. And right this very minute Jesus is looking down with the saddest eyes on the person who ate that chocolate. The Bible says that the worst thing that can ever possibly happen to us is to be separated forever from God's love. I hope you'll keep that in mind."

I just swallowed and didn't say anything. But before I went to bed, when Ma asked me again about that rabbit, I gulped and said yes, and she made me get down on my knees and ask God's forgiveness, which wasn't so bad. I honestly felt better afterward. But then she said that Jesus wanted me to go in the next room and tell Dara Lynn what I'd done, and Dara Lynn had a fit all over again. Threw a box of Crayolas at me and could have broke my nose. Called me a rotten, greedy pig. If *that* made Jesus sad, Ma never said.

Now as I study the darkness in the room around me, I'm thinking about lies again. I *hadn't* lied to

Judd Travers when I said I hadn't seen his dog in the yard today. That was the honest-to-God truth, because Shiloh hadn't been anywhere near our yard. But I also know that you can lie not only by what you say but what you don't say. Nothing I'd told Judd was an outright lie, but what I'd kept inside myself made him think that I hadn't seen his dog at all.

"Jesus," I whisper finally, "which you want me to do? Be one hundred percent honest and carry that dog back to Judd so that one of your creatures can be kicked and starved all over again, or keep him here and fatten him up to glorify your creation?"

The question seemed to answer itself, and I'm pretty proud of that prayer. Repeat it to myself so's to remember it in case I need to use it again. If Jesus is anything like the story cards from Sunday school make him out to be, he ain't the kind to want a thin, little beagle to be hurt.

The problem's more mixed-up than that, though. I'm lying to my folks as well. I'm *not* eating the leftover meat loaf I've put away. Every bit of food saved is money saved that could go to buy Dara Lynn a new pair of sneakers so Ma won't have to cut open the tops of her old ones to give her toes more room. Every little bit of food wasted is money wasted. If we ever have the least little bit of money to spare that doesn't have to go for the care of Grandma Preston, first thing we all want is a telephone so we don't have to ride down to Doc Murphy's to use his. But the way I figure, if it's food from my own plate I would have eaten myself but don't, what's the harm in that?

Next morning when I get up to see Shiloh, I put the rope on his collar and lead him to the other side of the hill again, out of sight of all but God. Then I let him go, and we race and tumble and laugh and roll, stopping now and then just to lie in the clover, me on my back, Shiloh on his stomach, both of us panting and nuzzling each other.

Don't know if Shiloh's gettin' more human or I'm gettin' to be more dog. If Jesus ever comes back to earth again, I'm thinking, he'll come as a dog, because there isn't anything as humble or patient or loving or loyal as the dog I have in my arms right now.

We eat our Sunday meal, but by late afternoon, storm clouds roll in, and the rain beats down on the tin roof of our house, streaming down the window glass, making a small pond in the side yard.

I can't help staring out the window at the far hill. Will Shiloh—*can* he, even—leap that fence to try and go somewhere it's more dry? Is he smart enough to go under that lean-to I'd made for him? Have I built it right, away from the wind? What if he gets to howling?

In twenty minutes the rain stops, though, the sun comes out, the birds start to sing again—all those worms oozing up through the wet mud. Shiloh's stayed where he was, trusting me that where I put him was best. Being quiet, like he knows his life depends on it.

"Marty," Dad says, going outside with a rag to wipe off his Jeep. "I saw Mrs. Howard yesterday and she said David was back from Tennessee, wanting to know when you boys could get together. She said David would like to come up here someday next week."

I like David Howard fine, but I sure don't want him up here. David likes the hill; always wants to play there. He's not afraid of snakes the way Dara Lynn is. David, in fact, likes to go to the very top of that hill and then go running lickety-split down it, racing to see who's first to the fence at the bottom. Likes to climb the trees up there, too, and play lookout.

"Well, I'll go down to David's tomorrow," I say. "I'd rather do that."

"Why not do both?" Ma says, coming out to throw some mash to the hens. "You've hardly seen any friends all summer, Marty. Why don't you go down to Friendly one afternoon and ask David to come up here another?"

"There's nothing much to do up here," I say, not knowing how else to answer.

It was the wrong answer. Both Ma and Dad were looking at me now.

"You said just the other day you had plenty to do here," Dad tells me, wringing out his rag at the pump.

"Lots for me to do, but not much for David Howard," I say. *A lie.* That's a flat-out lie. Funny how one lie leads to another and before you know it, your whole life can be a lie.

I sit on the porch swing later, not even bothering to push it, and listen to the table being set inside.

"What you figure is wrong with that boy, Lou?" Dad's voice.

"Just being eleven, I guess," Ma tells him. "Eleven's a moody age. Was for me, anyways."

"You think that's all it is?"

"What pleases you one day don't please you at all the next. What more do *you* think it is?"

"Don't think he's got that dog on his mind still, do you?"

"Eleven's got about everything on its mind," Ma answers. And then the evening news comes on, and Dara Lynn and Becky come out to the porch, leaving the TV to Daddy.

Dara Lynn's got the devil in her tonight—little

bit bored with summer, but not quite ready for school to start. Just for devilment, she plunks herself down beside me in that swing and starts doin' everything I do. I sigh, she sighs. I rest my arms on my head, she does the same. Gits Becky doin' it, too, both of 'em laughin' to beat the band.

When I have my fill of this nonsense, I decide to go up the hill and see how Shiloh's doin', but as I go down off the porch, Dara Lynn gits up and makes as if to follow me.

I stop. "I'm lookin' to find me a snake stick," I say as if to myself.

"I'm lookin' to find me a snake stick," Dara Lynn says.

I don't pay her no mind at all. Just start walkin' along the edge of the yard, picking up a stick here, a stick there, Dara Lynn tagging along behind.

"It's got to have the longest handle and a good strong fork on the end," I say, "because that was the biggest, meanest snake I ever saw in my life."

Dara Lynn stops dead still. She couldn't say all that right if she tried, but she's not interested anymore in trying. *"What* snake?" she says.

"Snake I saw up on the hill this mornin'," I tell her. "Must have been four, five feet long, just lookin' for somebody's leg to wrap itself around."

61

Dara Lynn don't go a step farther. Becky don't even come down off the porch.

"What you going to do when you find it?" Dara Lynn asks.

"Try to keep it from bitin' me, first. Pick it up with my stick, second, put it in a sack, and carry it clear on up past the Shiloh schoolhouse, let it out in the woods there. Won't kill it unless I have to."

"Kill it!" says Dara Lynn. "Git your gun and blow its head off."

"You been watchin' too much stuff on TV, Dara Lynn," I tell her. "Even snakes got the right to live." I'm thinking how if I ever become a vet's helper, I got to take care of pet snakes, too.

Next day, to head off David Howard from riding up from Friendly on his bike, I go down to see him. I'd tended to Shiloh first, taking a fistful of scrambled eggs left over from breakfast, a bit of bacon, and a half slice of whole wheat toast that I stuck in my jeans pocket. It's not enough for the dog, I know, but probably more than he'd get from Judd.

It's not enough for me, either. Sneaking off half my breakfast, lunch, and dinner for Shiloh like I'm doing means me going half hungry all the time, but if I eat extra, then it means Shiloh's costing us money we can't afford. I fill my pockets with wormy peaches before I set out for Friendly, biting off each piece, spitting it out in my hand, and picking out the worms before I put it back in my mouth.

It pleased me that Shiloh was sleepin' in his lean-to when I'd gone up that morning. The ground was dry under there, and I'd brought up some old gunnysacks from the shed for him to lie on, made it seem more like a bed to him, more like a home.

The walk to Friendly takes a good long time unless I hitch a ride. I'm not allowed to get in a car with somebody I don't know, but Dad being the mail carrier for this part of the county, I know most everybody who goes by. The first person to come along this day, though, is Judd Travers.

When I hear the sound of a motor and turn to see his truck slowin' down, I turn forward again and keep on walkin', but he pulls up beside me.

"Want a lift?" he sings out.

"No, thanks," I say. "Almost there."

"Where you goin'?"

I couldn't think fast enough to lie. "David Howard's."

"Hell, boy, you ain't even halfway. Hop in."

I know I don't have to unless I want, but if he's already suspicious about me, that'll only make it worse. So I get in.

"See my dog yet?" First thing out of his mouth.

"I been lookin' over all the roads," I tell him in answer. "No beagle."

"Well, I don't think he'd stick to roads," Judd

says. "Not a dog as shy as him. Shy as a field mouse, 'cept when he's around rabbits. That's what the man said who sold him to me, and he sure was right about that."

"How much did you pay for him?" I ask.

"Got him cheap 'cause he's shy. Thirty-five dollars. Worth a lot more'n that as a hunting dog, if I could just keep that damned animal home."

"You got to treat a dog good if you want him to stick around," I say, bold as brass.

"What you know about it?" Judd jerks his head in my direction, then turns the other way and spits his tobacco out the window. "You never even had a dog, did you?"

"I figure a dog's the same as a kid. You don't treat a kid right, he'll run off first chance he gets, too."

Judd laughs. "Well, if that was true, I would have run away when I was four. Far back as I can remember, Pa took the belt to me—big old welts on my back so raw I could hardly pull my shirt on. I stuck around. Didn't have anyplace else to go. I turned out, didn't I?"

"Turned out how?" The boldness in my chest is growing, taking up all the air.

Now Judd sounds mad. "You tryin' to be smart with me, boy?"

"No. Just asking how you turned out, somebody

who was beat since he was four. I feel sorry, is what I feel."

Judd's real quiet a moment. The big old wad of tobacco in his cheek bobs up and down. "Well, don't go wasting your sorry on me," he says. "Nobody ever felt sorry for me, and I never felt sorry for nobody else. Sorry's something I can do without."

I don't say anything at all.

We reach the road where David Howard lives, and the truck slows down.

"I can walk from here," I tell him. "Thanks." I get out.

But as I come around the truck to cross the street, Judd leans out the window. "Like I said, that dog's a shy one. Don't think you'll see much of him near the road, but you keep your eye out for him in the fields. That's where he'll be, more'n likely. You see him, all you got to do is whistle. That's what I teach him. I whistle and he comes to me, he gits fed. But he does somethin' I don't like, I kick him clear to China. You see him, just whistle, then hang on to him and I'll come pick him up. You hear?"

"I hear," I tell him, and keep walking.

CHAPTER 7

David Howard's house is about twice as big as ours for about half as many people. Only him and his ma and dad. Mr. Howard works for the *Tyler Star-News* in Sistersville, and David's ma is a teacher. They're always glad to have me come down to visit, partly because David and I are best friends, and partly, I think, because their old house is so big, the three of 'em get lost in it.

It's got two floors—three counting the basement and four counting the attic. Has four bedrooms upstairs: one for David, one for his folks, one just for company, and one for his father's books, with a computer in it. Downstairs there's a big kitchen, a dining room with a fancy light hanging over the table, a parlor, and a side room with lots of windows just for plants, plus a porch that runs along three sides of the house. I told Ma once the Howards had a room just for company, a room just for books, and a room just for plants, and she said that was three rooms too many. First time I ever saw any envy in my ma.

David says the house used to belong to his great-

granddaddy, so I figure it'll get to be David's someday. Like maybe our little house and the hill and
meadow and the far woods will belong to me and
Shiloh, except I'd probably have to share it with Dara
Lynn and Becky and whoever they marry, and that's
a whole lot of people for four rooms.

"Marty!" Mrs. Howard says when I ring their
doorbell that sounds like church chimes. "We're *so*
glad to see you! Come on in!"

She always means it, too. It's as though she
thinks about me even when I'm not there. Then
David comes whooping downstairs, carrying the helicopter that flies when you pull a string, and pretty
soon we're out in the backyard, chasing around after
the helicopter and telling each other what we've been
doing the six weeks since school let out. I got to bite
my tongue not to let on about Shiloh.

We sit on David's back steps and eat Popsicles
his ma makes out of pineapple juice. I tell David
about the fox I saw with a gray body and a red head,
and he tells me about his aunt's Siamese cat that
yowls just for the pure joy of making noise. Then I
tell him about Judd Travers and how mean he is to
his dogs, not mentioning Shiloh, of course, and then
David says he's got this surprise to show me.

We go upstairs to his room and David says he got
a pet and asks do I want to hold it.

"Sure!" I tell him. "What is it?"

"Sit down and close your eyes and hold out your hands," says David.

I sit down on the edge of his bed and close my eyes and hold out my hands. I expect something warm and wiggly and furry to plop into my arms. Instead I feel something cold and round and plastic, and when I look, it's a fishbowl with sand in it and a hermit crab, scurrying around with a shell on its back. This is a *pet*?

"My first pet!" David says. "His name is Hermie. See all those shells in there? We bought them for him. At night he gets out of one and puts on another, just like changing clothes."

I look at David and I look at that crab in a fishbowl and I want to tell him about Shiloh and how we run up and down the far side of the hill every day and roll in the grass and how he licks my face, but I can't tell him anything. Not yet. Not ever, maybe.

Hermie's sort of fun, though. We get out David's old blocks—the kind you play with back in kindergarten—and we build this big maze with walls on both sides, and then we put Hermie in it. He skids along the maze, looking which way to go, and we laugh when he gets himself in a dead end. I guess any kind of pet's okay once you get used to it, but I wouldn't trade Shiloh for all the hermit crabs in the world.

"When can I come up to your house?" David asks me when we put the blocks away.

"I don't know," I tell him. "Ma's had this sort of headache lately, and she can't take any noise at all." Boy, I am sure asking for trouble with that one.

"We could stay out on that big hill," David suggests. "Chase around in that field. Play lookout."

"Don't think we ought to till she's feeling better," I say. "I'll let you know. But I can come down here again next week, maybe."

I tell Mrs. Howard I got to be home by late afternoon to help out, and she says surely I can stay for lunch, which is what I was hoping. I sit down at the table with place mats, which are little doll-size tablecloths, one under each plate. Mrs. Howard's made us each a chicken-salad sandwich with lettuce and tomato, and toothpicks with olives on top to hold it all together. David's ma is like that. I think it's because she's a teacher—always looking for ways to make something better than it is.

She does the same with boys. She don't just leave us to eat by ourselves. My ma packs us a lunch and lets us eat it out in the woods. Mrs. Howard always sits down to eat with us and talks about grown-up things. Today she tells us about how we've got some new people elected to office who are going to be more honest, she hopes, than the people they defeated, and how the county's going to be better because of it, and so will the whole state of West Virginia. David's ma thinks big.

"You can't just go on electing people to government because they were friends of your father or grandfather," she says, chewing on a bite of celery.

Mostly I'm thinking about the food. I eat every bit of my chicken sandwich. I'm so hungry I don't even save some for Shiloh; then I'm ashamed of myself. Mrs. Howard notices the way I pick up every little crumb, and she says, "I've got enough chicken salad left for another half a sandwich, Marty. Would you like it?"

"Sure would taste good on the walk back home," I tell her, and she sets right to work wrapping it up for me. *Shiloh's dinner,* I tell myself.

But lunch isn't over yet. After the sandwich there's tapioca pudding and chocolate-covered graham crackers, which I love almost as much as Christmas. I don't see any way to get the pudding to Shiloh, so I eat that, but I ask can I take a couple cookies along to eat on the way home, too, and she opens the sack and sticks in six cookies. Ma would have blushed with shame if she heard me ask this, but seems I'm at the point where I'll do most anything for Shiloh. A lie don't seem a lie anymore when it's meant to save a dog, and right and wrong's all mixed up in my head.

Worse than that, when I leave David's house, I don't even head home. First I go down the street to the corner store and ask Mr. Wallace does he have any sort of old cheese or lunch meat he can sell me cheap. I got fifty-three cents for the cans I collected so far that Dad turned in for me, and I show Mr. Wallace how much I got.

"Well, Marty, let me see what I can find back here," he says, leading me into the little room behind the counter. He's sort of talking without looking at me, the way folks do when they don't want to embarrass you. "I got some stuff here that's not exactly spoiled, but it's too old to sell. Wouldn't want your family getting sick on it, though."

I blush then, 'cause my dad would die of embarrassment if he knew what Mr. Wallace is thinking— that I'm buying this food for our supper, but there's no way in the world I can let on about Shiloh.

I give him all the change I got, and he lets me have a big hunk of cheese, moldy on one side, a carton of sour cream, and half a package of frankfurters that somebody opened and bought five of. I'm happy as a flea on a dog. Somehow I know without asking that Mr. Wallace isn't going to go tellin' folks about it, because people around here tend to keep quiet out of someone else's business.

Next problem I got to solve, though, is how to

71

keep all this stuff from spoiling in the July heat. Can't keep it in our refrigerator or Ma would notice right off. When I get home, Ma's ironing and watching TV and Dara Lynn and Becky's out on the front swing with paper dolls spread out all over the place, so I fish around out in the shed till I find me an old Hi-C can.

I sneak off up the hill with the can and all the food I got with me. Then, with Shiloh watching, I put a rock in the bottom of the can to hold it down, set it in the cool stream, surround it with rocks, and put the container of sour cream, the frankfurters, and the cheese and cookies in there. Put the plastic lid on and set a large rock on top to keep the raccoons out. I'm so proud of myself I like to crow. Hungry again, too, but that half chicken-salad sandwich from Mrs. Howard is Shiloh's dinner, and I give it to him right off.

After that Shiloh and me go on a good long run over the meadow on the far side of the hill, and after I take him back, put fresh water in the pie pan, and love him good, I start down the hill. Halfway to the bottom, here comes Dara Lynn.

"What *you* doin' up here?" I ask her, heart starting to thump.

"Just wanted to see what *you're* doing," she complains. "You go off up here every day almost."

"You leave Becky by herself while Ma's ironing?"

"Becky's okay." She turns and follows me back down the hill. Shiloh, up in the pen, don't make a sound. That's how smart a dog he is.

"Well, I was lookin' for that snake again, but he's hiding from me good," I tell her.

"You *still* didn't get him?" she asks, and when I look back, she's got her eyes to the left, then to the right. "You didn't even take your snake stick," she says. *She's* a smart one, too.

"Got me a stick back up on the hill," I tell her.

"How many snakes you figure are up there, Marty?"

"Oh . . . 'bout twenty-nine that you can see. Baby snakes all over the place, though, hiding. Growing into big ones all the time."

Dara Lynn's walking faster now, hurrying to git on by me, watching every place she sets her foot.

I don't feel good about the lies I tell Dara Lynn or David or his ma. But don't feel exactly bad, neither. If what Grandma Preston told me once about heaven and hell is true, and liars go to hell, then I guess that's where I'm headed. But she also told me that only people are allowed in heaven, not animals. And if I was to go to heaven and look down to see Shiloh left below, head on his paws, I'd run away from heaven sure.

CHAPTER 8

Next two days go by smooth as buttermilk. Shiloh gets biscuits or toast and a couple bites of ham for breakfast, and then in the evening, I fix him up some frankfurters, cut up and mixed with sour cream, and little chunks of cheese. He don't much like the cheese. It sticks to his teeth and he turns his head sideways when he chews, trying to get it off. Licks his chops afterward, though.

He throws up the first time he eats the stuff—too rich for his belly, I guess—but after that he manages to keep it down, and all the while he's fattening out a little. Each day it's harder to see his ribs.

I know my secret can't go on forever, though. Only had the dog for six days, and that evening I find out that Judd Travers wants to hunt on our land. Up the hill and over in the far woods. Thinks maybe he could find himself some quail over there, he says.

When Dad tells us that piece of news at dinner, my whole body goes cold. I want to jump up and scream, "No!" but I just grip my chair and wait it out.

"Ray, I don't like that idea at all," Ma says. "You never ask to hunt on his land, and I don't want him hunting on ours. If we let him, we've got to let anyone else who asks, and one of those shots could find its way down here."

"I'll tell him no," Dad says. "Don't like the idea of it myself. I'll tell him the kids play up there."

I stopped gripping the chair, but my heart still goes on thumping hard. I'm thinking how maybe Judd Travers has hold of the idea that I got his dog hid up there and he's looking for an excuse to snoop around. Having Shiloh a secret is like a bomb waiting to go off.

Next day Dad comes home with more news—good news to him, bad news to me.

"Can't figure it out," he says, walkin' through the door with a sack in his hands. "Folks are taking to leavin' me food in their mailboxes, Lou. Used to be it was just Mrs. Ellison and her banana bread, but found me a ham sandwich today in Nora Klingle's box and half a baked pie in the Saunders'. I look thin to you or something?"

Ma laughs. "Maybe it's just you're the best mail carrier they ever had on the route."

"Well, we got half a pie for dessert tonight, anyways," Dad says.

Oh, brother! I say to myself. Maybe Mr. Wallace is doing more talking than I figured. He wouldn't come right out and tell folks I was in his store buying cheap food, but he might just pass it along that the Preston family's in hard times, and suddenly food starts appearing. That's the way it is here.

The next day, Ma rides into town with Dad, taking the girls along, and goes shopping for new sneakers for Dara Lynn and socks and underpants for Becky. First time I have the whole place to myself, and I let Shiloh run pure free. Bring him down the hill to the house, feed him the heels off a loaf of new bread, all the leftover sausage from breakfast, and a bowl of milk. Then I let him lick the oatmeal pan.

Show him every one of our four rooms, hold him in my lap on the porch swing, and laugh when he tries to stand up on the seat himself while the swing's moving. I let him smell the couch where I sleep and crawl under the front steps to sniff out the mole lives under there, follow him all over creation when he takes out after a rabbit. Then he gives up when he sees I'm not going to shoot that rabbit no way.

But I figure my luck's going to run out if I don't get him back to his pen soon, so about noon I take him back, and he goes right to the gunnysacks in the lean-to, he's so tuckered out.

It's just in time, 'cause when I get back and get the dishes done for Ma, the house picked up some, I look out and here she comes up the lane with Dara

Lynn and Becky and their packages. Somebody gave 'em a lift; you can always count on that around Friendly.

Ma's pleased I got the dishes done, I can tell. "Nice to come back to a clean house, Marty," she tells me. "Had good luck with my shopping, too. Wasn't a thing I bought that wasn't on sale."

Dara Lynn's wore her new sneakers home and got a blister already, but she don't care, she's so glad to have something new.

When I walk in the kitchen next, Ma's looking at her face in the mirror over the sink. Got her eyebrows raised high, then she pushes them low, then raises them again. When she sees me studying her, she says, "Marty, I got frown lines on my face? Tell me the truth now."

I look at her good. "Sure don't see any," I say. I don't neither. Ma's got a pretty face. Plain, but smooth.

"Well, I don't, either, but two people this morning asked me how I was feeling, and one of 'em wants to tell me what to take for headaches. I figure that if folks think I have headaches, I must be doing a lot of frowning."

Whomp, whomp, whomp. That's my heart. "Folks think they got a remedy for something, they'll tell it to you whether you need it or not," I say. Sound

77

so grown-up I hardly recognize myself. So scared inside, though, my stomach's shaking.

Ma's taking out all the things she's bought and putting 'em on the table, taking the price tags off Becky's underpants and socks. "I saw David's mother at the dollar store," she says, "and they've got relatives coming in tonight. She wanted to know if she could bring David up here tomorrow when the rest of them go to Parkersburg. I told her yes."

"Okay," I say, but all the while I'm thinking what I'm going to do with David to keep him off that hill. Take him up toward the old Shiloh schoolhouse, maybe, and walk along the river. Funny thing is, you've got yourself a dog, you sometimes feel like you don't need anyone else. Used to be I'd be waiting at the window for David Howard to come up here for a visit. Nobody else loves you as much as a dog. Except your ma, maybe.

That night Ma makes us fried chicken for supper. First time in a long while. I put away a wing and a thigh on a saucer—to eat later, I tell Ma—and add a spoonful of squash, which might be good for Shiloh's insides. He eats anything. The frankfurters and cheese and sour cream is all gone, so I got to be watching for table scraps again and go out can collecting soon.

Dad's working on the pickup after dinner—

changing the oil—Becky and Dara Lynn's turning somersaults in the grass, and Ma's cleaning the kitchen. Soon as her back is turned, I sneak the food off the saucer and head up the hill to see Shiloh.

I can tell Shiloh likes the fried chicken better than he liked the sour cream-frankfurter mess he'd been eating all week. Even eats the squash, and then he licks my hands and fingers to get all the salt off, anyplace I'd touched a piece of chicken.

Since I'd already taken him all over creation that morning, I don't feel he'll miss much if I don't take him out again, so I go around scooping up all the dog doo, like I do every day, toss it over the fence, and then I lie down on my back in the grass and cover my face with my arms, our favorite game. Shiloh goes nuts trying to uncover my face, nudging at my arms with his nose, tail going ninety miles an hour. Never whines like some dogs do, though. Even when we're out in the far meadow, racing the wind, he'll start to bark and I'll say, "Shhhh, Shiloh!" and he stops right off.

Wish I *could* let him make a little noise. It's not natural, I know, to keep an animal so quiet. But he's *happy*-quiet, not *scared*-quiet. I know that much.

I move my arms off my face after a while and let him rest his paws on my chest, and I'm lying there petting his head and he's got this happy dog-smile on his face. The breeze is blowing cool air in from the west, and I figure I'm about as happy right then as you can get in your whole life.

And then I hear someone say, "Marty." I look up, and there's Ma.

CHAPTER 9

I can't move. Seems as if the sky's swirling around above me, tree branches going every which way. Ma's face even looks different from down on the ground.

Shiloh, of course, goes right over, tail wagging, but all the steam's gone out of me.

"How long have you had this dog up here?" she asks. Not one trace of a smile on her face.

I sit up real slow and swallow. " 'Bout a week, I guess."

"You've had Judd's dog up here a week, and you told him you didn't know where it was?"

"Didn't say I didn't know. He asked had I seen him, and I said I hadn't seen him in our yard. That much was true."

Ma comes around to the trunk of the pine tree, unfastens the wire that holds the fencing closed, and lets herself in. She crouches down in the soft pine needles and Shiloh starts leaping up on her with his front paws, licking at her face.

I can't tell at first how she feels about him, the

81

way she leans back, away from his dripping tongue. Then I see her hand reach out, with its short, smooth fingers, and stroke him.

"So we've got ourselves a secret," she says at last, and when I hear her say "we," I feel some better. Not a lot, but some.

"How come you to follow me up here tonight?" I want to know.

Now I can tell for sure her eyes are smiling, but her lips are still set. "Well, I had my suspicions before, but it was the squash that did it."

"The squash?"

"Marty, I never knew you to eat more'n a couple bites of squash in your life, and when you put away a spoonful of that to eat later, I knew for sure it wasn't you doing the eating. And then the way you've been sneaking off every night . . ." She stops stroking Shiloh and turns on me. "I wish you'd told me."

"Figured you'd make me give him back."

"This dog don't belong to you."

"Mine more than Judd's!" I say hotly. "He only paid money for him. I'm the one who loves him."

"That doesn't make him yours. Not in the eyes of the law, it doesn't."

"Well, what kind of law is it, Ma, that lets a man mistreat his dog?"

Ma just sighs then and starts stroking Shiloh's

head. Shiloh wiggles a few inches closer to her on his belly, rests his nose against her thigh, tail going *whick, whack, whick, whack.* Finally Ma says, "Your dad don't know about him?"

I shake my head. More silence. Then she says: "I never kept a secret from your dad in the fourteen years we've been married."

"You ain't going to tell him?"

"Marty, I've got to. He ever finds out about this dog and knows I knew but didn't tell him, how could he trust me? If I keep this one secret from him, he'll think maybe there are more."

"He'll make me give him back to Judd, Ma!" I could hear my voice shaking now. "You *know* he will!"

"What else can we do?"

I can feel hot tears in my eyes now and try to keep them from spilling out. I turn my head till they go away. "Judd Travers ever comes here to get his dog, he'll have to fight me to get it."

"Marty. . . ."

"Listen, Ma, just for one night, promise you won't tell Dad so I can figure out something."

Can tell she's thinking on it. "You aren't fixing to run off with this dog, are you? Marty, don't you *ever* run away from a problem."

I don't answer, because that very thing crossed my mind.

SHILOH

"I can't promise not to tell your dad tonight if you can't promise not to run off."

"I won't run off," I say.

"Then I won't tell him tonight."

"Or in the morning, neither," I add. "I got to have at least one day to think." Don't know what good it will do, though. Have already thought till my brains are dry.

Ma puts out both hands now and scratches behind Shiloh's ears, and he licks her all up and down her arms.

"His name's Shiloh," I tell her, pleased.

After a while Ma gets up. "You coming back to the house now?"

"In a bit," I answer.

It's hard to say how I feel after she leaves. Glad, in a way, that somebody knows: that I don't have to carry this whole secret on my head alone. But more scared than glad. Have me just one day to think of what to do, and not any closer to an answer than I'd been before. I'd spent all my can money on stuff to feed Shiloh. Only money I have now to my name is a nickel I'd found out by the road. Judd won't sell me Shiloh's spit for a nickel.

My first thought is to give him to somebody else and not tell them whose dog it is, then tell Ma that Shiloh had run off. But that would be two more

lies to add to the pack. Word would get out somehow or other, and Judd would see David Howard or
Mike Wells walking his dog, and then the war would
really start.

All I can think of is to take Shiloh down to
Friendly the next day, draw me up a big sign that
says FREE: WORLD'S BEST DOG or something, and hold it up
along the road to Sistersville, hoping that some
stranger driving along will get a warm spot in his
heart for Shiloh, stop his car, and take him home.
And I won't ask him where home is, neither, so when
Ma asks me where the dog is, I can tell her honest I
don't know.

When I get back to the house, Dad's just washing up at the pump, using grease to get the oil off his
arms. He's yelling at Dara Lynn and Becky, who are
playing in the doorway, screen wide open, letting in
the moths.

I go inside and Ma's putting the dishes away in
the kitchen, lifting them out of the drain rack and
stacking the plates on the shelf. She's got the radio
on and is humming along with a country music song:

> *It's you I wanna come home to,*
> *It's you to bake my bread,*
> *It's you to light my fire,*
> *It's you to share my bed.*

85

She sort of blushes when she sees me there by the refrigerator, listening to her sing.

I know I'm not going to sleep much that night. I sit on the couch staring at the TV, but not really watching, while Ma gives Becky her bath. Then I wait till Dara Lynn is out of the bathroom so I can take my own bath. Don't know if I soaped up or not. Don't even know if I washed my feet. I go back in the living room, and Ma has my bed made up there on the sofa. The house gets dark, the doors close, and then just the night sounds come from outside.

Know there's a piece of cardboard somewhere out in the shed I can print on. There won't be any trouble getting Shiloh to Friendly, either. I'll put that rope on his collar, and he'll follow along good as anything. We won't take the main road, though, in case Judd's out in his truck. Take every back road I can find.

Then I'll plant myself on the road to Sistersville, holding that sign, Shiloh waiting beside me wondering what it is we're going to do next. What *am* I fixing to do, anyway? Give him to the first car that stops? Don't even know the person driving? Might even be I'll give Shiloh to somebody who'll treat him worse than Judd Travers. Now that Shiloh's come to trust me, here I am getting ready to send him off again. I feel like there's a tank truck sitting on my chest; can't hardly breathe. Got one day to decide what to do with Shiloh, and nothing I think on seems right.

I hear Shiloh making a noise up on the far hill in his pen. Not now, Shiloh! I whisper. You been good as gold all this time. Don't start now. Can it be he knows what I'm fixing to do?

Then I hear a yelp, a loud yelp, then a snarl and a growl, and suddenly the air is filled with yelps, and it's the worst kind of noise you can think of. A dog being hurt.

I leap out of bed, thrust my feet in my sneakers, and with shoelaces flying, I'm racing through the kitchen toward the back door. A light comes on. I can hear Dad's voice saying, "Get a flashlight," but I'm already out on the back porch, then running up the hill.

There are footsteps behind me; Dad's gaining on me. Can hear Shiloh howl like he's being torn in two, and my breath comes shorter and shorter, trying to get there in time.

By the time I reach the pen, Dad's caught up with me, and he's got the flashlight turned toward the noise. The beam searches out the pine tree, the fencing, the lean-to. . . . And then I see this big German shepherd, mean as nails, hunched over Shiloh there on the ground. The shepherd's got blood on his mouth and jaws, and as Dad takes another step forward, it leaps over the fence, same way it got in, and takes off through the woods.

I unfasten the wire next to the pine tree, legs like rubber, hardly holding me up. I kneel down by Shiloh. He's got blood on his side, his ear, a big open gash on one leg, and he don't move. Not an inch.

I bend over, my forehead against him, my hand on his head. He's dead, I know it! I'm screaming inside. Then I feel his body sort of shiver, and his mouth's moving just a little, like he's trying to get his tongue out to lick my hand. And I'm bent over there in the beam of Dad's flashlight, bawling, and I don't even care.

CHAPTER 10

Dad's beside me, holding the flashlight up to Shiloh's eyes. Shiloh's still alive.

"This Judd Travers's dog?"

I sit back on my heels and nod. Wipe one arm across my face.

Dad looks around. "Take those gunnysacks over there and put 'em in the back of the Jeep," he says, and then, still holding the flashlight in one hand, he slips his arms under Shiloh and picks him up. I can see Shiloh wince and pull back on his leg where it hurts.

The tears are spilling out of my eyes, but Dad can't see 'em in the dark. He can probably tell I'm crying, though, 'cause my nose is clogged. "Dad," I say, *"please* don't take him back to Judd! Judd'll take one look at Shiloh and shoot him!"

"Take those gunnysacks to the Jeep like I said," Dad tells me, and I follow behind as we go down the hill. I keep my mouth open to let the breath escape, crying without making a sound. Just like Shiloh.

Ma's watching from inside, the screen all covered with June bugs where they been buzzing about the light. Dara Lynn's up, standing there in her nightshirt, watching.

"What *is* it? What's he got?" Dara Lynn says, pestering Ma's arm.

"A dog," says Ma. And then she calls out, "Ray, is it alive?"

"Just barely," says Dad.

I put the gunnysacks in the Jeep, and Dad carefully lays Shiloh down. Without waiting to ask, I crawl in the Jeep beside Shiloh, and Dad don't say no. He goes in the house for his trousers and his keys, and then we're off.

"I'm sorry, Shiloh," I whisper, over and over, both hands on him so's he won't try to get up. The blood's just pouring from a rip in his ear. "I'm so sorry! Jesus help me, I didn't know Bakers' dog could leap that fence."

When we get to the bottom of the lane, instead of going up the road toward Judd's place, Dad turns left toward Friendly, and halfway around the first curve, he pulls in Doc Murphy's driveway. Light's still on in a window, but I think old doc was in bed, 'cause he come to the door in his pajamas.

"Ray Preston?" he says when he sees Dad.

"I sure am sorry to bother you this hour of the

night," Dad says, "but I got a dog here hurt bad, and if you could take a look at him, see if he can be saved, I'd be much obliged. We'll pay. . . ."

"I'm no vet," says Doc Murphy, but he's already standing aside, holding the screen open with one hand so we can carry Shiloh in.

The doc's a short man, round belly, don't seem to practice what he preaches about eating right, but he's got a kind heart, and he lays out some newspapers on his kitchen table.

I'm shaking so hard I can see my own hands tremble as I keep one on Shiloh's head, the other on a front paw.

"He's sure bleeding good, I can tell you that," Doc Murphy says. He puts on his stethoscope and listens to Shiloh's heart. Then he takes his flashlight and shines it in the dog's eyes, holding each eye open with his finger and thumb. Finally he looks at the big, ugly wound on Shiloh's hurt leg, torn open right to the bone, the bites around Shiloh's neck, and the ripped ear. I turn my head away and sniffle some more.

"I'll do what I can," Doc says. "The thing we got to worry about now is infection. That leg wound is going to take twenty . . . thirty stitches. What happened?"

I figure Dad will answer for me, but he don't— just turns to me. "Marty?"

I swallow. "Big old German shepherd chewed him up."

Doc Murphy goes over to the sink and washes his hands. "Baker's dog? Every time that shepherd gets loose, there's trouble." He comes back to the table and takes a big needle out of his bag, fills it full of something. Something to make Shiloh numb, maybe. "This your dog, son?"

I shake my head.

"No?" He looks at me, then at Dad. Dad still won't say nothing, makes me do the talking. While the doc leans over Shiloh and slowly inserts the needle in his side, I get up my nerve.

"It's Judd Travers's," I tell him. I got to start practicing the truth sometime.

"Judd *Travers's*? This the dog he's missing? How come you brought it in?"

"I had him," I say.

Doc Murphy sucks in his breath, then lets it out a little at a time—*huh, huh, huh.* "Whew!" he says, and goes on about his work.

Don't know how long we're there in Doc's kitchen, Dad standing over against the wall, arms folded, me with my hands cupped over Shiloh's head while Doc Murphy washes the wounds, dresses them, and starts stitching the skin back up. Once or twice I feel Shiloh jerk, like it hurts him, but when he lays too still, I don't know if it's because he's numb or if he's dying.

"The next twenty-four hours, we'll know if this dog's going to live," the doc says. "You check with me tomorrow evening; we'll have some idea then. I can keep him here for a day or two, Ray. Then, if he makes it, you can take him on home."

I put my face down near Shiloh's again, my mouth next to his ear. *"Live,* Shiloh, *live!"* I whisper.

Hardest thing in the world is to leave Shiloh there at Doc Murphy's, the way his eyes follow me over to the doorway, the way his muscles move, like he's trying to get up when he sees me leaving. Second hardest thing is to crawl in the Jeep with Dad afterward.

There isn't a word passed between us till we get home. Once Dad turns the motor off, though, and I'm all set to get out, he says, "Marty, what else don't I know?"

"What?" I ask.

"You keeping Judd's dog up there on our hill— got a place for him all built, never letting on. What else you keeping from me?"

"Nothing, Dad!"

"How do I know that's not another lie?"

" 'Cause it's not."

"You saying so don't make it true."

I know then what Ma meant. But it's not all so black and white as Dad makes it out to be, neither. And sometimes, when I get mad, it clears my head.

"You would have thought more of me if I'd let that dog wander around till Judd found it again, kick the daylights out of 'im?" I ask. "That what you want me to do, Dad?"

"I want you to do what's right."

"What's right?"

For once in my eleven years, I think I have my dad stumped. Leastways, it seems to be thirty . . . forty seconds before he answers:

"You've got to go by the law. The law says a man that pays money for a dog owns that dog. You don't agree with the law, then you work to change it."

"What if there isn't time, Dad? Shiloh could be dead by the time somebody looked into the way Judd treats his dogs."

Dad's voice is sharp: "You think Judd Travers is the only one around here hard-hearted toward his animals? You think he's the only one who starves 'em or kicks 'em or worse? Open up your eyes, Marty. *Open your eyes!*" Now Dad half turns in his seat, back resting against the door, facing me: "How many times have you walked to the school bus and seen a chained-up dog in somebody's yard? How many times you ever put your mind to whether or not it's happy, its ribs sticking out like handles on the sides?

Suddenly you're face-to-face with a dog that pulls at your heart, and you all at once want to change things."

I swallow. "There's got to be a first time," I answer.

Dad sighs. "You're right about that," he says.

I'm pushing my luck, I know. "If Doc Murphy don't tell Judd about Shiloh, can we bring him back here and keep him? I could build him a better pen. Make the fence high enough so the shepherd can't get in."

Dad opens the Jeep door on his side. "No," he says, and gets out.

I get out, too. "Just till Shiloh's better, then? You know how Judd treats anything that don't work right. He'll shoot Shiloh, Dad! I found a dog once before over near Judd's place with a bullet hole in his head. We could at least get Shiloh well. I'm going to pay Doc Murphy's bill. I promise you that. You get all my can money for the next three years, and I'll deliver the county paper, too, if I get the chance. Honest! I promise!"

Dad studies me. "You can keep him here till he's well, that's all. Then we're taking him back to Judd." And he goes in the house.

My heart starts pounding again. *Thumpity, thump. Thumpity thump.* There's still time, I'm thinking. Shiloh's still alive, and I ain't licked yet.

CHAPTER 11

It's only after I lie back down on the couch that night that I realize what all I've done. To Ma and Dad, for one thing. Ma's still awake. I can see the light in the bedroom as Dad goes on down the hall. And then I hear their voices. Not all of what they say, but enough:

"Ray . . . told you I just found out about that dog myself. . . ."

". . . secrets from me, you and Marty."

". . . till tomorrow. I would have told you then. . . ."

". . . every day . . . the mail to Judd's place . . . mentions that dog to me, and all the time . . . up on my own property, me not even knowing. . . ."

I bring my arms up against my ears and hold 'em there. So many things going wrong, it's hard to remember anything going right. Doc Murphy knows I've got Judd's dog now, Dad's mad at Ma, and we won't know till tomorrow if Shiloh's even going to make it. Worst of all, I'd brought Shiloh here to keep him from being hurt, and what that German shepherd done to him was probably worse than anything Judd Travers would have brought himself to do, short of shootin' him, anyways. This time, when the tears come again, I don't even fight. Don't even try holding back.

I must have slept through Dad's going off to work the next morning, 'cause when I wake, Becky's standing beside the couch eating a piece of honey toast and breathing on my face. Dara Lynn's already told her about the dog, because she asks right off, "Where's it at, the doggy?"

I sit up and tell her the dog's at Doc Murphy's and we'll find out how he is that afternoon. Then I look in the kitchen at Ma. There's the set look about the lips that means trouble—that means don't mess with her, 'cause she's already in trouble with Dad.

I go outside, pick me a couple wormy peaches, and sit on the stoop, eating at them, spitting out the wormy places.

Dara Lynn comes out and sits beside me. Today she's all kindness.

"Judd Travers don't take care of his dog, Marty, no wonder it come up here," she says, trying to say the right thing. I can tell she's been figuring it all out, from what she could overhear between Ma and Dad and anything else Ma told her.

I take another bite of peach.

"It wasn't like you *stole* him," she says. "That dog come up here on its own."

"Just hush up, Dara Lynn," I say, which I had no business saying. I didn't want to talk to anyone, that's all.

"Well, you could have told me and I wouldn't have told anyone."

"Thanks."

"Ma says we've got to give him back to Judd Travers when he's better."

I get up and start toward the hill to clean up the ground where Shiloh was attacked. See if there's any way I can put some fence wire over the top of the pen to keep out the shepherd.

"What's his name, Marty?" Dara Lynn calls after me.

"Shiloh," I tell her.

I'm only halfway up the hill when I hear a car and turn around. It's Mrs. Howard's car, and David's in it. Soon as he sees me he jumps out—it still moving a little—and comes running toward me.

"I get to stay here today!" he yells, waving a kite he's brought with him. "Everyone else is going to Parkersburg and I didn't want to go."

I look over to where Ma and Mrs. Howard are talking, see Ma nodding her head. I get lonely sometimes up at our house, but today I want to be with that loneliness. Don't want to talk to Dara Lynn, to Becky, to Dad, or even to Ma. If we had a telephone, I'd be calling Doc Murphy every hour. As it is, I have to wait till Dad comes home from work before I can find out about Shiloh. Can't go down there pesterin' Doc, him with patients to see.

"What do you want to do?" I ask David, trying to dig up the least little bit of enthusiasm. David and I are in the same grade, even though he's taller and heavier and looks like junior high already.

"Try out this kite over in your meadow," he says.

I lead him around the long way, away from Shiloh's pen, and he doesn't even notice because he's unwrapping his kite, made of silk or something, which one of his relatives brought him.

We stand out in the meadow flying the kite, and I watch the blue-and-yellow-and-green tail whipping around in the breeze, and I'm thinking about Shiloh's tail, the way it wags. You get a dog on your mind, it seems to fill up the whole space. Everything you do reminds you of that dog.

When we bring the kite down later, though, David sees a groundhog, and next thing you know he's after it—the groundhog zigzagging this way and that, David yelling like crazy.

"I'm taking your kite back down to the house, David," I yell when I see him getting near Shiloh's pen.

99

He goes on running and yelling.

"I'm going to get me a handful of soda crackers. You want to make some peanut-butter-cracker sandwiches?" I call out, trying to get him to follow.

And then his yelling stops. "Hey!" he says.

I know he's found the pen, and I walk over.

"What's this?" David asks. He looks at the blood on the ground. "Hey! What happened here?"

I go over and yank his arm and make him sit down. He's looking at me bug-eyed.

"You listen to me, David Howard," I say. Whenever I say "David Howard," he knows it's serious. Only did it twice in my life—once when he sat on the paper flowerpot I'd made for Ma at school, and once when he saw me with my pants down in the bathroom. That really made me mad.

But today I'm not mad, I'm serious: "Something awful and terrible happened in there, David, and if you ever tell anyone, even your ma and dad, may Jesus make you blind."

That's the kind of talk my folks can't stand, but I got it from Grandma Preston herself. Ma says Jesus don't go around making anyone blind, but Grandma Preston always used it as a warning and she went to church Sunday morning and evening both.

David's eyes about to pop out of his head. *"What?"* he asks again.

"You know Judd Travers?"

"He was *murdered*?"

"No. But you know the way he's mean to his dogs?"

"He killed one of his dogs in there?"

"No. Let me *tell* it, David. You know how he's missing a dog?"

"Yeah?"

"Well, it come up here on its own and I let him stay. I built him a pen and kept him secret and named him Shiloh."

David stares at me, then at the blood in the pen, then back at me again.

"Last night," I tell him, "Baker's German shepherd jumped the fence and tore him up. We took Shiloh to Doc Murphy, and Judd don't know."

David's mouth falls open and hangs there. "Wow!" he says, then says it again.

I tell David how hurt Shiloh was and how we've got to wait till tonight to see how he is, and then we go in his pen together, and David helps me clean up the blood—pull up all the grass with blood stains on it and throw it over the fence into the woods.

It's easier somehow with David helping. With David knowing, even. If it was me by myself, I'd be thinking again and again how this never would have happened if Shiloh could have got away from the shepherd. I look at David and think we're friends for life. Then I think of how there are exactly seven people now who know I have Judd Travers's dog, and it's only a matter of time before somebody lets it out. Probably Becky. She'll warble it to the first person coming up the lane. Did you ever notice how the more a little kid tries not to tell a secret, the sooner it gets out? Nothing that child can do about it. A secret is just too big for a little kid.

What I didn't expect was that at three-thirty, before Dad come home, here's Doc Murphy's car chugging up the lane, and he's got Shiloh in the backseat. I'm standing out by the oak tree with David, taking turns on the bag swing, when I see the car and Shiloh's head raised up in the backseat. I'm over to that car in three seconds flat.

"Shiloh!"

No cry ever sounded so happy as the one that come up out of my throat.

All of us, we're crowding around the car—Ma and Dara Lynn and Becky and David Howard, and all of us are saying, "Shiloh! Here, boy!" and holding out our hands, and Shiloh's trying to lick everything in sight.

"Patient recovered faster than I thought he would," Doc says, getting his big belly out from behind the steering wheel and standing up. "So I figured I'd bring him on over myself." And then, to Mother, "Had patients coming in and out today, and don't know that I wanted them to see the dog."

She nodded.

"I'm going to pay for this, Doc Murphy," I tell him. "You send the bill to Dad and he'll pay it, but then I'm payin' him."

"Well, son, that's a generous thing to do, with a dog not even yours," he says.

"Is he all well now?"

"No. Not by a long shot. Think it's going to take a couple weeks to heal, and I can't promise you he'll walk without a limp. But I got him sewn back up and full of antibiotics. If you can keep him quiet for a few days and off that leg, I think he'll pull through just fine."

If Ma was mad at me before, she's not now, not the way Shiloh's licking her all over both arms, getting a quick lick in at her face every time she bends close. Becky's sticking her hand out for Shiloh to lick, and when he does, she squeals and pulls back. Shiloh's tail going like crazy.

It's like a welcome-home party. Ma has me bring in this cardboard box from the shed and we put an old pillow in the bottom of it and cover it with a clean sheet, and Doc Murphy lays Shiloh down inside it.

SHILOH

Shiloh seems to know he can't walk too good, because as soon as he tries to stand up, he sits back down again and licks at his leg.

I'm glad Shiloh's back, I'm glad he's going to get better, and that we can keep him till he's well. But the more I sit there petting his head, feeling his happiness, the more I know I can't give him up. I won't.

CHAPTER 12

Sure seems strange having Shiloh in the house that night, after trying so hard to keep him secret. Strange, too, the way Ma takes to him. Seems like she can't hardly pass his box next to the stove without reaching down to pet him, making low sympathy noises in her throat, way she does when Dara Lynn or Becky or me gets sick.

Dad don't say much. He come home to find Shiloh there, he just stands off to one side, listening to what Doc Murphy said about him; he don't get close enough for Shiloh to take a lick.

But when supper's over and I go off to the bathroom to brush my teeth, I peek back through the doorway, and Dad's over by Shiloh's box, letting him lick his plate clean. Dad crouches there a minute or two, scratching all down Shiloh's back and up again.

What I'm figuring, see, is by the time Shiloh's better, everybody will love him so much they just can't let him go—even Dad. I'm hoping Dad will go over to see Judd Travers, make him an offer for

Shiloh, and then he'll be ours. The trouble with this kind of thinking, though, is we don't have the money.

I'll probably be through junior high school, almost, before I earn enough to pay Doc Murphy's bill. To buy Shiloh from Judd, even if Judd's willing to sell, I'd have to collect aluminum cans all through high school, too. Can't make very much with cans. I try to think about what other kind of work I can do that would pay me more, but except for delivering the county paper on Friday afternoons, nothing else comes to mind. And somebody's got that job already.

It's sort of like Shiloh's there and he's not. In the next couple of days, everybody's pettin' him every chance they get. Becky feeds him the crusts off her toast—breaks off little bits, and shrieks every time she feels Shiloh's mouth slurp them out of her fingers.

Ma's putting up beans in jars, and all the while she hums to Shiloh like he's a baby in a cradle, not a dog in a box. Dara Lynn's got an old hairbrush, and she just can't seem to brush that dog enough. Even Dad sits down one evening and gets out every tick Shiloh's got on him. Takes a little dab of turpentine and rubs it on the tick's rear end, and the tick backs out of Shiloh's skin mighty quick.

The thing that makes it seem like Shiloh's *not* there is that nobody except me and Dara Lynn and

Becky talks about him. Ma and Dad don't even once mention his name out loud, as though saying it makes him ours, which he ain't. As though if you don't talk about him, maybe he'll disappear as quietly as he come that day in the rain.

What everyone's waiting for, I guess, is something to happen. Every day Shiloh's getting a little stronger. Two days after Doc Murphy brought him here, Shiloh's up limping around on his bad leg. Ma puts some papers beside his box for him to do his business on, but he won't, so for the first couple days I pick him up, carry him out to the yard, and after he's done his business there, I bring him in again. But now he's pushing open the back screen himself and going down into the yard, then comin' back and tapping on the screen with one paw, so we'll let him in. Somebody, sometime, is bound to see him. Becky, sometime, bound to say something. Even David Howard, when his ma came to pick him up the other day, opens his mouth right off and says something about Shiloh.

"Who's Shiloh?" she asks, and David realizes he's let it slip.

"Old stray cat," he says, and now I've got David lying.

Worse part about having Shiloh here in the house where I can play with him anytime I like is that it's hard to leave him when I go out collecting cans. But I've got to earn money now more than ever, so each day, when Shiloh takes his long nap, I set out with my plastic garbage bag hanging out one jeans' pocket.

One day I walk all the way to Friendly and ask at the grocery, where the county paper is dropped, if they'll put in my name as a carrier. Mr. Wallace says he'll turn my name in, but he's already got six names ahead of me, and one of 'em is a grown man with a car. Don't see how I can match that.

I study the bulletin board at the back of the store where people put up notices. Stand on one foot and then the other reading the whole danged board, and seems like everybody got something to sell, or want to be hired, nobody wants to buy. Only two jobs listed, one for an appliance salesman and some woman who wants her house painted.

Mr. Wallace sees me looking at the board, and he comes over and takes down the notice about a woman wanting her house painted.

"That's already taken," he tells me.

That night, while we finish supper, Shiloh's going around the table, putting his nose in everyone's lap, looking mournful, waiting for somebody to slip him something to eat. I can tell Ma and Dad's trying their best not to laugh. Ma won't let us feed him at the table.

What I'm dying to ask Dad is did he tell Judd Travers about his dog being here. Dad don't mention it so I don't ask. Maybe I don't want to know, I tell myself.

And then, just as Ma's dishing up a peach cobbler that we're going to eat hot with milk, I hear a sound outside that makes my bones feel like icicles inside me.

Shiloh hears it, too, and I know right away it's what I think it is, because Shiloh sticks his tail between his legs, puts his belly low to the floor, and climbs back into his box.

Ma and Dad look at Shiloh. They look at each other. Then there's the slam of a truck door outside, footsteps on the ground, footsteps on the porch, and a *rap, rap, rap* at the back door. Everybody stops eating, like we was all froze to death in our chairs.

Dad gets up and turns on the porch light, and there he is, Judd Travers, looking as mean and nasty as I ever seen him look. He don't even ask can he come in; just opens the screen and steps inside.

"Ray Preston," he says, "somebody told me you got my dog."

Dad's looking serious. He nods and points toward the box by the stove. "Over there, Judd, but he's hurt, and we've been taking care of him for you."

Judd stares at Shiloh and then at Dad. "Well, I'll

be danged," he says, almost softly. "Somebody knows my dog is missing, takes him in, and don't even have the decency to tell me?"

"We *were* going to tell you," Dad says, and he's looking straight at Judd. "Nobody wants to hear his dog's been hurt, though, and we wanted to make sure he was going to pull through." Then he turns to me. "Marty," he says, "you want to tell Mr. Travers how his dog come to be here?"

He knows I don't. He knows I'd rather swim a river full of crocodiles than face Judd Travers. But it's my story to tell, not Dad's, and he always did make us face up to what we'd done.

"Your dog come over here twice because you been mistreatin' it," I say, and my voice don't sound near as strong as Dad's. Sort of quavery. I clear my throat and go on: "So second time it come over, I built it a pen up in the woods and Dad didn't know it, and that German shepherd of Baker's got in and fought Shiloh."

"Fought who?"

"The beagle. Shiloh, that's what I've been callin' him. And Shiloh got hurt bad. It was my fault for not making the fence higher. We took him to Doc Murphy and he patched him up."

Judd Travers is still staring around the room like he never saw the likes of us before. Finally he lets out his breath through his teeth and slowly shakes his head: "And I got to find out all this from Doc Murphy?"

I couldn't believe Doc would go tell him.

"Somebody goes to the doc the other day and sees a beagle lying out on his back porch. Tells me about it later. Says he thinks maybe the dog's mine. So I ride over to Doc's this evening, and he tells me it was you who brought him in."

Judd walks across the kitchen, and at the thud of each footstep, Shiloh huddles down farther and farther in the box, like maybe he can make himself disappear. His whole body is shaking. Ma sees it, I know, because she watches for a minute, then turns her face away quick.

Judd stares down at Shiloh—at his bandage and the shaved place where he's all stitched up—the rip on his ear. "Look what you done to my *dog*!" he yells at me, eyes big and angry. I swallow. Nothin' I can say to that.

Travers squats down by the box. He puts out his hand, and Shiloh leans away, like he's going to be hit. If that don't prove the way he treats 'em, I don't know what would, but Judd's saying, "I never mistreated my dogs. This one was shy when I got him, that's all. I sure never caused him an injury like this one. Wouldn't never have happened if you'd brought him back like I told you." I close my eyes.

When I open 'em again, Judd's putting his hand

on Shiloh's head, roughlike, sort of patting him, and you can tell he ain't got that much practice being kind. Still, hard to prove Shiloh wasn't mistreated *before* he got to Judd's. How do you go about proving something like that?

"It was wrong of Marty to pen up your dog, Judd, and we've already talked about that," Dad says. "He's the one who's going to pay Doc Murphy for patching him up, and soon as the dog is strong, we'll drive him over to your place. Why don't you let us keep him until then, in case he needs more care?"

Judd stands up again and looks at me. I stare back, but I don't say nothing.

And then Ma can't take it anymore. She says, "Judd, Marty's got awful attached to that dog, and we'd like to know how much you want for it. Maybe we can scrape up the money to buy him."

Judd looks at her like she's talking some kind of nonsense, like we are all getting crazier by the minute.

"That dog's not for sale," he says. "Paid good money to get me a hunting dog, and he could be one of the best I've had. You want to keep and feed him till he's better, okay with me. It's you that got him all tore up, and you paying the bill. But I want him back by Sunday."

Screen door slams again, truck starts up, and then he's gone.

CHAPTER 13

I'm back to not sleeping again. Everything I can think of to try, I've already thought on and turned down. Even thought of Dad and me driving to Middlebourne and going to the county courthouse to report a man who's mean to his dogs, thinking maybe they wouldn't let Judd have Shiloh back again. Dad says that's where we'd have to go, all right, but how am I going to prove it about Judd? Think about that, he says.

I been thinking about it. Do I really suppose they'd send an investigator all the way out from Middlebourne to see about a man said to kick his dogs? And if they did, do I think Judd's going to tell the man yes, indeed, he does kick them? Do I think the investigator's going to hide out in the bushes near Judd Travers's place for a week just to see for himself?

Tyler County hasn't hardly got the money to investigate reports of children being kicked, Dad says, much less dogs. Even if I told the animal-rights people that I found a dog with a bullet hole in its

113

head up near Judd's house, don't prove that Judd was the one who killed it.

I go out to talk to Dad about it some more while he's chopping wood, and he just says, "Son, it's hard, I know, but sometimes you just got to do what has to be done. It's Judd's dog and there's no getting around it."

Ma tries to make me feel better. She says at least I brought some joy and kindness into the life of a dog that never had any before, and that Shiloh will never forget me. But that even makes it worse. Wish he *could* forget. Keep thinking of how Shiloh's going to look at me when we drive him over to Judd's, and my eyes fill up again. Becky, she's been crying, too. So has Dara Lynn. The one good thing about it now is that the whole family loves Shiloh and we can talk about him out loud, but there's not one thing we can do. Three more days and we have to give him up.

I walk down to Friendly on Friday to talk with David Howard. David feels almost as bad as I do. I hardly finish telling about Shiloh and he's got tears in his eyes already. David Howard's thirty pounds heavier and bigger than me, and he still don't care who sees him cry.

"I been thinking, David," I say. "You got relatives in Ohio, don't you?"

He nods.

"You think any of them would take Shiloh?

Could you call 'em up and ask could they drive down here tomorrow and take him back with them, and I'll tell Judd we let Shiloh out one day and he never come back?" More lies.

But David's shaking his head already. "It's only Uncle Clyde and Aunt Pat, and she's allergic to dogs. They had one once and had to give him up."

On the way back home, I'm thinking about someplace really good I could hide that dog. The old gristmill, maybe, up by the bridge. The door's pad-locked, but it don't take much to get in, 'cause the top of the building's open where some of the roof's blown away. I bet I could hide Shiloh in there for ten years and he'd never make a sound. But what kind of life is that? Couldn't never take him anywhere except after dark. Even then, he'd be so close to Judd's place, the other dogs would probably sniff him out.

Slowly the minutes and hours of Friday tick by, then it's Saturday, and our last day with Shiloh. We give him every little treat we can think of, a wonder we don't make him sick, and after supper we sit out on the back porch like we usually do. Becky and Dara Lynn are rolling around in the grass, and Shiloh limps out there to join in the fun. I show Becky how if you lay down on your stomach with your arms up over your face, Shiloh will work to turn you over. Both girls have to try it, and Shiloh does just like I

115

said, trying his best to get those girls up on their feet.

"If Becky ever fell in the creek, I'll bet Shiloh would pull her out," Ma says.

"If I ever saw a snake, I'll bet Shiloh would kill it for me," says Dara Lynn.

I got a sadness inside me growing so big I feel I'm about to bust. That night I sleep a little bit, wake a bit, sleep a bit, wake some more. About dawn, however, I know what I got to do.

I get up quiet as can be. Soon as Shiloh hears me, of course, he's out of his box.

"Shhh, Shiloh," I say, my finger to my lips. He watches me a moment, then crawls back in his box, good as ever.

I dress, pull on my sneakers, take me a slice of bread from the loaf on the counter and a peach off the tree in the yard. Then I take the shortcut through the east woods toward Judd Travers's.

It's the only thing left to do. I'd talked to Dad, to Ma, to David, and nobody's got any more idea what to do than they did before. What I'm fixing to do is talk to Judd Travers straight and tell him I'm not going to give Shiloh back.

Rehearsed my lines so often I can say 'em by heart. What I don't know, though, is what Judd's going to say—what he's going to do. I'll tell him he can beat me, punch me, kick me, but I'm not going to give that dog up. I'll buy Shiloh from Judd, but if he won't sell and comes to get him, I'll take Shiloh and head out in the other direction. Only way he can get his dog back is to take me to court, and then I'll tell the judge how Judd treats his animals.

Halfway through the woods, I'm thinking that what I'm about to do could get my dad in a whole lot of trouble. Around here it's serious business when you got a quarrel with your neighbor and you got to carry it as far as the law. Folks ain't that fond of Judd, and most of 'em likes my dad, but when it comes to taking a man's property, I figure they'll side with Judd. I'm not makin' life one bit easier for my parents or Dara Lynn or Becky, but I just can't give up Shiloh without a fight.

Will he shoot me? That thought crosses my mind, too. Some kid got shot down in Mingo County once. Easy as pie for Judd Travers to put a bullet hole in my head, say he didn't see me. I got my feet pointed toward Judd Travers's place, though, and they ain't about to turn back.

Still so early in the morning the mist is rising up out of the ground, and when I come to a stretch of field, looks like the grass is steaming. Sky's light, but the sun hasn't showed itself yet. You live in hill country, it takes a while for the sun to rise. Got to scale the mountains first.

I'm practicing being quiet. What I hope is to get to Judd's house before he's wide awake, take him by surprise. He sees me coming a half mile off, without Shiloh, he's likely to figure what I got to say and have his answer ready. I want to be sitting there on his porch the moment he gets out of bed.

A rabbit goes lickety-split in front of me, then disappears. I went out hunting with Dad once, and he said that when you first scare up a rabbit, it hops a short way, then stops and looks back. That's when you got to freeze. Can't move nothing but your eyeballs, Dad says. What you have to look for is that shiny black dot—the rabbit's eye. If you look for the whole rabbit, you almost never see him because he blends into the scenery.

So I don't move a muscle and look for the shiny black dot. And there it is. I wonder what's going on inside that rabbit—if its heart's pounding fierce. No way I could tell it I wasn't going to do it harm. So I go on, back into the second stretch of woods, heading for that second field.

I'm just about to come out of the trees when I stop dead still again, for right there in the meadow is a deer, a young doe. She's munching on something, and every so often she stops, looks up, then goes on eating again.

Hardest thing in the world for me to see how

118

anybody could shoot an animal like that. Then I think of a couple winters ago we hardly had any meat on our table, and I guess I can see how a father with three kids could shoot a deer. Hope I never have to, though. I'm just about to step out into the meadow, when *crack!*

It's the sound of a rifle. It splits the air and echoes back against the hills.

The doe takes out across the meadow, heading for the woods. Its front legs rear up, then its back legs as it leaps, its tail a flash of white.

Crack!

The rifle sounds again, and this time the deer goes down.

I can't move. One part of me wants to go to the deer, the other part knows that somebody's out here with a rifle shooting deer out of season. And before I can decide whether to go on or turn back, out of the woods on the other side steps Judd Travers, rifle in hand.

CHAPTER 14

He's wearing this army camouflage shirt, a brown cap, and the weirdest grin that could fit on a human face.

"Whooeee!" he says, holding the rifle up with one hand as he plows through the weeds. "I got 'er! Whooeee!"

I know he wasn't out shooting rabbits and happened to get a doe instead, because he doesn't have his hounds with him; Judd Travers had gone out that morning with the clear intention of getting himself a deer. I also know that if the game warden finds out about it, Judd's in big trouble, 'cause the deer he shot out of season wasn't even a buck.

He slogs over through waist-high weeds to where the doe lays. Bending over, he looks at her, walks around her a little piece, then says "Whooeee!" again, soft-like.

That's when I come out of the woods. He's got his back to me now, his hands on the doe's front legs, trying to see can he pull her himself. Drags her a little way and stops. And when he looks up again, I'm right beside him.

He whirls around. "Where'd you come from?" he says.

"Was on my way over to see you," I tell him, and for the first time, standing next to Judd Travers, I feel taller than I really am.

He looks at me a moment like he don't know if he's glad I'm there or not. Then I guess he figures me being there, only a kid, don't matter. "Look what I got!" he says. "Found her eatin' at my garden this morning, and I chased her over here."

"That's a lie," I say. "I was back in the woods watching her eat. She was comin' down from the hills the other way. You went out deer huntin' for anything you could get."

"Well, supposing I did!" says Judd Travers, and he hates me worse'n snot.

"Deer ain't in season, that's what," I answer. "There's a two-hundred-dollar fine for killing a doe."

Judd Travers is staring at me like he's about to crack me across the mouth. Way we're raised around here, children don't talk back to grown folks. Don't hardly talk much at all, in fact. Learn to listen, keep your mouth shut, let the grown folks do the talking. And here I am, shooting off my mouth at five-thirty in the morning to a man holding a rifle. Am I crazy or what?

"Not unless the game warden finds out, there's not," Judd says. "And who's going to tell him? You?"

All at once I realize I got Judd Travers right where I want him. One way you look at it, it's my duty to report a killed doe. The way folks up here look at it, though, that's snitching. And if I *might* could tell, but bargain not to, it's something else again: It's blackmail. But, like I said, I'd got to the place I'd do most anything to save Shiloh.

"Yeah," I say, my heart pounding like crazy. "I'll tell. There's a free number to call." There is, too. It's on Dad's hunting regulation papers. Boy, I sure didn't know I was going to step into all this when I come up here this morning.

Now Judd's looking at me good, eyes narrowed down to little slits. "Your pa put you up to this?"

"No. This is me talking."

"Well, ain't you something now! And who's to believe you?"

"I'll get the game warden up here, show him the spot the doe was hit, the blood, and when he finds the deer at your place, he'll believe me." The words are coming out quicker than I can think, almost.

"I'll tell him he was eatin' my garden."

"And I'll say different. The new game warden won't make any allowance even if the deer *was* eating

122

your garden. You just don't shoot deer out of season no way. 'Specially a doe."

Now Judd's really angry, and his words come at me like bees. "What you trying to do, boy? Start up trouble? You think I can't put you in your place mighty quick?"

"So what you going to do?" I ask. "Shoot me?"

Travers is so surprised his jaw drops. But I'm cooking now. Nothing can stop me. Braver than I ever been in my life.

"Going to shoot me like that dog I found up here six months back with a bullet in his head?"

Travers stares some more.

"I know whose bullet that was, Judd, and I told Dad, and if folks find me up here with a bullet in me, Dad'll know whose bullet that is, too."

I can't hardly believe the words that's coming out of my mouth. Been scared most my life of Judd Travers, and here I am, half his size, talking like a grown person. It's because I know Shiloh's still got a chance.

"So what you waiting for?" Judd says finally. "Go get the game warden." And when I don't move, he says, "Come off it, Marty. Here. You take one of those legs, I'll take another, we'll drag it to my place, and I'll give you half the meat. And don't tell me your ma won't be glad to get it."

"I don't want the meat. I want Shiloh."

Now Judd's really surprised and whistles through his teeth. "Boy, you just come up here to set me up, didn't you?"

"Didn't have an idea in this world you was out with your rifle," I tell him, and that's one of the first truths I told in two weeks. "I come up here because it's Sunday, the day you said to bring your dog back, and I wanted you to know you got to fight me first to get him. Now I'm telling you I mean to keep him, and you expect to keep that deer without a fine, you'll make the trade."

"Whoa!" says Travers. "That's no kind of trade at all! If I *hadn't* got me a deer this morning, what would you have bargained with then?"

I didn't have an answer to that because I hadn't been thinking about a deal. Judd had already said he wouldn't sell Shiloh.

Judd's eyes narrow down even more till it almost looks like he's asleep. "I just bet you *would* tell the game warden, too."

"Jesus' name, I would."

"And you're sayin' if I let you keep my huntin' dog, you're going to keep this deer a secret?"

I begin to see now I'm no better than Judd Travers—willing to look the other way to get something I want. But the something is Shiloh.

"Yes, I will," I tell him, not feeling all that great about it.

"Well, you got to do more than that, boy, because I paid thirty-five dollars for that dog, and I want forty to let him go."

For the first time, I see a thin ray of hope that maybe he'll let me buy Shiloh. "I'll get you the money somehow, by and by," I promise.

"I don't want the money by and by. I want it now. And you haven't got it now, you work for me and pay it off."

You make a deal with Judd Travers and you're only eleven years old, you take what you can get. But all I'm thinking is *dog*.

"You got a bargain," I tell Judd, and now my feet want to dance, my face wants to smile, but I don't dare let the delight show through.

"You listen here," says Judd. "I'll pay you two dollars an hour, and that comes to twenty hours to earn forty dollars. And the work ain't easy."

"I'll do it," I say.

"Beginning now," says Judd, and I can tell he's gettin' a bit edgy that someone else might come through the field, wondering about those rifle shots, and see how he got a doe. "Help me get this deer to my trailer."

I'm so glad to be gettin' Shiloh, I can hardly think straight. But I'm thinkin' straight enough as I help drag that doe to Judd's to know that by lettin' him get away with this, I'm putting other deer in

danger. He kill this one out of season, he'll figure
maybe he can kill some more. To save Shiloh, I'm
making it harder for deer. I swallow. All I got to do,
though, is think of the way he'd look at me, I ever
give him back to Judd, and then I get on with my job.

When we get to the trailer at last, we carry the
deer around to the three-sided shed Judd's got in his
backyard. First thing Judd does is bleed the doe, keep
the meat from spoilin'. Then he goes out and messes
up the tracks with his foot, kicking up the grass
where we'd matted it down, and covering the trail of
blood with dust.

"I git home from work every day at three," Judd
says, "and I want you here when I pull up. You work
for me two hours a day, five days a week. I want that
wood back there stacked. I want the weeds cut and the
grass mowed. I want my beans picked, the corn hoed.
. . . Whatever I think of to be done, that's what you
do. And I want you here startin' tomorrow."

"I'll be here," I says. "But I want it in writing
that after I do twenty hours' work for you, Shiloh
belongs to me."

Travers grunts and goes in his trailer. He comes
out with a piece of grocery sack and the words "Beagle hunting dog to Marty Preston for twenty hours
work. J. Travers."

It occurs to me suddenly that maybe after I

do the work, he'll try to pay me off with one of his
other dogs.

"Write 'Shiloh,' " I tell him.

He gives me a pained look and crosses out "beagle," writes "Shiloh" in its place, but don't spell it
right. Leaves off the "h" at the end.

I take the paper and put it in my pocket. "I'll be
here tomorrow," I say.

"And you ever tell *anyone* about this deer,
boy, you're going to be more'n sorry you opened
your lips."

"You got my word," I say, which, considering all
the lying I'd been doing lately, didn't seem like it
amounted to much. It did, though.

I walk away from Judd's trailer in a sort of zigzag
line, half expecting a bullet in my back any moment,
even though I'm pretty sure he wouldn't. Soon as I'm
out of sight, though, I race through the woods, heart
going *thumpity-thump.* Can't keep the smile back no
longer.

Shiloh's mine! The words keep coming back
again and again. He's safe!

Should feel even more joyful, though. Thought
once if I could just get Shiloh for my own, it would
be the finest day of my life. In a way it is, in a way
it isn't.

Could be Judd gave in 'cause he couldn't think

of nothing else at the moment to do. Said I could have Shiloh just 'cause he needed some help with that deer. Could be that once he got rid of the evidence, he'd tell me to go ahead and get the warden, that I wasn't to have the dog. Could even say he never wrote that on the grocery sack, that I'd wrote it myself.

I don't think so, though. What worries me most is that Judd could go through with the bargain, give Shiloh to me, but then someday, when Shiloh's running free in the woods by himself, Judd might put a bullet in his head, just to spite me.

CHAPTER 15

Closer I get to home, though, the bigger the grin on my face, and when I burst in the kitchen, I got a smile from ear to ear.

Dad's having his coffee and Ma's in the living room listening to the Sunday morning service by Brother Jonas. She watches him every Sunday at seven, which tells me what time it is already.

"Where you been?" says Dad, and I can tell Ma's paying attention, too. "You up and gone, we got to worrying."

I slide into my chair and almost have to push my cheeks in to keep the smile from going all the way around my head.

"Went to see Judd Travers," I say, still breathless, "and I'm buying his dog."

Ma gets up and comes to the kitchen doorway. "What?"

"Thought he wasn't selling," says Dad, looking at me hard.

"He wasn't, but I talked him into it. He needs

help around his place, and he says if I work hard for him for twenty hours, at two dollars an hour, that will pay the forty dollars he wants for Shiloh."

Ma's smile getting broader by the minute. "I don't *believe* it!" she says. "Shiloh's yours?"

"Not yet, but he will be, and we don't have to take him over to Judd's." Before I can get the last word out, she's got her arms around me, squeezing the breath from my chest, almost.

I think Shiloh can smell Judd Travers on me. He can smell the deer's blood, too; I know by the way he sniffs my shoes. But finally he just can't stand it no more. He's joyful I'm back, and he's lickin' me, welcoming me home.

But Dad's still studying my face. "I can't figure it, Marty. Judd seemed pretty definite about keepin' that dog. What was said between you?"

I really didn't want to lie no more. If I tell Ma and Dad everything except about the deer, that's lying by omission, Ma says: not telling the whole truth. But if I tell about the deer after promising Judd I wouldn't, then I would have lied to Judd. Rather lie to Judd than my folks, but I figure it this way: Dad wouldn't report Judd even if *he* saw him shoot a doe out of season, because that's the way it's always been around here. That don't necessarily make it right, of course, but with him feeling that way, nothing's going to change if I *do* tell him about Judd and the deer, and because I promised not to, I don't. Right now, the most important thing to me is Shiloh.

"Told him I wasn't going to give Shiloh back no matter what," I tell Dad.

They are sure staring at me now, him and Ma.

"You said that to Judd Travers?" Dad asked, scooting back in his chair.

"Only thing left to say. Only thing I could think of to do I hadn't tried already. Was going to tell him he could take me to court, and I'd tell the judge how he kicked his dogs. But didn't have to go that far. Guess he needs help around his place."

Ma turns to Dad. "You know, I think it's because Shiloh was hurt. I think he figures that dog's never going to be what it was, and that's why he was willing to let it go. Figured he got rid of a lame dog, and the best of the bargain, too."

"That's what I figure," I say.

And at last Dad begins to smile. "So we got ourselves a new member of the family," he tells me, and that's about the nicest thing I heard said in this house in my life.

Then Becky and Dara Lynn wakes up, sad faced 'cause they think we got to take Shiloh over to Judd's. I tell 'em the news, and Dara Lynn, she starts dancing. Becky joins in, whirling herself around, and then Shiloh, smiling his dog-smile, everybody whooping and carrying on.

Ma turns off the TV and makes waffles, with a big pat of margerine in the center of each one and hot homemade brown-sugar syrup filling the plates. She even makes a waffle for Shiloh. We're going to make that dog sick if we're not careful.

"Now all we got to worry about is how we can afford to feed him as well as ourselves," Dad says finally. "But there's food for the body and food for the spirit. And Shiloh sure enough feeds our spirit."

We about pet Shiloh to death. Everytime he turns around, someone's got a hand on him some-wheres. I take him out for his first gentle run since he got hurt, and once up on the hill, him running free, the good feeling inside me grows bigger and bigger and I have to let it out. I hunch up my shoulders and go, "Heeeowl!"

Shiloh jumps and looks at me.

"Heeeowl!" I go again, out of joy and jubilation, the way they do in church. And suddenly Shiloh joins in with a bark. A pitiful kind of bark, like he's got to be taught how, but it's a happy bark, and he's learnin'.

Only bit of sadness left in me is for the deer. Wondering, too, about whose business it is when someone breaks the law. Wonder if Dad wouldn't never tell on Judd no matter what he done. Bet he would. There's got to be times that what one person does is everybody's business.

Monday afternoon at three o'clock, I'm waiting on Judd's porch when he pulls up. All his dogs is chained out to the side of the house, and they get to barkin' like crazy. I don't try to get near 'em, 'cause a chained dog can be mean. I've already restacked Judd's woodpile, but he wants me to do it again, put the big pieces here, the little ones there. He is looking mean and grumpy, like maybe he's disgusted with himself for lettin' me have that dog so easy.

When I finish the woodpile, Judd hands me the hoe. "You see that garden?"

I nod.

"You see that corn? I want the dirt chopped up so fine I can sift it through my fingers," he tells me.

Now I see what he's getting at. He's going to make it so there's no way I can please him. I'll put in my twenty hours and he'll tell me my work wasn't no good, he wants his dog back.

I hoe till I got blisters on both hands, sweat pouring down my back. Wish I could do my work in the early morning before the sun's so fierce. But I don't complain. I take off my T-shirt finally, wrap it around my head to keep the sweat out of my eyes, and

133

I keep on. Shoulders so red I know they'll hurt worse'n anything the next morning, and they do.

Next afternoon, Judd sets me to scrubbing down the sides of his trailer and his porch, shining up the windows, raking the yard. He sits on a folding chair in the shade, drinking a cold beer. Don't offer me nothing, even water. I hate him more than the devil. My mouth so dry it feels like fur.

Third day, though, he puts out a quart jar of water for me when I go to pick his beans. I bend over them rows so long, dropping the beans into a bucket, I think I'm going to be bent for life. When I'm through, Judd sort of motions me to the porch, like I can sit there if I want while I drink my water.

I almost fall onto that porch, glad to be in the shade.

"Looks like you got yourself some blisters," he says.

"I'm okay," I tell him, and take another long drink.

"How's Shiloh?" he asks. First time he's called the dog by that name.

"He's doing fine. Still got a limp, but he eats good."

Judd lifts his beer to his lips. "Would have been a good hunting dog if I could just have kept him home," he says. "The other dogs never run off."

I think about that awhile. "Well," I say finally, "each one is different."

"That's the truth. Kick one and he just goes under the porch for an hour. Kick another, he goes off and don't come back."

I'm trying my best to think what to say to that. Like how come he has to kick them at all? Then I figure nobody likes to be preached at, no matter how much he needs it, least of all Judd Travers, who is thirty years old if he's a day.

"Some dogs, it just makes 'em mean when you kick 'em," I say finally. "Other dogs, it makes 'em scared. Shiloh got scared."

"Never beat my dogs with a stick," Judd goes on. "Never did that in my life."

I don't say anything right away. Finally, though, I ask, "How *your* dogs doing?"

"Rarin' to go out rabbit hunting," Judd says. We look over at his three dogs, all pullin' at their chains and snarlin' at each other. "That biggest dog, now," Judd goes on. "He's the loudest squaller I got. I can tell from his racket whether he's following a fresh track or an old one, if he's runnin' a ditch, swimmin', or treed a coon."

"That's pretty good," I say.

"Littlest one, he's nothin' but a trashy dog— he'll run down most anything 'cept what I'm after.

Hope the others'll learn him something. And the middle dog, well, she gives a lot of mouth, too. Even barks at dead trees." The dogs were fighting now, and Judd throws his Pabst can at 'em. "You-all shut up!" he yells. "Hush up!"

The can hits the biggest dog, and they all scatter.

"Don't much like bein' chained," Judd says.

"Guess nobody would," I tell him.

I put in ten hours that week, meaning I make up twenty of the dollars I owe him; got one more week to go. When I leave of an afternoon for Judd's, Shiloh goes with me just so far, then he gets to whining and turns back. I'm glad he won't go on with me. Don't want him anywhere near Judd Travers.

Monday of the second week it seem like Judd's out to break my back or my spirit or both. This time he's got me splittin' wood. I got to roll a big old piece of locust wood over to the stump in his side yard, drive a wedge in it, then hit the wedge with a sledge-hammer, again and again till the wood falls apart in pieces to fit his wood stove. Then another log and another.

I can hardly get the sledgehammer up over my head, and when I bring it down, my arms is so wobbly my aim ain't true. Almost drop the hammer. This ain't a job for me, and if Dad saw what Judd was makin' me do, he'd tell him it wasn't safe.

But Judd's out to teach me a lesson, and I'm out to teach him one. So I keep at it. Know it takes me twice as long as Judd to split that wood, but I don't stop. And all the while, Judd sits on his porch, drinking his beer, watching me sweat. Sure does his heart good, I can tell.

Then he says somethin' that almost stops my heart cold. Laughs and says, "Boy, you sure are puttin' in a whole lot of work for nothin'."

I rest my back a moment, wipe one arm across my face. "Shiloh's somethin'," I tell him.

"You think you're goin' to get my dog just 'cause you got some handwritin' on a piece of paper?" Judd laughs and drinks some more. "Why, that paper's not good for anything but to blow your nose on. Didn't have a witness."

I look at Judd. "What you mean?"

"You don't even know what's legal and what's not, do you? Well, you show a judge a paper without a witness's signature, he'll laugh you right out of the courthouse. Got to have somebody sign that he saw you strike a bargain." Judd laughs some more. "And nobody here but my dogs."

I feel sick inside, like I could maybe throw up. Can't think of what to do or say, so I just lift the sledgehammer again, go on splittin' the wood.

Judd laughs even harder. "What are you, boy?

137

Some kind of fool?" And when I don't answer, he says, "What you breakin' your back for?"

"I want that dog," I tell him, and raise the sledgehammer again.

That night when I'm sittin' out on the porch with Ma and Dad, Shiloh in my lap, I check it out. "What's a witness?" I say.

"Somebody who knows the Lord Jesus and don't mind tellin' about it," says Ma.

"No, the other kind."

"Somebody who sees something happen and signs that it's true," Dad says. "What you got in mind now, Marty?"

"You make a bargain with somebody, you got to have a witness?" I ask, not answering.

"If you want it done right and legal, I suppose you do."

I can't bear to have Dad know I was so stupid I made an agreement with Judd Travers without a witness.

"What you thinking on?" Dad asks again, hunching up his shoulders while Ma rubs his back.

"Just thinking how you sell something, is all. Land and stuff."

Dad looks at me quick. "You're not trying to sell off some of my land for that dog, are you?"

"No," I tell him, glad I got him off track. But I

sure am worried. Every trace of that deer's gone now. Don't know what Judd done with the meat—rented him a meat locker somewhere, maybe. But there's no bones around, no hide. I report him now, I can't prove a thing.

Next day Judd Travers calls me dumb. Sees me waiting for him on his steps and says I must have a head as thick as a coconut; didn't he already tell me that the paper wasn't worth nothing?

I just look straight through him. "You and me made a bargain," I say, "and I aim to keep my part of it. What you want me to do today?"

Judd just points to the sledgehammer again and doubles over laughin', like it's the biggest joke he ever played on somebody in his life. I can feel the sweat trickle down my back and I ain't even started yet.

Four o'clock comes, and I finally finished all that wood, but Judd pretends he's asleep. Got his head laid back, mouth half open, but I know it's just another way he's got to trick me. Wants me to sneak on home; then he'll say I never kept to my part of the bargain. So I go in his shed, put the sledgehammer back, take out the sickle, and go tackle the weeds down by his mailbox. Work on them weeds a whole hour, and when five o'clock comes, I start back toward the shed. See him watching me. I walk over.

"Sickle's gettin' dull, Judd. You got a whetstone around, I could sharpen it for you."

He studies me a good long while. "In the shed," he says.

I go get it, sit out on a stump, running the whetstone over the blade.

"Past five o'clock," says Judd.

"I know," I say.

"I ain't going to pay you one cent more," he says.

"It's okay," I tell him. Never saw a look on a man's face like I see on his. Pure puzzlement is what it is.

Thing I decide on when I head for Judd's again the next day is that I got no choice. All I can do is stick to my side of the deal and see what happens. All in the world I can do. If I quit now, he'll come for Shiloh, and we're right back where we started. I don't want to make him mad. No use having a winner and loser, or the bad feelings would just go on. Don't want to have to worry about Shiloh when he's running loose and I'm in school. Don't want to feel that Judd's so sore at me he'll think up any excuse at all to run his truck over my dog.

Only sign in this world we're making progress is the water Judd puts out for me. This day it even has ice in it, and Judd don't say one more word about a witness. In fact, when I'm through working and sit down on his porch to finish the water, Judd talks a little more than usual. Only bond we got between us is dogs, but at least that's somethin'.

I decide to say something nice to Judd. Tell him how good-looking his dogs are. Givin' a compliment to Judd Travers is like filling a balloon with air. You can actually see his chest swell up.

"Forty, thirty, and forty-five," he says, when I tell about his dogs.

"Those are their names now?"

"What I paid for 'em," he says.

"If they had a little more meat on their bones, I figure they'd be the best-lookin' hounds in Tyler County," I tell him.

Judd sits there, turnin' his beer around in his hands, and says, "Maybe could use a bit more fat."

I nurse my water along a little, too. "When'd you first get interested in hunting?" I ask him. "Your pa take you out when you was little?"

Judd spits. Didn't know a man could drink beer and chew tobacco at the same time, but Judd does. "Once or twice," he says. "Only nice thing about my dad I remember."

It's the first time in my life I ever felt anything like sorry for Judd Travers. If you weighed it on a postal scale, would hardly move the needle at all, but

141

I suppose there was a fraction of an ounce of sorry for him somewhere inside me. When I thought on all the things I'd done with my own dad and how Judd could only remember hunting, well, that was pretty pitiful for a lifetime.

Thursday, when I get there, Judd's meanness has got the best of him again, because I can see he's running out of work for me to do, just giving me work to make me sweat. Dig a ditch to dump his garbage in, he says. Hoe that cornfield again, scrub that porch, weed that bean patch. But close on to five o'clock, he seems to realize that I'm only going to be there one more time. I'd worked real hard that day. Did anything he asked and done it better than he asked me to.

"Well, one more day," Judd says when I sit down at last with my water and him with his beer. "What you going to do with that dog once he's yours?"

"Just play," I tell him. "Love him."

We sit there side by side while the clouds change places, puff out, the wind blowin' 'em this way and that. I'm wondering how things would have turned out if it hadn't been for that deer. If I'd just knocked on Judd's front door two weeks ago and told him I wasn't giving Shiloh up, what would have happened then?

To tell the truth, I think Ma's right. Judd would have sold him to me by and by because of Shiloh's limp. Judd's the kind that don't like that in a dog, same as he don't want a dent or a scratch of any kind on his pickup truck. Makes him look bad, he thinks. His truck's got to be perfect, to make up for all the ways Judd's not.

The last day I work for Judd, he inspects every job I do, finds fault with the least little thing. Keeps pesterin' me, makin' me hang around, do my work over. When it's time to go, I say, "Well, I guess that's it then."

Judd don't answer. Just stands in the doorway of his trailer looking at me, and then I get the feeling he's going to tell me I can take that paper he signed and use it for kindling. Tell me I can call the game warden if I want, there's not a trace of that deer left. The two weeks of work I put in for him was just long enough for rain to wash away the blood, for the field grass to spring back up again where the deer was shot.

He still don't say anything, though, so I start off for home, chest tight.

"Just a minute," says Judd.

I stop. He goes back inside the trailer, me waiting there in the yard. What am I going to say, he tries that? What am I going to do?

And then Judd's back in the doorway again, and he's got something in his hand. Comes down the steps halfway.

143

"Here," he says, and it's a dog's collar—an old collar, but better than the one Shiloh's got now. "Might be a little big, but he'll grow into it."

I look at Judd and take the collar. I don't know how we done it, but somehow we learned to get along.

"Thanks a lot," I tell him.

"You got yourself a dog," he says, and goes inside again, don't even look back.

I get home that evening, and Ma's baked a chocolate layer cake to celebrate—a real cake, too, not no Betty Crocker.

After dinner, Ma and Dad on the porch, the four of us rolls around on the grass together—Dara Lynn, Becky, Shiloh, and me. Becky tries to give Shiloh her butterfly kiss, but he don't hold still long enough to feel her eyelashes bat against him, just got to lick everywhere on her face.

And long after Becky and Dara Lynn goes inside, I lay out there on my back in the grass, not caring about the dew, Shiloh against me crosswise, his paws on my chest.

I look at the dark closing in, sky getting more and more purple, and I'm thinking how nothing is as simple as you guess—not right or wrong, not Judd Travers, not even me or this dog I got here. But the good part is I saved Shiloh and opened my eyes some. Now that ain't bad for eleven.

SHILOH
SEASON

SHILOH
SEASON

by
PHYLLIS
REYNOLDS
NAYLOR

ATHENEUM BOOKS FOR YOUNG READERS

With special thanks to the staff of Seven Locks Animal
Hospital, Potomac, Maryland, for their information and help,
and to Frank and Trudy Madden, once again, for their love
and care of the real Shiloh.

Atheneum Books for Young Readers
An imprint of Simon & Schuster Children's Publishing Division
1230 Avenue of the Americas
New York, New York 10020
Text copyright © 1996 by Phyllis Reynolds Naylor
All rights reserved including the right of reproduction
in whole or in part in any form.
Book design by Becky Terhune
The text of this book is set in Goudy.
First Edition
Printed in the United States of America
20 19 18 17 16 15 14 13 12

Library of Congress Cataloging-in-Publication Data
Naylor, Phyllis Reynolds.
Shiloh season / Phyllis Reynolds Naylor. —1st ed.
p. cm.
Sequel to: Shiloh.
Summary: When mean and angry Judd, who has never known kindness,
takes to drinking and mistreats his dogs, Marty discovers how deep a hurt
can go and how long it takes to heal.
ISBN 0-689-80647-7
[1. Dogs—Fiction. 2. Kindness—Fiction. 3. West Virginia—Fiction.]
I. Title.
PZ7.N24Sgg 1996
[Fic]—dc20
95-32558

To my granddaughters,
Sophia and Tressa Naylor,
with love

One

After Shiloh come to live with us, two things happened. One started out bad and ended good. The other started out good and . . . Well, let me tell it the way it was.

Most everybody near Friendly, West Virginia, knows how Judd Travers treats his dogs, and how he bought this new little beagle to help him hunt, and how the beagle kept running away from Judd's kicks and curses. Ran to me.

They know the story of how I hid the dog in a pen I made for him up in our woods and named him Shiloh. Judd just calls his dogs cuss words. And everybody in Tyler County, almost, heard how a German shepherd jumped into that pen and tore up Shiloh something awful, and then the secret was out. My dad drove Shiloh over to Doc Murphy, who sewed him up and helped him live.

And then, because my friend David Howard has the biggest mouth from here to Sistersville, most everybody knows how I worked for Judd Travers two weeks to earn that dog. So now he's mine. Mine and Ma's and Dad's and Dara Lynn's and Becky's. We all just love him so's he can hardly stand it sometimes; tail wags so hard you figure it's about to fly off.

Anyway, the thing that started out bad and ended good was that I promised Doc Murphy I'd pay him every cent we owed him for fixing up Shiloh. I looked for bottles and aluminum cans the whole rest of the summer, but only earned two dollars and seventy cents.

When I took it to Doc Murphy, though, so he could subtract it from our bill, he says I can work off the rest, same as I worked for Judd. Next to Judd telling me I can have Shiloh for my own, that was the best news I'd heard in a long time.

And now for the good part that turned bad and then worse: after figuring that everything's okay now between me and Judd Travers—he even gave me a collar for Shiloh—Judd starts drinking.

Not that he didn't drink before. Got a belly on him like a watermelon sticking out over his belt buckle, but now he's drinkin' hard.

First time I know anything about it, I'm coming up the road from Doc Murphy's, Shiloh trottin' along ahead or behind. That dog always finds something old he's got to smell twice or something new he ain't smelled at all, and his legs can hardly get him there fast enough. I think he was down in the creek while I was working at Doc's, and he's trying to make like he was with me the whole time.

I'm following along, thinking how happiness is a wet dog with a full stomach, when I hear this truck coming up the road behind me. I can tell by the sound that it's going faster than it should. My first thought, as I turn my head, is that if it don't slow down, it won't make the bend, and then I see that it's Judd Travers's pickup.

I take this flying leap into the field, like I'm doing a belly flop in Middle Island Creek, and for a couple seconds I can't even breathe—it's knocked the wind right out of me. I watch the truck go off the road a couple feet farther on, then weave back on again, over to the other side, and finally it starts slowing down for the bridge.

Shiloh comes running back, licks my face to see if I'm all right. The question in my mind is did Judd try to run me over or didn't he even see me, he's that drunk? And if Shiloh had been behind me instead of up front, would I be looking at a dead dog right now?

"Judd almost ran me over!" I say that night at supper.

"He *what?*" says Ma.

I tell my folks what happened.

"He do it on purpose?" asks Dara Lynn. Ma's fixed white beans and corn bread, with little chunks of red ham in the beans, and Dara Lynn's counting out the pieces of ham on her plate. Wants to be sure she got as many as Ma gave me.

"I don't know," I tell her.

Ma looks at Dad. "This is serious, Ray."

Dad nods. "I guess I've been hearing right, then. They say Judd's been stopping off at a bar down near Bens Run. Does his drinking nights and weekends."

Ma's anxious. "You'd best keep off the road, Marty," she says. "You, too, Dara Lynn. You hear his truck coming, give him plenty of room."

"All he's going to do is get himself arrested," I say. "Why's he start drinking so hard all of a sudden?" Even I know that when a person does that it means he's bothered.

"Maybe he's thirsty!" says Becky, and we all laugh.

Becky's three. Dara Lynn laughs, too, even though it's something she might have said. Dara Lynn's seven. I'm four years older than that, and supposed to set an example for my sisters, says Ma, which is why it was so hard on my folks when they found out I'd been hiding Judd's dog up in our woods.

"I think Judd drinks because he's unhappy," says Ma. She smooths out the margarine on her piece of corn bread, then takes a real slow bite.

"Maybe he misses Shiloh," says Becky, trying again. I wish she hadn't said that.

"Why?" asks Dara Lynn. "He's got all those other dogs to keep him company."

Ma chews real thoughtful. "I think he looks in the mirror and don't like what he sees," she says. "The fact that his dog kept running away and coming to you, Marty, and the way you kept on working for Judd even though he called you a fool—I think that made him take a good hard look at himself, and it wasn't pretty."

Becky nods her head up and down. "Judd's not pretty," she says, real serious, and we laugh again.

All this time, my dad is breaking up his corn bread over his pile of beans, and then he eats it mixed together, and I notice he's the one not laughing.

"What's worrying me is that Judd's been hunting up in our woods, I think. Rabbits, I expect. I found a beer can up there, the brand Judd drinks, and heard a couple shots yesterday, same as last weekend."

"We've got those woods *posted*!" Ma says, meaning we got signs up around the property saying we don't allow any hunting. But poachers sneak in there sometimes anyway.

4

Up in our woods, and even in our meadow on the far side of the hill.

Her gray eyes are fixed on Dad now. "Ray, you've got to tell him! I don't want him up there drunk, firing his gun off every which way. One of those bullets could end up down here."

"I'll talk to him," Dad says.

I'm real quiet then. In fact, I'm through with the beans on my plate. Been thinking about taking a second helping, but suddenly I'm not hungry anymore, so I go outside and sit on the steps. It's been real warm and dry for September, and I like to catch a breeze.

Shiloh comes over and lies down beside me, head on my leg. Then he takes this big contented sigh and closes his eyes.

What my folks don't know—what nobody knows except me and Judd Travers—is how the only way I got Judd to let me keep his dog was that I saw him shoot a deer out of season. A doe it was, too. And when he knew I could report him to the game warden—I *would* have, too—he said I could keep Shiloh if I kept my mouth shut about the doe and if I worked for him two solid weeks. I swear Judd must have laid awake nights thinking of the hardest, meanest jobs he had for me to do, but I did 'em, every one.

So a promise is a promise, even if I shouldn't have made it in the first place. There wasn't any point in telling the secret now anyway. The doe and all traces of the killing were long gone.

I lean against the porch post and stroke the top of Shiloh's head, smooth as corn silk. Here I'd thought now that Judd and me were almost, but not quite, friends—you couldn't be *real* friends with a man like Judd Travers—I wouldn't have to worry anymore. But Ma says drink will make a person do things he never in this world thought he'd do, and you put drink in Judd Travers, you got a bomb just waiting to blow up. He might not try to run over Shiloh, or shoot him out of spite, but what if he's up in our woods hunting and Shiloh runs through? What if Judd shoots at the first thing that moves?

After supper Dad comes out, and he's carrying this beer can he found in our woods. He puts it on the front seat of the Jeep, then climbs in and heads down the driveway.

I watch the Jeep pause way out by the road, then turn right and go past the mill. It crosses the rusty bridge to the old Shiloh schoolhouse that's been closed as long as I can remember. After that it's out of sight and I know that in two or three minutes Dad will pull up outside the trailer where Judd Travers lives.

I listen. Yep. About two minutes later, way off in the distance, I hear all Judd's dogs barking at once, which means they hear the Jeep. All those dogs are mean as nails, 'cause the only time Judd don't keep 'em chained is when he takes 'em hunting.

I figure that about this time Judd's looking out his window, wondering who's driving up to see him at seven o'clock on a Sunday night. Then he'll get up and come to the door in his undershirt.

Dad'll walk up the boards that serve as Judd's sidewalk, and they'll stand on Judd's steps awhile, talking about the kind of weather we've been having, and are the apples going to be any good this fall, and when is the county going to fix that big pothole just this side of the bridge.

And finally, after they say all that, Dad'll show Judd the

beer can and say he's sure Judd didn't mean to wander off up in our woods when he was hunting, but Dad figures the beer can is his, and he's been hearing these shots. He surely would appreciate it, he'll say, if Judd wouldn't hunt in our woods. He don't like to make a fuss, but when a man's got children, he's got to look out for them.

My mind can think up about a dozen ways Judd could answer back, none of 'em polite, but I don't let myself dwell on it. I'm running my hand over Shiloh's head real slow, and I can tell by his eyes how he likes it. If Shiloh was a cat, he'd purr.

Becky comes out to sit beside me, and pulls her dress way up to let the cool air fan her belly.

"Shouldn't do that way, Becky," I tell her. You got to start teaching her young or she'll do like that down in Sistersville sometime, not think twice about it.

"Why?" says Becky, smartlike, and pushes her face right up against mine.

"'Cause it's not ladylike to show your underpants, is why," I tell her. I figure that's how Ma would answer.

Dara Lynn's out on the porch now, still eating a handful of cornbread crumbs, and she hears what I say to Becky. I can tell by her eyes she's up to mischief. Wipes her hands on her shorts, then sticks her thumbs down inside the elastic and starts snappin' it hard as she can—*snap, snap, snap*—the elastic on her shorts and underpants both, just to rile me.

Of course Becky laughs and then she's doing it, too, both of 'em snapping away at their underpants in a wild fit of the giggles. Girl children are the strangest people in the world sometimes.

But then I hear the Jeep coming back. Dara Lynn hears

7

it, too, and stops bein' crazy. Finally Becky gives up and we all watch Dad's Jeep—the one he delivers his mail in—come across the old rusty bridge again, on up the road, then turn in at our driveway.

Ma comes out on the porch, hands resting on her hips. "Well?" she says, as Dad gets out. "What'd he say?"

Dad don't answer for a moment. Just walks over to the house and throws the beer can in our trash barrel.

"Might be a good idea if the kids didn't play up in the woods for a while," he says.

Ma stares after him as he goes inside.

TWO

Miss Talbot's new to our school this year, and I've got her for sixth grade. She's young, younger than Ma, but she's got the same kind of cheekbones up high on her face. Wears her hair the same, too, pulled back on top and fixed with a barrette, then hanging loose around her shoulders.

David Howard and I sit next to each other. Miss Talbot said we could sit wherever we liked, but it was up to us whether or not she'd let us stay there. Just a polite way of saying that if we cause any trouble, she'll change our seats faster than you can spend a nickel.

Since she didn't know any of our names yet that first day, she asked each of us to tell her something about ourselves, and you wouldn't believe what some of the kids thought to tell.

Sarah Peters told how she fell off a swing last year and broke a tooth. Now who do you figure cares about that? Tooth's been *fixed*! Ain't nothing to see!

Fred Niles said they've got a new baby sister at his house, which wasn't exactly the biggest news in the world, 'cause he's got five sisters already.

Then David Howard told how his family flew to Denver the last week of August, and Denver's called the Mile-High City, because the state capitol's a mile up in the air, only nobody believed him. So Miss Talbot got out the encyclopedia and showed us he was right. Then she told us something else we didn't know: there's a Denver, West Virginia, too. In fact, *two* Denvers, one in Preston County and one in Marshall. Miss Talbot's sister lives in one of 'em, she said.

When it was my turn that day, I told about Shiloh and how I worked two weeks to make him mine, and then Michael Sholt told how there was this drunk man who drove by their house sometimes and once even knocked over their mailbox.

Everyone started whispering then, and the whisper went around the room: ". . . Judd . . . Judd . . . Judd. . . ." it went, one person to the next.

Miss Talbot didn't know who Judd was. Somebody's father, maybe? So she just said she hoped that whoever this person was, he wouldn't get it in his head to drive the next time he was drinking, 'cause he might run over a child or a little dog. And since I was the only one who had told about a dog, she looked right at me, and it didn't make me feel one bit better about leaving Shiloh alone all day.

There's times I wish we could just keep Shiloh in the house while I'm at school. But Ma says when you love someone, you don't keep him locked up, not a dog like Shiloh who likes to run; when you love, you got to take chances.

Every day when school lets out in Sistersville, the bus rolls alongside the Ohio River till it gets to Friendly, then turns and winds up the road toward the little community of Shiloh, which is where I found my dog. Which is why I named him what I did. One by one, sometimes two and three at a time, kids get off. David, of course, gets off in Friendly. Then Sarah and a few of the others, then Michael, then Fred, till at last it's only Dara Lynn and me. The bus goes as far as the old mill and turns around.

And always, there's Shiloh, barreling down the drive-way to meet us, his legs can hardly go any faster. Skids sometimes, whole body leanin' sideways, gravel flying out from under his paws, but he's standing there with his tongue out the minute Dara Lynn and me step off that bus, ready to lick us up one side of our faces and down the other.

I love this dog more than I ever loved anything in my whole life, I think. Except Ma and Dad. And Becky. And . . . well, I suppose, even Dara Lynn. One night I dreamed Judd Travers come to me with his shotgun, said he was going to shoot either Shiloh or Dara Lynn, which would it be? And I woke up in a cold sweat—still couldn't decide. Suppose I'd save Dara Lynn, it ever come to that, but boy, she'd have to work the rest of her life tryin' to make it up to me.

I get out the scrap of sandwich I always save in my lunch bucket and make a game of it with Shiloh. Take it out, cupped in my hands, then lie down in the grass, hands under my chest. Shiloh tries every which way to roll me over and get at that crust of bread, little sliver of ham still stuck to it.

After he gets it, though, Dara Lynn has to go through her hugging business, and Shiloh puts up with that, too.

11

"How's my wittle Shiloh-biloh-wiloh?" she sings, picking him up in her arms like a baby. He washes her face clean with his tongue, 'specially the corners of her mouth where there's still the flavor of lunch.

Too disgusting to watch, you want the truth, so I go on up to the house and Dara Lynn comes after.

On this day Becky's on the porch swing playing airplane or boat, either one. Looks maybe like she's playing boat, 'cause she's got a string hanging down over the side, like she's fishing.

When I get in the house, Ma's on the phone with Dad's sister over in Clarksburg. First time we've had a telephone in three years. Ever since Grandma Preston's mind started to go, Aunt Hettie had to have a nurse come in while she was at work to watch Grandma all the time. It was Dad who paid for that nurse, every spare cent we had.

Last month, though, Grandma Preston had a stroke, and what little sense she had left all but went. Not only that, but her kidneys failed. Got a bad hip so she can't get in and out of bed no more by herself, and Aunt Hettie was up half the night with her, still trying to work days.

"Your mother needs more care than you can give her," the doctor says finally to Aunt Hettie, so Dad drove down, and he and Aunt Hettie put Grandma in a nursing home.

Weird thing is, though, long as we were all trying to care for Grandma Preston ourselves—Aunt Hettie doing the work and Dad sending the money—we didn't get any help. Now that Grandma Preston's in a nursing home, not one penny to her name, the government pays for the nursing home and Dad says we can afford a telephone again and a few other things we've had to do without.

Dara Lynn and I sit down at the table, taking turns

easing our hands into a box of graham crackers and listening to Ma.

"She *did*, Hettie? Oh, land, what next?" Ma's saying.

Becky comes in and we give her a cracker. But soon as Ma's off the phone, I say, "What happened?"

Ma shakes her head. "I want the three of you to promise that I ever get to acting crazy, you'll remember me the way I am now."

Dara Lynn gets this gleam in her eye. "*I'll* remember you acting crazy!" she says.

"What'd Grandma do?" I ask. "How much trouble can she get into when she's in a wheelchair?"

Ma sighs. "She's been wheeling herself into other people's rooms uninvited. *Men's* rooms. She's got it in her head that Grandpa Preston's still alive and they're hiding him somewhere."

Becky stares, but Dara Lynn laughs out loud, and it's all I can do not to grin.

"Aunt Hettie's afraid if Grandma don't behave herself, they'll put her out, but those nurses know what to do. They understand."

Nice thing about a telephone is it helps you make plans. Before, when I wanted to say something to David Howard, I'd have to give the message to Dad, and Dad would tell it to David when he put the mail in their box. Then I'd have to wait all day for Dad to get home to find out what David said.

Now when the phone rings, everybody wants to answer.

Becky, when she gets there first, puts her mouth right up to the phone and says in this tiny little voice, "Hi, I'm Becky and I'm three years old and . . . and I have a dog." Somethin' like that. You almost have to sit on her to wrestle that telephone out of her hand.

The phone rings again and I answer. It's David.

"Why don't you stay at my house Friday night and I'll stay at yours on Saturday?" he says.

I ask Ma. She says yes, if I be sure my socks and underwear are clean.

So Friday of that week, I put my toothbrush in my pencil case before I leave for school, and when Shiloh follows Dara Lynn and me down to the end of the driveway, I'm thinking how when the bus gets back that afternoon, I'm not going to be on it.

I kneel down in the grass beside my dog.

"Listen, Shiloh," I say. "I'm not comin' back tonight. I'm staying over with David Howard, but I'll be home tomorrow, okay?" As though he understands a single word. I'm thinking that maybe he understands *something's* going to be different, even though he don't know what.

The bus comes then around the bend, and Shiloh barks and backs away. He don't much care for the big yellow monster that gobbles us up weekday mornings, and spits us out again each afternoon.

After I get on and the bus turns around, I always go to the back window and look out. See Shiloh trotting up the driveway, tail between his legs. He stops every so often and looks back, then goes a few steps more.

And I'm thinking that much as I like David Howard, much as I like going to his house, I sure don't like the thought of me being gone a whole night, Shiloh at home without me, and Judd Travers maybe out there in the dark.

14

Three

Kids are always wild at school on Fridays. Restless to get the weekend started—go poking along the bank of Middle Island Creek, maybe—borrow someone's rowboat and row out to an island, if the water's deep enough. Could wade across, if it isn't.

Funny, but as long as I can remember, Ma's called it "the river." Dad told us, soon as she laid eyes on it after he married her and brought her here, she says, "That's no creek to me; it's wide as a river." So we kids forget sometimes and call it "the river," too.

On the bus going home, Michael Sholt's got another story about Judd Travers getting in a fight down in Bens Run a couple nights back, but I don't hear the end of it, 'cause I get off with David Howard, and Dara Lynn rides the rest of the way without me.

I always feel a little strange at David Howard's. It's a big house, for one thing—all kinds of rooms in it. A whole room just for David. Another room for his father's books and computer. Even a room for plants! I told Ma about that once and she said if it was her house, she'd put some of those plants outside where they belong and make more room for *people*.

Meals are fancier at David Howard's, too. The food doesn't taste any better than it does at home, but Mrs. Howard has placemats under all the plates and cloth napkins rolled up in plastic rings. The way I eat at David Howard's, I watch what everybody else does before I start in.

His folks are nice, though. His dad works for the *Tyler Star–News*, and talks to me a lot about basketball, even though I like baseball better. He always forgets. Asks me about the New York Knicks when it's the White Sox I got my eye on.

Mrs. Howard's a teacher, and she can't help herself: she sees something wrong, she corrects it.

"Shiloh don't like to see me climb on the bus each morning," I say at dinner, about the time she's passing out the dessert.

"He *doesn't*, Marty?" she says. "He *doesn't* like to see you climb on the bus?"

"No, he don't," I answer, my eyes on the chocolate pie, and then David giggles and I know I goofed again.

After dinner, David and me go outside and play kick-the-can with some other kids till after dark, and when we come in, Mr. Howard teaches me some moves on a chessboard. After that we eat some more and watch a video, *Homeward Bound*. Then we take turns in the shower and have to mop up the floor.

That night I'm lying on the top bunk in David's room and I can't believe I'm homesick. Thinking about my

16

family, what they had for supper, whether or not the telephone rang, and who answered. What crazy thing Grandma Preston done this time, and whether Shiloh's watching the door, waiting for me to come home.

I'm thinking Ma will give him extra love tonight. She don't know this, but once—when Shiloh was healing his hurt leg—I woke real early in the morning from where I sleep on our couch, and across the room I saw my ma in the rocking chair. She had Shiloh on her lap, and was rocking and singing to that dog like he was a baby. I figure Ma's just getting herself ready for the day Becky, Dara Lynn, and me are grown and gone.

Haven't heard a peep from David Howard for a while down on that bottom bunk, and I figure he's probably already asleep. We played so hard and so long he's a right to be tired.

I wasn't, though. Hard to sleep with cars going by every few minutes, the beam from their headlights traveling along the wall. I'm lying there on my side, about to close my eyes, when suddenly this horrible face with red eyes and green lips pops right up beside me, not five inches from my own, and bobs up and down—a floating head.

I yell. Can't help myself, and then David's having a laughing fit down below.

"Settle down, you guys," comes Mr. Howard's voice as he passes our door.

I want to know how David did that, though, so I crawl down the ladder and push my way onto David's bed, punching his arm. David's got his head under the covers, he's laughing so hard.

"How'd you do that?" I whisper.

David shows me this rubber Halloween mask. He puts

17

it on and holds a flashlight under his chin. Then, when he moves around and all that's lit up is the mask, it looks like a floating head. I'm thinking how I can't wait to try that on Dara Lynn.

We lay on our backs on David's bunk and talk some more about school and the story Michael Sholt was telling, about Judd getting in a fight with someone. We talk about the way he's been drinking lately, and I tell him Ma's guess—that Judd looks in the mirror and don't like what he sees.

David raises up on one elbow. I can just make out his face in the dark. His eyes are wide open.

"You know what *that* means!" he says.

"What?"

"He's a vampire!" David says, his eyes about to jump out of his head. Even when David *knows* it's crazy, his imagination still runs off with him.

"You're nuts," I say.

"Vampires *hate* mirrors. If they ever look in a mirror, they die or something."

"Then if he was a vampire he wouldn't even *have* one!" I tell David.

"Oh," David says, and lays back down. A minute goes by and David pops right up again.

"A werewolf!" he says.

"David, you're as crazy as Grandma Preston," I say, and then I'm ashamed. It's not like she *wants* to be.

But David's excited all over again. "It figures, Marty! He looks in the mirror and sees fur and fangs, and he just goes a little crazy. The only way to find out . . ."

I know what's coming before David ever says the next word.

"I'm staying at your place tomorrow night. We'll go check out Judd then. Okay?"

"Okay," I tell him.

David don't think Judd Travers is a werewolf any more than I do. He just likes the idea of spying on him—stirring up a little excitement.

I crawl back up in the top bunk and can hear David snoring after a while. I fall asleep some time later, but don't know how long it's been 'cause all at once, middle of the night, there's this loud yell.

My eyes pop open, and the yell seems to hang in the air like an echo.

Can't figure out where I am. The bed's smooth, not lumpy like our couch. Then I remember I'm at David Howard's, and figure it was me who yelled. Wondered if I'd woke him up.

The dream was so *real*. Dreamed I'd just got up out of bed and walked home. Seemed to be half light—early morning, maybe—and I was hoping Ma would be up, tell me Shiloh was okay. But nobody seemed to be around, and I could see Shiloh sleeping out on the porch.

Whew, I'm thinking. He's all right.

Everything looks calm and natural, but just as I get close to the house, I see this long stick there in the bushes. . . . Looks like a branch has fallen out of a tree, maybe, and then I see it's not a stick at all, it's a gun, and it's pointed straight at Shiloh.

It's the kind of dream where your legs don't move, and you yell and yell, but no sound comes out.

Except I must have made some noise, because next thing I know I hear footsteps out in the hall and our door clicks open.

"Everything okay in here?" comes Mr. Howard's voice, real soft.

"Yeah," I say. "We're okay."

Mr. Howard closes the door again and I look at the clock. Four fifteen. Can't wait for it to turn light so I can go check on my dog.

Four

D ad come by in the Jeep next morning to take me home. Six days a week he picks up the mail in Sistersville for two hundred and eighty families, and after he delivers that, he picks up the mail for three hundred and sixty more outside of Friendly.

We don't go directly home, of course. I got to wait while he stops at every mailbox between David's house and ours. Could've walked it, but I like to open boxes for Dad, stuff the mail in.

What I like most, though, is finding a loaf of banana bread or half an apple pie that folks sometimes leave in their boxes for Dad. People like my dad because he delivers their mail no matter what. Can be seven o'clock in the evening, snowing like you wouldn't believe, but Dad'll be out there in his Jeep, getting that mail through.

Soon as I slide on the seat beside him, though, and we give the mail to David Howard, I ask, "Shiloh okay?"

Dad's moving the Jeep on to the next house. "Looked fine to me this morning," he says. "Why?"

"Just wondering," I tell him.

"You have a good time with David?"

"Sure. I always do."

I'm looking forward to Mrs. Ellison's box, which is coming up soon, because she leaves a piece of cake for Dad almost every day. Sure enough, I reach my hand in her box and pull out a loaf wrapped in foil, and my mouth's watering already. Then I read the label she's put on it: ZUCCHINI BREAD, it says.

"Why'd she have to *ruin* it?" I say. "Who would put squash in a cake loaf?"

Dad just chuckles. "You take a bite of that, you won't even notice," he says, but I figure I can last the morning on the pecan waffles Mrs. Howard made for our breakfast.

I get the mail ready for the next box. "Did you know there are two Denvers in West Virginia?" I say.

"Wouldn't surprise me if there are even a couple more," Dad says.

"How can there be two places named the same in one state?" I ask.

"If you don't incorporate, you can call a place most anything you want," he says. "We could call our own place Denver if we wanted."

"Could we call it New York City or Chicago?"

"Expect you could. Postmaster down in Friendly would have a laughing fit, that's all," says Dad.

After I put the mail in Mrs. Ellison's box and turn up the red flag on the side so she can see she's got mail, I ask, "Dad, what happened at Judd's last Saturday when you went over?"

Dad gives a sigh. "Let's just say that Judd wasn't himself, Marty."

"He was drinking again, wasn't he?"

"He'd been drinking some, yes."

"Did he say he'd been hunting up in our woods?"

"Conversation didn't exactly go the way I'd planned."

"So what'd he say?"

"Oh, he rambled on about how you took the best hunting dog he ever had. Just nonsense, Marty."

I can feel my chest tighten, though. It was the one thing I didn't want to hear.

"I earned that dog fair and square!" I say.

"Of course you did. Judd was just jawin' again. But I don't want you and Becky and Dara Lynn up in those woods till I've got this settled. Don't want you up in the meadow either. Next time I hear gunshots, I'm going up there myself and check."

Didn't make me feel any better.

It's nice to be riding along with my dad on a warm September day, though—breeze coming in one window and floating out the other. When we get up as far as our driveway, I decide I'll go on across the bridge with Dad this time and help deliver the mail on the road where Judd lives. Figure this will give Judd a second chance to say something about Shiloh if he's got a grudge building up inside him. Maybe if we can talk it out, things'll be okay.

But when we get up to his trailer, an old brown-and-white thing with rust stains on the roof, Judd's nowhere to be seen. We know he's not out hunting because all three of his dogs are chained. They go crazy when they see the Jeep. Leap and growl and bark, teeth showing, chains jerking.

I put the mail in Judd's box and watch the door, thinking maybe he'll hear all the ruckus and come out. His truck's there. But there's no sign of him, living or dead, and I wonder if he's even fed his dogs this morning.

"Judd don't work Saturdays?" I ask as the Jeep starts up again.

"Think he works every other Saturday, something like that."

"What kind of work does he do?" I try to think what kind of job would be right for a man like Judd Travers. Rattlesnake handler, maybe. Alligator wrestler . . .

"Mechanic," says Dad. "Works on trucks and cars down at Whelan's Garage. I hear he's right good at it."

I guess a man can be good at some things and horrible at others. Good with car and truck engines, and bad with dogs and people.

Dad's route ends a couple miles down at a ford where water comes over the road, and that's where we turn around and head back. After we come across the bridge by the old mill, I take our mail and zucchini bread and head on up to the house, 'cause Dad's got a couple hours of deliveries yet to do.

And here come Shiloh to meet me, legs flying out from under him. I pinch off a piece of the zucchini bread and he gulps it right down. That dog'll eat anything. You give him a piece of bread made of spinach and brussels sprouts, bet he'd gobble that down, too, beg for more.

I go up the driveway beside Shiloh. I'm thinking how he's always in a good mood. Always ready to jump to his feet and do any fool thing you got in mind. Don't matter how tired he is or how hot or cold it is outside, he'll be right there at the door waiting to go with you. You treat a dog right, and he's your friend for life.

Better natured than sisters, that's for sure. Dara Lynn gets up some mornings, looks like she's about to break your arm you even look at her cross-eyed.

I eat lunch—Ma's got some turkey sandwiches waiting—before I head over to Doc Murphy's to do my work.

"What'd you do at David's?" Dara Lynn asks me, mouth full of bread.

"All kinds of stuff," I tell her.

"Did Mrs. Howard have a good dinner?" asks Ma.

I'm only eleven, but I know that when your ma asks about somebody else's cooking, you got to be real careful.

"The chocolate pie was good," I say, and Becky and Dara Lynn both start squealin' about why don't we ever have chocolate pie? "But the rest wasn't anything special," I finish.

"What was it?" Mothers have to know the *details*.

"Some kind of meat, I guess. Some kind of vegetables," I tell her. She don't look so interested after that.

Shiloh follows me down toward Doc Murphy's. Before we get to the end of the driveway, though, I see Judd's pickup coming across the bridge on the right. It gets down at the bottom of our driveway and stops.

Thump . . . thump . . . thump. . . . Hard to tell sometimes if it's your heart beating or your knees knocking, or both of them together. It'd be cowardly to turn around and go back now, so I just keep walking. Shiloh don't, though. He stops dead still.

"Hey, Marty!" Judd opens the truck door and puts one foot out. "Come on down here."

I don't know whether to go or not.

"What you want?" I call.

"Want to show you something."

I don't want much to go, but then Judd gets out and walks around behind his truck. He's pointing to the back, so I go down and walk over.

"Look there," says Judd.

Somebody's taken a nail or screwdriver or something and made a long, deep scratch in the paint all the way from Judd's license plate to the door on the right-hand side.

I give a little whistle.

"You have any idea who might'a done this to my truck?"

Judd Travers is uglier than a snake. Not face-ugly, exactly, but mean-ugly. He ever try being anything but mean, he might not look too bad. Eyes are all bloodshot, though, and his breath—whew! You put your nose down inside a beer bottle, that's his smell.

I shake my head.

He looks at me hard. "You think of any boys who could've done it?"

"Nobody I know."

"Well, you listen around, and if you find out who scratched my truck, you tell me, hear?"

"I'll listen," I say, but I don't promise nothing.

Judd gets in his pickup and drives off, and it's not till he's out of sight that Shiloh comes on down. Don't take a lot to prove that Judd Travers isn't the most popular person in Tyler County.

That man can scare you so bad that even if you haven't done something, you almost wonder if you might. The kind of man you keep imagining all sorts of horrible things happening to, and then you feel guilty you enjoyed it. I'm

26

asking myself if it's such a good idea for David and me to go sneaking around Judd's tonight.

I walk on down to Doc's. He's got an office there in his house, but he don't see patients on Saturdays unless it's an emergency. His wife died ten years ago, and he tries to keep up the grass and flowers, just for her.

Doc figures I owe him about ninety-nine dollars for fixing up Shiloh after he was tore up by the German shepherd. I get three dollars an hour and work three hours every Saturday. Worked two Saturdays so far, so I got nine more to go.

"How's the patient doing?" Doc says, stepping out on the porch when he sees me coming. He's a heavy man, and he grunts some when he reaches down to pet my dog, check where he sewed him up. One of Doc's friends is a veterinarian down in St. Marys, and Doc checked with him after Shiloh was hurt, made sure he was doing right.

"Looks good, Shiloh," he says. "You keep out of trouble, now."

Today Doc wants some bushes transplanted from one side of his yard to another where they'll get more sun. He digs awhile, then I dig. Shiloh just lies on the grass in the shade, smiling at us, mouth open, and we laugh at the way he's watching us work.

"That dog sure has an easy life," Doc Murphy says, stopping to wipe the sweat off his forehead.

I'm wondering what kind of life he would have had if I'd turned him back over to Judd—if Shiloh would even be alive at all, the way Judd used to kick him and starve him every time he run off. Can't help thinking of the three dogs Judd's got left, all chained up, yelping and snarling at one another.

Doc begins digging again, and I hold on to the bush so's

27

it doesn't fall over while he works at getting the tip of the shovel down under the roots.

"You suppose the rest of Judd's dogs are ruined for good?" I ask. "I mean, once you chain a dog and he turns mean, is he going to be mean forever?"

"That I don't know, Marty," Doc says. "Sometimes I figure there's not all that much difference between a man and an animal. One has two legs, the other four—maybe that's the sum of it. I suppose some dogs and some people are born with meanness in them—something in their bloodline, maybe. . . ." He gives a final grunt, and the dirt ball lifts up. ". . . But a lot fewer than folks believe, I suspect. My own guess is that a little kindness will fix almost anything wrong with man or beast, but I wouldn't swear to it."

I lift the last forsythia bush up out of the ground and carry it over to the hole we dug for it on the other side of Doc's driveway. We work together to set that bush straight. Doc is going to a symphony concert in Wheeling this evening, so I finish the bushes myself, packing in loose dirt in each of the holes, making sure the bush is standing up straight.

Feel like an old man when I'm through, my back so sore. I head home at four, and Ma says I stink. Got to take a bath before David gets here, so I'm smelling sweet as a rose when David's mom drives up to our house. Shiloh never barks at the Howards' car—he's always glad to see David.

"You just have a bath or something?" David says, seeing my hair all slicked down.

"Sweet as a *rose*," I say, drawing out the "o," and I stick my armpit in his face. "Smell."

He laughs and pushes me away.

Ma comes out to talk with Mrs. Howard a few minutes, while David and I take turns on the bag swing we got hanging from our beech tree.

David climbs up the maple close by and sits out on a limb. Then I take the gunnysack hanging by a rope from the beech tree and toss it up to him, high as I can throw. David catches the rope, wraps his legs around the sack stuffed with straw, then slides right off the branch, hanging onto that rope for dear life. Swing swoops down toward the ground and way up in the air on the other side.

"Wheee!" yells David.

I should be having a good time, but I keep thinkin' about what David and me are going to do later.

He don't have any sisters or brothers, so he thinks Dara Lynn and Becky are cute. And they put on such a show of cuteness it almost makes your stomach sick.

Becky's got to sing the ABC song for him, only she always forgets what comes after the "L-M-N-O-P," so she starts all over again. Then Dara Lynn's got to get in the act, and after she shows David Howard all her scabs and bruises, she asks him jokes:

"How do you keep a bull from charging?" she says, grinning.

"I don't know," says David.

"Take away his credit card!" Dara Lynn shrieks.

She don't even know what a credit card is.

At supper, Ma's got apple dumplings for dessert, and we pour milk over them while they're still warm. David runs his finger around the bottom of his dish when he's done to get every last bit.

"What are you two boys planning to do this evening?" Ma asks as she clears the table.

29

"Fool around outside," I tell her.

I don't have to ask David Howard what he wants to do. David's got it all worked out in his head like a detective story, I can tell. And soon as we close the screen, he turns to me and asks, "How long will it take to get to Judd Travers's?"

Five

I figure when David Howard grows up, he'll be an explorer, a detective, or a spy.

Whenever there's a game where you have to crawl under a bush or slide on your belly or hide in a tree, that's what David wants to play. And because we have a lot more places to hide on our land than he does on his, that's why David Howard likes to come to our house.

Dad's reading Becky a story and Dara Lynn's helping Ma with the dishes. Only reason I got excused was I got a guest, and you can be sure Dara Lynn'll see to it that I have to do 'em two nights in a row.

"Takes about twenty, twenty-five minutes to walk to Judd's from here," I tell David.

"Okay. We'll need a canteen, a map, and a pair of binoculars," says David, his voice low.

"A map?" I say. "David, all we're doing is crossing the bridge and walking along the road till we get to Judd's."

31

"Not the way *we're* going!" says David. "How are you going to spy on someone if they see you come walking right up the road?"

So to please David Howard, I take the back of a used envelope and make a map of the bridge, the old Shiloh schoolhouse, and the road where Judd lives, plus the small private cemetery back in the trees behind someone's house.

David's brought his own canteen and his ma's field glasses, and I tell him if we don't set off right soon, Dara Lynn'll have all the dishes wiped and be begging to go with us.

We don't have to worry about Shiloh, though. Shiloh trots along beside us as we go down the driveway, but when we turn right instead of left, he pauses, not too sure, then lags ten feet behind us all the way to the bridge.

We stop to look at the pothole in the road. Been there since last spring. Must be seven inches deep, and three feet around.

"Wow!" says David Howard. "Looks like a sinkhole, Marty! I'll bet there's a cave under there, and the roof's falling in."

So of course we have to crawl down the bank and poke around in the weeds and bushes to see if there's a hidden entrance to an unexplored cave that nobody knows about. Every so often you read of someone discovering a new cave. Maybe his foot drops down in it when he's out hiking through a meadow, or his dog falls in and folks hear it whining. If we found a cave here under the road, with passages and waterfalls and stuff, we decide we'd name it the Howard–Preston Caverns.

We waste a good half hour of daylight lookin' for a cave that isn't there, and then climb back up to cross the bridge.

Shiloh won't go, though. Makes this pitiful-sounding whine in his throat. He tucks his tail between his legs and slinks off toward our driveway again. It hurts me to see how scared he still is of Judd Travers. He won't set foot on that bridge for all the rabbits in Tyler County.

"I'll be back, boy," I tell him. If I could just make him understand.

We set off down the road toward Judd's. David stops and takes a drink of water from his canteen, but I can tell he's not even thirsty. Just pretending he is, like we're working so hard and all.

We creep along through the bushes between the road and the creek, darting from tree to tree and waiting till the coast is clear before making a run for the next one. The coast is clear all up and down the road, of course—not a soul outside except an old woman sitting on her porch, and she don't have her glasses on. Don't even see us.

It's fun, though—all the spy talk.

"Agent XRX, Agent XRX. Come in, XRX," says David, holding one fist up to his mouth like a microphone.

"Read you, QZT," I say.

"How close are we now?" asks David.

"'Bout five houses more, I think. It's a brown-and-white trailer."

Problem is the houses are all so far apart up here you can't see Judd's trailer even when it's next one in line. Same as our house.

"Let's cut to the cemetery," says David.

We cross the road, go round behind a house, and creep through a lady's backyard, backs bent while we run like soldiers dodging enemy fire, hills looming up on our left. We pass this little cemetery plot with a low iron fence

33

around it. I mean, it's only two feet high; you can step right over it. There's a whole generation buried there, I guess, and all the names are Donaldson except one.

"Wait!" says David Howard, grabbing my arm.

I stop.

"Which way is the wind blowing?" he says.

"I don't know."

David licks his finger and holds it up in the air. He's still not sure, so he throws a handful of grass up and waits to see how it falls.

"We're going downwind!" he says, his eyes big, like we're on a ship that's sinking or something.

I try to look worried, too. "What do we do now?" I ask. "The dogs might smell us coming." There's no quick way to go around and get to Judd's from the other end, because we got hills on one side, Middle Island Creek on the other.

"We'll just have to be dead quiet," says David. "You want to risk it, XRX?"

"Roger," I tell him.

We get about fifty yards from Judd's trailer and we're down on our bellies, inching along through weeds two-feet high in the field right next to his yard. I'll probably have to explain the grass stains on my T-shirt to Ma, and I sure shouldn't have taken a bath, but it's worth it.

When we get close enough to Judd's trailer we wriggle around toward the road till we can see Judd's front door, and there he is, big as life, sitting out on the steps with a shotgun resting on his knees.

David and I just grab at each other and swallow.

Lucky for us, I guess, that Judd's dogs are chained on the other side, can't see us. They're quiet tonight. I guess when you're a dog, no matter how small your brain is or how full of meanness, you got sense enough to know that when a man's sitting out on his steps with a shotgun across his knees, you don't cause him any trouble.

"You think he's going hunting?" David whispers to me.

"Don't think so," I whisper back.

The scary thing is, Judd don't look like he's going anywhere. Not cleaning his gun either. Just sitting. And once in a while he spits. What's he waiting for? The person who scratched his truck, maybe? Just watching for someone to come along and try it again?

David Howard inches forward again, and I wish he wouldn't. I make my way up beside him and pull him back.

Then we realize Judd's talkin' to himself. Can't make out a single word, just a low kind of mutter. Every so often he slaps a knee or shakes his head, then he's quiet before he starts all over again. Not too hard to see he's been drinking.

It's right about then he suddenly jerks to attention and raises his gun, and I know for a fact I shouldn't be here. Shouldn't be anywhere near this place. But Judd's got his gun aimed at a tree in his front yard. At first I figure this shows just how drunk he is, mistaking a tree for a deer or something, but I raise my head in time to see two squirrels chasing each other around and around that tree trunk.

Judd lifts his gun and aims.

Bang!

One squirrel goes skittering on up the tree half crazy, and the other falls straight down and goes floppin' about the yard.

I can't watch. Put my head down on my arms and pray for that squirrel to die quick. But now all Judd's dogs are going nuts, yelping and barking, and above it all comes Judd's laugh.

"*Gotcha!*" he yells, and I can hear the slap of his hand on his knee again. He don't even stand up to go get the squirrel, or shoot it to put it out of its misery. I look up quick to see the squirrel still squirming, but then it lays still, only its tail twitching.

How can he *do* that way? I'm asking myself. To watch a living thing die slow like that, shot for no good reason at all? Wasn't as though Judd needed it for food—squirrel stew or something—because he don't even get off the step. Just spits again out the side of his mouth.

The other squirrel's comin' back now, probably to see what's happened to his pal, and just as Judd raises his gun again, I yell, "No, don't!" Can't help myself.

David pushes my head down. Judd jerks around.

"Who'zat?" he yells, but his words sound slurred. "Who said that?"

We hear him get up off the steps, and I think my heart's going to pound right through the skin on my chest. I'm about as frightened as I ever been in my life, because David and me weren't just walking down a country road where we've every right to be. We're lyin' belly down on Judd's property, and Judd could put some lead in us quicker than he could spit—say we were trespassing and he thought we'd come to rob him or something.

"Sound like Marty Preston to me," says Judd, and from where I'm lying, my chin on the ground, eyes turned up about as high as I can get 'em, I see Judd looking every which way, trying to figure out where that voice came from. "What you doing over here?" he yells again. "Your dad won't let me hunt on your land, so what you doing on mine?"

I press the side of my head to the ground, my whole

body as flat as it can get. All I can think of is Ma hearing that David and me were found with buckshot in our brains. This has got to be one of the stupidest things I ever did. I can hear Judd's big old boots comin' down the boards stretched across his yard.

Should I say something? I wonder. Call out and tell him we were just goin' by? And then I think how it will look, us just going by Judd's place flat on our bellies. I swallow.

The footsteps stop, don't come any closer. I tip my head so I can look up with one eye, and I see that Judd's so unsteady he's only gone as far as the end of the trailer. Got one hand against it, holding himself up, the other one's got the gun.

"I catch you foolin' around my truck, Marty Preston, I'll blast you to kingdom come!" he yells.

Finally, after the longest two minutes in the world, Judd goes back to the steps of the trailer again and then he goes inside.

David and I lie in the grass not saying a word—not breathing, hardly. Then slowly we inch backward out of those weeds the same way we came in, wondering all the while if Judd's got his shotgun aimed out a window, just watching for the weeds to wiggle.

When we're out of sight at last behind a lilac bush, we make a run for the little cemetery with all the Donaldsons in it, and from there, we cut on back out to the road.

We're breathing too hard to talk, almost.

". . . could of been us. . . ."

"Close as spit. . . ."

". . . squirrel hadn't done anything. . . ."

"Shouldn't have come. . . ."

". . . He knows it was you, Marty. . . ."

Both David and me feel sick inside. But there's one big thought taking up the whole of my mind, now that I seen Judd shoot the squirrel: squirrel season don't start till next month, so Judd's a little early; duck season starts in October; deer season starts in November. . . . But dogs? Not a thing on the charts about dog season. With Judd drinking every evening like he does, I tell myself, and now suspecting me of scratching his truck, he'll make his own rules. There could be a Shiloh season, and it could be any time at all.

Six

I don't sleep so good that night and neither does David Howard. When David comes over to spend the night, Ma opens up our couch to make a double bed, but it's got this bar down the middle inside the mattress, and every so often you hit it with your knee.

Shiloh, though, he sure likes to sleep down at the bottom of that bed. When you wake up in the night but your foot's still sleeping, you know you got a dog on it, that's why.

Both David and me wake early, and lie there talking while the house is still.

"You think we should tell?" David asks me.

"About the squirrel?" I say. He thinks *that's* bad, he should know what I know about Judd Travers.

He nods.

"You could, but it wouldn't do one bit of good. You ever hear of somebody getting fined for shooting a squirrel out of season, when you can walk from here to Friendly and find half a dozen dead on the road?"

It's a whole different thing, killing a squirrel or killing a deer. You can shoot only a few deer a year in West Virginia. During squirrel season, you can shoot six a day! Don't make it any more *right* to shoot a squirrel out of season. Just that the game warden isn't going to drive all the way up here because of a squirrel.

I guess it wasn't the fact that Judd killed a squirrel so much as the *way* he killed it. That's what made us sick. His plain delight in watching it flop about his yard while it's dyin'. What kind of kid was Judd Travers when he was growing up? I wonder. What kind of boy was he when he was fifteen? I'm puzzling over what his ma and dad were like, bringing up a son who could sit there and smile over a small creature's misery.

We must look pretty tired at breakfast, 'cause Ma says, "Were you boys up half the night playing games? You don't look very hungry to me. I don't see that bacon going anywhere."

David and I both reach for a piece of bacon just to show her we're awake and hungry, but we're not. Ma's biscuits are good, though. I show David how to mix a spoonful of honey with a spoonful of margarine—stir it up till it turns creamy, and then spread that on a hot biscuit.

We play on the bag swing till David's dad comes to pick him up. Dara Lynn gets up finally and watches us out the window, but our yelling don't wake Becky. She could sleep with a full brass band by her bed.

The Howards go to the Methodist church, and David's got to go home and change clothes first.

40

"See you at school Monday," David says as he gets in the car beside his dad.

"How you doing, Marty? You guys have fun?" Mr. Howard calls.

"Yeah," we both tell him. We did, too, but watching a squirrel die before our eyes wasn't part of it.

We like Sundays at our house 'cause they're slow. Dad's home all day, and he'll sit out on the porch swing reading the comics aloud to Dara Lynn and Becky. Takes all the different voices and makes us laugh.

Ma usually listens to Brother Jonas preach on TV, but now she's out in the kitchen making bread. She says that next to her children, she loves baking bread on Sundays about as much as anything she can think of.

She don't say so, but she loves Dad more'n she loves baking bread, too. And this morning after I listen to Dad read the comics, I go back in the kitchen where she's shaping the loaves and she's singing one of the country songs she likes so much:

> "If I could have three wishes,
> I'd spend 'em all on you.
> To love me when I'm lonely,
> To cheer me when I'm blue.
> To laugh with when I'm happy,
> Because I know you're true.
> If I could have three wishes, love,
> I'd spend 'em all on you."

I know it's not me she's singing about. I just smile and Ma smiles back.

I spread out my homework on the table across from her and do my arithmetic problems, trying not to let on that I'm worried:

Multiply: 687   1029   3998
             x .33   x .012   x 7.5
            _____   _____   _____

Divide: 687 by .33   1029 by .012   3998 by 7.5

I wonder if there is ever a time in my whole life that I will have 3998 of something and have to divide it by 7.5. I ask my ma.

"Even if you don't, Marty," she says, "arithmetic helps you think. It helps you learn to solve problems."

I'm thinking arithmetic can't help me solve the kind of problems we've got with Judd Travers. If that was true, I'd stay up to midnight every night just studying that arithmetic book.

The true fact is, I'm wondering if maybe some of Judd's drinking is because of me. The two weeks I'd worked for him during the summer, I'd got to know him some. And after a while we'd talk about his dogs and stuff, so that on the last day, I felt Judd was a little sorry to see me go. Sorry he wouldn't come home from work afternoons and find someone there he could talk to.

I'd figured to go back now and then to visit him—maybe even take Shiloh. But I could never get my dog to set foot over that bridge again, and since I wasn't all that eager to see Judd myself, a good idea just sort of washed away.

After we ate Sunday dinner, though, which at our house is about one in the afternoon, Dad lays down for a nap, Dara Lynn's got her paper dolls out on the swing, Becky's in bed, and Ma's got her feet up, reading a magazine. So I set out for Judd Travers's. I mean to come right out and tell him that yes, I was over there the night before, so he won't think I'm sneakin' around.

This time Judd's working on his truck. Got the hood up, and he's changing the oil. Don't seem like he's been drinking today. Leastwise, he's not drunk yet.

"Hi, Judd," I say.

Judd looks up and goes on tinkering under the hood of his truck. "What you up to?" he asks me.

"Nothin'. Just fooling around the creek," I tell him.

"You takin' good care of my dog?" he says.

Those are the very next words out of his mouth, and what I don't like are the words, "my dog."

"Shiloh's doin' fine," I tell him.

"Thought maybe you'd bring him by one of these days," Judd says. "How come he ain't with you now?"

How do you tell a man that your dog hates him more'n bee stings? "He's home playin' with Becky and Dara Lynn," I say. "They're fixing to spoil him."

Judd just grunts. "You don't take a dog hunting, he'll lose his touch."

"Dad'll probably take Shiloh with him when he starts hunting next month," I say. "Hunting season hasn't started yet, Judd. Only thing you can shoot in West Virginia this time of year is dove."

There's a sly grin pulling back the corners of Judd's mouth. "That a fact?" he says, and spits again as he wipes his hands on a rag.

What I'm trying not to look at is the remains of that squirrel. Pieces of squirrel all over Judd's yard. Looks to me like he got up this morning and threw that squirrel carcass to his dogs. Can just imagine those lean, mean dogs snapping and snarling at one another, eager to get a little blood on their muzzles.

I swallow. "Listen, Judd, I came to tell you somethin'."

"Yeah?" he says.

"David and me—he was over to my house last night—and we were playing spy. That *was* us you heard in your yard."

This time Judd raises up real slow. "So how come you didn't answer?"

"We were scared because you had that gun."

For a moment Judd don't quite know what to say. This amount of truthfulness is almost too much for him to handle. What I haven't counted on, though, is making Judd mad. His eyes get all squinty and the brows come together over the bridge of his nose.

"You expect me to believe that? You come all the way over here to play spy? You weren't *playin'*, boy, you were spyin', and wouldn't surprise me one bit your dad put you up to it."

"He *didn't!* He didn't even know we were here. But we shouldn't have been in your yard, and . . ."

He never even lets me finish. Judd's hollering now: "You and that boy come over here once, you've been here more'n that. And any two boys come sneakin' around my house, won't even answer, got something on their minds besides play. I'm no fool. It was you or that boy, or maybe the both of you, who scratched up my truck, I'm willing to bet, and I catch you over here again, I just may pull that trigger. A man's got a right to protect his property."

"Judd, I . . ."

"Go on home, you hear me?"

Judd's standing there with a wrench in his hand, and his face has gone from plain ugly to pure ugly—not a spark of kindness in those eyes at all.

When I don't move, he yells, "Git!" and takes a step forward, and that's when I turn and head for home.

Oh boy, I've done it now. I kick at a rock just about as hard as I can kick and send it flying into Middle Island Creek. I tell the truth, and look what happens.

Can't believe Judd would really put a bullet in me if he sees me over his way again, but I'm thinking he might could put a bullet in the living thing I love almost more'n anything else in the world. I sure can't go on like this, that much I know.

Dad's working outside when I get home, getting ready to mow. I stand over him as he pours gasoline in the mower.

"Somethin' on your mind?" he asks.

"I wonder if Judd's drinking on account of me," I say, trying to edge in easy on the subject. Dad won't like to hear that David and me were over at Judd's last night any more than Judd did.

Dad looks at me, screws the lid back on the gasoline can, then straightens up. "Now what put an idea like that in your head?"

"I was thinking how after I got Shiloh and worked for Judd, I never went back anymore. I think Judd sort of got used to me being around—somebody for him to talk to."

"Probably so, but I don't think a man starts drinking because an eleven-year-old boy don't show up. Judd's got problems that don't have anything to do with you, Marty. He sure wouldn't get no prize for getting along with people."

"But he says those things about Shiloh—about me taking his dog and all."

"Judd'll jaw on about anything, you give him a chance. You know that. You know and I know and he knows that you earned that dog. Why do you keep worrying about it?"

"I'm afraid he'll get drunk sometime and shoot Shiloh."

"Well, *I'm* worried he'll get drunk, go hunting up in our woods with his rifle, and a stray bullet will hit one of you kids," Dad says. "You want to worry about something real, take that one."

"But after all I did to protect Shiloh—the way that dog come to me—I just couldn't stand it if anything was to happen to him now," I say. I follow Dad as he pushes the mower over to a corner of our yard. "Couldn't we . . . well, invite Judd to dinner or something? Make like we're really friends?"

Dad's looking question marks at me. "Marty, no more'n two months ago, you were hating Judd Travers worse'n a rattlesnake, and now you want to invite him home?"

"Just to keep on his good side." I'm thinking maybe now is the time I should tell Dad I was over at Judd's, but there's something about him that stops me.

Dad rests his hands on the handle of the mower and takes in a big breath. "Fact is," he says, not looking directly at me, "when I was up to see Judd last week, I lost my temper. I'm not proud of it, but it happened. I showed him the beer can, and reminded him our woods and fields are posted, and all he did was cuss me out."

I'm staring. "He *cussed* you?"

"Said I was a sorry kind of neighbor to keep my land all for myself to hunt on. Said if he'd known what a miserly skunk I was, he'd never have let you have that dog at all. In fact, he says that because he *did* give him to you, he could hunt wherever he pleased. That was part of the bargain."

"That's not true!" I yell, my face hot.

"I know it isn't, Marty. Judd was drunk as a coot when he said that, and I should have come home and gone back again when he was sober. But I got a temper, too, when I'm riled. I told him I ever find him hunting on my land, I'm calling the sheriff. That's why I don't want him at our table right now. I'm not *asking* him to stay off my land; I'm *tellin'* him, and I don't want him to think I'm backing down."

I decide not to say anything just then about playin' spy.

Seven

It is sure quiet around our house. Dad never much held a grudge or carried on a quarrel with a neighbor. It bothers him to do it now.

What I don't like is not being able to take Shiloh up to the far meadow to romp and run. We're used to not going up there between Thanksgiving and Christmas when deer season is on, because—signs or no signs—hunters sometimes get in up there and they've got rifles. Shot from a shotgun and bullets from a rifle are different things entirely.

Shiloh can't understand why we've stopped going up to the meadow, though. I come home from school and he gets all excited—does his wiggle dance, front end going left and his rear end going right. Runs right off toward the path to the meadow, yipping for me to come, too. Runs back and forth to show me the way, get me to follow.

"Shiloh! No!" I say.

He just slinks down low, tail between his legs, like he don't know what he's done, but it's bad. Then when I reach down to pet him, he can't make sense of it, I can tell.

He's been running around some with a black Labrador, though, and it's nice to see him have a friend of his own. Those two dogs go off together and sometimes Shiloh's gone all day and half the night. Comes back with burrs and ticks, but eager to be off again the next time his friend comes around.

At school I find out more from Michael Sholt about Judd fighting at Bens Run. Michael says a cousin told him that a friend's uncle had a brother who said Judd owed him some money, and Judd said he didn't. I suppose that by the time a story's passed along to that many people, there's a little added on or a little left out, so I don't know how true it is. But they say Judd had been drinking and he took the first swing. Would have half killed each other if the sheriff hadn't shown up.

I can imagine that all right. Having seen Judd kill two living things now, I can imagine him *half* killing something without no second thoughts whatsoever.

Last week in September Miss Talbot tells us our school is taking part in a project called "Imagine the Future." The idea is to get kids thinking about their lives a little further than what they're going to do over next summer's vacation, she says.

All fifth and sixth graders in a dozen schools are supposed to choose the job they'd most like to have when they're grown. That's just for starters. Then we've got to write a paper on what it would be like to do that kind of work.

Sarah Peters chooses swimmer.

"Swimmer?" I say when she tells me on the bus. "What kind of job is that?"

"Swimming champion," she says.

Sarah took swimming lessons last summer at a camp down near Middlebourne and now she thinks she can go to the Olympics.

I ask David Howard what he's going to choose.

"Biologist, forest ranger, or football player," he says. "Haven't decided yet."

Didn't take me long to think up mine: veterinarian. It's all I can think of that would please me.

When I go to Doc Murphy's that Saturday I tell him what I picked, only I say I'll probably write down "veterinarian technician," 'cause it takes a lot of money to go to veterinary school. He's showing me how to use a soaker hose on his bushes—how to keep moving it every twenty minutes.

"It does take money, and it's real tough to get into veterinary college, Marty," he says, "but there's no harm in aiming high."

I finish watering all the bushes before I go home. David doesn't come over 'cause he's gone camping with his folks. He's decided to write a report on being a forest ranger, and his dad is taking him to visit a real ranger station so he can ask questions and write a good report.

At the supper table, we're talking about Grandma Preston again. Ma called Aunt Hettie over in Clarksburg and, as usual, Grandma Preston was in trouble.

"What's she done now?" asks Dara Lynn, eyes all shiny, can't wait to hear the latest.

Ma starts to tell, then stops: "Dara Lynn Preston, I don't

want this told all over second grade," she warns. "This is *family* business."

"I *won't!*" says Dara Lynn.

"Well," says Ma, and then she looks straight at Dad. "Your mother," she says, "has been stealing."

"Stealing?" says Dad.

"The nurse opened the drawer in Grandma's bedside table and found five pairs of eyeglasses. Seems she's been going around from room to room collecting 'em."

Dad gives a loud cough and ducks his head, but you know he's tryin' to hide a chuckle, and we all laugh then. Can't help ourselves.

"She thinks they're hers!" Ma continues. "Says the other patients have been stealing from *her!*"

"I don't never want to get old," says Dara Lynn.

"Well, most old people don't act like that," says Dad. "Grandpa Preston lived almost as long, and he was smart as they come."

"Same with Grandma Slater," says Ma, talkin' about her own ma. "She hadn't gone out picking beans in the rain and got pneumonia, she'd probably be alive yet."

"If she was so smart, how come she was picking beans in the rain?" asks Dara Lynn.

I see Dad cover his mouth, but Ma gets a little testy.

"All of us do things now and then we shouldn't," she says.

"That's the truth," says Dad.

It's right about then the phone rings, and because Becky's just slid from her chair, ready to go out and play, she grabs it and answers.

"Hi!" she says. She's holding the mouthpiece right under her nose. "My grandma . . ." she begins.

"Becky!" yells Dara Lynn.

"Get that phone away from her, Marty," says Ma.

I'm already reaching around for it, but Becky's turned her back to me and is facing the wall, her tight little fists closed around that telephone.

"Hi," she says again. "What's your name?"

And then I hear his voice: Judd Travers.

"You turn that phone over to your daddy!" he says.

I am trying to wrestle the phone away from her, and Becky is screeching at the top of her lungs. She stops long enough to ask, "What's your *name?*" again, then screeches some more.

"You never mind my name!" We can hear Judd's voice over the whole kitchen. "Give that phone to your daddy, like I said!"

Dad's on his feet now. He's removing the fingers of Becky's right hand from the telephone, one by one, and I'm removing the fingers of her left. Becky gives a final squeal, enough to make your ears sing, and goes out on the porch bawling. Screen slams after her.

"Hello?" says Dad.

The rest of us wait.

"Ray Preston, I come home this evening to find my mailbox pushed flat over on the ground. Not a scratch on it, so I know no car backed into it by mistake. I'm saying I think your boy was over here today and knocked over my box. Maybe him and that kid from Friendly."

I stare openmouthed at my dad.

"What makes you think Marty had anything to do with it?" asks Dad.

"Because somebody scratched up my truck a week or two back, and I'm thinking it's Marty who done it. I want

52

him over here tomorrow digging me a new hole, and I want that post set in cement."

"If Marty did it, you can be sure I'll have him put it up, but hold on while I talk to him," says Dad. He turns to me.

"I didn't do it, Dad! I didn't scratch up his truck, neither!"

"Sure of that, son?"

"Yes, I'm sure!"

"You know who did?"

"No."

Dad studies me a moment, then puts the phone back to his ear. "He says he didn't do it, Judd."

"You believe a kid who'd come over here hiding on my property, spying on me, then saying he don't know nothing about my mailbox?" Judd is shouting now. "What's he over here for, then? He and that kid from Friendly? You ask him that."

"Look. I'll talk to him, Judd. If he did it, we'll both come over and put that box to rights. But I think you've got the wrong boy. It just might be, you know, that since you've knocked down a few boxes of your own lately, the way you've been driving, someone's trying to settle the score. I'm just guessing."

"Well, I'm guessing your kid, and until he puts up my box, you've got yourself some trouble," says Judd. And hangs up.

Ma and Dara Lynn are staring first at Dad, then at me. Even Becky's stopped her squalling and is standing outside the door, nose pressed flat against the screen, 'fraid she'll miss something.

"Marty, let's you and me go outside and have a talk," Dad says.

Boy, I want this talk about as much as I want poison ivy on the roof of my mouth. But Ma brings Becky in, we go out, and we sit on the porch swing on this cool September night, one square of yellow from the window shining on the floorboards.

"That true what Judd says—that you and David were over there on his property, spying on him?"

"We were just playing," I say. Even my voice sounds guilty.

"What did you do?"

"We were crawling along in the grass—making like spies. David wanted to see what Judd does at night."

"What does he *think* he does at night?"

I'm looking down at my hands, rubbing my two thumbnails together. It's so silly it's embarrassing. I shrug. "See if he turns into a werewolf or something."

The swing jiggles slightly as Dad half turns and stares at me.

"Judd was sitting on his steps with a shotgun, and we saw him shoot a squirrel," I go on. "When he started to shoot another one, I yelled, 'No, don't!' Couldn't help myself. But David pushed my head down and we stayed hid that way. Judd tried to find us there in the weeds, but he was too drunk."

This long, long sigh comes out of my dad—almost like it's got no end to it. He sounds plain tired. Worn down.

"If you tried, you couldn't have picked a worse time to do something like this," he says. And then, "Marty, *did* you have anything to do with Judd's mailbox, or scratching up his truck?"

"No! I already told you!"

"But how do I know you're telling the truth? Because

you say so?" He's looking at me there in the dim light, and I'm remembering how I kept Shiloh secret from him when the dog first come to me. Thinking how I'd told Dad I hadn't seen Judd's dog in our yard when he asked, not mentioning I'd seen it up in our woods. Not for one moment letting on that I *had* him up there.

"You lied once, you know."

"I know. I lied then, but I'm not lying now."

"So, I've got to decide whether what you're saying now is the truth," says Dad.

Neither of us is pushing the swing. I can see Dara Lynn's shadow just inside the door, standing close as she can get to hear what we're saying.

"What we've got here," Dad goes on, "is a man who's drinking heavy, doing things when he's drunk he don't even remember, and getting ready for hunting season, if he hasn't started shooting already. Until I give the word, I don't want you so much as crossing that bridge. I want you as far away from Judd Travers as you can get. I've got enough problems on my hands without you making more. You got that understood?"

"Yes," I tell him.

Dad gets up from the swing and starts inside.

"Dad?" I say.

He stops.

"I didn't mess around with his truck or mailbox. If there's some way to make you believe that, just tell me."

"Keep out of trouble," Dad says. "That's all I ask."

Eight

Sunday we're restless. Shiloh's tried four times to lure me up to the far meadow where he runs himself in circles, and each time I say, "No, Shiloh!" He's confused. We all hear a gun go off somewhere that afternoon. Don't think it's in our woods, but we can't be sure.

Even Dara Lynn's got an ache to go up there, 'fraid as she is of snakes. Last summer you couldn't lure her there with ten ice-cream sundaes. But today there's something in the air tells us fall is coming. The wind'll get cold, and the path to the meadow will be ice all the way up. If we don't go soon, we'll lose our chance. But we can't, and that's why we've got the jumps.

It's just after Sunday supper, still light in the sky. Becky's getting cranky, and Dara Lynn's pestering me to play hide-and-seek with her. I'm hanging on the bag swing, listless like, twirling myself around and around and letting one toe of my sneaker drag the dirt. Ma and Dad are inside listening to some man on TV who wants to be the next governor of West Virginia.

"Who we going to play hide-and-seek with?" I ask her. "You hide and then I hide and then you hide . . . where's the fun in that?"

"Becky can play," Dara Lynn says.

"Yeah!" yells Becky. "Let me play, Marty! And Shiloh can play!"

Shiloh hears his name and pads over, ready for something, he don't know what. Why wasn't I born into a family of nine boys? I'm thinking. A baseball team! I think of my ma being one of nine children, and how they must never have lacked for something to do, someone to do it with.

The swing keeps turning around and when I face forward again, there's Dara Lynn and Becky and Shiloh, all lined up looking at me with begging eyes.

"Okay," I say. "I'm 'it.' You two go hide."

I lean my forehead against the rope as the swing goes on its lazy circle around and around. "Five . . . ten . . . fifteen . . . twenty. . . ." I say.

"*Hide*, Becky!" I hear Dara Lynn screech.

I get to a hundred and still hear Becky running around up on the porch. Count to two hundred.

"Here I come, ready or not!" I yell, and open my eyes.

Becky's on a chair on the porch, got a pillow over her, feet sticking out. I smile and play like I don't see her. Go after Dara Lynn instead.

I'm looking around in back of the chicken coop, the shed, but all this time she's behind one of the tires on Dad's Jeep. I get just far enough away from that bag swing, and in she comes, her skinny legs flying. That girl can run!

"Free!" she yells, pounding one hand on the bag swing. Becky slides down off the porch chair and I make like I'm trying to beat her to the swing. I let her pound her little hand on it.

"Fwee!" she sings out.

"Okay, I got to be 'it' again," I say, and drape one leg over the swing, circling around, my eyes closed. "Five . . . ten . . . fifteen. . . ."

Out of the corner of my eye I can see Becky starting up the path to the far meadow. "Don't you go up there, Becky!" I call.

She stops and turns around. I bury my head again and go on counting.

Then Dara Lynn stubs her toe—Ma *tells* her not to go barefoot—and she's howling like she broke a leg.

I get up off the swing again—Becky's sitting down now on the path—and go see whether Dara Lynn's going to live or die.

Ma comes to the door with her scolding look.

"We're *trying* to hear what this man has to say!" she says, and I tell her I can handle it, so she goes back to the TV.

I get Dara Lynn to sit down on a stump and take a good look at her toe. She's dislocated it, is what she's done, 'cause the end part sort of hangs loose, bent to one side. Happened to me once—twice, I think—so I know. Dara Lynn looks down at it, too, and then she's howling again.

"Dara Lynn, shut up," I tell her. "If you stop yelling for one minute, I'll fix it."

She stops, but she's got her mouth open, ready to let loose with the next.

"This is going to hurt for two seconds and then it'll be okay," I say.

She's crying now, shaking her head and holding her foot.

"You got a choice," I say. "Either you let me put your toe back in place—it'll hurt for two seconds—or you go to Doc Murphy. Which you want it to be?"

Dara Lynn scrunches up her face something fierce, closes her eyes, and tips her head back so she can't peek. "Fix it," she says.

I hold her foot in my hand, then gently take hold of the end of her bent toe and give it a little tug.

Dara Lynn yelps and jerks her foot, but when she looks down again, the toe's back in place. Maybe I *should* think of becoming a vet, not just a helper.

"Okay," she sniffles. "You got to count to three hundred this time, though, 'cause I have to run slower, and I got the perfect hiding place."

I sit down on the swing again and count to three hundred. "Five . . . ten . . . fifteen . . . twenty. . . ."

When I go out hunting for the girls again, Dara Lynn's got a good hiding place all right—inside Dad's Jeep—but it's too hard to get out of in a hurry, and I beat her back to the swing.

Then I go looking for Becky. Look behind the bushes, under the steps, on the porch.

"Allee, allee in come free!" I yell after a while. "You're home free, Becky. Come on in."

But nothing happens.

"Becky?" I call.

Dara Lynn joins the search. But Becky's gone.

Nine

It's when I remember I last saw Becky sitting on the path to the far meadow that my legs like to give out.

"Becky!" I yell again.

Dad comes to the screen. "What's the matter, Marty?"

"We can't find Becky," I say. "We were playing hide-and-seek and I can't find her."

He comes out on the porch. Then Ma.

"What?" says Ma. Her face looks all pulled around the edges.

I tell it again.

"Where did you *see* her last?" asks Ma, hurrying down the steps.

"Up on the path." I point to the steep dirt trail that leads to the woods and the far meadow. "I told her not to go up there, and she sat down. Then Dara Lynn hurt her toe, and I don't remember if I saw Becky after that."

Ma's running now, heading for the path. The sky's got that in-between look. Isn't day, isn't evening. Everything looks in sharp focus, but you know it's not for long.

"Where's Shiloh?" Ma calls over her shoulder. "If Becky wandered off, how come he didn't go with her?"

Shiloh is stretched out on the ground between the house and the shed, just enjoying himself.

"Why isn't he *with* her?" Ma cries again, and she looks with such anger at my dog it scares me. "What good is he if he can't protect Becky?"

"Ma . . . !" I say.

Then she turns on me. "You should've *watched* her!"

"Get the flashlight, son," says Dad. "Dara Lynn, you go in the house in case she shows up there. Don't let her wander off again."

I tear into the house and grab the flashlight from off the top of the refrigerator, then run back out. Shiloh sees all the excitement now, and he's up on his feet, ready to join in.

I feel empty and rattly, like all my ribs are knocking together. How much should you expect from a dog, after all? How does he know where Becky's supposed to go and where she isn't? He's only been with us a month or so.

"Becky?" Ma's yelling into the bushes on either side of her, and I follow her up the hill.

"Becky!" yells Dad. "Where are you? Yell so we can hear you."

Somewhere far off I hear a gun again. At least I think it's a gun. Could have been a firecracker, I suppose. It's hard to tell sometimes. I look at Dad, though, and he heard it, too. It's a gun. I can tell by his face.

We get to the fork in the path. Go left, you end up in

61

woods, up near where I hid Shiloh—where I built his pen. Go right, you'll come to the meadow where I'd run him sometimes, nobody could see us from below.

"Marty," says Dad, "you just sit right here and keep your eye on the yard. What I don't want to happen is for Becky to wander back home, think we're all gone, and go off again."

"O-Okay," I say, and hand over the flashlight to him. He heads for the woods, Ma takes the meadow, and I sit down on the big flat rock at the fork where David and I used to play spaceship sometimes.

I don't sit down so much as I sink. I just got a thought so terrible that it makes my knees give out in earnest.

What if Judd Travers is up here hunting deer with a light? Some hunters do that way, which is about the lowest way you can hunt a deer—stun it with a powerful light and when it stops dead still in front of you, shoot it with a rifle.

But that's not the terrible thought, that's just for starters. What if, because I didn't report Judd to the game warden when he killed that doe out of season, he feels he can get away with it again? If I'd reported him, maybe they would have taken away his license or something. But because I wanted Shiloh so bad, I didn't say nothing. And maybe saying nothing is why Becky's missing now. Maybe one of those stray bullets found her, and I traded Becky for Shiloh.

I bend over, hugging my stomach, like I got belly cramps. So scared my arms are shaking. How can you think you're doing the right thing, and it's maybe not right at all?

Down below in the yard, I can see Shiloh standing up, looking around. I'd thought he'd follow us up here, been wanting so bad to come. Guess when you scold a dog four times in one day, he learns a little something. But why couldn't he have learned to stick with Becky? Why wouldn't he just naturally know that Becky, being the smallest, needed him most?

"Becky! Becky!" I can hear my ma yell.

There's no answer.

It's going to get dark right soon, now. It's already black back in the trees. I can see the spot of yellow from Dad's flashlight from time to time, then it disappears again.

Ten minutes go by. Which is worse, I'm thinking— sitting here waiting for Becky, or lying in the weeds beside David Howard when Judd was yelling, "Who's there?" and was starting over with his gun to find us?

I think I'd choose to be back there and take my chances at Judd's. At least what was happening, or going to happen, would take place before my eyes. Here I don't know. All I can do is sit.

Dad's coming back through the trees now, then I hear Ma's footsteps not far behind.

"I'm calling the sheriff, ask for a search party," Dad says, and I hear a tremble in his voice. Ma's starting to cry.

We make our way down the steep path, and Dad's talking out loud. Praying, I guess he is, closest he comes to prayer: "I wish to God I hadn't riled Judd; wish to God I'd handled that better."

I can see right off I'm not the only one feeling responsible. Guess I'd thought that when you get to be thirty-eight, like Dad, you don't have these questions. You just *know*. Now I'm seeing the other side of things.

"Ray," Ma sobs, her nose all clogged up. "You don't think Judd would come through those woods and just *take* Becky, do you?"

"No, not even drunk. I don't think so." Dad puts an arm

63

around Ma to steady her, but his voice gives him away. Needs a little steadying himself.

Shiloh's standing down at the bottom of the path waiting for us, tail wagging, tongue hanging out, glad to see us coming back.

But Dad's not glad to see him. In fact, seems to me that Dad's right foot sort of reaches out and gives that dog a push. Not blaming Shiloh, exactly, but not feeling so kindly toward him, neither.

Dara Lynn's standing at the screen door bawling 'cause she don't like being left in the house by herself at night, and nobody's paying her much mind. Dad steps up on the porch and goes straight for the telephone. Ma's telling Dara Lynn to hush.

I go up on the porch and wait for Shiloh to follow us in, the way he does when we're all on the porch in the evening. But he just trots back down the steps, goes over to the shed, and stands there wagging his tail.

And suddenly my heart begins to beat faster. I leap off that porch, not even bothering with the steps, and open the door of the toolshed a little wider.

There's Becky, sprawled out on the dirt floor, head on a bag of chicken feed, her lips letting out little fluttery sounds while she sleeps.

I'm so happy I shout. Then I hug Shiloh and get the wettest kiss this side the Mississippi. I shout once more. The shout don't even wake Becky up. Her body jolts for a second, then drops right back into sleep.

But now Ma is coming out of the house, then Dara Lynn and Dad.

"I found her!" I yell. "Shiloh was looking out for her all the time. Led me right over to the shed."

Everyone comes running, and I can't tell who's hugging who. Ma's hugging Becky, Dad's hugging Ma, Dara Lynn's hugging Shiloh, but I'm not hugging Dara Lynn. Not that far gone. I guess I'm hugging Shiloh, too.

Dad picks up Becky in his arms and carries her into the house and she don't even open her eyes. Bet you could operate on her brain and she wouldn't even feel it.

Ma takes off Becky's shoes and lays her down on her bed, clothes and all, and then the only thing left to do is have some ice cream. Dad calls the sheriff again to tell him the search is off, and Ma's dishing up big helpings of fudge ripple. Shiloh gets the first dish.

"Would have saved us a lot of grief and worry if that dog could talk," says Dad. He's smiling now.

"He did talk, we just didn't ask the right questions," I say. "He knew Becky was in that shed the whole time. She must have gone in there to hide and fell asleep. He was watching over her, not making any fuss. It was when we all went in the house without her that he figured he ought to let us know."

"Well, if I don't see Judd before next weekend, I'm going over there and settle this whole thing peaceably," Dad says. "Can't go on worrying this way every time a gun or firecracker goes off."

I sleep real good that night.

Ten

The *Tyler Star–News* says that rabies has been reported in Tyler County, and Dad says it's time we took Shiloh to a vet, make sure he has all his shots.

We know for a fact that Judd never takes his dogs to a vet unless he has to. Says with his dogs being chained and all, how are they going to get rabies?

Judd'll do most anything to keep from spending a nickel he don't have to, but Ma says if he took the money he spent on beer and spent it on his dogs instead, he'd have a lot happier, healthier animals. Happy and healthy ain't what interests Judd, though. Hunting is.

Doc Murphy gives us the name of his veterinarian friend down in St. Marys, and we make an appointment for Tuesday afternoon late. Dad goes to work early that morning to get his mail delivered in time, and about four o'clock, after Dara Lynn and me get home—have some pop and cheese crackers—Dad and Dara Lynn and me put Shiloh in the Jeep and drive to the vet's.

John Collins is his name and, just like Doc Murphy, he uses part of his house for his clinic. Shiloh is not one tiny bit happy about going, let me tell you. He's happy about gettin' in the Jeep, though, and likes to ride up front with Dad, his head out, the wind blowing his ears. Dara Lynn and me laugh at the way spit drops off the end of his tongue. Jeep gets going fast enough and the wind'll blow that spit right into the backseat. Dara Lynn lets out a shriek when some of it smacks her arm.

Once we get to the clinic, Shiloh knows something is up. Don't know how dogs can tell that, but they seem to. Not a place he's ever been before, that's one thing. The scent of other dogs around, that's another. Scared dogs, too.

We're walking up the sidewalk with Shiloh on a leash, and the more he smells the bushes, the more scared he gets. By the time we reach the door, his tail's so far tucked in between his legs he can hardly walk. Dara Lynn picks him up in her arms and carts him inside.

Dad signs in at the desk, and a young woman in a blue shirt rubs Shiloh on the head, but that don't fool him one minute. He knows right off this is a place he don't want to be. Knows it for sure when a fifteen-pound cat reaches out and swats at him as we go past.

We sit in a row on the plastic chairs and Shiloh's sitting on the floor between my feet. I sort of press the calves of my legs close around him like a hug, but I can feel him shaking. I reach down and pat Shiloh on the head. He licks my hand, but it's not a very strong lick. Think he's saying, "I thought you liked me. How come you're bringing me here?"

Dad's reading some pamphlets on distemper, rabies, and something called hepatitis. I'm looking at a dog chart over on the wall. Shows a side view of a dog, and every part of him is named—parts of a dog I never even heard of before. Figure if I'm going to be a vet I got to know them all, so I start memorizing 'em right here—the hock joint, loin, croup, withers, brisket, stifle, flews. . . . Should've brought my notebook, I'm thinking, so I could put it all down.

Dara Lynn, though, is reading about worms. She sits there with her mouth full open, eyes big as quarters, and nudges me in the side.

"Marty," she whispers, "you know that puppies have *worms* in 'em?"

"Yeah," I tell her. "I know dogs can get worms."

"*Live* ones!" says Dara Lynn, eyes like fifty-cent pieces now. "Crawling around *inside* 'em!" She's looking more horrified every minute. Then she looks over at me. "Maybe Shiloh's got 'em."

"I suppose he could have."

"How would they know?" she asks me.

I lean over and whisper: "You have to look in his poop."

"EEeeuu!" Dara Lynn cries, and claps her hands over her mouth.

Only thing I like better than teasing Dara Lynn is making her sick.

Now it's our turn to take Shiloh into an examining room. I get up and tug on the leash, and Shiloh follows, looking about as mournful as a dog can look.

The vet is a tall man—must be six feet four, I'll bet—and he's got on a blue shirt, too. Got a big head, big ears, and a big smile.

"Well, well, so this is Shiloh!" he says in a friendly, calm kind of voice as Dad lifts our dog up and puts him on the examining table. "This the one Doc Murphy told me about?"

"He's the one," says Dad.

The first five minutes all John Collins does is pet Shiloh and talk real soft. Runs his hands behind his ears, smooths his head, and pretty soon Shiloh's feeling like maybe this isn't going to be so bad. Starts frisking up a little, tail begins to wag, and then he's lickin' John Collins all over his hands and chin. The vet laughs.

He asks us questions about Shiloh, about how many shots he's had, and of course we don't know the answers because we don't know who had him before Judd. Wants to know what we feed him, and I can tell he don't like the idea of table scraps.

"You've been taking real good care of him, but he'd be even healthier if he had more protein in his diet," John Collins says, and tells us what kind of dog food we should be buying and where we can get it cheapest.

Then he gives Shiloh a couple of shots—Shiloh's right good about it, just flinches a little—and tells us never to give him bones, make sure he has fresh water, clean his food dish every day, what to do for fleas. . . .

When Dad and Dara Lynn take Shiloh out to the desk to pay the bill, I say to John Collins, "Something I've been thinking on: Chaining dogs makes 'em mean, don't it?"

"It makes them scared, so they act mean," the vet says. "When you chain a dog, he feels trapped. If other dogs or people come over and he thinks he might be attacked, he tries to pretend he's big and fierce in order to scare them off."

"And these dogs just stay mean for life?" I ask.

John Collins shakes his head. "They don't have to. Once you unchain a dog, he doesn't feel so threatened. Knows he can get away if he has to. He may not settle down right then, but if he learns to trust you, knows you'll treat him right, he can become a loyal, gentle dog."

We go home and I sit at the kitchen table and write all that down for my report. We got a vet now; I can call him and ask questions, and I'm thinking how maybe some day *I'll* have an animal clinic—my name there on the door. Folks will bring their pets in with all kinds of problems, and I'll know just what to do. But two days later, something happened and I sure didn't know what to do then.

It's after school on Wednesday—a common kind of school day. Couple kids give their reports for their "Imagine the Future" project.

Sarah Peters stands up and reads how she is going to be a swimmer and swim the English Channel. Miss Talbot says that's an interesting goal, but what about the rest of her life? She has to be thinking about what else she could do with swimming even after she becomes a champion.

Sarah turns her paper in, and Fred Niles reads the report he's written. He wants to be a policeman, and if he can't get on the police force, then he'll settle for rescue squad.

Miss Talbot says this is a good example of how you can use your desire to help and protect people in several different ways. The boys all give Sarah our smart look, but then Laura Herndon gets up and says she wants to own a restaurant. If she can't own her own restaurant, she says, she'd like to be a cook. If she can't be a cook, she'll be a waitress. And if she can't get a waitress job, she'll start out as a dishwasher and work her way up. Boy, Laura sure knows how to please a teacher. Miss Talbot likes Laura saying how she's willing to start out small and work up.

David Howard and I look at each other and figure

maybe we better do a little more work on our reports before we give them.

It's about five o'clock that afternoon that something happens.

Dad's not home yet. Ma's in the kitchen cooking some turnips and onions, and listening to the news.

Dara Lynn has a wire strung between the chicken coop and the shed, and she's got these little cereal boxes fastened to it like cable cars or something, and she's running 'em back and forth. Sort of neat, really. Wish I'd thought of it myself.

Becky's rolling around in the grass with Shiloh, who's looking about as bored as a dog can look and still be polite about it. Becky rolls over his back and then rolls the other way. Each time Shiloh sort of braces himself, digging his paws in. Don't even protest. Just turns around and licks her now and then.

I'm trying to pick enough apples off our two apple trees to see if there's enough for Ma to make applesauce. The peaches are all gone now, but Ma wants every last apple I can find.

I've found about six, when I hear this barking and carrying on. Sounds like it's far away but coming closer. Shiloh turns his head in the direction of the sound and stands up, body all tense, and Becky rolls right off in the grass.

"Who's that? Your friend?" I ask Shiloh, thinking of the black Lab.

But the noise is too much for a single dog. Gets louder and louder, and I'm wondering what it could be when suddenly, here come these three dogs through the trees back beyond the house. I know the minute I see them that they belong to Judd Travers.

Eleven

There's not even time to think. I grab Shiloh up in one arm, Becky in the other, and run up on the porch.

"Ma!" I yell, and she's already halfway to the screen. She opens it for me and I drop the two inside. Shiloh runs over to a window and stands up on his hind legs, front paws on the sill, wanting to see.

"Dara Lynn?" calls Ma.

I turn around on the porch to see Dara Lynn backed up against the chicken coop, like her body's frozen, dogs all around her snappin' and snarlin', and first thought in my head is that Judd's sicced 'em on us.

Ma goes charging down the steps and grabs the clothes pole that props the line up on wash day. I grab my baseball bat from off the porch and we're running over to that chicken coop.

Dara Lynn's screamin' now, elbows up over her face, and

this one dog, the black-and-white one, lunges forward and nips her arm.

Whack! Ma brings down the clothes prop on the black-and-white dog. The others snarl and turn our way, but I'm swinging that bat out in front of me ninety miles an hour and Ma's bringin' that clothes prop down a second time. The dogs back off.

Air is filled with noise. Dogs are yelping, Ma is shouting, Dara Lynn's screaming, Shiloh's yipping, Becky's standing at the screen squalling, and the hens are all carrying on in the chicken coop.

The black-and-white dog seems to be the leader. As Ma's pole comes down again he hightails it out of the yard, and the others follow.

Ma grabs Dara Lynn and rushes her in the house, cleans that bite with soap and water.

About this time Dad comes home.

"Whose dogs are those running up the road?" he asks.

"Judd's!" I tell him. "They got loose and come over here, and one of 'em bit Dara Lynn."

She's sobbing. "I didn't do nothing! All I was doing was playing out in the yard and those dogs come up and bit me."

"You sure they were Judd's?" Dad asks.

"I'd know 'em anywhere," I tell him.

Ma calls Doc Murphy and he says to call the sheriff and get those dogs picked up. The one that bit Dara Lynn'll have to be kept locked up for ten days to see whether or not he's got rabies. If he does, Dara Lynn's got to have shots. If we can't find the dog, she'll have to have 'em anyway.

Dara Lynn howls again.

Dad calls the sheriff and he says someone already

73

reported them, that those dogs killed somebody's cat. He's got a man out looking for them.

Dara Lynn's sobbing now and Becky squalls, too, just to join in. Shiloh runs from window to window, whining, standin' up on his hind legs. Meanwhile Ma's turnips have boiled dry and the pan's starting to scorch.

Ma turns off the fire, takes Becky out on the swing, and tries to cool her own self down.

"Let's just sit out here a spell and rest," she says. "Becky, it wasn't you got bit, so quit squallin'. Dara Lynn, you're not going to die anytime soon, so just come sit here by me. Let me have five minutes of peace and quiet or my head is going to fly straight off."

Becky looks up at Ma's head and starts suckin' her thumb.

Dad and I come out on the porch then with Shiloh, and we sit on the steps while Shiloh goes trotting all around the yard, smelling for a trace of those dogs. Guess a dog's nose tells him a whole lot we don't know anything about.

"Wonder how in the world those dogs got loose," Dad says. "Judd had chains on 'em that would have held a grown man. Were they dragging their chains, Marty, or what? I didn't notice."

"No. Looked to me like they were all unhooked at the collar," I tell him.

And just when we thought we'd had about enough excitement to last us a while, here come Judd's pickup turning into our drive.

"Well, look who's comin'," says Dad.

Shiloh stands so still it's like he's turned to stone. He knows the sound of that pickup better'n he knows his own name, almost. And soon as it stops beside Dad's Jeep and

74

Judd puts one foot out, Shiloh races over to our steps and crawls underneath. Seem like he don't even trust that I can save him. Got to get to some deep dark place away from the reach of Judd Travers.

Judd comes stompin' across the yard in his cowboy boots, and his face looks like thunder. If you was to give Becky her crayons and tell her to draw it, she'd choose purple.

"Ray Preston, I accuse you of turning my dogs loose," Judd says right off, a voice three times too loud.

"Now calm down, Judd. I did no such thing," Dad tells him.

"You put your boy up to it, then."

"Marty didn't have anything to do with it."

"Well, somebody come by and unhooked the chains on all three of 'em, and a neighbor says he saw my dogs coming off your property."

Now Ma speaks up: "They were here all right, and one of 'em bit my daughter. Show him, Dara Lynn!"

Dara Lynn holds up her arm and gives a loud sniffle.

"If Marty hadn't got Becky, no telling what they might have done to *her*," Ma continues.

But Judd don't believe it.

"That is a put-up lie, I ever heard one. Sheriff tells me he finds my dogs, he's keepin' the one in a cage for two weeks. That's my second-best hunting dog, the black-and-white."

"It's the only way they can tell for sure whether or not the dog has rabies," Dad says. "Any dog that bites someone has to be watched."

"I see what you're up to, don't think I don't!" Judd goes on, like he never heard one word. "You took my best hunting dog and now you're cooking up some story about my second-best. I'm going to lose two good weeks of hunting because of this, and I want you to loan me that beagle. I can use him."

My heart almost explodes inside my chest.

"No!" I say.

"Judd," says Dad, "why don't you sit down? We can talk this over man-to-man without getting all hot-under-the-collar."

"I'm not sittin', and I have nothing to say, except you owe me the use of that dog."

Becky slides down off the swing. "You can't have him!" she says, her little neck thrust out, face all screwed up. She's sassing this big old man in the cowboy boots, but I notice she's got one hand still holdin' fast to Ma's skirt.

"Hush, Becky," Ma tells her.

"Judd," I say, trying my best to reason with him. "Even if we were to let you, Shiloh wouldn't go."

"He'd go, all right," says Judd. "Where is he?" And he gives a whistle.

Under the steps, Shiloh don't move. I wonder if he's even breathing.

"See?" chirps Dara Lynn. "He won't even come out!" and she points to the steps. I could have drowned Dara Lynn.

Judd goes over to the side and gets down on all fours. I'm just close enough I can smell the beer on his breath. Don't think he's drunk, but he's been drinking.

"Here, you!" Judd yells, and whistles again. "Come on outta there, boy! Come on!"

I'm wondering what Shiloh's thinking right now. Does he think I'm lettin' this man come get him?

Stay there, Shiloh, I whisper. But I'm remembering the way he looked first day I found him back in the weeds over near Judd's, crawling along on his belly. Only thing that brought him to me was to whistle. What if he's so scared of Judd, of what will happen if he doesn't obey, that he comes out? Am I going to just sit here and let Judd take my dog, even for ten days? Will Dad let him?

I'm glad to see that nothing's happening. Shiloh's probably scrunched up in the far corner beneath the steps as far away as he can get.

Judd gets up off his hands and knees, cussing to himself, and goes to get the clothes pole. He comes back with it, ready to poke my dog out.

"No!" I say again, and this time I stand up. "You ain't goin' after my dog with that pole."

"Now, Judd, put that down." Dad gets up too, and his voice is strong. "That dog belongs to Marty now and you don't have permission to take him. I know you're upset about your dogs getting loose, but acting this way is not going to help."

And Ma says, "We got a daughter with a bite on her arm, but we're not going to press charges, so there's no 'cause for us to be mad at each other."

Judd stands there a full fifteen seconds, the pole in his hand. He glares at Dad. Then at me. He even glares at Ma and the girls.

Suddenly he throws the clothes pole to the ground.

"I ain't through with you, Ray Preston," he says. "I know you and that boy are behind this, I'll bet a week's pay. You ain't heard the last from me, you ain't seen the last, and I'm tellin' you now you'll be sorry."

He goes back across the yard, gets in his pickup, turns

around on our grass, and with a loud roar and a squeal of tires, he barrels on down our driveway, the dust from the gravel rolling off to the left.

Shiloh creeps out and comes up the steps, tail between his legs. He huddles against me, 'bout as close as he can get, and I put my arm around him.

We don't say a word, none of us. Just sit there watching that cloud of dust till Judd gets out to the road again and makes his turn.

Twelve

Everybody's talking about Judd's dogs the next day on the school bus. Dara Lynn, of course, had to go up and down the aisle showing off the place where Judd's black-and-white dog had bit her. To hear Dara Lynn tell the story, it had her arm in its teeth and had twisted it almost off before Ma whacked the dog with the clothes prop.

It was Michael Sholt's daddy who caught the black-and-white dog. After that the two other dogs scattered and were soon picked up. Michael's daddy said if someone else hadn't let loose Judd's dogs, he might have been mad enough to do it himself, on account of Judd's running into his mailbox twice. Guess there were a lot of folks starting to get mad at Judd Travers.

We all felt bad about the cat, though. Belonged to Mrs. Donaldson over there near Judd. Sarah heard that the cat had just been sitting out on the steps, sunning itself, when those dogs got hold of it and broke its neck. I reckon Mrs. Donaldson buried it back in her private cemetery with the rest of the Donaldsons. Don't know how many of 'em were cats.

Fred Niles heard that it was the man who'd got in a fistfight with Judd down in Bens Run who went up there and turned those dogs loose while Judd was at work, but I don't know that anyone could prove it.

David Howard's imagination gets going, though, it just never stops. After he got on the bus and heard the story about Mrs. Donaldson's cat and Dara Lynn's arm and the man from Bens Run, he says, "If those dogs snatched up a cat, they could snatch up a baby."

"What baby?" I say.

David shrugs. "Any baby! I'm just saying they *could*. What if someone put a baby out in a carriage and when they came back it was gone? If we hear of any baby missing, I'll bet Judd's dogs took it."

By the time that bus rolls into the driveway at school, we have cats missing, babies missing, girls with their arms torn clear off their bodies, and a whole pack of men from Bens Run all out lookin' for Judd Travers.

I'm still thinking about Judd's dogs, though. Wonder if once they start running in a pack like that and get a taste of blood, you can really change 'em. I'd like to put that in my report if I could, so when I get home from school I call John Collins.

I have to wait for him to come to the phone, his assistant tells me, 'cause he's working on a dog with a snake bite. But when he answers, I ask him about pack dogs, and can even a dog as mean as that be changed? How would a vet go about doing that?

"It's harder," says the vet, "but I've seen it done. What

you have to do, once you separate the dogs, is work with them one at a time. Sometimes when a dog is really mean and hiding out somewhere, you start by leaving food where he can reach it. He may not take it right away, but by and by he'll get hungry. Once he starts accepting your food, he'll listen for the sound of your voice and get to know you. And after he learns to trust you, he'll let you pet him. Just takes time. You have to be patient."

I thank John Collins and put it all in my report.

Since the whole class is still talking about Judd at school the next day, Miss Talbot asks us the difference between truth and gossip.

Truth, she says, is what you see with your own eyes and hear with your own ears. Gossip you get secondhand. Gossip may or may not be true, because it's coming to you from another person. It could even be *half* true, with parts left out now and then, and little extras tacked on to give it flavor.

I think about that a while, and then I figure there's another difference: truth's more important, but gossip's more interesting.

David Howard and me both get good grades on our reports because we actually talked to a forest ranger and a veterinarian.

When the bell rings for recess, though, Miss Talbot says, "Marty, I wonder if I could see you for a few minutes?"

What can you say but yes, so after everyone else goes out to play kickball, I got to sit over at the reference table where Miss Talbot's waiting for me.

After I sit down I see that she has my report in front of her, and there are big red circles all over it. She don't look mad, though.

"Marty," she says, "you and I come from the same kind of families, where the talk is slow and quiet and as soft and beautiful as a summer day. But it's not the way most people talk. If you spell the way you speak, people might have trouble reading what you write."

Then she shows me all the words she's circled in red—all the places where "don't" should be "doesn't," and "nothin'" should be "nothing" and "ain't" should be "aren't" or "isn't" and I don't know what all.

"It's okay to talk like that at home," she says. "That's personal talk; family talk. When I go back to my grandma's down in Mississippi, and we're all sitting around relaxed and happy, my tongue just slips into that easy way of talking, and everyone there knows exactly what I mean."

She smiles at me and I smile back.

"The problem," Miss Talbot says, "is that when you talk one way at home and another way at school, you've just got to be more careful, that's all. If you want to go to college and become a veterinarian, then you have to learn to speak and write and spell correctly."

Any other time a teacher told me to stay behind at recess, I would be thinking I was in big trouble. But when I leave the room and go out to get in that kickball game, I feel like Miss Talbot really wants to see me make something of myself.

"What'd you do, Marty, break a window?" Fred Niles calls out.

"Naw. She just wanted to talk about my report," I say.

The problem at our house now is that Dad's so quiet. I hardly ever seen him this quiet for so long. Looks to me like he can't put his mind to anything because he's troubled by something else. He sits down to watch TV and after a while you see his eyes are looking out the window, not at the screen.

"Sure wish this mess with Judd was cleared up," he says that Sunday out on the porch. It's getting cold now. You sit out too long, you'll need a coat. Couple weeks more and we won't be sitting out on the swing at all. "You were right, Marty," Dad goes on. "Maybe if we'd invited Judd to dinner before this thing got out of hand, we could have talked it out and come to some agreement. Yesterday he saw me pause at his mailbox, and he called, 'You just put that mail in there, Ray, and move along. Got no interest in talking to you.'"

"Somebody put his mailbox back up?"

"I expect Judd did. Nobody else was going to do it."

Knowing my dad, I figure he'll think of some way to patch things up with Judd Travers. Never saw a problem yet he couldn't lick. Only thing is, his job is a whole lot tougher now that Judd's mad. And *my* worry is that whatever they decide, if they *do* agree to something, they might make Shiloh part of the deal.

Seeing Dad worry reminds me of the way I felt when I was working for Judd, worrying that even after I'd put in my twenty hours, he still might not let me have the dog.

It was blackmail, pure and simple—me telling Judd that if I didn't get Shiloh I'd report the doe. I'd never in this world have done that if it weren't for Shiloh, and me wanting to save him.

It's the same with Dad. He'd let a neighbor hunt on his land before he'd work up a quarrel. But when it comes to protecting his children, Dad did and said things that weren't like him at all. Now all of us just seem to be sitting around waiting for what'll happen next.

"Dad," I say. "No matter what happens, you won't make me give back Shiloh, will you?"

Dad grunts and shakes his head, but I sure would have felt better if he'd come right out and said no.

Couple nights later at the supper table, Becky looks around and asks, "Why are we so quiet?"

"*I'm* not quiet!" says Dara Lynn, ready for some action. "You can talk to me, Becky."

"Want to hear my ABC song?" Becky asks.

"Becky, don't talk with your mouth full," says Ma. "Here. I want you to eat a little spinach with your meat."

Becky stares down at her spinach. "It looks like poop," she says.

"Becky!" scolds Ma.

Dara Lynn giggles so Becky says it again.

I guess Ma figures she's got to rescue the dinner conversation before it gets any worse, so she says to Dad, "I heard from Hettie today."

"What now?" says Dad, trying to liven up a little, too. Smiles. "They put Grandma in solitary confinement or something?"

"She *escaped?*" asks Dara Lynn.

"Dara Lynn, your grandma's not in prison," Ma says.

"Well, what'd she do?" I ask.

"Stealing again," says Ma.

"Money?" I ask.

Ma looks at Dad. "Teeth. False teeth."

Suddenly we just can't help ourselves. We all burst out laughing. The thought of Grandma Preston rolling her wheelchair from room to room and swiping people's false teeth is just too much to hold in.

"How'd they know she was *doing* it?" asks Dad.

"The nurse tried to talk to her but Grandma Preston wouldn't open her mouth. They finally got an orderly to help pry her lips open, and she had two pairs of teeth in there, her own and her neighbor's."

Dad is laughing so hard he's got tears in his eyes. I think part of me is feeling bad because we know Grandma Preston didn't mean to be this way at all and it sounds like we're making fun of her. But the other part of me says that sometimes things can happen that are sad and funny both. You can feel sad that her mind is gone, and still laugh at the stuff that's funny.

The laughter helps. I notice that when Dad's drying the dishes for Ma later, she's singing, and I know by the way Dad watches her that he likes to hear her sing.

And I'm feeling right angry at Judd Travers just then. Thinking how if it wasn't for him, we'd be like this every night: Happy.

It still ain't—isn't—too cold to romp around outside with Shiloh, so I take him for a run. Every so often I just got to test his legs. I go down the front steps and stand there beside my dog.

"Ready . . . !" I sing out, and Shiloh looks up at me. "Get set . . ." Shiloh's body starts to quiver. "Go!" I yell, top of my lungs.

We go racing down our driveway like a pack of wolves is on our heels. Guess maybe I'm testing my legs as much as Shiloh's, 'cause all the while I'm running, I'm counting by fives real slow, trying to get down as far as Doc Murphy's by the time I reach two hundred. Never done it yet. Two hundred thirty-five is closest I've come, but I figure if I keep practicing, I'll do it one of these days. Hate to say so, but I'll bet Dara Lynn could do it now. She can outrun me, but it's probably 'cause her legs are so skinny.

Road's near empty this hour of evening—everybody home eating supper—so it's a good time to practice our run. Shiloh's ahead of me, and he seems to know right where we're headed. I got sweat dripping from my eyeballs, almost, but Shiloh's going like a wind-up toy. Just won't stop. By the time we get to Doc Murphy's place, though, his sides are heaving.

We sit down on a log to rest. It's an old telephone pole, I think, that Doc rolled out there near the road to keep cars from cutting across the corner of his lot. I'm sitting there sweating something fierce, and Shiloh's on the ground, 'bout six feet away, his tongue hanging out, little drops of saliva dripping off the end. I got to be sure he's got plenty of water in his bowl when we get back, I'm thinking.

Shiloh looks at me like, "Is it time to go home yet?" and I say, "In a minute, Shiloh." Want to get rid of the ache in my side first. I wipe one arm across my forehead, and I'm just about to get up, when . . .

Pow!

Something hits the log so hard it jolts, and I don't know whether it's the log moving under me or the noise, but I tumble backward onto the ground. Shiloh hops over the log and scrunches down beside me. I know even before I can think it that somebody took a shot at us.

My heart's already pounding hard from the run, and now it's like to explode. Don't know whether to stay where we are or try to crawl up to Doc's house. Didn't see any lights on at his place, so he's probably not even home. I'm afraid if I try to move, Shiloh will make himself a target for whoever's out there.

And then I hear the sound of an engine starting up. I know, as I lie there, leaves in my face, that it's Judd Travers's pickup turning around on the road and heading back over the bridge.

It's only when the truck is gone that I sit up. I crawl back over the log again, looking for the place the bullet hit, and I find it—a small hole as round and clean as a gun barrel.

I let out my breath and pull Shiloh onto my lap. I can feel my knees shaking. Judd must have been coming over the bridge when he saw me and Shiloh racing down the road. He probably pulled over, got out, and followed us with his rifle.

There are three main thoughts going through my head, all trying to get my attention at the same time: first, this is the closest Judd ever came to trying to hurt Shiloh or me; second, I don't know whether he was trying to kill one of us, but his aim was way off the mark, so maybe he was only trying to scare me—either that or he's drunk; and third, I'm not tellin' my dad.

I can't. Tonight for the first time in a long while I heard my dad laugh, and telling him this wouldn't help nothing. Dad's going to patch things up with Judd; I know he will. In the meantime, though, I'm going to stick near our house. Keep myself and Shiloh off the main road altogether, especially at night. Don't want to give Judd any excuse whatsoever to try again.

Thirteen

I got to go to Doc Murphy's on Saturday, though, to help him lay some slab side timbers along his garden out back. There's something in me seems to be growing bigger and bigger and I feel I just can't hold it in no longer. It's not Judd taking a shot at me, neither.

So when Doc and I take a break—he's got this jug of fresh cider on his back steps—I take a sip from my glass and say, "I done something I shouldn't have done, but if I had it to do over, I don't know that I'd do any different."

Doc glances over at me, then takes a good long drink. "Well, we've all got a story or two like that, I guess."

"Not like mine," I say, and the more I talk the more I'm feeling this *has* to come out. If I don't tell it, it'll rip a hole in my chest.

I swallow. Swallow again. "You know how . . . after the German shepherd tore into Shiloh and we're taking care of him till he gets better? Well, I went up to Judd Travers the

Sunday I was supposed to give Shiloh back. I went up early morning to tell him I wanted to keep that dog. I was ready to do whatever it took to get Shiloh for my own. Even fight Judd, if I had to. I wasn't going to give him back."

Doc's giving me a puzzled look, like how can an eleven-year-old boy fight a two-hundred-pound car mechanic? Something I hadn't figured out either, to tell the truth.

"What happened, though, I came across Judd out in a field and I saw him kill a deer. A doe."

"In summer? He killed a doe?"

"Just shot it with his rifle. It wasn't anywhere near his garden, the way he said."

"There's a real stiff fine for that," Doc says.

"I know. I blackmailed him."

Doc sets down his glass of cider, arms resting on his knees and he looks at me for a long time.

"Judd's not real happy when I step out of the woods and he knows I seen him do it. I tell him that doe's not in season, and he wants to know what I'm going to do about it. I say I can tell the game warden, and he offers to divide the meat with my family if I keep quiet about it."

"Hmm," says Doc.

"I tell him I don't want that meat, I want Shiloh. So, the deal is I'll help him drag that doe to his place, keep my mouth shut, and work for him for two weeks. After that the dog's mine. So I do. And I never told my dad."

"I see," says Doc.

"Now you tell me something," I say. "Which do you suppose is right? Tell the game warden about that deer, and have to turn Shiloh back over to Judd? I never saw a dog so scared of a man as Shiloh was of him."

"Well, it seems to me, Marty, that you thought it over and did what you thought was best."

"But was it *right?*" I ask. "I didn't report Judd killing a deer out of season, and now I suppose he'll go right on doing it. Dad says he's been hunting some up in our woods lately, even though we got it posted. Might even be going up there drunk. What if he gets to firing crazy and one of his bullets comes down and kills Becky?" I take a deep breath. "Sometimes I don't sleep so good, just worrying about it."

What I don't tell Doc is that maybe if I'd reported Judd, they would have taken his rifle away, and then what Judd did out on the road last night wouldn't have happened. I don't guess they'd take his gun, though.

"Some folks," Doc's saying, "think they know what's right for every occasion. They say there's a right and wrong for everything. Well, it's good if things work out that way, but sometimes they don't."

"Even for you?" I ask.

Doc smiles just a little. "Especially for me. I grew up learning to tell the truth, Marty. My dad ever caught me in a lie, I'd get a whipping. Went through high school and college and medical school, and never once cheated on a test. The real tests, it seems, came later."

I realize I'm getting paid for sitting here in the shade on Doc's steps, drinking cold cider and listening to him talk, but he don't—doesn't—seem to care.

"There were a lot of them . . . tests. But not like the ones you get in school. There was a man with a sickness I couldn't cure. I knew that most people like him didn't have much time left to live. But he kept talking about how he was going to get well, and his wife said she knew he was going to get well, too, and when they asked me how he

90

was doing, I'd just . . . I'd just beat around the bush. Figured I wasn't going to be the one to make them sad."

"And then . . . ?"

"He died. Got real sick on a Sunday and was gone by Monday. Hadn't left a will. Hadn't taught his wife to drive or what to do about his business. And the wife came to me and said, 'Why didn't you *tell* us he was going to die? It would have made things so much easier.' "

"But you thought . . ."

"Yes, but I thought wrong. So when I had another patient I couldn't cure, I decided to tell her the truth. She was a painter. Had shows all over the state—Huntington, Charleston, Morgantown—even in New York City. I knew she didn't have a lot of time left, and figured she must have a lot of business to take care of. So the next time she was in my office talking about some pain she was having, I told her, as gently as I could, that she ought to get her affairs in order because she might not make that next big show she was talking about."

Here Doc takes a deep breath and puts his elbows on the step behind him.

"Well, she died five months later, and her friends sent me an angry letter. Why did I have to tell her? they asked. She was working on three paintings, her very best work, and after I told her the news, she never picked up her brush again. Just sat at home with the blinds drawn for five months and then died."

I sat thinking about that. "Maybe you could have said something sort of in-between," I suggested.

"Oh, I've tried that, don't think I haven't. I say, 'Only God knows when we're going to die.' Said that to a man just the other day and he looks me right in the eye and says, 'I know, Doc, but in your experience, how long does a man as

91

sick as me usually live?' Could hardly ask it plainer than that. Yet I wonder, does he really want to know?"

Doc picks up his glass again and drains it. "If folks know what's right and wrong for themselves, I've no quarrel with that. And we've all got to obey the law. But beyond that, what's right in one situation may be wrong in another. *You* have to decide. That's the hard part."

I realize when I go home that afternoon that Doc never did tell me what I should have done about that doe. And I see that no matter how old you get, you'll always meet up with problems and they won't have easy answers.

David Howard calls.

"Why don't you come over tomorrow?" he says. "I got this puzzle last year for my birthday that I never opened—a map of the ocean floor."

That's the kind of presents David's folks give him. No wonder he never opened it.

"You know how deep the deepest place in the ocean is?" asks David.

"No."

"Guess."

"A mile?"

"Almost *seven* miles!"

"You're lying, David."

"Come over tomorrow and see. Come around two o'clock and I'll show you. There're mountains and valleys on the floor of the ocean just like there are on land."

It was sounding more interesting now. "Okay," I tell him. "I'll come."

Dara Lynn's feeling good 'cause she's only got four more days to wait to see if Judd's black-and-white dog has rabies, and it don't look like he does. So she probably won't have to have shots. She's sliding around the kitchen in her stocking feet, pretending she's on ice skates, and then she grabs Becky's hands, and they're both slipping and sliding on Ma's waxed floor.

"Fine with me," says Ma, eating an apple in our living room. "They'll just shine it up all the prettier."

They have to get Shiloh into the act, though, and pretty soon they're trying to put Becky's socks on his paws and then they got a pair of Dara Lynn's underpants on him and a "Wild and Wonderful West Virginia" T-shirt. They're screeching and giggling and looking around for a cap and some sunglasses. I figure any dog who puts up with all that should get a medal of honor.

Dad comes home with news. Heard on his mail route today that Judd Travers went to work drunk one day this week, and his boss tells him it better not happen again.

Seems like every new thing Judd does is worse than the one before. First he runs into mailboxes. Then he picks a fight. Drives drunk and goes to work drunk. Maybe he'll get fired and move away from here, I'm thinking, and that would be just fine with me. Meanwhile, I'm not going out there on the road any more than I have to, and I'm not telling Dad what happened, neither. Dad would go see Judd and end up making him madder, and maybe he'd shoot at Becky next.

I sit up late that night watching TV with Ma and Dad. The nice thing about having the couch for my bed is I get to stay up as late as they do. That's not very late, of course, 'cause Dad starts his mail route early, so he's always in bed by ten o'clock. Saturdays, though, he'll stay up till eleven.

'Course, you don't get many TV channels up here above Friendly, unless you have a satellite dish, which we don't. So on Saturday nights we either all watch TV together, or Ma and Dad sit out in the kitchen talking after I spread out my blankets on the couch.

Lately Dad's been talking some of selling off a few acres of our land and maybe building on another room to our house—a new bedroom for him and Ma. Then I could have their old one. I'd like that. Seems like everyone who wants to live up here already does, though, so nobody's much interested in our land.

I'm lying on the couch thinking how it would be to have a room, just Shiloh and me in it together. I'm wondering what rabbits Shiloh's sniffing out tonight. Or maybe he's with that black Labrador and they're exploring all over the place. I listen to the sounds of our house after Ma and Dad go to bed—the refrigerator and the hot water heater, buzzing and clicking. I fall asleep about eleven thirty, I guess, dreaming of that puzzle of the ocean floor, and wondering if it's got mountains and valleys down there, like David says.

Then I hear the noise.

It's the kind of loud, scary noise that if you are sound asleep when you hear it, you think your heart is going to stop. You can't tell if your eyes are staring into the blackness of the room or the blackness inside your eyelids.

All you know is you hear something—a loud bang and then a thump and another and another.

You are so scared your chest hurts. Your heart is beating so loud you can hear it. You can hardly breathe. Is somebody breaking in? Are you the only one awake? Why isn't your dad getting up? you wonder.

And then, an even worse sound than that.

Shiloh.

Fourteen

I don't think I can stand this again—Shiloh getting tore up by that German shepherd in the middle of the night. He ain't penned up now! Shiloh can run!

But there's the sound again, a dog sound, a yipping, yelping, dog noise, and it just won't stop.

Shiloh season?

I leap off the couch.

Dad and Ma are awake now, too, coming down the hall. I race over and turn on the porch light, expecting to see my dog with his ear half off, but Shiloh's not there. He's close by, though. I can tell.

"What is it?" asks Ma, pulling her arm through the sleeve of her robe.

"I don't know," I say, slamming my feet into my shoes. "I got to find him."

"Wait a minute," says Dad. "I'll go with you."

Ma gets the flashlight, hands it to me. Her hair is

all loose around her face, eyes sort of sleepy-surprised.

The Shiloh noise comes again and I just go cold all over. Could he be poisoned? But I wonder. It's not a whine, not a howl, not a bark—or maybe it's all three. More like talking, is what it is.

Dad comes out of the bedroom. He's pulled his pants on over his pajamas, and we both put on our jackets.

"Please be careful," says Ma.

We start down the driveway, but in two seconds I've started to run, and Dad trots along beside me.

"Did you hear that noise? That bang?" I ask.

Dad nods. "Couldn't figure out what it was. Thought maybe it was thunder, the way it rolled on. That dog's not afraid of storms, is he?"

"I never saw Shiloh afraid of a storm. Maybe there're hunters out," I say.

The sky's cloudy. When the moon breaks through, though, we can see pretty good. Nothing looks different or strange all along our driveway, but then we pick up Shiloh in the beam of the flashlight.

He's standing out on the road, and he's got his tail tucked between his legs like he's done somethin' really bad.

I run over and bend down.

"Shiloh!" I cry. "You hurt?"

That noise comes out of his throat again. Second time that night my heart almost stops beating. I run my hands over his head and ears. All over his body, feeling for wounds. Feel his legs and paws. No bones out of place.

He's not foaming at the mouth or anything. He keeps looking to the right, though, so Dad shines the light up the road.

I can see there's something in it—some small thing, a

'possum, maybe. We go over to check. Shiloh goes along with us a little way, but then he hangs back.

We get up to that big pothole in the road, just before the bridge, and I see that the thing I caught in the flashlight beam is an old muffler dropped off somebody's car, that's all.

"Don't see anything else," says Dad.

Shiloh's stopped still now, won't come any farther.

I shine my flashlight slowly all around the road, the bridge, and then we see the weeds over on the side. They're all mashed down like some big steamroller come by. There's something else in the weeds. We walk over. It's the rest of the muffler. I shine my flashlight on down the bank. There at the bottom is Judd's pickup, turned on its side.

"Oh, no!" breathes Dad.

We are scrambling down that bank. We can tell from the smell of oil and gasoline that the accident just happened. Engine's still hot. Then we know that was the bang we heard, Judd's pickup hitting the pothole and rolling over and over before it hit bottom.

I got to tell the truth, and the truth is that all the while I'm climbing down that hill behind Dad, same bank I scrabbled down with David Howard, lookin' for a cave, I'm thinking how if Judd could just be dead, our problems would be over. Wouldn't have to worry about his hunting on our land, wouldn't have to wonder if he'd drive by drunk some night and run over Shiloh. Wouldn't have to be scared he'd take another shot at me.

But as soon as the thought come into my mind, I'm ashamed, and saying, "No, Jesus, I didn't mean it."

If Jesus is getting one prayer from your lips and another

from your heart, which one is he going to pay attention to? That's the question.

We get to the bottom and Dad grabs the flashlight out of my hand and shines it on the truck. A man's leg is sticking out from underneath the cab of the pickup. The leg don't move.

I'm down on my hands and knees, trying to see into the cab. Dad gets down beside me and shines the light through the windshield.

Looks to me like Judd's upside down, pinned between the steering wheel and the side. Smells like a brewery in there.

Dad gets the door on top open and leans way in, feeling for Judd's wrist.

"I got a pulse!" he says.

Then he's making his way around to the other side, and pushes on the truck to see if he can rock it. "See that big old limb over there?" he says. "Drag it here, Marty, and wedge it under, right next to Judd's leg. He's going to lose that leg if we don't prop the truck up a little."

He rocks the truck again, and I get the thick part of the limb wedged under. Figure the door on Judd's side must have come open as the truck rolled.

"You run home and call emergency," he tells me. "Do it quick, Marty. And then you call Doc Murphy in case the rescue squad takes too long getting here. Tell Doc that Judd's still alive, but he's unconscious."

I run like the wind, Shiloh beside me. He's been waiting up on the road, won't come down. But now he thinks it's a game almost. Looks happy again.

All the while I'm running, though, I'm wondering: Did Judd see Shiloh trotting along the road and try to run him over? Put on the gas, maybe, and that's when he hit the pothole?

That's my guess. All I really know is that if Shiloh hadn't carried on like he did, I wouldn't never have got up. Would've laid there a while, maybe, wondering if that bang I heard was thunder, but I would have gone right back to sleep. If Judd lives, it's because of Shiloh.

Ma is standing at the screen, and Dara Lynn's beside her, rubbing her eyes and looking cross.

"Marty?" calls Ma.

"It's Judd!" I yell, more out of breath than I realize. "His truck went down the bank by the bridge. Call emergency, and then call Doc Murphy."

Ma finds another flashlight for me, and I go out to the road, wait until I see Doc's car coming real slow, looking for where it is he should stop.

Doc gets out at the bridge. He's got his pajamas on, too, and a robe on top. Got his black bag with him. I help him down the bank and through the weeds and brush to Judd's pickup. Dad's got the door open, and Doc leans way in with his stethoscope as best he can. Takes the flashlight and checks out Judd's eyes.

"Internal injuries, that's my guess," Doc says. "No way I can examine him without crawling in there, and doing more harm than good. . . ."

It's about then we hear the far-off sound of a siren, and I climb back up the bank to wait for them, show them where we are. I see that Shiloh didn't come back with me; stayed home with Ma and Dara Lynn.

Then there's lights and yelling and a truck motor running. Men are coming down the bank with a stretcher, the radio's blaring. Floodlights are turned on me and Dad and Doc, all in our pajamas. Nobody cares.

The pickup is gently set upright again. Splints are being

put on Judd's neck and back before they place him on the stretcher. Then the men are carrying him up the bank, and at some point Judd opens his mouth and groans. Says something, but all I can make out is a cuss word.

"Sure sounds like Judd Travers," one of the men says, and three minutes later the rescue truck is heading for the hospital in Sistersville.

Fifteen

"Is he dead?"

First words out of Dara Lynn's mouth when we get back to the house.

"No, but he's unconscious," Dad says, and tells them what happened.

"What about his truck?" Ma asks.

"Whelan's will send up a tow truck tomorrow."

"Do you think he's badly hurt, Ray?"

"Likely so. Got a broken leg, I can tell you that."

"Was the bone all sticking out?" asks Dara Lynn. I tell you, I got the strangest sister.

"All I know is that the truck came down on it when it turned over," Dad says.

Dara Lynn sticks around long enough to see if there're any more gory details, then ambles off to bed. Becky, of course, sleeps through the whole thing.

Ma and Dad talk a little more out in the kitchen, then

turn off the light and go back to bed. I lay on the couch, staring up into the dark. I'm having this conversation with Jesus again, only I'm doing all the talking. One minute I hope He's listening, and the next minute I hope He's not.

"Help him get well," I'm saying, because I think I should. Because you're supposed to pray for somebody who's been hurt.

Then I find myself thinking, *Just don't let his leg get well enough to ever go hunting again.*

Can you ask God to heal things, but only so much?

Next morning a tow truck comes up from Whelan's, and people stand around to watch. It's Sunday morning, so word hasn't spread too far yet. Dad and me and Dara Lynn all go over to watch—Dad wants to be sure there's nothing left in the weeds belonging to Judd. Finally the truck's up on the road again, being towed to the garage where Judd works. Truck don't look as bad as Judd did. Bet he didn't even have his seat belt on.

After Sunday dinner, Dad drives me down to David Howard's, and soon as I see him out on the porch, I run up.

"You hear what happened?" I say. Can tell by David's face he hasn't.

"What?" he says.

"You know that big pothole this side of the bridge?"

"It caved in?" whoops David.

"No, but you know Judd's truck?"

"It fell through?"

"No, David, let me tell it! Judd was driving drunk again last night, and his truck must of hit the pothole and gone out of control."

Then I tell him how the sheriff figures it hit the bridge first, then rolled on down the bank, Judd with it.

"Wooooow!" says David Howard, and the way he says it, dragging it out, sounds like air coming slow out of a bag.

We go in and tell his folks, and Mr. Howard calls his newspaper to be sure they've got the story.

David and I work at putting together his puzzle of the floor of the Pacific Ocean. Takes about two hours, with Mrs. Howard helping sometimes, and when we're all done, all we've got is a lot of light and dark lines; looks like blue burlap up close, with names printed on it: Galapagos Fracture Zone, Continental Shelf, Bounty Trough, Bonin Trench. Heck, I figured there would be fish and pirates' treasure chests and sunken ships on the bottom, not just lines.

Mrs. Howard, though, she's pointing out the Marianas Trench on the map.

"That's the world's greatest ocean depth," she says. "Almost seven miles deep."

I'm thinking what it would be like to go seven miles straight down in the ocean. Ma's granddaddy worked in a coal mine, but he didn't go down any seven miles. Quarter mile, maybe, and that's scary enough.

Dad was supposed to pick me up at four but it's almost four thirty when he shows up. I don't mind, 'cause Mrs. Howard gets out some pumpkin pie, and this gives me time for a second piece.

When I get in the Jeep, Dad says, "Didn't mean to be late, but I drove down to the hospital to look in on Judd. Took longer than I thought. Doctor wanted to talk to me."

"What'd he say?"

"Wanted to know if Judd had any relatives around here, and I couldn't think of one."

"How is he?"

"They operated on him last night. Had some internal injuries, like Doc Murphy said. Ruptured spleen, couple broken ribs, left leg broken in two places, fractured collarbone, skull fracture. . . . Still, his condition is stable."

"He's going to live, then?" I sure didn't sound very pleased.

"I think so. But it's going to be a while before he can go back to work."

"How about hunting?" I ask.

"That I don't know, son."

Then I know I have to do it.

"Dad," I say. "I got something to tell you." I swallow.

Dad looks over at me, and then he pulls the Jeep off the road and turns off the engine. Don't say nothing. Just sits there studying me.

I take a big breath and tell him everything. Tell him how I'd blackmailed Judd into giving me Shiloh by promising not to report him to the game warden. And when I get all that out of my system, I tell him about Shiloh and me out on the road by Doc Murphy's, and how I'm pretty sure it was Judd who took a shot at us.

Didn't exactly plan it this way, but when you got two things to tell, one of 'em scarier than the other, it's the scary one your dad will fix on every time.

"He *shot* at you, Marty?" he says. "He *shot* at you and you never told me?" He's so worked up he forgets all about the blackmail. "Why *didn't* you tell me?"

" 'Cause I didn't see it would help. Just make you mad and Judd madder. I figured I'd stay clear off the road till we got this thing settled."

Dad tips back his head and closes his eyes.

"Marty," he says finally. "Sometimes I'm stubborn and sometimes I'm cross, but don't you ever keep something like this from me again. Somebody takes a shot at one of my children, I want to hear about it. I want you to *promise* . . ."

"I promise," I say, quicker than he can blink.

And when Dad starts up the engine again and don't say one word about the blackmail, I'm so happy and relieved to have it out and over with I almost start to whistle. Then I figure that with a man in the hospital, half his bones broke, it's no time to be whistling, no matter *what* I think of him.

It's the talk of the school on Monday. Everybody's heard by then, and everyone's added a little something extra to the story.

"You hear about Judd?" says Michael Sholt. "Drove his truck right off the bridge and into the creek."

"Split his head wide open," says Fred Niles.

Sarah Peters says Judd's dogs were with him and all of 'em drowned, and by the time the bus pulls into the school yard, we got Judd Travers dead and buried already, dogs along with him. I see now the difference between truth and gossip.

Miss Talbot tries to sort out fact from fancy, but because I'm the only one who really saw Judd lying inside his truck, she takes my version and says we'll find out later what the newspaper has to say.

Then she says it might be nice to make a big card and send it to Judd from our sixth-grade class. The thing about folks from the outside is that as soon as they move to where we live, they want to change things—make them better. And there's nothing wrong with that, I guess, except she don't—doesn't—understand how long we've been hating Judd Travers.

The room is so quiet you can hear Michael Sholt's

stomach growl. Fact is, it might be "nice" to make a card, but there's not a single person wants to sign it.

Miss Talbot senses right away what the problem is. She says that the wonderful thing about the English language is there are enough words to say almost anything at all, and if you don't want to say something one way you can say it another.

"What could we say that would be both helpful and honest?" she asks.

"We hope you get well?" says Sarah, but the rest of us shake our heads. Nobody wants him driving drunk along the road anytime soon.

"We're sorry about your accident?" says David.

But the truth is we're not. Nothing else seemed able to stop Judd Travers from knocking over mailboxes and backing his truck into fences. He could have run over Shiloh.

Finally I raise my hand. "What about 'Get Well'?" I say.

We vote for that. It's more like a command than a wish. Miss Talbot gets out this big sheet of white drawing paper and folds it in half. On the outside, in big green letters, she writes, "Get Well!" And on the inside, in different colored pens, we take turns signing our names.

Some of the girls draw flowers at the ends of their names. Fred Niles draws an airplane, which don't make a bit of sense. When it comes my turn, I do something I didn't plan on, but somehow it seems right: I put down two names: *Marty and Shiloh.*

By the time Judd comes home from the hospital, the leaves are beginning to fall. Halloween's come and gone. (I was a pizza and David was a bottle of ketchup.) Judd's black-and-white dog didn't have rabies, and the county says they'll keep it until Judd can take care of his dogs himself.

The neighbors on one side of Judd took one of his other two dogs to care for, and the neighbors on the other took the third. Still another neighbor drives his tractor mower over to Judd's and mows his grass, and Whelan's Garage fixes his truck up for him and parks it in front of his house for when he's ready to drive again. All the dents are gone.

It was Dad who drove Judd home from the hospital. Ma had shopped the day before and sent along two big sacks of groceries. Dad helped Judd get into the house with them.

Told us later that Judd said hardly a single solitary word to him the whole time. Just sat looking straight ahead. Got his neck in a brace, of course, and a big old cast on his leg. Sits without turning left or right because his ribs are mending.

"Did you tell him we were the ones who found him?" I ask.

"I did," says Dad, "but it didn't seem to make much difference to him, one way or another."

I rake leaves at Doc Murphy's that Saturday. He asks if I know how Judd is doing.

"Ma says there's a visiting nurse comes twice a week," I tell him.

Doc shakes his head. "Some people seem to have a string of bad luck they can't do anything about, and other folks have a string of bad luck all their own doing," Doc says. "Guess Judd's had a little of both."

I can only think of the kind he got himself into. "What's the kind he couldn't do anything about?" I ask.

"Getting born into the family he did," says Doc.

"Did you know 'em?"

"Knew who they were. Lived in a house couple miles from here, other side of the creek. Mostly I heard stories from some of my patients, but the stories were so much alike there was bound to be a little truth in them."

"What did they say?"

"Mostly about old man Travers beating his kids. They get out of line, he'd take a belt to them. The buckle end, mind you. Neighbors said they could hear those kids yelling sometimes clear down the road. Once or twice somebody called the law, but nothing much was done."

"What happened to them? Where did they all go?"

"Most of the kids ran away as soon as they could, moved away, or got married. Judd was the youngest, and when the others left and old man Travers got peeved, Judd got his share of it and the others' share as well. Then there was a fire, and that house went up like a torch. Mrs. Travers died, but Judd got out, and his dad, too, but old man Travers died a week later of a heart attack. That's when Judd moved on down the road into that rental trailer. Been there ever since. Far as I know, he doesn't have a girlfriend. Hardly any men friends either. Just him and those dogs, and the way he treats 'em, you could hardly call them friends."

"You'd think that a man who missed out on kindness would want to be kind to his dogs," I say.

"You have to *learn* kindness, Marty, same as you learn to tie your shoes," Doc says. "And Judd just never had anyone to teach him."

I think about that a lot. All I can figure is that Judd would rather be the grown-up who does the beating, not the kid who's getting beat. Doesn't seem to realize they ain't—aren't—the only two choices he's got.

That afternoon when Dad comes home from delivering the mail, I ask if maybe we can go visit Judd.

"I don't think I'd try it, Marty," he says. "I've been taking his mail right up to his door so he don't have to climb down those steps to get it. I always rap on the door, ask how he's doing. I know he's there. But he never answers. Neighbors tell me he does the same with them."

"You figure he'll stop drinking now?"

"I doubt it, but I hope I'm wrong. They say a man has to reach bottom before he stops. If this isn't bottom, I'd sure hate to see what is."

What I'm wondering is whether Judd looks in the mirror each morning and decides he can't stand what he sees. Never wanted a dog that was lame in any way. Never wanted a dent or a scratch in his pickup. Now it's him that has the scratches and bruises and broken bones. I heard a couple men talking about how Judd might get it in his head just to shoot himself, and I'm wondering how I'd feel if he did.

Don't know that I'd be too sorry, 'cause once he's well, we got the very same problems we had before. Judd'll be just like he was, only meaner.

Sixteen

The next day, though, just because I ask, Dad and I get in the Jeep and drive over to Judd's. Seems strange to park across the road from his trailer and not be greeted by a bunch of yelping, snarling hounds.

November sun is shining down on Middle Island Creek, and you'd never think that inside that trailer is a man as wretched and mean and sad as a man can get. His grass has been mowed again, probably for the last time this year, but all his shades are pulled, like he don't want one ounce of sunlight trying to sneak its way into his house and cheer him up.

We start across the road to where Judd's board sidewalk begins. The trailer door opens. There is Judd, big cast on his leg, holding his shotgun.

"What you want, Ray Preston?" he calls. Still wearing a neck brace, I see.

We stop dead still. "Marty and I just wanted to stop by, say hello," Dad calls back.

"Well, I don't need no hellos," Judd says. He's not exactly pointing the gun at us, but he's not pointing it away, neither.

"You need any groceries, Judd? Anything I can pick up for you?" Dad asks.

"Don't need nothing."

"Well . . . okay. We're just concerned about you. Everyone is."

Judd gives this little laugh—so weak you could hardly call it that—and closes the door again.

"Well, son?" says Dad. "Looks like that's that."

But something in me just don't give up. If kindness has to be learned, then maybe Judd's got some lessons coming. If I don't try, and Judd ever hurts Shiloh, how am I going to feel then?

Soon as we get home, I say, "Ma, you suppose we could fix up something every day to leave there on the steps along with Judd's mail? Something to eat?"

"I think that's a fine idea, Marty," she says. "When I was making bread this morning, I was thinking of giving him some."

That evening, I wrap up a loaf for Judd, and next day Dad takes it along with him and puts it right outside Judd's door.

On Tuesday, though, Dad reports that the bread he'd left on Monday's still there. Judd had taken in his mail but left the bread outside. And you know what I'm thinking? It's not just the world he's mad at; he's mad at himself. Oh, it's part-ly that he don't want to take any kindness from the Prestons, 'cause he don't—doesn't—know how to give any back in return. But when a man's sunk about as low as he can get, I'll bet he feels he don't even have a right to that bread.

"What did you do with the chicken I wrapped up for him this time?" I ask Dad.

"Just set it right there beside the bread," Dad tells me.

Well, I thought, just like John Collins says, you leave it there long enough, he'll get hungry.

On Wednesday, Dad says that both the bread and the chicken are gone. Judd could've thrown 'em out, of course, but sometimes you got to take chances.

"What kind of mail does he get?" I ask my dad.

"Oh, magazines, mostly. *Guns and Ammo. Shooting Times.* Junk mail, bills."

"He ever get any letters?"

"None I can remember."

After the first week of leaving food outside Judd's door, I decide I'll start sending a little note under the rubber band on the food package:

> *Last month a bee was chasing Shiloh. You should have seen him. Was running and looking behind him both at the same time, and he run into a bush. Thought that bee would drive him right down to the creek. Think Shiloh put his nose too close to a nest somewhere. He'll be a little more careful after this.*
> *Marty*

We weren't the only ones taking food to Judd. Heard that some of the neighbors had been leaving casseroles and cakes outside his door from time to time. The food seemed to disappear, so we figure either Judd was eating it or burying it, one or the other.

Still, we wonder, what's a man thinking and feeling when he don't never come to the door, don't never say thank you, sits in his house all day with the shades pulled? Sits there hating himself, I'll bet. Knows if he keeps up the way he was doing, he'll lose his job, and then he'll lose everything—trailer, dogs, guns. . . .

Doc Murphy told me that he'd heard Judd was healing nicely. His body, that is. It would take some time for that leg to heal, but the visiting nurse said he was moving around a whole lot better than he had been.

I'm thinking about Shiloh and when I first saw him— all slunk down in the brush, so trembly and scared of me he couldn't stop shaking. Wouldn't even let me pet him—just crawled away on his belly. No trust left in him at all.

Thinking, too, of the other three dogs of Judd's— the way he'd chained them up, so fearful something or somebody was going to come along and start a fight they couldn't win. All snarlin' and snapping, trying to keep themselves from being hurt.

And now that we got Judd all shut up in his trailer, I'm thinking how slowly, a little bit at a time, we got to teach him kindness. He was taking the food we left for him. That was a start.

Seemed like the only thing I could think of to write about in my notes to Judd was about Shiloh. Thinking back on things, it was the only thing we both cared about, though I guess we cared about Shiloh in different ways.

I told him how much Shiloh weighed now, when we took him to the vet. How we're not supposed to feed him table scraps, but buy him this balanced dog food, make his coat shiny. Told how we laughed ourselves sick once watching Shiloh take off after a mole burrowing along just beneath the ground. Fast as Shiloh could dig, that mole was tunneling away from him. Every last thing Shiloh ever did that would interest a live body in the least, I put down on paper. I figure if a man don't get any other letters, he's got to be interested in the only ones he gets.

The blinds come up in Judd's trailer. Nobody's seen him at a window yet, but he can't hardly keep from seeing out.

One day I decide that all these notes I've been writing about Shiloh are just so much noise—just writing around and around what it is I really want to say to Judd. And what it is I want to say is that here's this little dog he kicked and cussed and starved, so scared of Judd he won't never even cross the bridge leading to the road Judd's house is on. Yet one night he meets up with Judd's truck out on the road. I still don't know whether Judd had been drunk and had hit the pothole the wrong way, or whether he'd seen Shiloh trotting down the road and was trying to hit him.

But here's this man pinned under his truck at the bottom of a bank, dead of night, quarter mile from any house except ours, and Shiloh could have sneaked on home without a sound. Judd could have died in the wreck that night. Might have, too. Nobody would have discovered him till the next morning. Maybe not even then.

But instead, the dog starts crying and whining, scared as he is of gettin' within a hundred feet of Judd Travers, and wakes us up. I don't expect Judd to jump up and down, I say in my letter. Shiloh don't expect no reward. Judd don't have to go around praising my dog. I just think he ought to

114

know that it wasn't my dad and me who saved him that night, it was Shiloh.

I stick the note under the rubber band on the raisin rolls I package up for Dad to put on Judd's doorstep the next afternoon.

A day goes by. Two days. And then, on a Friday afternoon when Dad gets home from work, I say to him, "I want to go see Judd Travers."

"Now, Marty," says Dad. He's still sitting in the Jeep. "You know what happened last time. What makes you think he'll let you in?"

"Nothin'. Just want to try, is all," I say. "I don't want to go on fighting with Judd and worrying myself sick about Shiloh."

"Well, hop in. Might as well go now as later," he says.

"Wait just a minute, I'm takin' something," I say. And I go back to the porch where Shiloh is sitting, happy as a beetle on a rosebud, and gather him up in my arms.

"We're goin' visiting," I say.

Shiloh licks my face.

I get in the Jeep, but I don't put Shiloh on the seat by Dad and crawl in the back, way I usually do. I fasten my seat belt and hold my dog in my lap.

Dad's giving me his puzzled look. "You sure about this, son?"

"No. But it's only a visit," I say.

Shiloh wriggles right over to the window and sticks his head out as Dad starts the motor.

"Be right back," I yell to Ma. She and the girls have their coats on, picking up black walnuts over by the shed.

Shiloh hangs out the window, one paw on the sill, and

the happier he looks, the more I wonder: Am I doing the right thing?

Shiloh's happiness lasts just till we get to the end of the driveway, because as soon as Dad turns right, he backs away from the window and looks up at me.

I stroke his head.

"It's okay, Shiloh," I say. I hold onto him, because I'm afraid when we go to cross the bridge he might try to jump out the window or something, run back home. I roll up the window. It's cold, anyway.

Dad eases the Jeep around the pothole, and as we start over the bridge, the boards makin' loose rattly sounds beneath the truck, Shiloh sinks down in my lap, like all the wind is going out of him.

"It's okay," I say again.

He licks my hand.

Once across the bridge, though, when we turn right again, Shiloh starts to whine—a high, soft whine down in his throat. I stroke his back. I'm remembering how, when he come to me for the first time, Dad made me take him back to his rightful owner. Owner, anyway. And how he had hunkered down on my lap, just like he's doing now.

I want in the worst way to let him know that this time is different. That I wouldn't let Judd have him for all the money in the world. Wouldn't never even loan him out. Just payin' a visit, is all. But there's no way Shiloh can understand. All he's got in his memory is the time I took him back before, and how Judd had kicked him when I let him out of the Jeep—kicked him and shut him up in his shed and didn't feed him for a couple days.

I swallow. Just hearing my dog whimper and feeling his body shake, I think, how can this be the right thing to do?

We get to Judd's and park on the creek side. Shiloh is really whimpering now, scrunched up on my legs like he's trying to grow roots.

I hug him in my arms as we get out.

"I'm not puttin' you down," I say. "You're mine for as long as you live. I promise you that."

He licks my face again.

We cross the road and go up the board sidewalk to Judd's trailer. Go up the steps.

Dad knocks on the door, and Shiloh snuggles up against me, don't make a sound. Figure he's thinking if he don't make any noise, Judd may not notice.

Nobody comes. I know Judd's there, 'cause I can hear the TV going.

Dad knocks again.

The TV goes off. Nothing happens.

"Judd," Dad calls. "Got a visitor here to see you."

Still no answer. I'm thinking maybe this is a sign that I should turn around right this minute and go back. Think maybe Judd is going for that shotgun. Will tell himself that if it wasn't for the dog, he wouldn't have started drinking heavy, and if he hadn't started drinking heavy, he wouldn't have hit that pothole the way he did, and if he hadn't hit the pothole, he wouldn't be laid up with a broken leg right now.

Then the door opens, but only a crack.

"What you want?" Judd's voice.

Shiloh is shaking so hard I think he is gonna shake right out of my arms.

"Got someone here to see you," Dad says pleasant-like, and steps aside. I move over to where Judd can see me through the crack in the door.

There is not a sound from inside, but the door don't close. Shiloh's grown bigger and fatter and sleeker since he became my dog, but right now, burrowed down almost as far as he can get in my arms, he looks almost like a pup.

"We just came for a visit," I say, to make it plain right off that no way am I giving Judd this dog.

And finally, when the quiet gets almost embarrassing, Judd opens the door a little wider. "Well, come on in for a minute," he says. And it's Judd who's embarrassed. First time in my life I ever saw a look on his face that says he's ashamed of himself.

First time I been in Judd's trailer, too. And the thing I notice is it smells. Smells like the home of a man who don't empty his garbage or wash his socks when he should.

I see he's not wearin' the neck brace anymore, but he still walks stiff, and he's still got this big cast on his leg.

He leans over and picks up some magazines on the couch, throws 'em on the floor. "Sit down, if you want," he says, and lowers himself into the straight-back chair beside the couch, broke leg out in front of him.

I'm trying to hold Shiloh as tight as I can to give him the message that he won't get loose. That I don't *want* him loose. But he's still shaking. Wouldn't surprise me none if he peed on my leg.

"It's good to see you up and around," Dad says, sitting on the couch beside me. "Things are healing all right, are they?"

"Doing okay," says Judd, his voice low. He don't take his eyes off Shiloh, though.

I wonder what he thinks about this scared, trembling dog, hunkered down on my lap, silent now and limp as a leaf. Wonder if he's thinking about when this dog was his—

118

the way he treated him then, the way Shiloh kept running away.

"So he's the one that found me," Judd says.

"Yeah," I tell him. "Just kept on making those noises till we come out and found your truck."

All the while I'm talkin', I'm rubbing Shiloh's silky head, scratching gently behind his ears, running my hand along his back, then starting all over again. Judd's watchin'.

"I suppose he remembers me," says Judd.

I don't answer. The way Shiloh's shaking, there's no doubt.

Judd leans forward a little, and I think I see his hand move. Slowly he reaches out, and I can feel Shiloh flinch. I swallow as I see him shy away, drawing back from Judd's touch.

But Judd lets his fingers rest lightly on top of Shiloh's head, just the way mine did. And then, he begins to stroke my dog.

At first I think Shiloh's too numb to feel it, too scared to breathe. All he wants to do, I know, is get out of there, make sure he's not going to be left behind.

I figure that Judd's going to give him a couple more strokes and pull his hand away, but he don't. Just keeps stroking Shiloh's head, like he's found somethin' here he needs, and I can begin to feel Shiloh's body easing up some, feel his legs relax.

He sits real still, looks straight ahead. Judd's strokes get more even, not so jerky. The palm of his hand strokes lower now, down on Shiloh's nose, then slowly moves up over the forehead, before the fingers settle behind Shiloh's ears and do a little gentle scratching.

I glance over at Judd, a quick little look, and for just a

moment, his eyes seem wet. I look down at my dog again. Don't want to embarrass Judd.

Does Shiloh know I wouldn't never leave him? That this is only a visit, and that he's mine forever and ever? I think he does, because the next time Judd's fingers come forward to stroke his head, Shiloh—for the very first time—reaches up and licks Judd's hand.

Saving
SHILOH

Saving
SHILOH

by
PHYLLIS
REYNOLDS
NAYLOR

ATHENEUM BOOKS FOR YOUNG READERS

Thanks to our friends, the Maddens,
of Friendly, West Virginia

Atheneum Books for Young Readers
An imprint of Simon & Schuster Children's Publishing Division
1230 Avenue of the Americas
New York, New York 10020

Book design by Nina Barnett
The text of this book is set in Goudy.

First Edition
Printed in the United States of America
10 9 8
Library of Congress Cataloging-in-Publication Data
Naylor, Phyllis Reynolds.
Saving Shiloh / Phyllis Reynolds Naylor.—1st ed.
p. cm.
Sequel to: Shiloh season
Summary: Sixth-grader Marty and his family try to help their
rough neighbor, Judd Travers, change his mean ways, even though
their West Virginia community continues to expect the worst of him.
ISBN 0-689-81460-7
[1. Dogs—Fiction. 2. Family life—West Virginia—Fiction.
3. West Virginia—Fiction. 4. Prejudices—Fiction.] I. Title.
PZ7.N24Sav 1997
[Fic]—dc21
96-37373

To anyone who ever tried
to make a difference

One

There's one last thing to say about Shiloh before the story's over. I guess a dog's story ain't—isn't—ever over, even after he dies, 'cause if you lose a pet, you still go on loving him. But I couldn't bring myself to tell this part until now; of all the stuff that's happened, this was the scariest, and just thinking on it starts my hands to sweat.

When I first tried to get Shiloh from Judd Travers, who was treating that dog meaner than mud, at least there was a chance that if I couldn't have him for my own, Judd would let him live.

And even after Judd turns his beagle over to me, then starts drinkin' and talkin' ugly, there's hope he never meant it. But sometimes hope seems out of human hands entirely, and when the third thing happened . . . well, here's all that's left to tell.

Next to Christmas, I guess, Halloween is big in West

Virginia—out where we live, anyway, which is the little community of Shiloh, up the winding road from Friendly there on the Ohio River. It's because I first saw the little dog here in Shiloh that I named him what I did.

To get to our house, you go through this place called Little—you'll know it by the church—and you keep going along Middle Island Creek, wide as a river, till you see this old falling-down gristmill. It's right by this rusty bridge, and just over the bridge, you'll see the old Shiloh schoolhouse. SHILOH SCHOOL—1920–1957, reads a sign above the door, like a gravestone or something. I seen plenty of buildings got the date on them when they were built, but I never seen a building got the date when it died.

We live on the side of the creek near the mill, up the lane in a two-bedroom house. You sit out on the steps of an evening, don't move even your little finger, and pretty soon a buck will step out of the trees, a doe or two behind him, and parade across your field just as grand as you please. Now you tell me how many sixth-grade boys in the United States of America got somethin' like that to look on!

"What you going to be for Halloween next year, Marty?" asks Dara Lynn at supper. Halloween is over and gone, see, and already my skinny seven-year-old sister is thinkin' about the next. With her there's never no question. She dresses up like a witch every single year just so Ma can paint her fingernails black.

"I don't know," I tell her. "A ghoul, maybe."

"What's a ghoul?" asks Becky, who's three.

"Halfway between a ghost and a zombie," I say.

"Like a vampire?" asks Dara Lynn. Dara Lynn's big on vampires.

"Naw. Its skin is green, and it don't suck blood," I say.

2

"Marty!" Ma scolds, nodding toward my littlest sister.

We're having biscuits with sausage gravy for dinner, and there's nothing in the world I love more than sausage gravy. Except Shiloh, of course. And Shiloh loves that gravy, too, 'cause all through supper he's sittin' beside my chair with his muzzle on my leg, just waiting for me to finish up and pass that plate down to him so's he can lick up every last bit.

"I'm going to be a bunny," says Becky.

"Bunnies don't scare no one!" says Dara Lynn. "Why don't you be a pirate or something?"

"I don't *want* to scare no one," says Becky.

I guess there are *two* things I love more than sausage gravy: Shiloh and Becky.

Dad's washing up at the sink. We wait for him if we can, but sometimes his mail route takes longer than he thinks, and Becky gets hungry, so we eat.

"Passed by Sweeneys' house on the way home, and two of those straw men they rigged up on their porch have fallen over and been dragged out in the yard by their dogs," Dad says, sitting down at the table. "Look like a couple of drunks keeled over on the grass."

"Those straw men in overalls don't scare nobody," says Dara Lynn. "I want a dead man on our porch next Halloween with a face as white as flour."

"What's Shiloh going to be?" chirps Becky.

"He ain't going to be anything but his own self," I tell her. "Nobody messing with my dog."

"All this talk of Halloween, when Thanksgiving's right around the corner!" says Ma.

I guess there isn't that much to holler about where we live, so when a special day comes along, you want to hang on to it—keep Halloween stuff around till Christmas, and

Christmas lights goin' till Easter. I'm thinking how Ma wouldn't let us go trick-or-treating this year, though—not by ourselves.

"Houses too far apart for you kids to be walking out on the road," she'd said.

Well, the houses weren't any farther apart this year than last, and Dara Lynn and me went out then. But this time Dad drove us to the Halloween parade in Sistersville, and we had to do all our trick-or-treating there. I knew Ma was thinking of Judd Travers and the accident he'd had a month ago out on the road, drunk as he was. Knew she didn't want some other drunk to run his car into one of us.

Dara Lynn must have guessed what I'm thinking, 'cause she jokes, "We could always stuff Judd Travers and put him up on our porch. He'd scare off anybody."

"Hush," scolds Ma.

"There's enough talk going around about Judd Travers without you adding your two cents' worth," says Dad.

My ears prick up right quick. "What kind of talk?"

"None that makes one bit of sense," Dad tells me. "The man paid his fine for drunk driving, he busted up his leg and his truck besides, and as far as I can tell, he's trying to turn himself around. You'd think folks would want to help."

"I thought they were," I say. "Whelan's Garage fixed his truck up for him; people were takin' him groceries. . . ."

"That was when he was flat on his back, when he was really down. Now that he's on his feet again, there's the feeling around here that he got off way too easy. Heard Ed Sholt say as much down at the hardware store last week. Said we ought to keep Judd on the hot seat, let him know his kind wasn't wanted around here, and maybe he'd move somewhere else."

4

That sure would solve a lot of problems, I'm thinking. Ma wouldn't be so afraid for us kids out on the road, Dad wouldn't have to worry about Judd hunting up in our woods where a stray bullet could find its way down to our place, and I could rest easy that Judd wouldn't look for excuses to take Shiloh back; that he wouldn't hurt my dog out of spite, he ever got the chance. I think maybe I like the idea just fine.

"But what if he *doesn't* move?" says Ma. "What if everybody starts treatin' him worse'n dirt, and he stays right where he is?"

And suddenly I see a meaner Judd Travers than we ever saw before. Madder, too. I think how he used to kick Shiloh—even took a shot at the log where Shiloh and me were sitting once. A meaner Judd than that?

"Way I look at it," Dad goes on, "is that Judd's doing fine so far, and we ought to wait and see what happens."

Dara Lynn's got a mouth on her, though. "Ha! He's still got his leg in a cast," she says. "Get that cast off, and he'll be just as bad as before."

"Well, I believe in giving a man a second chance," Dad tells her.

"Beginning now," says Ma, fixing her eyes on us. "Your dad and I have talked about it, and we're inviting Judd here for Thanksgiving dinner."

Dara Lynn rolls her eyes and falls back in her chair. "Good-bye turkey!" she says, meaning she won't have no appetite come the fourth Thursday in November. As for me, I lose my appetite that very minute and set my plate on the floor.

TWO

On the school bus next day, I tell David Howard who's coming to our house for Thanksgiving.

"Judd *Travers?*" he yells, and David's got a mouth bigger than Dara Lynn's. Every last person on that bus takes notice. *"Why?"*

" 'Cause he don't have no other place to go," I mumble. All the kids are looking at me now.

"He'll probably show up drunk and drive right into your porch," says Fred Niles.

"He'll bring his gun and shoot your dog," says Sarah Peters.

Michael Sholt says, "If it was us, *my* dad wouldn't let him in the house! Judd was the one who knocked over our mailbox when he was drinking. And it was Dad who caught his black-and-white dog when somebody turned Judd's loose. Said it was almost as mean as Judd."

"He's just coming for dinner," I say. "It ain't like he's movin' in." I wish I'd never said anything. David Howard's my best friend, but he sure is loud.

In school, we're learning far more about Pilgrims than I ever wanted to know. All our spelling words for the last two weeks have had something to do with Pilgrims, so I have to learn words like "treaty," "colonist," "religious," and "celebration."

What I do like, though, is learning about the two Indians, Samoset and Squanto, who taught the Pilgrims how to plant corn. And how, except for the Indians, every single person who lives in the United States is either an immigrant himself or his great-granddaddy, maybe, came from a foreign country. Us Prestons are mostly English, a little Scotch and Irish thrown in. Miss Talbot says a lot of the early colonists were convicts, people who had been in jail in England, and were deported to America. I'll bet you anything Judd's great-great-great-great-granddaddy was somebody who'd been in jail.

Thanksgiving morning, I can smell the turkey roasting before I even open my eyes. We got a sixteen-pounder on sale, so Ma gets it in the oven early. I guess being hunkered down on a warm sofa, which is where I sleep, smelling turkey and knowing I don't have to go to school is about as close to heaven as I can get. Shiloh must think so, too. He's asleep against my feet, and every so often I can feel his paws twitch, like he's dreamin' of chasing rabbits.

Once Becky's awake, though, I don't sleep anymore, 'cause she'll come right over to the couch and stand with her face two inches from mine. She knows she's not supposed to wake me, so what she does is just stand there, her hot breath warming my eyelids. If I don't wake up right off, she'll start blowin' real soft—short little puffs—and then I know that whatever sleep I ain't had yet, I'm not gonna get.

I scoot over to one side so Becky can climb up and watch cartoons on TV. This morning, though, she's not content just to blow, her breath smelling of Cheerios and sleep; she's got to tap me on the cheek with the edge of the cardboard Pilgrim Dara Lynn brought home. I'm beginning to wish I'd never heard of Thanksgiving or Pilgrims, either one.

My job is to crack the bag of walnuts somebody give us so Ma can make a walnut pie—we always have us a walnut pie and pumpkin both. As soon as I'm dressed and get some cinnamon toast in me, I begin. Dara Lynn's settin' the table, putting little toothpick and marshmallow turkeys she's made by each plate. Dad slides the extra leaf in the table so there's room for Judd, and Shiloh just hangs around the kitchen, smelling that turkey. He don't know who's coming for dinner, and it's just as well.

Usually Ma sings when she's feeling good, but I notice she's not singing today. There's a frown-line that shows up on her forehead, and she bites her bottom lip as she tests the pie.

About two o'clock Dad says, "Well, I better drive over there and pick up Judd. Marty, why don't you come along?"

There's no reason I can think of why I should, but when Dad says that, it's 'cause he's got something to say to me. So I get my jacket.

I climb in the back of the Jeep. Judd, with his left leg in a cast, is going to need room up front to stretch himself out. As soon as we start down the lane, Dad says, "Now Marty, you being the oldest, Dara Lynn and Becky are going to take their cue from you. You treat Judd with respect, your sisters will learn a little something."

What's he think? I'm gonna start some kind of argument right there at the table? I don't respect Judd, but I can be polite.

"What I mean is," Dad goes on, "if he says something about Shiloh, don't go getting hot under the collar. Let's see if we can't get through this meal at least being good neighbors."

I want just as bad as anyone else to make peace with Judd, but there's one condition: "Long as you don't let him borrow Shiloh to go hunting," I say.

"Judd won't be doing any hunting this season, you can bet," says Dad. "He's got even more injuries besides that leg to heal up."

We reach the road, turn right a few yards, go around the big pothole that sent Judd's pickup truck rolling down the bank last month, then cross the bridge by the old mill. We turn right again and keep going till we get to the brown-and-white trailer where Judd lives.

He's already out in the yard, hobbling about on his cast and crutches. He's got brown hair, eyes that look smaller than they are on account of being so close together, and a mouth that don't seem to open as wide as it should, the words sliding out the corners when he speaks. Judd comes down the board walkway holding a gunnysack in one hand.

"Brought the missus a little somethin'," he says, sliding in after Dad leans over and opens the passenger door. He eases himself onto the seat—I'm wondering should I get out and help him—then pulls his crutches in after him, and rests the bag on his lap. Black walnuts, I figure.

9

"You seem to be getting around a little better," says Dad, making a U-turn and heading back toward the bridge.

"Doin' okay, but I'm still mighty sore," says Judd.

"How long you got to wear that cast?" I ask.

"Another month, I'm lucky. Longer, if I'm not."

I sure am glad to hear that—that he'll have that cast on all through deer season. There's only 'bout a week and a half of it left.

Middle Island Creek is on the other side of us now. Dad and Judd are talking about Judd's work at Whelan's Garage where he's a mechanic, and how wasn't it a good thing Whelan kept his job open for Judd while his bones heal—kept his job open and fixed up his truck, both. Then we're heading up the lane toward our house, and there's Shiloh standing out by the porch, tail going back and forth, his rear end doing this little welcoming dance.

But suddenly his dancing stops, tail goes between his legs, and he's up on the porch, whining to get in. Don't take no genius to know he's got a whiff or a look or both of Judd Travers, and is scared the man's come to take him back. I wouldn't let that dog go to save my life.

Ma opens the door for Shiloh, then comes out herself. "Happy Thanksgiving, Judd," she says, and when she smiles, she's got this dimple in one cheek. "I got dinner on the table. Hope you're hungry."

Judd thunks up the steps and hands Ma the gunnysack. "Brought you somethin'," he says.

Becky and Dara Lynn are hangin' back by the door, but they get wind there's a present, they're right out there, tryin' to see in the bag.

"Why, thank you, Judd," says Ma. She opens the sack and starts to put one hand in, then draws it out real quick.

"Eeeuuu!" cries Dara Lynn, getting herself a look. "What *is* it?"

"Squirrel," says Judd, mighty proud of himself. "They're already bled. Woulda skinned 'em, too, if I'd had the time, but I shot 'em not long before Ray come over."

I see now where the blood's stained one side of the gunnysack.

"Those'll make a fine-tasting stew," says Dad, and he takes the bag himself and sets it on the porch. "I'll skin these after dinner." And then, "Didn't know you could hunt with that leg like it is."

Judd laughs. "Not much hunting to it. I just picked those squirrels off while I was sittin' on my front steps." And he follows my folks inside.

I'm feeling sick at my stomach. I'm remembering how David Howard and me were over at Judd's once, before the accident, and saw him shoot a squirrel just for the pure mean joy of it. Didn't even cook it, just threw it to his dogs.

"Well," says Ma. "Guess we can all sit down at the table, if you're ready."

Becky takes the long way around the kitchen so she don't have to get within four feet of Judd. Shiloh's nowhere to be found; usually he'd have his nose right at the edge of the table, waiting for a piece of that turkey to stand up and walk his way.

It sure ain't—isn't—what you'd call a comfortable Thanksgiving. About the way the Pilgrims must have felt with Indians there. Or maybe the way Samoset and Squanto felt with the Pilgrims—everybody a little too polite.

Ma usually has us do somethin' special on Thanksgiving. Like last year, we each had to think up three things we were thankful for, and the year before that, we had to say some-

11

thing nice about the person on our right, except that Becky couldn't talk yet, and the person on *my* right was Dara Lynn. Only nice thing I could think to say about her was that she didn't look too bad with three teeth missin'.

This year, though, with Judd there, Dad offers the prayer he usually prays on Sundays. He thanks God for the food before us and says, "Bless it to nourish our good. Amen." Dara Lynn don't even bow her head, she's so afraid somebody's going to get the drumstick she's set her eye on.

Everyone smiles when the prayin's over, and Ma says, "Now Judd, you just help yourself to whatever you see before you, and we'll start the platters around. I've sliced some white meat and dark meat both." And the eatin' begins.

With all that food coming at me, I almost forget for a time that we got Judd to look at across the table, but once we get a little in our bellies, I can see the conversation isn't going very far.

First off, Judd's embarrassed. I think he likes the food, all right, but he don't especially like being at our table. It's like he owes us somethin' for finding him after his accident, and Judd don't like to owe nobody nothing. Guess he figured if he was to refuse our invitation, though, it'd be like a slap in the face. And bad as he is, even he's got a limit to rudeness. I look across at him, shoveling that food in like the sooner he gets it down the sooner he can leave, and I'm tryin' to think of a question to ask that'll give everybody a chance to say somethin'.

But right that minute Becky says, "What was the turkey's name?"

We all look at her.

"Only pet turkeys have names, Becky," Dad says. "We bought this turkey at the store."

12

That gives Judd something to talk about. "I got me a fine wild turkey last year. Bought one of those turkey callers, and after I got the hang of it, I bagged a thirteen-pounder."

Dara Lynn's thinkin' that over. "You make a call like a turkey, and when a real one shows up, you blow its head off?"

"That's about it," says Judd.

Ma never looks up—just goes on cutting her meat, her cheeks pink—but Becky stops chewing her turkey wing and she is glaring at Judd something awful. Boy, you get a three-year-old girl lookin' at you that way, she's got a scowl would stop a clock.

I'm just about to ask Ma to pass the sweet potatoes when I hear Becky say, "We'll blow *your* head off!" and suddenly there is quiet around that table you wouldn't believe.

Three

Well, Thanksgiving sure went downhill after that. You wouldn't think a three-year-old could say anything that would cause much trouble, but it just seemed to put into words the feeling we had about Judd Travers.

Judd looks over at Becky and says, a little sharp-like, "Hey, little gal, you ain't havin' much trouble eatin' that turkey, I see. Somebody had to kill that."

Becky looks at the turkey wing and slowly lowers it onto her plate, then turns her scowl toward Judd again, her bottom lip stickin' out so far you could hang a bucket on it.

Everybody starts talkin' at once. Ma asks wouldn't Judd like some more gravy, and Dad wants to know if he's going to watch the football game that afternoon, but their voices seem too loud and high. By the time Ma cuts the pie, we don't have much taste for it. I don't, anyway. Judd eats one piece of pumpkin, and Ma says she'll send a piece of the wal-

14

nut home with him. Then her cheeks turn pink again, 'cause it sounds like maybe she can't wait for him to go, and she says, "But of course you're staying to watch the game, aren't you?"

Judd don't say yes or no, but when Dad turns on the TV, the picture's fuzzy on account of we don't have us a satellite dish. Judd's got one in his yard that's bigger'n his trailer, almost. And that gives him a real fine excuse to say no, he thinks he'll go on home, prop up his leg, and watch the game there.

Now that he's leavin', we're all smiles and politeness, standing around waiting for Judd to get his jacket on.

"Where's that dog of yours?" Judd says to me, pulling his sleeve down over the cuff of his shirt. That's about the first time he ever admitted that Shiloh was really mine.

I decide Shiloh's gonna say good-bye if I have to drag him out, and I do. I go behind the couch where he's lyin', about as far back in the corner as he can get, and I have to take two of his paws and tug. He's shaking already, but I hold him tight so he'll know he belongs to me.

Judd looks him over. "Shyest dog I ever seen," he says. But again, just like he did when we went to visit him after the accident, Judd puts out his hand and strokes Shiloh on the head. He's still awkward about it, but he's learnin'. It was Shiloh who barked when Judd's pickup rolled down the bank, really Shiloh who saved his life, and Judd knows that. And once more, Shiloh licks his hand. It's a feeble sort of lick, but Judd likes it, I can tell. I figure Judd's a person who don't get no kisses and hugs from anyone.

After Dad and Judd get in the Jeep, Ma moves about the kitchen, her lips pressed together like she's seen better Thanksgivings, so Becky and Dara Lynn make themselves scarce. They go in the next room and gather up all the Thanksgiving cutouts Dara Lynn brought home from school. They make like they're paper dolls, the Pilgrims riding around on the big cardboard turkey, and the Indians sittin' on this pumpkin.

When Dad gets back, though, he takes out after me! I can't believe it!

"Marty, you didn't say more'n five words to Judd the whole time he was here."

I bet I said fifty, maybe, but I'll admit, I didn't say a whole lot. "What're you yellin' at me for?" I ask. "It's Becky you should be scolding for sayin' too much."

He knows it and I know it, but truth is, you can't hardly scold a three-year-old girl for anything, and Dad would rather cut off his thumb than make Becky cry.

Then Ma chimes in: "Marty's right, Ray. Don't take it out on him."

Dad turns on her then: "Why do you always side with Marty? We have a guest for dinner, I expect everyone to pitch in and be sociable. Can't me be doing all the talking."

I know he's not really mad at Ma, either. He just wishes the day had gone better—we was all so stiff.

But that's enough to set Ma off. "Well, if you want to stand out here in the kitchen and do all the cooking next time, *I'll* sit in the other room and talk. How about that?"

Oh boy, this is the worst Thanksgiving I can remember. Dad turns on the TV to watch the game, then turns it off again, picture's so bad. Becky's leaning over a sofa cushion, sucking her thumb and twisting a lock of hair—ready for a nap.

And then I realize that not a single word's been aimed at Dara Lynn. If *she* had opened her mouth, no telling *what* would've come out; she can sass the ears off a mule. How

16

come *she* got through Thanksgiving without even a look? I find myself gettin' all churned up inside, and when she comes out of the kitchen with the wishbone—the Thanksgiving turkey *wish*bone—and asks Becky to pull it with her, it's all I can do not to reach out and sock her arm.

"Make a wish, Becky, then pull," she says.

This ain't no fair contest, 'cause Dara Lynn's holding that wishbone right close to the top, and Becky's little hand hardly has a grip on it. Guess who wins.

"I got the center, so now you got to tell your wish," Dara Lynn crows.

Becky stands there looking at the broken wishbone in her hand and starts to cry.

"It's *supposed* to break, Becky!" Dara Lynn says, but Becky goes on bawling, and finally Dad snaps at Dara Lynn. Nicest thing that's happened all day.

I hate it when Ma and Dad aren't talking, though—feel all tight inside. Shiloh feels the same way, I can tell. Lies down on his belly with his head on his paws, his big brown eyes travelin' back and forth from Ma to Dad. Every so often, when their voices get extra sharp, his ears will twitch. But that evening, after we have us some turkey sandwiches, Dad says to Ma, "Why don't you go put your feet up, and Marty and I will make stew out of that squirrel meat."

Last thing in this world I want to do, but I put on my jacket and go out on the porch with Dad. He shows me how you skin a squirrel by cutting a ring around the back legs at the feet, then around the top of the base of the tail. He lays the squirrel on its back, puts his foot on its tail, grabs its back legs and pulls, and the skin comes off like a jacket, right up to the neck. I think I am going to throw up.

"You get the other two done, you call me," I say, and go

17

back inside. Why Judd Travers would bring over three dead squirrels as a present to my ma, I don't have a clue. But the thing is, Dad's a hunter, too, so I got to be real careful what I say. When he comes back in, he's cut off the heads, the back feet, and the tails of those squirrels, he's gutted them, and now we got to soak them. I fill a pan with water.

It's later, after Ma's put Becky to bed and is reading a story to Dara Lynn, that Dad and me cut up the squirrel meat. I feel like a murderer.

"I don't think I want any of this after it's cooked," I say finally.

"Nobody's going to make you eat it," says Dad.

"Bet I could be a vegetarian," I say. "I could live just fine on corn and beans and potatoes."

"For about a week, maybe," Dad tells me. "You'd be first to complain."

"Would not!" I say. "I just can't see going hunting. I can't see how you can shoot a deer or a rabbit or anything." I sure am getting smart in the mouth, I know that.

Dad's voice has an edge to it. "You like fried chicken, don't you? Like a good piece of pot roast now and then?"

I think about all I'd have to give up if I gave up meat. Forgot about fried chicken.

"Judd was right about one thing," Dad goes on. "Just because we didn't kill the meat we get from the store don't mean it died a natural death. The hamburger you eat was once a steer, don't forget. Somebody had to raise that steer, send it to market, and someone else had to slaughter it—just so's you could have a hamburger."

I'd have to give up hamburgers, too? I'm quiet a long time trying to figure things out. "Well, if I wanted to be a vegetarian, could I?"

Dad thinks on this awhile as he drops the meat in a pot of water he's got boiling on the back of the stove. "Suppose you could. But of course you'd have to get rid of that cowboy hat I bought you at the rodeo. Your belt, too."

"Why?" I say.

"They're leather; it's only fair. You don't want animals killed for their meat, then I figure you don't want 'em killed for their hide, either. And you know those boots you had your eye on over in Middlebourne? You can forget those, too. Same as that vest you got last year at Christmas, the suede one with the fringe around the bottom."

Man oh man, life is more complicated than I thought. One decision after another, and no matter which way you lean, there's an argument against it. What it comes down to is that I like to eat meat if I don't have to know how the animal died. And I sure don't want to give up my rodeo hat.

"Well, one thing I know," I tell my dad as we set to work cutting up the potatoes and carrots, "I don't want Shiloh turned into a hunting dog."

Dad don't answer right off, but I can tell by the way he's chopping that I struck a nerve. "He was already a hunting dog before you got him," he says. "I was hoping I could take him coon hunting with me some night."

"He's not going to be no hunting dog!" I say louder.

"Well, he belongs to you, Marty. You got the right to say no, I guess." And then, after we put the vegetables in the fridge, waiting to go in the pot when the meat's tender, Dad says, "Tomorrow, I want you to take some of this stew over to Judd, and thank him for the squirrels."

I figure this is my punishment, and maybe I had it coming.

19

Four

When I get up next morning, Ma's got this big waffle sittin' on my plate, a sausage alongside it, little pools of yellow margarine melting in the squares. Syrup's hot, too.

Still, a waffle can't make up for the fact that on a day off school, wind blowin' like crazy, I got to hike over to Judd's place and give him the remains of what I wish he hadn't shot in the first place.

To make things worse, Dara Lynn's sittin' across from me in her Minnie Mouse pajamas and, knowin' I got to go to Judd's, crows, "I'm not gonna go outside alllll day! I'm just gonna sit in this warm house and play with my paper dolls." And when that don't get a rise out of me, she adds, "*Alllll* day! I don't have to go nowhere."

I asked Ma once if Dara Lynn had been born into our family by accident or on purpose, and she said that wasn't the kind of question you should ask about anyone.

Accident, I'm thinkin', looking at her now. Nobody'd have a daughter like that on purpose.

Shiloh starts dancin' around when I put on my jacket and cap. He thinks we're going to take a run down to Doc Murphy's or somethin', but I know that as soon as I turn right at the end of the lane, he'll start to whine and go back. Surprises me, though. This time he goes halfway across the bridge before he stops. I finish the rest of the trip alone.

I'm thinkin' how when a man wrecks his truck and his leg both, and almost loses his job—his life, even—he's sunk about as low as he can get. Dad says either he'll hate himself so much he'll decide to change, or he'll hate the way other folks feel about him, and turn that hating onto them. Sure hope he don't turn his hating onto me.

I'm passing by the house of one of Judd's neighbors, the family that took two of his dogs to care for till Judd's better. I see the smaller one at their window now, barkin' at me, but his tail's wagging. Never saw any of Judd's dogs wag their tails before.

I get to Judd's and have to knock three times before he comes to the door, and then I see I woke him up.

"What you doin' out this early?" he asks, hair hangin' down over his face, his pants pulled on over a pair of boxer shorts bunched up above his waistband.

"Dad wanted me to bring over this squirrel stew," I tell him, handing him the jar. "Thought you ought to have a share of it."

That pleases him then—as much as you can please a man you just woke up. "Can get some more squirrels where those come from—pick 'em right off the tree," he says, and laughs.

It's then I know this is one big mistake.

"Well," I say, "actually, we don't eat all that much meat. But Ma didn't want the stew to go to waste." Trying to be polite and honest at the same time is hard work.

Judd quits smilin'. "She *didn't* like it then, so you're giving it to me?"

Uh-oh. "No! She likes it fine. Just wanted you to have some." Right this minute I am wondering what the difference is between a fib and a lie. Last summer, when Shiloh run away from Judd and come to me, and I hid him up in our woods, I told Judd Travers I hadn't seen his dog. Didn't tell my folks I had Shiloh, neither, and they claim I lied. What am I doing now? I'd like to know. Ma don't appreciate those dead squirrels any more than I do. If I stand here and tell Judd Travers the naked truth, though, I'll get my britches warmed pretty quick when I get home, you can bet.

"Well, you tell your ma that anytime she wants some more, let me know. I can't hunt nothing else, I can at least shoot squirrel."

"I'll tell her," I say. And I head back home.

There's somethin' good waiting for me when I get there. Ma says David Howard called and wants to know can I spend the day at his place. His ma will be picking me up about eleven.

"Ya-hoo!" I say, throwing my jacket in the air, and Shiloh dances around, too; if there's any happiness going on, he's a part of it.

"Change your shirt and comb your hair," says Ma.

I go into the girls' bedroom where I got a bureau in the corner, all my clothes in it. I get out a sweatshirt with BLACKWATER FALLS on it, and put it on.

Dara Lynn's still in her pajamas—she and Becky. Got their paper dolls spread all over the bed.

"Where *you* goin'?" Dara Lynn asks.

"Over to David's," I say. And then, not even looking at her, "Can't wait to have lunch at David Howard's: chicken salad with pineapple in it, pickles and potato chips, and a big old fudge brownie covered with coffee ice cream and chocolate sauce." Truth is, I don't know what we're havin' for lunch, but figure that's close.

Now I done it. Dara Lynn slides off the bed and goes hollerin' out to the kitchen to ask why don't we never have fudge brownies and chocolate sauce, and I get away just in time.

David's in the car with his mother when they pull in. For the second time that day, Shiloh thinks he's going somewhere, but don't even get out of the house. I give him a hug and tell him we'll have a run when I get home, and then I slide in the backseat beside David. Since we usually play up in David's room, his ma don't appreciate a dog runnin' around inside the house.

"How was Thanksgiving, Marty?" she asks. Mrs. Howard's got blond hair, and she's wearin' a heavy white sweater. She teaches high school. David's dad works for the *Tyler Star–News*.

"Yeah," says David. "How was dinner with Judd?"

"Nothing special," I say. "It was okay."

"Was he drunk?"

"'Course not, but he's still banged up pretty bad. He'll be wearing that cast another month, at least."

"Do you see any change in him, Marty?" asks Mrs. Howard, and I can tell by her voice she don't expect much.

"Not a lot, but Dad says he's tryin'," I answer.

David and me each tell what all we ate on Thanksgiving—how many rolls and helpings of stuffing, and after the car goes back down the winding road, through Little, and past the post office in Friendly, we get to David's house, which is two stories high (four, counting the attic and basement), and has a porch that wraps around three sides of it.

David whispers he has a secret but won't tell me till we're in his room, so while his mom gets lunch, we go upstairs. David's room has a map of the universe on one wall and a globe on his bookcase. Except for the bunk beds, David Howard's bedroom looks like a school. Got his own desk and chair, bulletin board, and encyclopedias.

As soon as we're alone, he closes the door. "Guess what? You know that fight Judd Travers was in, back before his accident?"

"Yeah?" I say. "With the guy from Bens Run?"

"Yes," says David. "Well, the man's missing. It's going to be in the newspaper this week."

"So?" I say. "What's Judd got to do with it? He's been laid up for weeks now with that broken leg."

David's eyes gleam like two small penlights. "The man's been missing since *before* Judd's accident. His family just now reported it. What do you bet Judd killed him?"

"*What?*"

"I think Judd was trying to wreck the evidence along with his truck."

"Go on!" I say. "And maybe kill himself in the bargain? You're nuts!"

"Marty, we've got to check it out! I'll bet we'd find blood on the seat or something." David gets excited about somethin', he almost shoots off sparks.

"If there's blood on the seat, it's Judd's," I tell him.

David shakes his head. "Here's how I figure: Judd and the man from Bens Run had another fight, and Judd kills

24

him. Maybe he didn't mean to, but he did. Throws the body into the cab of his pickup to hide it, then buries it and tries to rig up an accident so any blood in the truck will look like his own."

David's imagination has got us in trouble before, and I know what would happen if Judd catches us snooping around his truck.

"Nope," I say. "Whelan's Garage fixed that truck up for him after the accident. Cleaned the inside and everything. If there was any evidence, it's long gone. Besides, he wouldn't stuff a body in the cab. He'd put it in the back."

David sighs. He don't like to give up a good idea. "Judd could've buried that body down by the creek!" he says.

"Well, the fella from Bens Run must not have been too popular if nobody reported him missing for a month!" I say.

"His family thought he'd gone to visit a cousin in Cincinnati. That's why they didn't report him missing before now," David tells me.

Must be nice, I'm thinking, to have a reporter for a dad—learn all the news before it comes out in the paper.

"There's nothing to say we can't take a look around the bank where Judd's truck went down," David goes on.

"I suppose we can do that," I answer.

Mrs. Howard calls us to lunch then, and this time it's turkey sandwiches with turkey soup. I think I've seen enough turkey to last me awhile, but the real disappointment is there's leftover mince pie for dessert. Just about the time I'm wondering if she invited me to help eat up leftovers, though, David's mom says, "Now if you'd rather have chocolate chunk cookies, Marty, I've got those, too."

"I'd rather have the cookies," says David.

"Me, too," I tell her.

She smiles and takes the pie away and comes back with a plate of homemade cookies and two bowls of mint chocolate-chip ice cream.

Only thing I don't like about being at David's house is I got to watch how I talk. Mrs. Howard don't—doesn't—correct me the way Miss Talbot does at school, but she'll repeat my words using the right ones, and then I know I made a mistake.

"Well, deer hunting season began last Monday," she says as she removes a tea bag from her cup. "At least Judd Travers won't be out there shooting. I suppose your dad will go hunting this weekend?"

"Maybe," I say. "He don't hunt as much as some folks."

"He doesn't?" she says, and I know I got to say it over.

"No, ma'am, he doesn't," I tell her. David grins.

Miss Talbot tells me I'm smart enough to be almost anything I want if I just work on my grammar, so I'm trying.

After lunch we fool around up in David's room. He's got this revolving light, and if you close all the shades and turn it on, it sends sparkles of light, like snowflakes, swirling over the walls and ceiling.

It's time to go home before I'm ready—we're having a really good time—but when Mr. Howard pulls up, David's mom says he's driving me home. David gets his coat and goes along.

"They find out any more about that man from Bens Run?" David asks his dad.

"I haven't heard anything. Only that the cousin in Cincinnati says he never showed up there."

"Is the sheriff investigating?" asks David.

"He's asking around," says his dad.

Just before I get out of the car, David whispers, "Remember! Next time I come over, we check out the creek bank."

Five

Saturday mornings I work for John Collins, the veterinarian down in St. Marys. Dad drops me off early and I change the paper in the pens, scrub the floor, clean the dog run, refill the water and food bowls, and answer the phone. Sometimes, if his assistant's busy, I'll put on the thick gloves Doc Collins keeps around and help get a balky cat out of a cage or something.

I got to know Doc Collins when we took Shiloh in for his shots, and it was him who told me how to get a dog settled down and trusting again after Judd's other three dogs were set loose once. Never did find out who did it, but could have been anyone. Michael Sholt's dad said he might of thought of it himself just to get even with Judd for all he did when he was drinking. Judd sure made a lot of enemies. The talk is that it was the man down in Bens Run who'd had a fight with Judd that did it. Now, of course, the man from Bens Run is missing.

The longer I work for John Collins, the more I want to be a vet. A vet's assistant, anyway. This morning I'm counting sacks of dog and cat food in the supply room so we'll know how much to order.

John Collins is so busy he hardly knows what to tackle first. No sooner get a dog vaccinated or a rabbit patched up than here come a parrot or a snake. The way I see it, a vet has to know a whole lot more than a people doctor, 'cause what's a parrot and a snake got in common? I'd like to know.

Eleven o'clock and John Collins pours himself a cup of coffee.

"Doc Collins," I say, "a few more weeks and Judd Travers is going to get his three dogs back. I was wondering how he could keep them from turning mean again, now that somebody's been kind to 'em."

"Well, just like people, you can't always predict what they'll do," he says. "Some folks who grow up in the worst kind of homes manage to make something of themselves, and others lash out—want to treat everybody the way they were treated. Same with a dog."

"So what should Judd do?"

"For starters, I'd fence my yard so I wouldn't have to chain them up again. You chain a dog, he knows he's not free to fight if he's attacked, so he tries to appear as ferocious as he can. And Judd should certainly stop kicking them around the way he used to, beating on them with a stick. That's just common sense."

Dad picks me up at noon in his Jeep and drives me home along his mail route. Takes about ten times as long to get home this way as if we just drove it straight—Sellers Road, Dancers Lane, Cow House Run Road—but I don't complain. He hands me the mail to put in the boxes, and I turn up the little red flag on the box to let folks know there's something in it, so they don't have to come all the way down their driveway if there's not. Out where we live, the houses are little, but the land is big.

You feel real bad for people who don't get any mail at all. Some folks are tickled just to get a catalog. What I like, though, is finding something in the box for Dad—a piece of pie, maybe. This morning Mrs. Harris leaves a paper plate with five chocolate cupcakes on it. She waves to us from her window up on the hill, and we wave back. I eat my cupcake right away.

"Judd's going to be getting his dogs back soon," I say, wiping my hands on my jeans, and I tell Dad what John Collins says about how chaining a dog makes it mean.

Dad gives a sigh. "Marty, don't you never quit? You're makin' an old man of me, I swear it. You couldn't rest till you got Shiloh for your own, and now you're worrying about those other three dogs."

"But they've settled down some, Dad. Be a shame to chain 'em all over again."

"Maybe so," says Dad, "but I know better than to tell a man how he should be raising his dogs. And I got a whole lot of other things to think on besides that."

I got other things to think about, too, and soon's I get home, I stretch out on the floor, my head on Shiloh, and put my mind to Christmas. He makes the best backrest! I got eighteen dollars saved so far from working for John Collins. Work for Doc Murphy, too, only he takes my pay off the bill I owe him. It was him who stitched up Shiloh after the German shepherd tore him up last summer. At Doc's I'd trim the grass around his fence. He don't mind the mowing, but hates the trimming. With winter coming on, though, he finds other jobs for me to do.

I'm trying to think what to get Dara Lynn. Got the other gifts decided on. Becky's was easy—a tiny yellow bear, the kind you hang on a tree, fluffy as a new mitten, holdin' a box with two Whitman's chocolates in it. Got Ma a cassette tape of her favorite country singer, and for Dad, a giant-sized coffee mug.

Dara Lynn's gift, though, is giving me fits because the pure truth of the matter is I don't want to waste a nickel on her. Far back as I can remember, she's envied every nice thing that ever happened to me and rejoiced in the bad. Like the time I found a dollar bill at the county fair, and she was mad as hornets it wasn't her that saw it first. And then, when I lost it on the Ferris wheel—it blows right out of my hand and goes floating down over the crowd—she almost falls out of the seat laughing.

Nothing makes her smile as wide as when I got to go outside in the cold to do a job I don't like, and she gets to stay indoors eating buttered popcorn. Don't know why the feeling grew up between us like it did, but lately it's been worse than ever.

Dara Lynn's my sister, though, and I got to get her something, so I settle on a cocoa sampler I seen in Sistersville, three different flavors in a little wooden box.

I don't offer up one word about inviting Judd Travers to our house for Christmas, and at dinner that night, I'm glad to hear Ma say that Doc Murphy told her Judd was going off to visit friends at Christmas. Only Doc don't believe him, because as far as anyone knows, Judd don't have hardly any friends. Not the kind to invite you for Christmas, anyway.

"What I think," says Ma, "is that Judd made the story up so nobody would feel sorry for him. One thing he can't stand is people feeling sorry."

I got one hand under the table giving Shiloh a bite of

30

my chicken, feelin' how glad I am he belongs to me and not to Judd. Do you know how lucky you are, dog? I'm thinkin'. You know how hard I had to work to make you mine? But just when I'm most grateful that Judd won't ruin *this* holiday, I find out it's going to be ruined anyway.

"We're going to have a different kind of Christmas this year," Dad tells us. "Going to drive to Clarksburg on Christmas Day and have dinner with your Aunt Hettie, then go see Grandma Preston in the nursing home."

There is nothing I can say, because I know it's kind and good to go, but there is not one small inch of me that wants to visit a nursing home on Christmas. I don't say a word because I know Dara Lynn will do it for me. She sets up such a howling you'd think she caught her finger in the door.

"Not the whole daaaay!" she wails. "I don't wanna sit in a nursing home with an old woman who goes around steal- ing false teeth!"

Grandma Preston's got quite a reputation in that nurs- ing home for takin' things from other people's rooms.

"Dara Lynn, your grandma wouldn't do half of what she does if she had her mind back," says Dad. "She might not even know who we are, but it's not fair that Hettie has to spend all her holidays alone with Mother. We're going to do what we can."

"Good-bye, Christmas!" Dara Lynn sings out, and it's a miracle to me she don't get a slap on the mouth.

It snows on Sunday—first big snow of the season. Not some little half-inch job where you can still see sticks and stones underneath, but four or five inches of stuff so white you got to squint your eyes when the sun's on it. Wind blows it high against the shed.

Ma hates to see snow ruined by footprints, but she

31

knows we got to go try it out. She helps Becky on with her boots and jacket, and when we find our caps and mittens, she turns us loose.

We spend the first five minutes just laughing at Shiloh—the way he leaps up over the snow, disappearing down into a snowbank, then makin' another leap and another. He looks like a porpoise. Ma and Dad come out on the porch to watch.

A big clump of snow falls off a tree and lands on Shiloh's head. We throw snowballs at him then, and he tries to catch them in his mouth. He's running and barking and chasing and skidding, and by the time Dad gets out our sled, there are dog-crazy tracks all over the place.

Dara Lynn drags the sled to the top of our hill and I haul up Becky. I settle myself on the sled, Becky between my knees, heels dug deep in the snow. The plan is that Dara Lynn'll give us a push, then jump on behind me, but when I lift my feet and Dara Lynn pushes, she goes down on her knees and the sled takes off without her, Dara Lynn screechin' bloody murder.

I take Becky and the sled back up and this time Dara Lynn gets in the middle and I crawl on behind. We are flying down that hill, coming to a stop between the henhouse and the shed. We've just started back up for a third time when the crack of a rifle sings out, then another. Way up at the top of our hill, we see a buck go leaping across the field.

"Marty!" Dad yells from the doorway. "You kids get in here! Now!"

We leave the sled where it is, and run for the house. We know it's not Judd Travers up there, but even though we got the woods posted, there are always other hunters, other rifles.

"I wish this season was over," says Ma, closing the door behind us.

Six

It stays cold and windy, so David Howard don't come to check out the creek bank like he'd said. We decide we'll wait till after Christmas.

Usually our family cuts our own pine tree to bring inside, but this year—with us driving to Clarksburg and all—Dad says why don't we just string lights on the cedar outside the window? No need to do all that decorating when we won't be here on Christmas Day.

Becky hasn't had enough Decembers yet to care, but Dara Lynn sets up a bellow could've attracted a moose.

"We have to sit outside and open our presents in the snow?" she wails.

But there's new snow come Christmas Eve, and the lights of the tree shine on the ice and make a prettier tree than we ever had inside.

So we just sit at the living room window Christmas morning, eating our pancakes and opening our gifts. Ma loves the cassette I give her, Dad uses my mug for his coffee, Becky eats her Whitman's chocolates, and Dara Lynn even likes the cocoa. I bought a box of doggie treats for Shiloh, and we hide them under all the wrapping paper. He goes nuts trying to trace the smell. Paper and ribbon all over the place. He finds the box and I toss the treats up in the air, one at a time—make him snap at them. Whew! That dog's breath is somethin'!

Ma and Dad give me a new pair of jeans, a Western shirt, and a Pittsburgh Steelers watch.

We change our clothes to go to Aunt Hettie's and, leavin' Shiloh behind, climb in the Jeep. He don't like it one bit when we go off without him; follows the Jeep right down to the road, like any minute we're going to realize we left the most important thing and whistle for him to climb in. When we don't, he trots back up to the house, tail between his legs. I sure do wish dogs could understand English, you could explain things to 'em.

I don't like Shiloh bein' left outside during hunting season, but Ma says it's good to have a dog guarding your house when you're away. Anybody come up our drive with the wrong idea in mind, he might think twice if a barking dog comes out to meet him.

We're only a couple miles down the road when Dara Lynn's got to go to the toilet.

"For heaven's sake," Ma scolds. "If it was Becky, I could understand, but you're almost eight now, Dara Lynn!"

"It's not like I planned it," she shoots back, and we got to stop at Sweeneys' house, ask if we can use their bathroom. Ma takes Becky in, too, for good measure, and I stay in the car with Dad, my faced turned toward Middle Island Creek, embarrassed.

We start off again, Becky's car seat in the middle of the back so's to separate me and Dara Lynn. But she'll stretch her body from one side of the Jeep to the other just to rile me. I'm sitting here minding my own business, and I can feel Dara Lynn's shoe kickin' my leg. She's wriggled down so far that her seat belt's up under her armpits.

"Get on over there where you belong," I say, giving her leg a punch.

Dara Lynn sits up, but this time she spreads her arm across the back of the seat behind Becky so that she's rapping me on the side of my head.

"Stop it, Dara Lynn!" I say, punching her arm, but my elbow bonks Becky, who gives a squeal.

"Marty, keep it down back there. I can't drive and be referee, too," yells Dad. Ma turns and gives us a look.

It's always me gets the blame 'cause I'm the oldest. I wish Dara Lynn could be the oldest for one whole day. I'd get her in so much trouble she'd beg to be let off.

In Clarksburg, Aunt Hettie's waiting at the door, and she don't look anything like Dad, which makes me feel better, 'cause I sure don't want to look like Dara Lynn when I'm grown. Don't want anyone to know we're related. Hettie's wide about the hips, and her arms are round, but she's got Dad's smile, all right. When she hugs you, you know you been hugged.

"You just get on over here and see what's under the tree," she says.

Mostly it's candy, the homemade kind—lollipops for Becky, fudge for me, and peanut brittle for Dara Lynn. Dara Lynn hates peanut brittle, and her mouth turns down so at the corners Ma has to give her a nudge. But Aunt Hettie has dinner waiting with roast beef so juicy I wish Shiloh was there so I could share mine with him.

"Now you've got to be prepared for that nursing home," says Aunt Hettie as we finish her caramel spice cake. "It's not the finest in the world, but the nurses do the best they can."

We go see Grandma right after we eat, before Becky turns cranky, needing her nap. I guess what hits you when you walk in a nursing home—this one, anyway—is that it don't—doesn't—smell so good. Like the bathroom needs cleaning and the food's overcooked. There's eight or ten people in a room with a television in it, all of 'em watching a boys' choir singing "O Holy Night." Two of the women are asleep, and one old lady, tied to her wheelchair with a bed-sheet, is tapping on her tray with a spoon.

We sign in at the desk, and a young woman in a red Santa Claus cap says that Grandma's around somewhere, and then here she comes, flyin' down the hall in her wheel-chair, banging her gums together 'cause she hasn't put her teeth in yet, asking everyone did they see her snow shovel.

Dad goes over and stops the wheelchair before she can run into the artificial tree.

"Merry Christmas, Mother," he says, kissing her cheek. "I brought the family to see you."

"It was right outside my door," says Grandma, not making any sense.

"What was, Mother?" asks Dad.

"My brand-new snow shovel, right outside my door," she says, and fastens her eyes on me. "You take my shovel?"

"No, ma'am," I say.

Becky's backing away, trying to squeeze behind Ma's legs, but Dara Lynn's just staring, her eyes bugging out like a frog's.

"We brought you a present, Grandma," says Ma, putting a box in her lap.

Grandma tears away at that wrapping paper, got fingers like claws, almost, nobody to cut her nails except Hettie, and Ma leans down to help get the ribbon off. Grandma pulls out a robe, a rose-colored robe with a flower on each pocket.

"It's got to have pockets," says Grandma, handing it back to her, "I don't want a robe without pockets." Ma tries to show her the pockets, but Grandma's talkin' about somethin' else now. It pains Ma, I can tell.

The nurse comes over and suggests we wheel Grandma around the nursing home so she can see the decorations in the dining room and parlor. It gives us something to do. Ma and Aunt Hettie stay in the reception room to talk, but Dad pushes Grandma's wheelchair, and us kids troop along.

Becky's got the idea that we come to see Santa, and now she spots some old man with a beard sitting at his window.

"There's Santa!" she yells excitedly. The man turns and laughs.

"Come here, sweetheart," he says, holding out his arms, and I take Becky inside his room to say hello. She sits on his lap and tells him what all she got for Christmas, and he's so tickled. Becky don't even notice he only has one leg.

But Grandma wants to go. "That man is *no good!*" she says to Dara Lynn. "He stole my change purse."

"Mother, your change purse is right there in your pocket," Dad tells her as we start off again, and Becky waves to the man with the beard.

But Grandma goes on about how she lives in a den of thieves and liars, and how if Dad really loved her, he'd get her out of this place.

It hurts Dad, 'cause it was more than Aunt Hettie could

37

manage to care for Grandma at home, and it'd be even worse for Ma, with a family to look after, too.

"I ever get old and crazy, just shoot me," murmurs Dara Lynn.

After we tour the whole building and take Grandma back to her room, we read the Bible together and then we all sing "Silent Night." For the first time, Grandma gets real quiet—studies us hard while we're singin'—and I see tears in her eyes, like maybe for the first time she remembers who we are.

But by the time we get our coats, she wants to roam around in her wheelchair again. She's got her new robe over her shoulders like a cape now, won't let nobody touch it, and says she's got to go see the man with the beard and get her change purse back.

The attendant winks at us. "You go on," she says. "I'll handle this."

So we go back out to the Jeep, and spend the rest of the day at Aunt Hettie's. Becky takes a nap on her bed, and Dara Lynn and me put together a jigsaw puzzle of a pepperoni pizza, and I'm thinking how Dara Lynn and me are getting along fine right now, why can't we get along like this all the time? I wonder does it have anything to do with Shiloh being my dog, when all the while what Dara Lynn really wanted was a kitten?

We have a light supper before we leave—cold roast beef sandwiches—and then we set out. Sky's almost dark, but the snow gives off light so it don't seem as late as it is. Starts to snow some more, too.

Ma says, "It's always hard to visit Grandma and it's always hard to leave." Her own ma died a few years back, so Dad's is the only ma she's got.

We see we left the lights shining on our outdoor Christmas tree when we pull in the drive, and it's a welcome sight, but I'm lookin' around for Shiloh. Usually he'd be dancin' down the drive by now, head goin' one way, tail the other.

"Where's Shiloh?" Becky asks, missing him, too.

"Probably running around with that black Labrador, I'll bet," says Ma. "Nice that he's got a friend."

I'm thinking, though, that it's not often our whole family's gone the way we were today. Usually Ma's home while Dad's at work and we're in school. But this time we've been gone from almost eleven in the morning to eight at night, time enough for a dog to wonder if you're ever comin' back. Go lookin' for you, maybe.

We walk inside and turn on the TV to get the last of the Christmas music we'll hear all year, and when my Steelers watch says ten o'clock and Shiloh's still not back, I put on my boots and jacket and go out on the porch.

First I just stand on the steps and whistle. Never did learn to whistle like Dad can, though. Mine's a puny little noise that don't travel much beyond the cedar tree.

"Shiloh!" I call, and my voice echoes against the hills. "Here, boy! Shiloh! Come on, boy!"

Nothin' stirs but the bushes, branches blowin'.

I clump down to the end of the drive, hands in my pockets, shoulders hunched.

"Shiloh!" I yell, loud as my lungs will let me. "Shi . . . loh! Shi . . . loh!" Air's so still I figure that dog should be able to hear me a half mile off.

Then I stand real still and listen. Used to be I could hear his feet scurrying through the field or down the path from the meadow, but I know that with all the snow, that dog could be right behind me and I wouldn't hear a thing 'cept his collar jingling.

I walk to the bridge and yell some more, then go left and follow the road in the other direction, bellowing like a new calf.

Nothin' answers but the wind.

Seven

It's hard to sleep that night. Our sofa's got more lumps than bean soup, and every time I turn over, I pull out the blanket from the bottom.

I get up about two in the morning and stand at the window. Moon's almost full, and the snow sparkles like diamonds. I'm not lookin' for moonlight or snowlight, though—only Shiloh. We keep the shed door open on nights like this so he can go in there and sleep if he comes back late. But I know my dog; he'd make at least one detour up on the porch first to see if somebody was awake to let him in. Not a fresh paw print anywhere.

I'm thinking of the hunters we heard up in our woods. Deer season's over now, but there's possum and coon to hunt; rabbit and groundhog, too. What if a hunter took it in his head to steal Shiloh? You ride along and see notices posted on trees about a dog missing, and most of the time someone's made off with it—someone who wants a good hunting dog, or a watchdog, or both.

I get this sick feeling—what if I never see Shiloh again? What if somebody's got him chained, beatin' on him like Judd used to do? All I got to remember him by are yesterday's paw prints, most of 'em half covered now by new snow. I lay back down and fall asleep out of sheer sadness.

Don't have to go to school till the second of January, so Ma lets us sleep in next day. Can't believe I sleep till nine thirty, and I only wake then because I hear dogs yipping out in the yard. I sit straight up.

"Shiloh's back!" says Ma from the kitchen. "My stars, what's that dog got now?"

I leap off the couch and run to the door. There's Shiloh and the black Lab. Shiloh's got a piece of orange rag in his mouth, and they're playin' and tuggin' at it. Thing about dogs, they can get enjoyment out of the most common ordinary object you could ever imagine. I'm so happy to see him I pull on my jeans, push my feet in my shoes, and grab my jacket. I run outside and wade through the snow to where Shiloh and the Labrador are chasing each other around and barking.

Rag looks like a piece of vest a traffic cop wears. I'm hoping those dogs didn't get in somebody's clothes basket or, worse yet, run off with somethin' belonging to the sheriff. I stick the rag in my jacket pocket and reach down to hug my dog. "You're weird," I tell him. "You and your friend both." He gives me the wettest kiss this side the Mississippi.

When I go in the house, Shiloh follows for his breakfast,

42

and the Labrador trots off, lookin' for some other mischief. Becky's up, wantin' me to play Candy Land with her—most boring game in the whole world, but I do.

Ma's feeling good this morning, I can tell. Shiloh's back, Christmas is over, she's done her duty by Grandma Preston, and she's in the kitchen making cinnamon rolls. She sings along with the cassette I give her:

> "The roughest road in the valley,
> Longest I ever did roam,
> But the sweetest path in the country,
> Because it leads me home."

I tell Dara Lynn it's her turn to play Candy Land with Becky, and I call up David Howard. After I hear what he got for Christmas, my presents don't sound all that much. He got two computer games, a pair of Nike Air Gridstar crosstrainers, a basketball, a sleeping bag, four books, a Chicago Bulls T-shirt, and a horn for his bike. And that was just from his folks. He still has presents coming from his grandparents.

"Why don't I come over to your house tomorrow, and we'll check out the creek bank where Judd had his accident?" says David.

"Okay with me," I tell him.

Dad's got the *Tyler Star–News* with him when he comes home, and while he sits in the kitchen talking to Ma, I take the paper in on the sofa and look through it, see if there's anything more about the missing man from Bens Run. Don't find anything of interest except a story about a car crash up in Wheeling, an escape from the county jail, a robbery up in Sistersville, and a hunter who shot a man over in

Marion County by mistake. Nothing about nobody from Bens Run.

David Howard's mom drives him over the next morning, and it's the kind of gray winter day that can't decide if it's going to rain or snow. We plan to head out for Middle Island Creek soon as we eat lunch. Becky, of course, goes and asks David to play Candy Land with her, but he don't have little sisters, and don't know you got to let Becky win. When it's him doing the winning, Becky slides down off the chair and runs in the bedroom, then comes back out later with a towel over her head so no one can see she's been cryin'. David must think I got the strangest family!

Ma says lunch is ready. It's only hot dogs and soup, but there's cinnamon rolls for dessert, the frosting still warm.

"You boys playing in or out this afternoon?" Ma asks.

"Out," I tell her. "Maybe do some hiking."

We put on our jackets and head down to the bridge, Shiloh trotting along behind. I point out the place the pickup went over, and we crawl down the bank, our feet turned sideways.

"Nothing to see!" I say to David. "Everything's covered with snow."

But David keeps going. The thing about David Howard is he don't let real life get in the way of his imagination. If he wants to find clues that Judd Travers murdered the man from Bens Run, then David'll find plenty; just won't happen to be the right clues, that's all.

Shiloh's comin' down the hill after us, glad to be doin' whatever we are, though he's no idea in the world what that is.

David turns and points at Shiloh. "Sniff!" he says.

Shiloh wags his tail.

"What you doing, David?"

"I'm telling him to sniff. If there was a dead body buried down here, I'll bet a dog could find it."

I laugh. "Shiloh don't even know the word 'sniff,'" I tell him. So David says it again, and gets down on all fours, trying to show my dog what to do. I fall down in the snow laughing my head off, and Shiloh falls on top of me, joinin' in the fun.

We're rolling around on the bank, havin' a wrestling match, when all of a sudden my knee hits somethin' hard.

"Ow!" I yell, and push David off me.

Shiloh comes runnin' over like a snowplow, pushin' up snow with his nose, and before you can blink, he's dug up a man's boot, frozen hard as cement.

Eight

David and I sit on our knees in the snow, turning that boot over and over.

"Evidence!" says David, his eyes snappin'. "This could put Judd Travers behind bars for life."

That's the way folks feel about Judd, see. They remember how he was—and maybe still is, far as I know. His meanness to dogs and people, the way he cheated and lied. When you've done all the things Judd did, how do you get folks to start trusting you? It's true he might be tryin' to change, but the tryin' part still needed a lot of work.

"David, you don't even know whose boot that is!" I say. David Howard's case against Judd is as stupid as flypaper in winter. "Even if it *does* belong to that man from Bens Run, and even if Judd *did* murder him, just 'cause he wrecked his truck here don't mean that's where the man is buried. The one don't have a single thing to do with the other."

Even Shiloh's laughin'. Sittin' there in the snow with his mouth open. Sure looks like a grin to me.

But David says, "You know how a criminal always returns to the scene of the crime? He just can't help himself! Same with Judd Travers. Maybe his conscience drove him here."

If I was a teacher and this was homework, I'd give David a failing grade. One thing sure, he's never going to let himself be bored, and that's what I like about David Howard: He don't have enough excitement, he'll make it up.

We walk upcreek for a spell, watching a flock of ducks fly low over the water. Probably going to light down on one of the islands out in the middle. A little farther on, we can make out Judd's trailer across Middle Island Creek.

"Who named this a creek instead of a river? Paul Bunyan?" says David. "Sure looks like a river to me."

"We walk far enough, we'd get up to Michael Sholt's cousin's house," I tell him. Michael lives down toward Friendly, but his cousin lives way upcreek and takes a different bus to school.

"If we walk far enough we'll get to the North Pole!" says David. Think he's getting a little tired of all this hiking. Getting cold, leastways. Probably got his mind on Ma's cinnamon rolls.

"Want to go back?" I ask.

"Yeah," he says. "But keep the boot."

I don't know what I'm going to do with a frozen shoe, but I throw it under the porch steps when we get home, and we eat a plate of cinnamon rolls.

On Sunday, Ma's listening to Brother Jonas preach on TV and Dad's cleaning his razor. Dara Lynn and Becky have pulled bedsheets over a couple chairs in their room to make a tent, and they're pretending that Shiloh's a bear, tryin' to get in. The more they squeal, the more Shiloh wiggles about, tryin' to get his nose under the edge of the sheet, tail going ninety miles an hour. If that dog had wings, he'd fly, except his propeller would be on the wrong end.

"I'm going over to visit Judd—see how he's doing," I tell Dad.

Dad don't look at me, just frowns a little at his razor. "You could always pick up the phone," he says, not too sure, I guess, about me goin' over alone to visit a man like Judd, no matter how many chances he'd give him.

"I might could give him a hand with somethin', help him out," I say.

"Well, don't stay too long," says Dad.

Outside, I pull that boot out from under the steps, tuck it under my arm, and start off.

I cross the bridge, Shiloh beside me, and watch to see if he'll come ahead or turn back. This time he goes a few steps beyond the other side, then sits down in the snow and whimpers. I walk on about fifty yards and look back over my shoulder. Shiloh's trottin' back across the bridge. Guess he's decided not to freeze his bottom waiting for me.

Sky is bright, but cold. Sun don't seem to warm me at all. The thing about West Virginia is it takes so long for the sun to come up over those hills on one side of the creek that it don't seem any time at all before it's sliding down behind the hills on the other. Boy, you live in Kansas, flat as an ironing board, I'll bet the sun comes up in the morning before you even open your eyes. You go to bed, it's still got a way to go before it's down.

Then I realize I'm not cold from the weather, I'm cold

48

from fear. The goose bumps I can feel popping out on my arms under my jacket don't have nothing to do with the snow. Shiloh had the right idea turning back. What I am fixing to do is walk right up to Judd Travers holding the one piece of evidence he just might kill for to get. Could be he's thinkin' on digging around over on that bank himself as soon as his leg gets better, and here I am, showing him what I got, what David and me know.

I got this far, though, I got to go on. If Judd's looking out of his trailer now, he's already seen me comin', knows what I got. I wonder if there's a rifle pointed at me right this very minute.

Climb the steps to his trailer and knock, but I don't hear any sound at all from inside—no TV, no radio. Can hear my teeth chattering. I hug my arms tight around my body, the boot still tucked under my arm, and knock again. Then I hear this engine. I turn around, and here come Judd's pickup. He gets out, hauling his left leg down first, then his crutches. The cast is a dirty white, but nobody's wrote his name on it or anything, the way they'd do at school. He don't have his gun with him, and that cheers me right quick.

"Hey!" I call. "You're driving now!"

"I can get where I want to go, that's about it," Judd says. He unfolds himself like an old man. Got a paper sack in his hand, and I hope it's not whiskey.

I knew that as soon as Judd could start driving again, he would, because he loves his truck almost more than anything else in this world. Washes it every weekend, and finds any excuse he can to drive to Friendly and back, just ridin' around, listenin' to his radio. Last summer, on the Saturdays he wasn't working, wouldn't be anything at all to see Judd passing three

49

or four times out on the road, goin' nowhere in particular.

He's comin' slow up his board walk, cast and crutches tapping a rhythm like old Peg Leg the Pirate. "What you doin' over this way?" he wants to know.

"Just came to say hello, see how you're doin'."

"Well, I'm alive," he tells me.

Judd goes in first, leaves the door open behind him, and I figure that's all the invitation I'm gonna get, so I go in, too. Close the door. I guess what I plan to do is show him the boot and ask does he know who it belongs to. I figure I can tell by the look on his face if it belongs to that man from Bens Run, and if Judd's the reason he disappeared. With Judd hobbling about on that leg of his, I can be out the door and in the bushes if he gets mad.

Judd puts the sack on his table, then reaches inside and pulls out a half gallon of milk, some bread, and a tin of sardines.

"What you got there?" Judd asks, nodding toward the boot.

I swallow. "Oh, just somethin' I wonder if you'd recognize," I say, and hold it up. Wonder if I'm sounding smart-mouth.

Judd's jaw drops and he stares at it for a moment. "Where'd you find it?"

"Over by the creek." I study his face, my heart thumpin' hard. "Know who it belongs to?"

"Of course," says Judd. "It's mine."

Talk about feelin' stupid! I don't tell him what David Howard figured.

"Never thought I'd see *that* again! Couldn't wear it anyway, it's soaked up so much rain and snow. Most of my clothes, they just cut them off, you know. In the emergency

50

room, they don't fool around." He takes the boot and throws it back into his bedroom.

"Didn't you miss it when you dressed to come home from the hospital?"

"Missed it before then, so a guy from work brought me a pair of his old sneakers to get home in. You want a pop or somethin'?" Judd asks me.

"Okay." I sit down on Judd's couch, remembering how only a few months past, he had me workin' out there in the summer sun in order to earn his dog, and then, when I'm about done, tells me I can't have Shiloh after all—that nobody witnessed our agreement, and I'm a fool to do all that work. Guess I'd have to say it was the worst day of my life. No—the worst hadn't happened yet; I'm gettin' to that—but it was a time I'll never forget.

Judd gets me a 7Up from his refrigerator and pours himself a mug of leftover coffee. Then he sits down, his jacket still on, 'cause he keeps his trailer cold. Holds the cup under his chin, lettin' the steam warm his face.

"So how's things?" he asks.

"Okay," I tell him. "I been working for that vet down in St. Marys on Saturday mornings. Learnin' a lot about dogs."

"Yeah?" says Judd.

"We see a lot of dogs that have been chained up, and most of 'em are mean as nails. John Collins—he's the vet—says it's because they feel trapped that way. If something came along to attack 'em, they'd be in a tough spot 'cause they can't fight free, so they act real fierce to scare you off."

"That a fact?" says Judd, and I'm tryin' to read his face as he takes another drink of coffee. "Well," he says at last, "I sure know how it is to feel cornered. Know what it's like to feel trapped."

I don't say nothing. I'm remembering what Doc Murphy told me about how he knew the Traverses when Judd was a little kid, and how the father used to whip those kids with the buckle end of a belt.

Judd stares out the window beyond my head like he don't hardly see me at all. And suddenly he stands up and says, "Well, I'm goin' to take a nap, Marty." That's a good-bye if I ever heard one, so I set my empty pop can on the floor.

"Okay," I say. "See you around."

I'm halfway across his yard when I realize what I've done. My hands feel all clammy. Why do I think I can believe Judd Travers? If David Howard *was* right, and Judd done something to that man from Bens Run, and if that boot belonged to him, you can bet Judd'll burn it faster than a dog can pee. Why didn't I ask to see that other boot—see if it matched? I can't believe how stupid I am—just handed the evidence right over!

Figure I got to steal a look in the back of his pickup as I walk by, see if there're any clues in there. Judd keeps all sorts of stuff in there, but he's got a tarp over it now, and the tarp's covered with snow. I manage to lift a corner and peer underneath. Piece of plywood, a coil of rope, truck battery, tires, roofing shingles, iron pipe, canvas. . . .

And then I see Judd Travers watchin' me from his window. I drop that tarp right quick, give him a wave, and head on home. Feel like the worst kind of fool.

But I feel even worse later. Walk in the house and Ma says, "David called, Marty. Wants you to call him back right away."

I go out in the kitchen and dial David's number.

"Marty!" he says. "Guess what?"

I kid around. "They found the guy from Bens Run with a bullet in his head?"

There's silence from the other end. Then, "There wasn't any bullet, but they found him. And he's dead."

Nine

I don't see David again till we go back to school after New Year's. By then I'm ready for vacation to be over. Becky's come down with chicken pox, and Dara Lynn's stepped on my Steelers watch and broke the glass. Now we got to send it all the way to the factory for a new face cover, which means I can't wear it on the first day back to school.

Big news is that the man from Bens Run died of a blow to the head, says the *Tyler Star–News*, and David and I been on the phone to each other most every day about it. Body was found down along the Ohio River by a highway maintenance crew, but the man's shoes were missing. Murder weapon's missing, too, and David's sure Judd's the one who done it. I'm not so sure about the shoes—they could have come off and floated most anywhere. I'm thinking about the murder weapon. What I'm remembering, and wish I wasn't, is that piece of iron pipe in the back of Judd's pickup.

School bus comes up our road as far as the bridge, then turns around. Anybody living on the other side has to walk over here or catch another bus somewhere else. I think it's because that old bridge might not hold a bus full of kids. Fire truck come up once makin' a safety run, and had to empty its tank before it crossed, then fill up again from the other side of the creek.

Driver picks up anybody who's ready on the way up, and everybody else on the way back, so that kids who live along this route got two chances to catch the bus.

"Happy New Year, Marty," says Mrs. Sims, the driver. "How you doin', Dara Lynn?"

Dara Lynn never smiles at nobody before nine o'clock in the morning, and she don't say nothing, but I wish Mrs. Sims a Happy New Year, too, and go sit across from Michael Sholt. Out the window I can see Shiloh trotting back up the lane to the house. Ma says that sometimes after we're gone in the mornings, she picks that dog up and rocks him like a baby. Don't many dogs have a grown woman who'll do that, I'll bet.

"Heard the news?" Michael crows as soon as I step on the bus. "The man from Bens Run was found murdered, and they think Judd did it."

"*Who* thinks?" I say.

"*Everybody!*" says Fred Niles. "Everyone's talking that it's Judd!"

Sarah Peters is up on her knees on the seat so she can see around the whole bus. "The sheriff's questioning a whole lot of people, and one of 'em's Judd. It was on the news this morning." I see pretty quick that whether Judd done it or not, the feelin's going against him.

"Just because they questioned him don't mean he did it," I say.

"How come you're stickin' up for Judd, Marty?" asks Sarah. "Thought you used to hate him worse'n poison."

"Maybe he's tryin' to change. You ever think of that?" I ask her. But I don't even know that myself.

One by one, other kids climb on, and everyone's wearin' a little something they got for Christmas—a jacket or sneakers or cap. By the time David gets on, the other kids are looking at Michael Sholt's baseball cards and telling what all they got for Christmas. David sits down beside me.

"Anything new?" I ask.

"Judd was called in for questioning, but the sheriff released him," David says. "Doesn't mean he's innocent. It just means they haven't charged him with anything yet."

"Do they know where he was when the guy was murdered?" I ask.

"They don't even know the exact day. It was about the time of Judd's accident, but it could have been a week before or a week after." He looks at me. "I think we better turn that boot over to the sheriff."

I swallow. "I don't have it," I say.

"Where *is* it?"

I'm so miserable, my stomach hurts. "Judd said it was his, so I gave it to him."

David slides down in the seat, can hardly believe it. "We could've been on the witness stand, Marty!" he says. "Maybe we could have solved the case!"

"Just be quiet about it," I say. I'm feeling low enough as it is.

David don't tell the other kids what I did, but he is sure disgusted.

At school, Miss Talbot's wearin' something new she got for Christmas, too. It's a diamond ring, and all the girls got to gather round her desk and make her turn her hand this way and that, see the diamond sparkle. She's engaged to a high school teacher over in Middlebourne.

Soon as the kids start talking about Judd Travers being guilty, though, she puts a stop to it. "This class is not a court-room," she says, and we know that—ring or no ring—she means business.

At home, Dad won't let us talk about Judd being the murderer, either.

"That Ed Sholt!" he says. "Shootin' off his mouth . . . !" Dad kicks off his shoes and sinks down on the sofa. "Saw him at lunch today in Sistersville, and he's worked out the whole thing in his head—all the different ways the man could have been killed, and he's got Judd doing the killing in every one of 'em. 'Pipe down, Ed,' I tell him. 'A man's innocent till proven guilty, you know. He's a right to his day in court, it ever gets to that.' But he says, 'You're the one who should worry, Ray. You live closer to Judd than the rest of us. If it were me, I'd get a good strong lock for my door and keep a gun handy.'"

I swallow. "You talk to the sheriff yet?"

"Yes, and he's guessing Judd's not the one. They can't tell when the man was killed exactly, not when a body's been dead this long, but they figure he probably died some-time after Judd's accident; somebody thinks he may have seen him later than that, anyway."

I'm wondering what it's like to have everybody suspect-ing you of a crime you didn't do—just when you're tryin' to be better. Maybe you think, what's the use? If everybody figures you're bad, might as well go ahead and be bad. But if Judd gives up now, those dogs of his, when he gets 'em back, are going to have a worse time of it than before.

Judd'll hate everything and everybody, includin' his dogs. On the other hand, what if he *did* do it? What if he really is a killer?

I try not to let myself think on that. The only thing I can see to do—for Judd's dogs, anyway—is to get Judd Travers a fence. Once I do something for *all* Judd's dogs, I can stop feelin' so guilty about saving only the one. So I say to Dad, "You know anybody got some old chicken wire stuck away that we could use to fence in Judd's yard for his dogs?"

Dad turns the TV down and looks at me. "*Chicken* wire? You got to have somethin' stronger than that, Marty! You need regular fencing wire and metal posts, and nobody I know has a whole fence just sittin' around, I can tell you."

Seem like everything I think of to do has got a hitch to it.

All week the weather stays mild, and the snow's disappearin' fast. "January thaw," Ma says. Tells us that for a few days most Januarys, it seems, there's a mild spell to give us a promise of spring before the next big snowfall.

The sun shines on into the weekend, and Saturday afternoon, after I get back from the vet, I decide that I'm going about this fence idea all wrong. If nobody's going to keep an old fence around after they take it down, then I got to find somebody with the fence still up that he'd just as soon wasn't there.

I walk over to Doc Murphy's, Shiloh frisking alongside me, tryin' to get me to run. I'm thinking how last September, when I was helpin' Doc in his yard, he'd said now that his wife wasn't there to garden anymore, he wished he didn't have a fence around that vegetable plot, just a nuisance when he mowed.

Doc's got a couple of men patching his roof and cleaning

his gutters, and he's out there scattering grass seed on all the bare patches of lawn. Shiloh goes right over and waits for Doc to pet him. I wonder if in his little dog brain he remembers that Doc saved his life after the fight with the German shepherd.

"Hello there, Marty," he says, scratchin' Shiloh behind the ears. "I'm getting a jump on old man winter. Figure if I can get this seed in the ground before the next snow, it'll be the first grass up come spring."

"Too bad that fence is still there, or you could plant right over the postholes," I tell him.

"I was thinking the same thing," says Doc. He lets Shiloh go, and scoops up another handful of seed from his bag.

"I could maybe take it down for you," I offer.

He gives this little laugh. "That's not a job for a kid. Lot of wire there, and those posts are heavy."

"I bet I could. Would haul it away for you, too."

Doc studies me over the rim of his glasses. "Your dad wants this fence?"

"It's for Judd Travers. To keep his dogs happy when he gets 'em back. He won't let 'em run loose, 'cause they're his hunting dogs, but John Collins says they wouldn't be half as mean if they weren't chained—if they had a yard to play in."

Doc Murphy don't say anything for a minute. Just turns his back on me and goes on scattering that seed. Finally he says, "Tell you what: I'll have Joe and Earl there" —and he nods toward the men on the roof— "take that fence down if you can have it off my property by tomorrow. I don't want a pile of fencing sitting around here. Then I can get the whole place seeded in this warm spell. Deal?"

"Deal," I say. "Dad and me'll come pick it up in the morning."

59

I don't even have time to be happy, because I realize Judd Travers don't know a single solitary thing about any of this. You don't just show up at a man's house and start fencing his yard.

Only thing I can think of to do is walk on over to Judd's and ask. I'm not real eager to go over there by myself, though. I mean, what if that boot we found *did* belong to the dead man, and Judd knows that I know what it looked like? Where it was found? 'Course, why would Judd kill a man, leave his body by the river, but bury his boots someplace else? That don't make a whole lot of sense, either.

I walk back up the road and my mind's goin' around and around, first how Judd must have done it for sure and then how he didn't, like to drive me crazy. I cross the bridge, but when I head for the brown-and-white trailer, Shiloh turns back. I get to Judd's about the time he's sittin' down to lunch.

Any other man would ask me to come back later or invite me to share his food. Judd Travers invites me in to watch him eat, I guess, 'cause I sit at his table and he only offers me a pop. And right off he says:

"What you want? Everybody else seems to think I killed a man. That what you come to say?"

"No," I tell him. "'Course not." Already my heart's knockin' around beneath my jacket.

"Then what were you doin' snoopin' in the back of my truck last time you were here?"

My breath seems to freeze right up inside my chest. One thing about Judd Travers, he don't forget. I decide to tell it straight. "Trying to figure where that other boot of yours was," I tell him. "To match the one I found."

"Why should you care?" asks Judd, his narrow eyes on me.

I shrug. "No particular reason. Just wondering, that's all."

"Well, I threw it out," Judd says. "When you think you've seen the last of one, not much use for the other."

Wonder just how far Judd trusts me; about as far as I trust him, I guess. I talk about somethin' else: "When do you suppose you'll get your dogs back?"

"Soon's I can get around without this cast," he says. "Doc's taking it off next Wednesday. I'll still be hobblin' around on crutches, but I figure I can at least tend to my dogs."

"You know," I say, "the way I hear it, the happiest dogs make the best hunters."

"Don't know about that," says Judd. "My pa always said to keep 'em lean and mean."

Can't help myself. "Maybe your pa wasn't always right," I say.

Judd pauses, a piece of macaroni on his fork. He looks at me for a minute, then puts the fork to his mouth, don't say nothing. I figure that don't get me no points.

"All I know is what I learn from Doc Collins, that chainin' up dogs is one of the worst things you can do," I say.

"Well, that's just a pity, because I don't have no money for a fence," Judd tells me, and takes a big swallow of water, wipes his hand across his mouth, and hunches over his plate again, like his macaroni and beef is a chore he's got to wade through.

"What I come to tell you is that Doc Murphy's having his garden fence took down this afternoon, wants if off his property by tomorrow. First come, first get. I asked him not to give it to nobody till I'd talked to you." I pray Jesus this isn't a true lie, just a social conversation.

61

"What's the catch?" asks Judd.

"Nothin'. He wants to plant grass seed over the post-holes during this warm spell."

"Well, I got the strength of a ninety-year-old man right now, and Doc knows that. I can't be fooling with a fence."

"Dad and me can bring it by. Put it up for you."

Judd gives this half smile and a "*Huh!* Nobody does nothing for free," he says.

"We're not askin' anything, Judd! Just see a chance to do a little something for those dogs."

"Why? They're not your dogs. You got Shiloh. You got an eye on them, too?"

"No! What you talkin' about? We're just bein' neighborly, that's all."

"Well, my dogs'll get along fine without you," says Judd, and goes on eating, and my stomach does a flip-flop.

I stand up. "If you don't want it, I know folks who do. What's the name of that man with all those hunting dogs over in Little—those really *fine* dogs? He knows they need a place to run, and he'd like that fence, I'll bet." I am stretching the truth so far I can almost hear it snap. Don't even know a man in Little.

I wait for two . . . three seconds, but Judd don't say a thing. I push my chair in and head out the door.

Ten

All the way home I am chewin' myself out. What am I, some kind of fool? Judd Travers don't care about his dogs any more than I care about mushrooms. Couldn't get that man to change if you was to hold his feet to the fire.

And now I feel a rage buildin' up in my chest that's almost too much for me to handle. All I am trying in this world to do is make life a little easier for Judd Travers's dogs, and what do I get? Trouble up one side and down the other. Bet he *did* kill that man from Bens Run. Judd's got enough meanness in him to do most anything.

Right this very minute Doc's got those men takin' down his fence. I cross the bridge and can look way down the road, see where one is digging up those posts, and the other is winding up that wire. And tomorrow morning my dad, who don't even know it yet, is to drive his Jeep over and pick up a whole yard of fence that Judd Travers don't want in the first place.

I am too mad to go inside our house. Too mad to look myself in the mirror. Shiloh comes out to meet me and I don't even say hello. Just march on by and head up the path to the far hill, Shiloh running on ahead, bouncing with pure joy.

"It's all because of you," I tell him, knowing all the while I'd do it again, even so. It's true, though. If it weren't for Shiloh, Judd Travers would be just somebody to stay away from when we could, say your howdys to when you couldn't. But because I got Shiloh, I am smack in the middle of all Judd's problems.

I'm remembering it was up here I saw that gray fox last summer with the reddish head. Suppose somebody's shot it by now, with all the meanness around. Every minute of every day there are folks like Judd Travers bein' born; every minute of every day they are thinkin' up ways to be worse than they were the day before.

What do I care what happens to Judd? I ask myself. What do I care what happens to his dogs? I am turnin' myself inside out to be nice to a man who hasn't an ounce of kindness in his whole body, and who's probably a killer, too.

All afternoon I stomp and storm around our woods and meadow, pickin' up every limb I can find and whackin' it so hard against a stump I send splinters every which way. Every log becomes a Judd Travers I got to kick and whack, till my feet and arms are tired.

Finally, when I been gone so long I know Ma will worry, when even Shiloh's laid down to rest himself, I turn around and start back. I get home about the time Dad's coming up the drive in his Jeep.

"You look like you been hiking some," Dad says as I fol-

64

low him into the house where Dara Lynn and Becky are watching TV.

"*Wondered* where you were, Marty," Ma calls from the kitchen.

I throw my jacket on the floor. "I don't want to have anything more to do with Judd Travers the whole rest of my life!" I say.

Now Dad's lookin' at me. "Marty, I don't think I want you going over there alone," he says. "Didn't have a fight with him, did you?"

"No, I didn't have no fight!" I say, a little too loud, and grab a box of cheese crackers from the cupboard like they was out to get me. Lean against the counter and stuff 'em in my mouth, hardly even tasting. I think again how that fence is waiting over there at Doc Murphy's, and figure I'm not just mad, I'm crazy. Whatever Grandma Preston's got wrong with her mind, I got it, too.

But Dad's been delivering the JCPenney spring catalog, and he's too tired to take on my worries. "You'd think it was Christmas all over again, the way folks were waiting for 'em," he says. And then, "Ooof," as he sits down at the table and pulls off his boots. "I don't ever want to get up again. Think I'll spend the night right here in this chair."

Ma laughs and rubs his shoulders.

"I am going to stretch out on that couch and not move except to eat," he tells her.

Telephone rings, and I answer.

It's Judd.

"What kind of fence did you say it was?" he asks.

I blink. Swallow. "Green yard fencing, the wire kind," I tell him, and swallow again. The cheese crackers are dry in my mouth.

"Well, I don't want no gate. Don't want anybody sneakin' in, lettin' my dogs loose again."

I stare at the clock above the sink. "What time you want us to come over tomorrow?" I ask.

"Not before nine, that's for sure."

"See you tomorrow, then," I say, and hang up.

I am suddenly so quiet my hand freezes there in the box of crackers. Dad is telling Ma about the deliveries he made that day, and I slip the crackers back on the shelf. Go stare out the window. Now how in the world am I going to tell my dad I volunteered him to put up fencing at Judd's?

"Ground's softening up," I say finally. "Good time to work in the yard."

Dad gives me a sideways glance. "You want to work in the yard, Marty, you got my blessing." He reaches for the mug of coffee Ma pours for him, warm him up a little.

I try again. "Dad, what if you was to find that tomorrow's your one good day to do a really fine deed for a person? And what if I said I'd help out?"

Dad slowly slides that coffee mug back on the table, turns to me, and says, "What in the world have you done now?"

I tell him about Doc Murphy's fence, and what a good thing this would be for Judd's dogs.

"Marty, just two seconds ago you even mention Judd's name, you're spittin' nails!" Ma says.

"Well, a person's got a right to change, hasn't he?" I plead, lookin' at Dad. "Didn't you say you believe in second chances?"

Dad gives such a long, drawn-out sigh you'd think there couldn't be that much air in a human lung.

"We'll see how I feel tomorrow," he says.

66

Tired as I am, I don't sleep so good. What if Judd changes his mind? What if we haul all those posts over to Judd's tomorrow and, out of sheer spite and meanness, he says to get 'em off his property, he don't want 'em there? Worse yet, what if after all this work, Judd *does* turn out to be the one who murdered the man from Bens Run, and I'm doin' all this work to please the devil?

Next day Dad says he feels better. Not good, but better. The sun helps, so he wants to start early, get it over with, and we drive to Doc's to load that fencing in the Jeep, then make trips back and forth to Judd's till it's all there. I know there's a hundred other things my dad would rather be doing, but when he's got a chance to do what's right or to do what's easy, he can work the legs off most any man in Tyler County.

Judd comes outside, and if he's not exactly friendly, he's helpful. But I never knew that putting up a fence could take so long or be so hard. First thing we do is measure to see just how much of it we can use, bringing it right up to Judd's trailer so's he can step out his back door and into the dog run. Then we lay those posts where they're going to go, and Dad and I take turns with the shovel, digging the holes and packing the dirt in around the posts till they're rock solid. Judd can't do any digging, but he helps uncoil the fencing and fasten it in place. We put the extra behind his shed.

It's well into afternoon before the job's done, and when Dad and me get home, we both stretch out on the living room rug and don't wake up till dinner.

"Judd was about as pleasant today as I've seen him," Dad says to Ma, helpin' himself to the black-eyed peas and ham.

"Maybe so, but I'm still uneasy about him," she answers.

I'm thinking that the sheriff's guess is right. Judd may

67

have had a fight once with the man from Bens Run, but he probably wasn't the one who killed him. 'Course, they could have had a second fight, and Judd killed him not meaning to. That's another way it could have happened.

That don't keep me from going over to Judd's on Wednesday after school to see the neighbor on one side of Judd bring the two dogs he's been keepin', and the folks on the other side bring over the one. Those dogs don't know which to smell first, the new fence or each other. They get to yippin' and runnin' around in wider and wider circles like they can't believe their freedom. We laugh at their craziness. I reach out every time a dog comes by, like I'm tryin' to grab him, and he just runs all the harder—knows I'm playin'.

"Look at the exercise their legs are getting, Judd," I say. "That'll make 'em all the stronger; they'll go up hills like nobody's business."

He points to his own leg, out of the cast now, but still weak. "Maybe I should get in there with 'em," he jokes.

Not no accident that each of his neighbors has a little something to say to Judd, things like: "Well, we're returning your black and white better-tempered than it was before," and, "Think we put a little meat on their bones; they look better fattened up some, don't you think?" and, "You treat these dogs right, Judd, you'll get many years of good hunting from them."

I wish they'd just leave; Judd don't need no sermon right now. But I know he figures he owes 'em something, so he just nods, and after a time they go home. Then Judd and me sit on his back steps watching those dogs enjoyin' themselves, and I sure do feel good. Still, can't help glancin' at

Judd's hands now and then and wondering, Those the hands of a killer? He the one who done it?

When I get home and tell Dad about Judd getting his dogs back, I can see he's feeling good, too. Glad to be on neighborly terms with Judd Travers again, no hard feelings between them.

Ma's not feeling too good, though.

"Tooth is actin' up again," she says.

"You ought to go have it looked at," Dad tells her.

"Well, the pain comes and goes. I got some oil of clove on it now," she says.

One thing about Ma, she sure hates to go to the dentist. Dad says he don't know how a woman who can stand giving birth to three children is so afraid of the dentist, but Ma says there's no comparison. Children you ask for; toothaches you don't.

What I'm thinkin' is that Ma's been hurting since yesterday—I could see it in her eyes, but didn't say nothing. I give more time to Judd Travers, who, if he's not ninety-nine percent evil is sixty percent at least, and paid no mind to her at all.

"I'll read to Becky tonight," I tell her, when Becky's beggin' for a story. Ma nods and hands me the book. So Becky, still scratchin' her pox, crawls up on my lap, Shiloh beside us. When Becky leans her head back against me and sits real quiet, one hand resting on mine as I turn the page, I can understand why Ma would go through pain to have children and still not like the dentist. Of course, she give birth to Dara Lynn, too, but that's somethin' else entirely.

Becky and Dara Lynn go off to take a bath together, and Ma gets out the quilt she's makin' and settles down in front of the TV with Dad. I finish my homework at the table. We give up on Pilgrims, and we're studying about Alaska now; I'm reading how it gets as cold as seventy-six degrees below in winter.

I try to figure how cold seventy-six degrees below is. Wonder if you spit, would it freeze before it hit the ground? After the lights are out and I crawl under my blanket on the couch, all that coldness gets to me. When I hear Shiloh's toenails clickin' about on the porch, I feel my way to the door in the dark to let him in; he makes one fine back-warmer.

As I close the door again, I see this little beam of light movin' way off in the direction of Middle Island Creek. Can't place where it is exactly, but it's there sure as I got eyes in my head. It's sort of bobbing around, like somebody's holding a flashlight. I watch for fifteen, twenty seconds, maybe, and then the light goes out.

Eleven

It's the next day on the school bus I tell David about the light. And even though it probably don't mean spit, David Howard can work up one heck of a story with it, I know.

"Like a signal or something?" he asks, eager.

"Well, it could have been," I say.

He's cautious, though. "How do you know it wasn't just somebody with a flashlight out jogging after dark?"

"It was movin' too slow for that. And didn't stay on more'n fifteen seconds."

"Like somebody looking for something?" asks David.

"Maybe."

"The other boot!" whispers David. "We found one, and now Judd wants to find the other."

"David, that don't make any sense at all!" I tell him. "Why would the killer leave a body out in plain sight, but go hide the shoes somewhere else?"

71

"The murder weapon, then," says David. "Maybe Judd buried it somewhere along Middle Island Creek, and now that the police are looking for it, he wants to be sure it stays buried."

I lean back against the seat and stare out the window, wondering if David could be right. The sheriff hasn't found enough evidence to arrest Judd, but everybody from here to Wheeling is ready to string him up, it seems. Maybe they got good reason.

"Besides," says David, lookin' over at me, "if somebody's looking for something, why would they go out at *night?*"

"That's what I'm *tellin'* you! We got a mystery on our hands. But it don't mean it's anything to do with Judd," I say. Deep inside, though, I'm thinkin' maybe it does.

What's fun is sitting in Miss Talbot's class, me and David, and having this secret. During math, we pass these notes back and forth.

How high off the ground was the light? writes David.

How in the world would I know that? I wonder. It was dark—couldn't even tell where the ground was. But I write back, *Three feet, maybe four.*

Then it was a man holding the flashlight, answers David. *If it had been a kid, it'd be more like two or three feet from the ground.* I tell you, he can find clues in almost anything.

"Marty?" says Miss Talbot.

"Three," I say, staring at the blackboard where she's pointing. I don't even know what the question is.

Somebody snickers.

"What I'm asking," says the teacher, "is whether you would multiply or divide."

"Multiply," I tell her, making a guess.

"Correct," she says, and I let out my breath real slow.

On the bus going home, David says he'll ask his ma if he can stay at my house this weekend. That way we can take turns watching for the light. So when I get home with Dara Lynn, and Shiloh comes dancin' and wigglin' down the drive to meet us, I'm not surprised to hear the phone ringing soon as I step inside.

"Mom says it's your turn to come to our house," David tells me. "I can't sleep over there till you come here."

I ask Ma can I spend the night at David's.

"I think it's his turn to come here," she says.

"He was just here!" I say.

"Not to spend the night," she says. Nothin' is ever simple with mothers.

"Well, I can't go down there till you sleep here," I tell David.

Finally Ma says I can go to David's house for an overnight if David will sleep over the weekend after that. And on Friday morning, I put my toothbrush and pajamas and some clean underpants in my book bag before I leave for school.

"You be polite at the Howards' now," Ma says as she hands me a plate of fried cornmeal mush, cut in slices, crisp around the edges. I slather on the margarine and then the hot syrup.

"Why don't anybody ever invite *me* to sleep over?" gripes Dara Lynn, glaring down at her fried mush.

" 'Cause you're a sourpuss, that's why," I tell her.

On the way to the bus stop, Dara Lynn says to me, "I wish you'd get run over and your eyes pecked out by crows."

"I wish you'd fall down a hole and pull the dirt in after you," I say.

If Shiloh hears the meanness in our voices he sure don't

show it. Happy as can be trottin' along beside us till he sees that school bus comin' to take us away.

"See you tomorrow, boy," I tell him, give him a hug.

Somebody on the school bus is passing out Gummi Bears, though, and Dara Lynn revives in a hurry. Sitting there beside a girl in third grade, eating Gummi Bears and swinging her legs, Dara Lynn don't look like such a poor neglected child to me.

Fred Niles gets on, and he's got a story to tell. Seems that somebody walked right into their house the day before and stole two jackets and a shotgun.

"Just walked right in while you were home?" asks Sarah.

"Ma was only gone two minutes," says Fred. "She walked down to the road to check the mailbox, and later we discovered what all was missing. We're locking our doors and windows from now on. Never had to do it before."

"Wouldn't surprise me if Judd Travers had something to do with it," says Michael Sholt. "Heard he got his cast off this week. Bet he's making up for lost time."

I got this feeling Michael may be right. But I say, "Could have been anyone at all."

"You know anybody else around here who would walk in a neighbor's house and steal from him?" Michael asks.

At school, we are so deep in Alaska I don't see we can ever get out. We're buying and feeding imaginary sled dogs for math, figuring how many pounds of food per day they're going to eat, and how many pounds they can pull. We're studying Eskimo paintings in art, and listening to Eskimo folktales, and for spelling I got to memorize words like "tundra," "Aleutian," "glacier," "petroleum," and "permafrost." Now I *know* I never want to feel what seventy-six degrees below zero is like.

I get off at David's house after school. David has his own key. His ma gets home a half hour after he does, and she's got a pile of papers to grade.

"Hi, Marty," she says. "There's chocolate pudding in the refrigerator if you boys want a snack."

"We already found it," David tells her.

I guess maybe everybody feels more comfortable at his own table in his own house. I know I feel a little awkward at David's. First off, there's always a tablecloth. I can't imagine a cloth on our table at home. Becky would drop spinach on it first off, and Dara Lynn would spill her milk. The Howards have napkins, too. Cloth napkins. And everything's in bowls that you pass around. Ma just sets a pan right from the stove on our table; it keeps the food hot, you want some more.

David's folks are nice, though. David and I tell his dad how we're studying Alaska, and he tells us about this dogsled race they hold up there every year called the Iditarod, and how you have to travel a thousand miles and sleep out in the snow and be careful your dogs don't drop off the ice and I don't know what all.

"You see much of Judd Travers these days?" Mr. Howard asks me finally when David's ma brings out the dessert.

"Some," I tell him.

"Wonder how he takes to all this talk of the murder."

"Don't take to it at all, same as you or me," I tell him.

Mr. Howard grows quiet after that.

Later we're lyin' on our backs on the top bunk in David's room, trying to make out the constellations on his ceiling. David and his dad got a package of those stick-on stars and planets, and they put them in just the right places so that the ceiling looks something like the sky would look if you stepped outside at night a certain time of the year.

"That's Orion, the Hunter," says David, pointing. "See those two bright stars there in the middle, and then the three bright stars below? Well, the two stars are supposed to be his shoulders, and the three stars are his belt."

Now who figured that out, do you suppose? How do they get a whole man out of five little stars? Why couldn't those two stars on top be the eyes of a wolf or something, and the three below be his mouth? Makes as much sense to me as a hunter.

And then, because we're talking about hunters, maybe, David says, "I'll bet it *was* Judd Travers who stole those jackets and that shotgun from Fred's house."

I roll over on my side, trying to see his face in the dark.

"How come whatever happens has to be Judd's fault?" I ask. "How come it all goes back to him?"

David thinks about that a minute. "I guess it's because anything that happened around here before was usually Judd's fault. The way he'd cheat Mr. Wallace over at the store. We've both seen him do that. Give him a ten-dollar bill, then get to talking, and when he got his change back, say he gave Wallace a twenty. Driving drunk and knocking over people's mailboxes. Kicking his dogs. Other people have done one of those things maybe once in their lives, but Judd can do all those things in a single month!"

"Yeah, but what if he's changed?" I say.

David thinks about that, too. "Maybe," he says. "But once you get a reputation, it follows you around like your shadow. That's what Mom says, anyway." He's quiet a moment. Then he tells me, "Mom said I can't come to your house anymore unless we promise not to go anywhere near Judd's."

Right then I see how I got connected in people's minds with Judd Travers.

"You haven't gone with me to his house since last fall,"

I tell David. "We can keep on not going there together. I don't care."

"I just wanted you to know," says David.

Next thing they'll suspect *me* of murder!

"You know, Marty, if he *did* have anything to do with killing that man, he could go to jail for a long time and you probably wouldn't have to worry about him ever again," David says.

I think about that awhile. Why *don't* I wish Judd would be found guilty? Why don't I wish he'd get sent to jail? David's right. It sure would solve a lot of problems, just like that. I wonder why I been trying so hard to take his side?

Because I think I know how Judd got to be the way he is, that's why. Once you know what happened to someone as a little kid, it's hard to think of him as one hundred percent evil. If Judd's the way he is because of what his dad done to him, though, maybe his *dad* was that way on account of what *his* dad done, and maybe the grandpa was that way because *his* father. . . . When's it going to end?

Dad picks me up early the next day before he starts his mail route and takes me down to the vet's in St. Marys. I'm stacking twenty-pound bags of cat box litter when John Collins comes in to scrub his hands, getting ready to operate on a collie that was hit by a car. The vet scrubs with a brush, even under his fingernails.

"What's happening up in Shiloh these days, Marty?" he asks me. "I've had two customers come in this week telling me that their homes have been broken into. Walk-ins, more like it. Somebody coming in when they weren't home, and helping themselves to whatever they want."

"You must be talking about Fred Niles's family," I say. "They got a shotgun and some jackets missing."

77

"No, hadn't heard about them. But one family's missing two twenty-dollar bills they kept on a shelf in their kitchen, and a woman tells me she came home to find half the food in her refrigerator gone. Drove her husband to work, she says, and came back to find a whole roast chicken, half a cake, and a pan of scalloped potatoes missing."

"Who do they figure took it?" I ask.

"Nobody knows. There's talk about Judd Travers doing it. Of course, as I said to Mrs. Bates, it could be more than one person. Could be a whole ring of housebreakers. I sure don't like to hear about that shotgun, though. Walking in a house when no one's there and helping yourself to a chicken is one thing; walking in with a gun, if they start using that shotgun, is something else."

Doc Collins puts on his surgical gown and then his gloves, and goes into the operating room. I go on with my stacking. Maybe it's me who's got his head in the sand, I'm thinking. Maybe I just don't want to face the fact it could be Judd. How long's he had that cast off now? Three days? And when did the robberies begin? Three days ago, exactly.

Twelve

David's got an idea about the light I saw over near the bridge. If Judd didn't murder the man from Bens Run, he says, maybe someone's trying to murder Judd.

He slips this note to me during history:

1. Let's say Judd didn't murder anyone, but suppose he knows who did?
2. What if the light you saw was the real killer's flashlight? I'll bet you he knows Judd could squeal on him, and he's setting a trap for Judd down by the creek.

I turn over my spelling paper and send a note back to David:

1. I think you're nuts.
2. I think that whoever the killer is, Judd or anyone else,

79

he threw his murder weapon down the creek bank, and now he's trying to find it before the police do.

I remember how David says he wants to be either a forest ranger or a biologist. I write a P.S.:

P.S. I don't think you're going to be a biologist or forest ranger either one. I think you are going to write detective stories. Bad ones.

David reads my note and laughs.

"David," says Miss Talbot. "May I see that note, please?"

I don't move. I can feel the color rise to my face. David don't move, neither. He sure don't want Michael Sholt and the whole sixth-grade class knowing about that light I saw and snooping around the creek themselves.

"I . . . I can't," he says. "It's . . . it's not my note to give."

"Who wrote it?" asks the teacher.

Now the whole class is watching.

"I did," I say.

"Then may I see the note, please, Marty?"

I swallow and shake my head. Everyone's staring.

"It's . . . private," I tell her. This is a real good secret David and I have going, and Miss Talbot just might pin it up on the bulletin board, the way she did Jenny Boggs's note last week.

"I see," says Miss Talbot. "And is this class a private place?"

"No, ma'am," I say.

"Then, because you were taking school time for private business, I suggest you stay in after lunch and use some of your personal recess time for your studies," she says.

That's fair enough, I guess. I see David stick the note in

his pocket. So while the other kids are playing kick-ball out on the playground, I've got to make a list of Alaska's natural resources and David's got to list the mountain ranges. Why do we have to study Alaska in January? I wonder. Why couldn't it be Hawaii? The only thing we've got to look forward to is the next weekend, first of February, when David gets to stay overnight at my place.

That night when I go to the door to let Shiloh in, I see the light again. Feel so cold inside my body it's like I had ice cubes for supper. Now I know this mystery's real, not just something David Howard and me put together to have some fun. Somebody's out there in the night doing something he don't want nobody to see. Looking for something he don't want nobody else to find, I'll bet. Maybe even studying our house like I'm studying the light from our window, standing in the dark. Is it the killer? Is it Judd?

I stay at the window watching till the light disappears, trying to figure just where it's coming from, but when there's nothing but blackness outside your window, you got nothing to pin it to. The old gristmill seems the most likely place.

Turns out David can't come for a sleep-over that weekend, though, on account of we're not home. We got to go to Clarksburg for Grandma Preston's funeral on Saturday.

"It was pneumonia," Aunt Hettie cries over the phone. Can hear her voice all over the kitchen. "It happened so fast! One day she had a cold, and the next thing we know it's pneumonia, and then she's gone—just like that. I should have been with her. I could have taken off work, and gone to that nursing home and stayed right by her bed. . . ." She cries some more.

"Now Hettie, don't you go blaming yourself for something you couldn't help in a million years," says Dad. "You did the best you could for Mother, and no one's faulting you now. We'll be there Friday evening, soon as I can get away."

"What about Shiloh?" I ask when my dad hangs up. Grandma Preston's dead, see, and first words out of my mouth are about my dog.

"I'll ask Mrs. Sweeney to come by and feed him," says Ma.

"But the whole family's never been gone overnight before," I say. "Shiloh might figure we're not coming back." All I can think of is that a lot can happen to a dog in twenty-four hours.

"Marty, that dog of yours is rompin' all over creation with that Labrador, and he won't even miss you," says Dad.

"Couldn't we just put him in the house?" I beg.

"And ask Mrs. Sweeney to let him out every few hours for a run?" says Ma. "What if he doesn't come back when she calls him, and her with that bad knee? It's enough she's asked to feed him."

There's not much to say after that.

Ma spends the rest of the week cooking food for the funeral dinner. "Here's one thing I can do for Hettie," she says, wrapping up a ham and a dish of sweet potatoes.

Dad tells the post office why he won't be in on Saturday, and I call Doc Collins. By five o'clock Friday evening, we're on our way to Clarksburg, and Ma's in the front seat, trying to answer our questions.

Dara Lynn's just told Becky we aren't going to see Grandma Preston ever again. "Not ever, ever, ever, ever, ever," she says.

"Why?" asks Becky.

" 'Cause she's dead," says Dara Lynn.

82

"What's dead?"

"It's when your body gets as cold and stiff as an icicle and somebody could put a red-hot iron on your leg and you wouldn't feel nothing," Dara Lynn says.

"Dara Lynn, shut up," I tell her.

Becky asks if *she's* ever going to die, and Dara Lynn says yes, and Becky starts cryin', says she don't want nobody putting a red-hot iron on her leg.

"Becky," Ma says from the front seat, "your grandma's gone to be with the angels, and there won't be anymore sickness or pain for her ever again. We can rejoice in God's love."

"She won't be stealin' nobody's false teeth anymore, neither," says Dara Lynn, and we can't help ourselves. Have to laugh. We all feel better after that.

We sit up late that night talking to all the people who drop by Aunt Hettie's to remember Grandma Preston, and we sit real quiet through the service at the church next day. Dara Lynn keeps her hands to herself and Becky hardly makes a peep. I'm beginning to think Dara Lynn's not gonna be too bad a sister after all, but when we get to the cemetery, I wish she'd never been born.

She's standin' there beside me at the grave while the preacher reads from the Bible, the coffin resting on one side of the hole, waiting to go in. But when the preacher asks us to bow our heads and begins his prayer, Dara Lynn inches right over to that hole and peers down inside. I can't believe it!

"Dara Lynn, get back here!" I hiss.

Just then the dirt gives way, her being so close to the edge. Dara Lynn's arms start goin' around like a windmill, and somehow, though one leg went over the side, she lands on her knees and keeps from goin' in. She just don't have any sense at all when it comes to danger.

Ma reaches out and grabs that girl and yanks her back beside us—Dara Lynn's white socks all dirty now and mud on both hands. I'm thinkin' what I said about how I wish she'd dig herself a hole and fall in, but my mind don't stop there. I'm thinking how what if nobody saw her, and what if she really did fall in, a whole pile of dirt on top of her, and then the coffin goes in and Dara Lynn's buried alive.

It's such an awful thought I can feel the sweat trickle down my back. Sometimes a thought comes to you that you just can't help, but you don't go to jail for *thinking!*

And then we're all back at Aunt Hettie's, and it's like a picnic supper. Everybody's bringin' more food—sliced cheese and a turkey, and little rolls to fold the meat up in. There's potato salad and cherry pie and burnt sugar cake and marshmallow Jell-O. Can't tell if this is a party or a funeral.

It's near ten o'clock when we get home that night. First thing I look for is my dog, but this time I can hear him before we even turn up the drive. He is barking his head off, and when we get out of the Jeep, he don't even come over— just stands back there by the henhouse, his nose toward the woods, his body jerking with every bark he makes.

"Shiloh!" I say, and he comes over to give me a lick, then goes right back to barking again. Even after we take him inside, he's jumpy. Goes from one window to the next.

"What in the world has got into that dog?" asks Ma.

She checks out the house. Our TV is still there—the money box, Dad's shotgun. Nobody's made off with the toaster or the radio or anything else that we can see.

"I'm going to get my lantern and have a look outside,"

Dad says. He takes a flashlight, puts his coat on again, and goes to the shed.

But a few minutes later he's back. "The lantern's gone," he says. "Somebody took my shears and my knife, too. If it weren't for Shiloh, that thief probably would have broken into the house."

I had goose bumps on my arms before, and now even the goose bumps have goose bumps. Was it because of Shiloh's barking that the thief didn't come in, or was it that we turned up the drive just about then? And if we *hadn't* come home when we did, would the robber have made off with Shiloh, too?

"Oh, Ray!" says Ma, and sits down hard on a kitchen chair. They stare at each other. "It's like someone knew we were gone."

"Well, I didn't go around telling everybody—just my supervisor at the P.O.," says Dad.

"I only told Mrs. Sweeney so she'd feed the dog," says Ma. "And Marty called the vet and David Howard, but that's all."

They stare at each other some more, and Dad don't even blink. "Only other person who saw us leave was Judd Travers," he says at last. "We passed his pickup just after we pulled out of the drive."

Thirteen

And then the blizzard comes. We go back to school on Monday, the TV talking three inches of snow, but by the time the bus lets us off that afternoon, it's five or six, and still comin' down.

"We gonna be snowed in!" Dara Lynn crows happily, dropping her coat on the floor.

Becky looks worried, but Dara Lynn grabs her hands and dances her round and round the kitchen, tellin' her how we might not have to go to school for a whole week. Then Shiloh gets into the act, skidding around the linoleum, his toenails clickin' and scratchin'.

"Well, I sure wish I'd got extra milk," says Ma. "I can always make bread, and I've got beans and salt pork enough for an army, but there's not much substitute for milk."

"We can always put snow on our cereal!" says Dara Lynn, laughing.

Ma decides to get in the spirit of things, too, so she gets out her valentine cookie cutter, and she and the girls make cookies while I carry in wood for the little potbellied stove in the living room. Our house has a furnace, but it don't work if the electricity goes out, so a couple years back Dad put in the potbellied stove.

"Next best thing to a fireplace," Ma says.

I know if I don't bring in the wood now and stack some more on the porch, I'm not going to be able to find the woodpile in another couple hours.

Shiloh goes out with me, and tries to tunnel through the snow with his nose. I stack wood on the porch first, then stamp the snow off my boots and make another couple trips from the porch to the stove inside. By this time Shiloh's had his fill of snow and comes when I call. He plops down close to that potbellied stove, giving out big contented sighs, his eyes closin'. He wore himself out.

Every time there's another report on TV about the blizzard nobody knew was comin', the weather bureau moves the number of inches up. Twelve to fifteen inches of snow, one of the weathermen says now, and, a half hour later, he's talkin' two feet.

Dad finally gets home about eight, and can hardly make it up the drive. He's got snow tires on the Jeep and four-wheel drive, but the wind's blowin' the snow in drifts across the road. I can tell by the look on Ma's face when she hears that Jeep that it's about the best music in the whole world to her.

Dad's real pleased to see all the wood I brung in.

"Good for you, Marty," he says. "Last I heard, we're goin' to need every stick of it. They're talking thirty inches now."

Dara Lynn squeals some more.

I wake up next morning and look out the window in

sheer wonder. Dad's stomping back in the house to say that he can't move the Jeep one inch—he'd have to shovel all the way down to the road, and then couldn't go anywhere. Plow hadn't been down there, either.

"Well, Dara Lynn, looks like you got your wish," Ma says, turning the French toast over in the skillet.

It's only the second time in all the years Dad's worked for the post office, though, that he hasn't been able to get his Jeep through, and he worries about people who are waiting for their pension checks.

"Even if the checks got through, nobody could get to a bank to cash them," says Ma.

David calls, of course, and tells me they haven't been plowed out yet down in Friendly, either, and his dad is still trying to get to the newspaper office. Then Ma calls Aunt Hettie in Clarksburg to make sure she's okay, and finally there's nothin' else to do but give in to being snowbound.

Snow finally stops about noon, and Dad goes out with a yardstick to measure where it's flat in the yard. Thirty-one and a half inches, not counting six or seven feet along the side of the house and shed where it's drifted. We shovel a path to the henhouse to get some feed to the chickens.

Us kids have to go out in it, of course. I take a shovel and dig a path from our porch to a tree, just so Shiloh can do his business. Dara Lynn and Becky, fat as clowns in their snowsuits, scarfs wrapped around their faces, only their eyes peeking out, set to work diggin' a cave at one side of my path, but Becky no sooner sits down inside it than the roof falls in on her. She's squallin', looks like she got hit in the face with a cream pie, and I got to carry her into the house. I sure wish David Howard was here. We'd dig a tunnel all the way down to the road.

We have a fine time—go out and come in so many times that Ma just puts our caps and mittens beneath the potbellied stove to dry out, so they'll be ready again when we are. House smells like wet wool and Ma's home-baked bread. Dara Lynn's cheeks are red as apples, her nose, too. She wouldn't be half bad-lookin' if she'd just keep her mouth shut.

By middle of the afternoon, though, Dad's gettin' calls sayin' that trees are down, and power lines as well. The snow's wet and heavy, like pudding, and plows can't get through till the trees are cleared off the roads. They got a substitute mail carrier deliverin' what mail he can down in Friendly, and I know Dad wants in the worst way to be doin' his own route. A matter of pride.

Ma's cheerful, though. Says we can toast marshmallows in the woodstove after supper, and then we watch a *National Geographic* special on alligators. But fifteen minutes from the end, the TV goes out along with the lights.

"Hey!" yells Dara Lynn. "What happened?"

"What do you suppose?" I say. "The electricity went off."

"Ray . . .?" says Ma.

Dad makes his way into the kitchen to get the flashlight. "Well," he says, "I imagine a transformer went out somewhere. Guess we're lucky it waited till we had our supper."

We hang round the stove till the fire dies down. Dad don't want to put in any more wood, in case the power's off a long time, and we need every bit of wood we can find.

"Why don't we go to bed early to stay warm, and maybe the electricity will come back on in the night," says Ma, and she gets out some candles to make an adventure of it. The girls go to bed without their baths, because we all got wells out this way, and the electric pump won't bring up the water if the power's off. The only water we got for drinking and cooking is what's left in the water heater right now.

Shiloh and me are lucky. Because the woodstove's in the living room, and we're sleepin' on the couch, we got the warmest place of all. But when we get up the next morning, the house is cold as an ice chest. Dad's got his coat on over his pajamas, and he's bringing in wood from the porch to feed the stove.

Ma tells me to dress without washing up, and nobody's to flush a toilet. Dara Lynn immediately sets up a howl.

"It's gonna stink in there!" she cries. "I ain't going to use no toilet that stinks!"

Ma turns on her suddenly. "Dara Lynn, I can think of a hundred worse things that could happen to you, and I don't want to hear another word. You don't want to use the bathroom, you can potty in the snow."

That shuts Dara Lynn up in a hurry. I smile; can't help myself—just thinking of Dara Lynn with her backside in a snowdrift. But I can see right off that today's not goin' to be near as much fun as yesterday. The woodstove's got a round top on it, not made for cookin', so Ma puts a pot over it upside down, and grills our toast on its flat bottom. Everything takes twice as long to make, though, and finally, cold as we are, we settle for Cheerios and the last of the milk. It's right about then we hear the sound of an engine grinding out on the road somewhere.

"Snowplow!" sings out Dara Lynn, looking toward the window.

No sight of anything, though. Don't look like there's any plow comin' along the country road. And then we see Judd's pickup, a plow blade in front, turnin' right up our driveway.

Slowly, his wheels spinning, Judd pushes his way

through the snowdrifts till he can't go no more, then backs up and makes another run at it. We all go to the window to watch, and Dad steps out on the porch and waves.

The pickup keeps comin', huge mounds of snow moving ahead of it. Every so often, Judd turns the wheel, ramming into the snowbanks with the plow to get rid of his load. The snow sure isn't doin' his truck any good, but Judd keeps at it, pushin' a little bit farther each time before he backs off and makes another run. Finally he gets up as far as our porch.

"Judd, I sure do appreciate this," Dad calls.

Judd rolls down his window. "Thought you might need to get out."

"Won't you come in and warm up?" Ma calls.

"Couple more folks I got to help out," Judd yells. "Thanks, anyway." And he makes a wide sweep to turn himself around, then heads off down the driveway, pushing more snow in front of him.

If people would just give him a chance! I'm thinking. See how much he's changed! But at the same time, I'm wondering is that a new jacket he's wearin'? And is that shotgun I see resting above the back window in the truck really his?

Fourteen

By next day, the electricity's still off, and we all sleep on the floor in the living room around the stove. Dad brings in a pail of snow and sets it by the toilet to flush it, but the bathroom's so cold the snow don't thaw. Now we got buckets of snow settin' all around the stove, coaxin' it to melt. Only good thing we've had to eat is hot dogs, 'cause you can put 'em on a stick and shove 'em right in the fire.

Dad gets out his Jeep to see how far he can go, but this time he's stopped by a tree that's down. Trees and wires all the way between here and Little, and when he tries to go the other way, across the bridge and on past Judd's, he come to the place where even Judd quit plowin'. Big wall of snow blocking the whole road. Drifts clear up over Dad's head.

"Sure am glad I'm not expectin' a baby in a blizzard like this," says Ma. I see her hand go up to her jaw and figure she's thinking a toothache would be even worse.

The bad part is we can't get no news on the TV or radio, neither, and with the sky that sick color again, like it's going to throw up more snow, we don't much feel like rompin' around outside. Takes too long to warm up afterwards. Even Shiloh hangs back when we open the door.

And then things slide from bad to worse. Our phone line goes out.

I know Ma's thinkin' that if one of us had an accident or something, there'd be no way to call for help. No way for anyone to get in with an ambulance, either. Last year down in Mingo County, a man got hurt during a snowstorm and they had to send a helicopter to pick him up. Almost worth knockin' Dara Lynn off the roof just to see a helicopter set down in our field. I smile to myself, but you sure can't say a joke like that out loud.

Everybody's tired of snow. We're tired of eatin' cold food, tired of settin' on a cold toilet seat, and of everybody crowded together at night on the living room floor just to stay warm, gettin' on each others' nerves. Dad's the only one half cheery. He says just pretend we're campin' out, but I can tell he's itchin' to get to work, and Ma just plain wants out of the house. And as if that ain't enough, it starts snowin' once more.

But then, fast as things got worse, they get better. The power comes on during the night. We're all sound asleep when suddenly the TV starts blarin' and the lights come on. We sit up and cheer. Hear the furnace click. By morning the phone's workin', too, and about nine, we hear chain saws goin' out on the road, crews workin' to remove trees that are down, and then the low grinding sound of the snowplow.

Dad gets to work about noon. Weatherman on TV says

the four more inches of snow we got is all it will be for a while, and suddenly the world looks good again.

Weren't all the roads in the county cleared, though, so the schools stay closed till Friday. Then everyone's got stories to tell of just how bad the blizzard was at his place, and I make a point of telling how Judd Travers come and plowed us out; plowed out some other driveways, too. To hear me tell it, Judd was part Paul Bunyan and part Jesus Christ, doin' all kinds of hero and wonderful things. No one says a bad word against him this time, but I don't hear no kind word for him, neither.

And then that evening, I see the light again over near Middle Island Creek. I stand at the window in the dark watching, and get the feeling like something real bad is out there. Why's it staying right across from where we live? Why don't it go somewhere else? How do I know that after I go to sleep at night, that light won't come floating and bobbing right up our driveway and around our place? I'm glad David Howard's comin' to sleep over the next day. Sometimes I feel we got us a mystery I'd just as soon not have.

I go to my job at the vet's Saturday morning, and when Dad picks me up at noon, we stop by David Howard's and get him. As soon as we finish our lunch, we're going to explore the gristmill, where I figure that light's got to be.

This time, though, Dara Lynn wants to go with us.

"No way," I tell her.

"Why not?" she says.

" 'Cause we're doing our own stuff. You go do yours."

"I'll just watch," says Dara Lynn.

"You will not!" I yell, as she follows us to the door.

Ma comes out of the bedroom. "Dara Lynn, you got things to play with in here," she says. "I'll mix up some flour paste, and you and Becky can cut pictures out of magazines, make a scrapbook."

"I don't want to make no scrapbook! I can play out in my own yard if I want!" Dara Lynn says.

David and I go out, but leave Shiloh inside so he won't give us away when we give Dara Lynn the slip. We're tryin' to beat her to the bridge, but we get halfway down the drive and here she comes, clomping along in her boots, not even buckled. So we have to make like we're going hiking along the creek in the other direction, hide behind some trees, then head back the other way using the same footprints in the snow to confuse her.

By now the thirty-one inches have sunk down to twenty or so, and melting all the time, but every step we take is still a high one. Finally we see Dara Lynn headin' back up toward the house, so we make our way toward the bridge, down the bank, and push our way through the tangle of bushes and trees and snow to the cinder block supports of the old mill.

The old white-shingled building is propped up on a dozen or so columns to keep it out of the water in flood season, and one whole side of it's been burned or collapsed out of sheer misery, can't tell which. Dad won't let us climb up in there—too dangerous—but we take a good look below.

We hold on to each other, 'cause we know that the ground slants toward the creek, and it's full of ruts and gullies. One wrong step, and we're in a snowbank over our heads. Can't even tell where the bank stops and the creek begins. You get thirty-one inches of snow falling down in this place, plus the four or five inches more, plus all the snow that blows off the road or was pushed down here by the plow, why . . . a person could get buried, and nobody find him till spring.

I take this old dead limb and dig out a path in front of us. Even without snow, it's hard to see just what's here. Imagine the waterwheel was on the side next to the creek, but we sure can't make out anything.

"Know what?" David says at last. "If anybody had been down here, either we'd find his footprints or he's buried at the bottom of this snow."

I stop and think. Without moving my feet, I twist my body all around, lookin' in every direction, and I don't see any footprints here at all, not around the gristmill nor the bank nor the path leading up to the road—only the tracks we made ourselves.

"Shoot!" I say, disappointed.

"If we dig, though, we might find a body under the snow," says David.

"Yeah," I say, not all that eager. We don't even know what we're lookin' for anymore—just talkin' nonsense. We both know we're not about to go back to my place, carry a shovel all the way down here, and start digging.

We claw our way back up the bank, same place we come down, and make a whole pile of snowballs—line 'em up on the bridge. Then we take turns seeing if we can hit a stick far out there on the ice.

We do a couple of throws, and I've just picked up my third snowball when suddenly there's this loud *whomp!*, like a whole house has rose up in the air and set down again.

David and I turn, starin' in the direction of the noise, just in time to see snow slidin' off the roof of the old Shiloh schoolhouse. We run over and wade through the school yard, and there's half the roof caved in, settin' there like it's been that way forever.

"Wow!" I say.

"It went just like that!" says David. "All that snow!"

"Let's check it out!" I tell him, and we go over and try the door. Locked, of course. Paint flecks scattered all about. Through the dusty window I can see an old refrigerator, a flowered armchair that the mice have nested in, some children's desks, a table. . . . We go around back to where the outhouse is. And then we stop dead still and stare, because there's a fresh path in the snow between the outhouse and a cellar window.

"Marty!" David whispers, his eyes half popped from his head.

We know what we're going to do. We check out the outhouse first, and my heart's like to jump out of my skin. The snow's been cleared away where the door's ajar, and I figure if anybody's in there hearing us talk, he'd probably pull the door to. But I know if we get up to that door and peer around it and see somebody sittin' inside, I will die on the spot.

We're lifting our feet so high with each step it looks like we're marching, and David gets to the door first.

Ready? he mouths to me. I nod. He hooks one finger around the edge of that door and slowly, slowly pulls it open.

Creeeaaak! it goes, just like in the movies.

"Whew!" I say, when I see the seat's empty.

Together, we turn and look at the school, knowing that somebody could be watching us that very minute. At the same time, we know as sure as we got teeth in our mouth that we're going to climb in there and take a look. You can see by that open window where somebody's been crawlin' in and out.

"Who's gonna go first?" asks David, meaning that he was the one who checked out the outhouse, and now it's my turn.

97

I get down on my knees, stick one leg inside, and back in. See that somebody's put an old bench below the window to step down on, and soon as both my legs are in, and then my back and head, I look around.

"What do you see?" David whispers.

"Junk," I tell him. "Broken-down chairs. An old blackboard. Rats' nests—pigeon poop." But I don't see a living soul. Don't hear a single sound except the creak of some boards where the wind blows through.

"Come on in," I say to David, and he climbs in, too. The floor above us is sagging, so we hug the wall wherever we can. Have to crawl over a ton of stuff to get to the stairs, and then we stick to the sides in case they give.

When we get to the top, we see where the roof's come down, spilling snow onto what's left of a classroom.

"David!" I say, and point. There is my dad's lantern, sittin' right on the floor beside a blanket. I'd know it anywhere—got a piece of tape at the back to hold the batteries in. We look around, and there's a shotgun, too. And some chicken bones and a box of crackers. Any minute now, I'm thinking, I'll feel a gun in my back.

I walk over to pick up Dad's lantern, but then my heart almost gives out and my legs start to buckle. All I can do is grab David's sleeve and point, 'cause there, sticking out from under one of the fallen rafters, with snow and shingles on top, are the curled fingers of a man's glove. And on down the pile of rubble, about where his foot would be, is half a man's boot showing.

Fifteen

Forget Dad's lantern. David and me tumble back down those steps, scrambling over junk in the basement, sure that any minute someone's goin' to snatch us by the ankles, pull us back. We get outside, and go floppin' and falling through the snow till we reach the road, then tear across the bridge and on up the drive, our breath comin' in steamy puffs.

We reach the house, scramble up on the porch, and we're both trying to squeeze through that door at once, falling over Dara Lynn's boots she's left right there on the rug.

"Marty, what . . .?" asks Ma, lookin' up from her sewing.

"Over in the schoolhouse . . ." I point. "The roof caved in from all the snow and there's a dead man under the rafters." I collapse on a chair, my chest heaving.

Ma rises from the sofa, her scissors sliding to the floor. "You sure 'bout this, Marty?"

"Sure as Christmas," says David, and we wait, starin' at each other while Ma makes the call to the sheriff.

Dara Lynn says she will never forgive us, not takin' her along.

"I never seen a dead person in my whole life!" she cries.

"You have too. You seen Grandma Preston," I tell her.

"I never seen one that got a roof caved in on him," she wails.

I am actually thinking of taking Dara Lynn over there and showing it to her, but Ma says David and me are not to go back till the sheriff gets here, and Dara Lynn's not to go at all. Not somethin' for a little girl to see. So we watch from the window, and when the sheriff's car shows up out on the road later, David and me go on over. They got a police dog with 'em.

Sheriff rolls down his window. "You the boys who found a body? Your ma called?"

I nod. I point to the schoolhouse.

Car moves on slow across the bridge, and David and me follow. We show 'em the path in the snow from the basement window to the outhouse, and one of the deputies points out another path leading off into the woods. David and I didn't notice that one at all.

"Okay, now," the sheriff says. "I want you boys to stay outside with Frank here while Pete and I go take a look." Frank's the man with the police dog, I guess.

David and I stand there watching, wondering how in the world Pete, the fat one, is going to get himself through that basement window—jacket, gun, belly, and all—but he does.

Frank lets us pet his dog while we wait. We can hear the other men talking inside, but can't make out the words.

Now and then a board creaks, something else giving way, I guess. Footsteps going back and forth across the floor.

After a while the men come out again, Sheriff crawling out first through that basement window, Pete behind him, dragging a leaf bag filled with stuff. I can see the shotgun sticking out of the bag. I tell 'em Dad's lantern is in there, but they say they've got to keep all the evidence for a while.

"So what you got?" Frank asks the others.

Sheriff grins at us. "Well, there was a glove and a boot, all right, but nobody in 'em. I'll admit, it sure looked like there was a body under there, but it was just some clothes."

But before David and I have a chance to feel really stupid, Sheriff says, "But look what else we found, Frank," and holds up a pair of bright orange pants.

Frank whistles, then smiles.

"Know what this is?" the sheriff asks David and me. "The uniform over at the county jail. We've been lookin' for those two escapees, and it appears this is where they've been."

My hand moves into my jacket pocket and deep down in one corner where I'd forgotten all about it, I find this piece of orange cloth that Shiloh and the Lab were playing with.

"There you go!" says the sheriff when he sees it. "Piece of the shirt! Where'd you find that?"

"My dog brought it home," I say, as David stares.

"Surprised they got this far," says Pete. "Probably dropped their clothes as soon as they could steal something else to put on their backs."

"Well, we figured they'd show up sooner or later, weather like this," says the sheriff, taking the piece of shirt in my hand and sticking it in the bag, too. "What I can't figure, though, is why two men, who only had thirty days to serve for disorderly conduct, would pull something like this. Walk off that work detail. Now they've got to serve even more time when we catch 'em."

"Heck," says Pete. "I'd choose jail just to stay nice and warm. Three square meals, a bunk and blanket . . . who knows what they were eating here!"

I'm wondering the same thing. I've been up to Middlebourne before with my dad, and the jail actually don't look too bad. Sort of like a castle snuggled there next to the courthouse, with the words, COUNTY JAIL in bright red letters. You put a wreath on the door, it'd look right cheery.

"But where are they now?" I ask.

"That's what Sergeant here is going to find out," Sheriff says, and he gives that dog a good healthy sniff of the jail clothes.

David and I watch as that dog buries his nose in the uniform, like he's drinking in the scent, and then he starts running around, nose to the snow. Pretty soon he's on the path to the outhouse and, after that, the path through the woods.

The story makes the next edition of the *Tyler Star-News*. There's a picture of the old Shiloh schoolhouse with its roof caved in, and the story says how two boys found the hideout. And then it tells how those men, who'd been arrested for disorderly conduct, turned out to be the chief suspects in the murder of the man from Bens Run. David was right about that much, anyway. They'd figured that the longer they were in jail, the better chance the sheriff had of connecting them to the killing, so they got away when they saw the chance. Seems they'd been gambling with the man from Bens Run, who owed them a pile of money, and when he said he couldn't pay them, they got in a fight. Whether they meant to kill him or not, the court, I guess, will decide.

The story says that the police dog found them a couple miles away, coming back through the woods with some more blankets and half a roast beef. Photographer wanted to come and take our picture, but Mr. Howard wouldn't let him. Dad wouldn't even let the newspaper use our names. Said he didn't especially want the men to know who the boys were who found the hideout, and where they lived.

But it felt pretty good to be a hero for a day—me and David both. Tell the truth, I'd forgot about those men escaping from the county jail, and never dreamed they'd got clear over to Shiloh lookin' for a place to hide.

The kids on the bus Monday morning want to hear all about it—don't take them long to figure out who the two boys were.

"It *was* you and David, wasn't it?" squeals Sarah Peters.

"You see 'em go in the schoolhouse, or what?" asks Fred Niles.

"They pull a gun on you?" Michael Sholt wants to know.

Tell the story all over again, but I guess I skim the truth a little by leavin' things out—like how David and me run like roosters when we saw that glove sticking out from under the rafter. But if I leave things out, David puts things in, and after he gets on the bus, each of us giving our account in our own way, we have a story rolling like you wouldn't believe.

One kid tells another, and he tells somebody else, each of 'em tacking on a little something, so that by the time the bus gets to school and the story reaches Miss Talbot, it seems David and me had trapped the vicious killers in the old Shiloh schoolhouse, and then we climbed up on the roof and tramped around so that it fell down, burying the men in snow up to their armpits.

But wouldn't you know, Miss Talbot made a lesson of it? She can make a lesson out of anything. First it's Pilgrims, then Alaska, and now we got to find out all about prisons—how many in the state of West Virginia, how you get there by doin' what, and how long you got to stay. Don't ever tell your teacher somethin' she don't need to know, or she'll make homework out of it quicker'n you can say, "My dog Shiloh."

Each time we tell the story, though, I say, "See? It wasn't Judd, after all! You had him all wrong. He's changin'! You should see all he's done for his dogs."

But the worst was right around the corner, and maybe, if I'd known what was comin' next, I wouldn't have said nothing at all.

Sixteen

Valentine's Day, and David and me get more valentines than any other boys in our class—most of 'em from girls. In sixth grade, we don't go much for valentines—just the gross and crazy kind—but here are all these hearts with our names on 'em. I even got a valentine from Sarah Peters with a stick of spearmint gum stuck to the front, and the words VALENTINE, I CHEWS YOU! Sarah Peters never give any boy a valentine before, namely 'cause she's so stuck on herself, and all because she can swim. On a swim team or something. But here's this big valentine with her name on it. Embarrassing is what it is, especially since I didn't give out any valentines at all.

On the way home, after David Howard gets off the bus, Dara Lynn comes and sits beside me. She's showin' me all her valentines, and then she reaches in her coat pocket and pulls out the one from her teacher. Got a whole Milky Way bar with a ribbon around it.

I can't believe her teacher gave everybody a big candy bar like that. Dara Lynn, of course, starts peelin' the wrapper off that chocolate real slow like, wavin' it around in front of my nose till I think I hate my sister worse'n spinach.

And then, all of a sudden, she breaks that candy in half and hands a piece to me. "Here," she says.

I look at the candy. Look at Dara Lynn. "That half got poison in it?" I say.

"No," she tells me, jiggling it a little. "Go on. You can have it."

I take the candy and look it over good. Seems fine to me. Take a bite. The purest, sweetest chocolate you ever did taste. Dara Lynn settles back in her seat, swingin' her legs and eatin' that chocolate bar, and I eat my piece, too, and think how if I live to be a hundred, I will never understand my sister.

Kids still talkin' about the men from the county jail hidin' out in the old Shiloh schoolhouse. All the stuff that they'd stolen was returned, and Fred Niles's dad got his shotgun and two jackets back.

"See?" I say to Fred. "You were accusing Judd for nothing."

"I'll bet he's taken stuff we don't even know of, though," Fred says.

I turn halfway round in my seat. "Why are you always tryin' to blame Judd for every little thing that happens?" I ask, angry.

But Sarah says, "The way he used to treat Shiloh, Marty, I'd think you and Judd would be enemies. Tell me one good thing he's done."

"He plowed us out after the blizzard. Plowed out a few more besides," I say, and try hard to think of something else.

106

Judd wasn't drinkin' anymore that I knew of. Wasn't knocking down anybody's mailbox. Wasn't going around stealing all the stuff people thought he had. Then I see that all I'm doing is thinking of things he *wasn't* doing. I was short on things he did.

"You know what I think?" says Michael Sholt, maybe jealous of all the attention David and me got that day. "I think you and your dad are afraid of him. No matter what he does, you say a good word. He's got you scared!"

Now I'm really mad. "Has not! I wasn't too scared to stand up to him and take Shiloh!" I say. "Dad wasn't scared to go tell him not to hunt on our land!"

"Well, *my* dad says the Traverses have been trouble ever since they been here—my granddad knew his granddad— and they are bad news, the whole lot of them! If a man goes driving around drunk, destroying people's property, you don't reward him by fixing up his truck and taking him food."

"But it worked, didn't it?" I say. "He's not driving drunk anymore! He didn't kill that man or rob those houses. What else do you want him to do?"

"Move to Missouri, as far from here as he can get," says Michael, and laughs. Sarah and Fred laugh, too.

At dinner that night, I tell Dad what Michael said.

"Well, Marty," he says, "a person's got to make up his mind: Does he want someone to change for the better or does he want to get even? And if you want to get even with somebody, you'll get back at him, he'll get back at you, and there's no stopping it."

"But I wish there was some way we could make people like Judd better," I tell him.

Dad don't answer for a moment. Puts a square of mar-

107

garine on his mashed potatoes and covers it all with pepper. "You can't *make* folks like you, Marty, and you especially can't make folks like somebody else."

I lay on the living room floor after supper over by the woodstove and wrestle with Shiloh. He had his head on my leg all through dinner, his big brown eyes watchin' every morsel of food that travels between my plate and my mouth, like why don't something make a detour down his way? And sometimes, when Ma ain't lookin', I'd slip him a piece of fat off my pork chop.

But now we both been fed, and Shiloh sure loves to romp after a good dinner. I lay down on the floor and hide my face in my arms, and that dog goes nuts. Tries every which way to roll me over, and finally he'll run his nose up under my arm and all down my side, and get to tickling me so I laugh and have to turn over, and then he's happy.

Ma's watching from over in her chair and smiling. "Maybe he thinks you're not breathing, Marty, lyin' so still. Maybe he's got to see you're still alive," she says.

Hard to tell sometimes if that dog's playin' or workin', but we roll around till we're both wore out, and then I lay still on my back and let him put his head on my chest. Stroke his ears and think how I must be one of the luckiest people in the whole state of West Virginia.

February turns to March, and every now and then we get a little taste of spring. Wind feels just a bit warmer. You walk outside and everywhere you hear the sound of running water. Snow sliding off the roof, ice melting on the shed, and all the extra water makes the creek run higher and faster, so the sound's louder than it was. Every day the heaps of dirty snow that the plow left at the side of the road get smaller and smaller, and now and then there's a good hard rain that almost melts it down while you watch.

In between the rains, the sun shines warmer and brighter, and all the water in the ditches and gullies shines back at you. Ma sees her crocuses starting to come up, and goes out to count them.

Judd works at Whelan's Garage every other Saturday, meanin' that every other week he's got the weekend off. Once in a while I hang around his place—help him wash his truck, maybe.

Can't say I see a huge change in the way he treats his dogs, but I see some. He don't cuss at 'em like he used to, and I don't see him kick 'em. Now and then he'll reach out to pet one of 'em, but they always shy away a little when he does that. Guess it's the same with animals as it is with people—takes them a long time to win back trust.

"I think your dogs are happier now that they got a yard to run in, don't have a chain around their necks," I tell him as I wipe the hubcaps on his pickup.

"Seem happy," Judd says. "Neighbors say they don't bark as much."

"Well, that's good, then," I tell him. "Fence holding up okay?"

"Yeah, but I wish I'd put a gate in it after all. When I'm in the backyard and want to go round front, I got to go in through the trailer first," Judd says.

"Well, we got the extra fencing behind your shed," I say. "Want me to help you put the gate on?"

"I'm going over to Middlebourne today, but you can come by tomorrow, you want to," Judd says.

"Sure," I tell him.

109

* * *

Sunday's on the cold side, but when the sun comes out from behind a cloud, the air takes on a different feel. Something about a March sun on the back of your neck, you *know* spring's not far off. Shiloh's out with the black Labrador somewhere, and I'm glad, 'cause we both seem to feel guilty when I head for Judd's—Shiloh, for not comin' with me, and me, 'cause I'm goin' somewhere without him. But today he don't have to watch me leave, and I tell Dad I'll be back soon as I help Judd put on that gate.

When I get to the trailer, Judd's dogs are having a fine time out in the yard. He's thrown 'em an old sock with a knot in it, and they are just chewin' it to pieces, growlin' and tugging and shakin' their heads back and forth, holding on with their teeth for dear life. Keeps 'em busy while we work on the fence. Judd's got pliers and a hammer, and he unhooks the wire from one of the poles. We roll it up and haul his gate into place. Got to move another pole over closer, and fasten some hinges on it.

It ain't as easy as it first seemed. I'm holdin' the gate upright and Judd's tryin' to hammer a pin down inside a hinge. His dogs are still at work on that sock, tumbling around and makin' like they're all so fierce. John Collins says that tug-o'-war's a game you shouldn't play with your dogs—makes 'em aggressive; turns 'em mean. But we done enough preaching already, and I'm not about to tell Judd how his dogs should *play*.

Suddenly—it happens so fast I almost miss it—Judd steps backward to test the gate, and the heel of his boot comes down hard on the left front paw of the black-and-white dog. Dog gives this loud yelp, Judd turns, lookin' to

110

see what's happened, and next thing we know, the black and white's sunk his teeth deep in Judd's leg.

Judd's bellowing in pain, I'm trying to call his dog off, the other dogs are barking, and a neighbor down the way opens her back door to see what's going on.

All the noise just seems to put the black-and-white dog in a frenzy. He's the biggest one of the lot, and he's tuggin' at Judd's leg like a piece of meat, growlin' something terrible. It's as though all the anger and meanness that dog's felt for Judd all these years is right now comin' up out of his mouth. Judd groans, swears, bellows again, tryin' to swing himself around, get the leg free, but he can't.

I'm about to run inside for a pail of water to throw on that dog when Judd lifts the hammer, hangs back a moment, then brings it down on the black and white's head.

The dog's legs give out from under him, his jaw goes slack, then he slumps to the ground and lays still.

Seventeen

I can't hardly breathe. Don't know who to head for, Judd or the dog, so I don't move at all.

"Clyde!" comes the neighbor's voice. "Judd Travers just killed that dog!"

That gets my feet moving. I go over to the black and white and put my hand on his chest to see if the heart's beating. Then I feel for the pulse on the inside of his hind leg, the way John Collins taught me. Nothing at all.

I look over at Judd. He's sittin' on the ground, arms on his knees, head on his arms. His pant leg's soaked with blood. The other two dogs have crept off to a far corner, just watching. Don't make a sound.

"Judd," I say, "you sit tight. I'm callin' Doc Murphy." And I run to the back door of his trailer.

"What's happened over there?" calls the neighbor's husband.

"Dog attacked Judd," I call back, but all the while I'm wondering, did he have to *kill* him? Judd's leg looks bad, though. Not the same leg that was broke, either. The other one. Now he's got *two* bum legs.

Doc Murphy says he's just about to walk out the door, going to visit his brother down in Parkersburg, and I say, "Doc, Judd's been hurt by one of his dogs and he's bleedin' pretty bad."

"Where you calling from, Marty?"

"Here at Judd's," I tell him. "He's out back."

I go out the door again. Judd is in the same position I left him, but he suddenly rears back and socks the fist of his right hand into the palm of his left just about as hard as a man can hit, cussing hisself out. Then he slumps again, and don't lift his head.

"Anything we can do?" the neighbor woman calls.

"Doc's on his way over," I yell back.

I sit down beside Judd. He's shakin' his head back and forth, back and forth, his shoulders twitching once or twice like he's about to hit himself again.

"My best hunting dog," he says. "Now I've lost two." I know he's counting Shiloh.

"This one ever do anything like that before?" I ask.

"Was always chained before. Don't know what got into him this time. I never meant to step on his paw."

"I know you didn't," I say.

He eases up his pant leg, and that is some bite. Big flap of skin just hanging there.

We hear a car coming down the road from the bridge, and it's not long before Doc Murphy makes a U-turn in front of Judd's and pulls his car off the pavement. Comes hurrying around to the back and walks through the opening

113

in the fence. Judd's other two dogs don't even bark. One of 'em's lying down now, head on his paws. Look like they're both too scared to move. They can tell something's happened to the black and white.

Doc Murphy grunts and sets his bag on the ground, then bends over Judd's leg and gives a whistle. His eye falls on the dead dog, blood oozing out one corner of his mouth, eyes fogged over. Sees the hammer, too, and shakes his head.

"You provoke that dog, Judd?"

"No, he didn't," I say, answering for him. "I seen the whole thing. Judd accidentally stepped on his paw. The dog bit him and wouldn't let go."

Doc sighs. "Well, we got trouble enough right here," he says. "Come in the house, Judd, where I can sew you up. Don't like to stitch up a dog bite if I can help it. Better to keep the wound open, keep it clean, but this one's going to take a whole bunch of stitches, I can tell you."

Seems like Judd just got through limpin' on one leg, and now he's limpin' on the other. I unwind that roll of wire fence back again and stretch it over the opening where the gate was to be so the other two dogs won't get out, and I fasten it good. Then I go inside. Soon as the yard's empty, I see the other dogs come over and sniff the black and white. One of 'em makes a whining sound in his throat. Don't tell me dogs don't cry!

I sit off to one side while Doc works on Judd. Got him sitting up on the table, leg stretched out on a towel where Doc can reach it. I get some more towels, and some hot water, scrub up good, and hand Doc things as he needs them.

"Okay, now, Judd," Doc says at last. "Don't want you to get that bandage wet. You come by in a couple of days, let me take a look at it, and we'll take the stitches out in two weeks or so. I got to pump you full of antibiotics now before I leave." He writes out a prescription, too. "And I got to take that dog with me; it's the law. Check him for rabies."

"Tell 'em I want him back," says Judd, real soft.

Doc turns around. "What you say?"

"I want the body back when they're done with it."

"Sure, Judd," Doc says. "I'll tell them."

I find an old box out back. Roll the dog's body into the box, and set it on the floor of Doc's car.

When he's gone, I go inside to wash up, see if Judd wants me to stay. He don't. He's on the couch, staring straight ahead.

Finally I tell him, "I'm sure sorry today turned out like it did."

But he don't answer, and I leave.

I tell my family what happened. Everyone's looking real sorry, even Dara Lynn.

Ma sighs. "Some people just seem to attract trouble," she says at last.

And Dad says, "Does seem like there should have been some other way to make that dog let go, but I don't know what. A dog get his teeth in you like that, he can tear you up mighty quick."

One good thing about bein' an animal is you don't have to know all the bad things happening around you. When Dara Lynn and me walk down to the school bus stop on Monday, Shiloh goes dancin' along beside us, frisky as you please. Don't even know one of his own kind was killed. But I see that all the sorry's gone out of Dara Lynn's eyes, too, and there's pure eagerness in its place.

"Listen here," I say. "I don't want you tellin' *any*body that Judd killed one of his dogs. Hear?"

"You can't make me not tell!" she says.

"If you tell what Judd did, I'll tell the whole bus how you threw up on your new shoes last summer," I say.

Dara Lynn's mad as hornets. "Okay!" she shouts. "I won't say he killed a dog!"

The bus comes and we get on, and the first thing out of her mouth is worse: "Judd Travers killed something yesterday!" And then, to me, "I didn't say *what*, did I?"

Fact is, couple of the kids had already heard, so the whole bus already knew.

"Just picked up a hammer and hit his own dog over the head. That's what his neighbor said," Fred Niles tells the rest.

"Listen!" I say. "I saw it happen. That dog was tearing up his leg. If Judd hadn't hit him when he did, he might not be walking now."

"Yeah, but why do his dogs hate him so much? Ask him that!" says Michael Sholt.

I worry a lot about Judd after that. Doc Murphy says he come by to have his stitches out, and the wound's healing nicely. The black and white didn't have rabies, the test showed, and as far as Doc knows, Judd's going to work every day. But when Judd's out in his truck and passes me on the road, it's like he don't even see me.

I go over once to ask if he wants to finish putting that gate on yet, 'cause the wire fencing's right where I left it, the gate swingin' in the breeze with no opening there at all. Judd's truck's out in front, but when I knock, nobody answers. I call, but nobody comes.

I go around in back to see if Judd's there. His two dogs

are inside the fence, but beyond that, out past his satellite dish, even, I see a little mound of fresh dirt at the edge of Judd's property. I walk back, hands in my pockets, and look down. There's a horseshoe stake driven in the ground at the head of this little grave, and around the stake is a dog's leather collar.

Eighteen

Seems like maybe we're back where we started with Judd Travers. Can't tell what's going on in his mind, 'cause he don't ever stop to talk to me. Saturdays I'll see him pass by out there on the road two, three times, but if I'm out there he don't even wave. Either he's mad at me, I figure, for bringin' that fence by in the first place, or he's grievin' for his dog.

Maybe all my work to be friendly and to give his dogs a better life is going to backfire, and when he looks at me, what he'll think about is how two of his dogs are gone.

"Just you stay away from him for a while," says Dad. "You got to give a man time to sort things through."

Closer it gets to April, the more it rains. Not a bit of snow left. Everything's mud, and just when you think there's not a drop of water could be left in the sky, it rains some more.

When it rains hard enough and long enough, Middle Island Creek overflows its banks and we get stranded. Being up the hill a ways from the road, our house don't get wet, but there's a stretch of road near the church in Little that floods when the creek is really high. "The Narrows," we call it, and Dad'll have to get to work another way. What we do is count the layers of stones in the supports that hold up the bridge here in Shiloh. If we can only see nine stones between the bottom of the bridge and the top of the water, we know the road down at Little will be flooded. More than nine, we're probably okay.

On Saturday when I go to the vet's, there's a litter of kittens somebody found along the creek. A mama cat had gone in one of those school bus shelters, no bigger than a phone booth, and had her babies, and the water was threatening to carry them off. She was meowing and somebody heard and brought 'em to John Collins. Hadn't even got their eyes opened yet.

I'm making sure each of those babies gets a turn at the mother's milk, and thinking how Dara Lynn wanted a kitten even before I wanted Shiloh. Can't believe I'm thinking what I am, but I say, "I'll take one of those kittens, Doc Collins."

"You get your pick, Marty," he says. "But you'll have to wait till they're eight weeks old. You don't want to take them from their mother too early."

Dara Lynn's got a birthday in May, and that'll be just about the right time to surprise her. But knowing my sister, she'll probably say something ugly—like how come she didn't get to choose it herself, or I got the wrong color. Sometimes you just have to take chances.

Somebody brings in a dog that morning to be checked

over 'cause he's tearing up the furniture. The man says that every time he comes home from work in the evening, the dog's destroyed something else.

I scratch the retriever's ears while John Collins talks to the owner—explains that dogs, like people, want a little more out of life than just hanging round waiting for somebody to come home, pay them some attention. They got to feel needed.

"Let your dog know that when you come home, it's his time, and you expect things of him," Doc says, "even if it's only to bring in the paper or chase the squirrels away from the bird feeder. Your dog wants to know he has a purpose."

The last Saturday in March, Dad picks me up after my job at the vet's and then we pick up David. Been raining all week, off and on, and the water's right high, lapping at the side of the road through the Narrows. When we get to the Shiloh bridge, we see there're only ten layers of stones showing on the supports between the floor of the bridge and the top of the water.

"It's close," Dad says.

He drops us off at the driveway and goes on to deliver the rest of his mail, and David and I run up to the house where Ma's got grilled cheese sandwiches and tomato soup waiting.

"Da-vid!" sings out Becky, all smiles, when she sees him. Girls always like to show off for David.

"Hi, Popcorn," says David.

Then Dara Lynn has to be her usual nuisance, and keeps kickin' us under the table and pretending it was Becky did it.

"Dara Lynn, will you stop it?" I snap, almost sorry I'm savin' that kitten for her.

120

"Dara Lynn, I'm not tellin' you again! Behave!" says Ma, and I notice she's holding her cheek. "I got no patience with you today." And then she gives this little half smile to David and says, "Sorry I'm not more cheery, but I got a toothache that is making my whole face sore."

I take a good look at Ma. "It's swelling up some, too," I say.

She feels with her hand, then goes and looks in the mirror. "Guess I ought to have gone to the dentist like your dad said," she tells me.

She goes back in the bedroom and lies down, and we try to keep it quiet in the living room. We spread out my Monopoly set on the floor and let Dara Lynn play, but when you get down on the rug like that, Shiloh thinks it's playtime, and he wiggles and rolls and tries to lick our faces, and soon the houses on Park Place are all over the board. Becky thinks it's funny, but Dara Lynn gets mad.

"Stupid old dog!" she yells, and hits at him hard. Shiloh gives this little yelp and comes around behind me. I swoop all Dara Lynn's houses and money off the board, and tell her the game's over. "Don't you ever, never, hit my dog!" I say.

"Oh, who wants to play Monopoly, anyway? Come on, Becky," she says, and the girls go off to their bedroom, get down the box of old jewelry Grandma Preston give them once, and try on all the pieces.

It's raining lightly outside, and David and me are waiting for it to stop. Then we're going back to the old Shiloh schoolhouse to see if we can find any more stuff those men left behind—keep it for a souvenir.

We horse around a little, try to teach Shiloh to help David take his jacket off, make himself useful. But Shiloh yanks too hard on one sleeve and a seam pulls out at the shoulder.

Ma comes out of the bedroom and makes some calls in the kitchen, then comes over to me.

"Marty, I've called the dentist and he says if I can get down there right now, he'll take me today. This toothache's gettin' worse and worse. I called Mrs. Sweeney, and she said she and her daughter are going to Sistersville and they think they can squeeze me in the cab of their pickup, too. Mrs. Ellison is going to come up here and watch you kids till I get back."

"We don't need a sitter!" I say, embarrassed.

"Maybe not, but the girls do, and I want you to behave for her now. Hear?"

She goes in the bathroom to brush her teeth, and by the time she's got her coat on, we can see Mrs. Sweeney's pickup coming up the drive. Ma goes out and gets in.

Great! I'm thinking. David comes for an overnight, and we get a baby-sitter! Mrs. Ellison's nice, though. Always leaves a little something in her mailbox for Dad when she bakes, and I'm thinking she might show up with a chocolate cake. At least Dara Lynn and Becky are having a fine time in their bedroom, and are leaving David and me alone for a change. We open a pop and watch a basketball game on TV.

Fifteen minutes go by, though, and Mrs. Ellison still hasn't come. Phone rings and she says, "Marty, your ma still there?" I tell her she's gone, and Mrs. Ellison says, "Well, the water here in Little is higher than I thought, and I'm afraid if I get over to your place in our Buick, I might not make it back again. Sam's on his way home right now, and he's going to drive me to your house in the four by four. Everything okay there?"

"Everything's fine," I tell her.

No sooner hang up than it rings again, and this time it's Michael Sholt.

"Marty!" he says. "I'm up at my cousin's, and there's a dead man floating down the creek! He just went by! Should be by your place in five minutes. Go see who he is!"

Nineteen

I drop that phone and David and me grab our jackets and run outside, Shiloh at our heels. The rain's tapered off, but there's mud everywhere. We don't care, though. We run up on the bridge and wait right in the middle, looking upstream. That is one wild-looking creek!

"You suppose dead men float on their backs or their stomachs?" I ask David.

"Stomachs," he says. "That's the way they do in the movies, anyway."

Who could it be? I wonder. Bet someone's called the sheriff already and there'll be men waiting down at the bend where the water slows—see if they can snag him, pull him in. Wouldn't it be something if David and me could find out who he is, and be the first to call the paper? And then the thought come to me: What if it's Judd Travers? Don't know what made me think that, but it just crossed my mind.

We stand out there on the bridge watching that muddy water come rushing at us and disappear under our feet. No one in the *world* would think Middle Island Creek was anything but a river now.

"You figure five minutes are up?" I ask David.

"Probably ten," he says. "What if Michael was kidding? Be just like him, you know. Get us standing out here on the bridge waiting to see a dead man, and him and his cousin laughing their heads off."

We stare some more at the water. You look at a river long enough, it makes you dizzy.

"There's something!" David yells suddenly, and I look hard where he's pointing. Sure enough, bobbing around the curve ahead is something about the size of a man. When it bumps a rock, we see an arm fly up.

"Jiminy!" breathes David.

We run to the far side of the bridge where it looks like the body is heading. Can't tell what color his hair is—can't even see his hair, just the shape of his head, and then his feet, tossing about on the current like the feet of Becky's rag doll.

"Here he comes!" yells David, just as I see Dara Lynn and Becky cross the road.

"Go on back!" I yell. "We're comin' right up." I turn toward the water again, and next I know, the body's coming smack toward us, sliding under the bridge, and we see it's no dead man at all, it's one of those dummies left over from Halloween.

"Ah, shoot!" says David, as we turn and watch it pop out from under the bridge on the other side, its straw-stuffed legs flopping this way and that. Even Shiloh's been fooled—runs across to the other side and barks.

125

"What was *that?*" Dara Lynn demands, hurrying over. She and Becky got their shoes on, but the laces are flopping, and Becky's jacket's inside out.

"It wasn't nothing—just somebody's Halloween dummy," I say. "Go on back to the house, I said!"

"Don't have to!" says Dara Lynn, sticking out her chin. "Ma didn't say I couldn't come down here. I can walk on the bridge same as you."

"We're all goin' back," I tell her.

But David's mad at Michael Sholt. "Bet he knew it was a dummy all along," he's grumbling. "Maybe he and his cousin dropped it in the creek themselves!"

Becky goes over to the edge of the bridge where the railing makes a diamond pattern. She's lookin' at a spiderweb strung in one of those openings. It glistens silver from the rain. I'm thinking that this water is rising faster than I ever seen it before, as though a couple more creeks have suddenly emptied into it up the way, and it's all of them together rushing under the bridge now.

"Come on," I say again, stopping to tie Becky's shoes for her. "We're goin' up to the house. Mrs. Ellison'll be along, wonder where we went."

Becky starts off again, Shiloh trotting ahead of her, and David catches up with me, talking about what he's going to do if Michael starts a story around that he saw a dead man in Middle Island Creek.

"Look at me!" sings out Dara Lynn behind us. I turn and see she's worked her head through one of those diamond openings in the railing, acting like she's a bird, going to sail out over the creek. Her big puffy jacket on one side of the opening, her head on the other, she looks more like a turtle. Girl can't stand not having all the attention on her.

126

"Dara Lynn, you cut that out and come on," I say. "Get on up to the house."

She just laughs. I grab her by the arm and pull her back through the railing just as the Ellisons' four by four turns in our drive and moves on up to the house.

"I got it!" says David. "If Michael says there was a dead man in the creek, we'll say we saw him, too. Only we'll make it different. Say it was a man with red hair and a blue shirt on."

I laugh. "His face all swole up. . . ."

"And he looked like he'd been shot in the heart!" says David. We both laugh out loud, thinking of Michael's face if we turn that trick around.

"'What'd I miss?' he'll be thinking," I say, "and . . ."

"Who-eeee!" I hear Dara Lynn whoop. I turn around and my heart shoots up to my mouth, 'cause right at our end of the bridge, Dara Lynn's climbed up on the railing, her skinny legs straddling it, one foot locked behind a metal bar to keep her balance. Both her arms are in the air, like kids do on a roller-coaster.

"Dara Lynn," I bellow, my voice cracking. "Get off there!"

She laughs, and in her hurry to climb up where I can't reach her, wobbles, grabs at the rail to steady herself, but misses. There's this short little scream, and then . . . then she's in the water.

"Dara *Lynn!*"

Stomach feels like I'm on a roller-coaster myself. Can't even swallow. I'm hanging over the rail, but Dara Lynn's too far down to reach. She's lookin' up at me with the wildest, whitest eyes I ever seen, her arms straight out at the sides like the cold of the water has paralyzed her. And then,

127

just like the straw man, she disappears beneath the bridge.

David's shouting something, I don't know what, and Becky's run screaming up our driveway, then turns around and screams some more. I can see Mr. and Mrs. Ellison running down the drive toward her. David is running over to the railing on the other side of the bridge, his face as white as cream.

"Where is she?" he asks, turning to me. "She didn't come back out."

I am running around the end of the bridge, slipping and sliding down the bank toward the high water.

"What happened?" Mrs. Ellison calls.

"Dara Lynn fell in," I yell, and it's more like a sob.

"Oh, Lord, no!" cries Mrs. Ellison in the background, offering up a prayer for all of us.

All I can think of is havin' to tell Ma that Dara Lynn drowned. Of having to remember every last awful thing I ever said to her, like wishin' she'd fall in a hole and pull the dirt in after her. I am praying to Jesus that if he will save my sister I will never say a mean thing to her as long as I live, even while I know it's not humanly possible. "Just don't let her die, please, please!" I whisper. She'll drown without ever knowin' I gave her a kitten.

I squat down, lookin' under the bridge. I see that Dara Lynn's been snagged by the small trees and bushes sticking out of the water near the first support. At that moment she feels herself caught, and her arms come alive, floppin' and flailin' to turn herself around, and finally she's holding on, screamin' herself crazy.

Mr. Ellison's beside me now, and he's shouting instructions to Dara Lynn to pull herself hand over hand toward the bank, to grab on to the next branch and the next, and not let go on any account, while he wades out into that swirling water as far as he can to meet her.

It's when Dara Lynn pulls herself close enough for us to grab her that I think maybe the thumpin' in my chest won't kill me after all. But then it seems my heart stops altogether, for I see Shiloh out there in the water, the current carrying him farther and farther away. I know right off he jumped in to save Dara Lynn, and now he's got to save himself.

Twenty

All I hear is my scream.

We're haulin' Dara Lynn out, her clothes making a sucking sound as she leaves the water, but I can see my dog trying to paddle toward us; the current's against him, and he can't even keep himself in one place.

Most times Shiloh could throw himself into Middle Island Creek, chasing a stick I'd tossed, and come right out where he'd gone in, the water moves that slow. But when the rains are heavy and the creek swells fast, the water just tumbles around the bend, and Shiloh's never been in nothing like this before. He keeps tryin' to turn himself around in the water and get back to us.

"Shiloh!" I'm yellin', while behind me, back up on the road, Becky sets up a wail of despair.

"Oh, Lord Jesus, that little dog!" cries Mrs. Ellison, praying again, while her husband takes off his coat and wraps it around Dara Lynn. Dara Lynn's crying, too—huge sobs.

Is God puttin' me to some kind of test, I wonder—saving my sister and drowning my dog? Did I trade one for the other? Lord knows I can't swim. Oh, Jesus, why didn't you make me go to the park in Sistersville and take lessons with Sarah Peters? Why'd I get to sixth grade and not even know how to float?

My mouth don't seem connected to my head. Can still hear it screaming. "Shiloh! Shiloh!"

All he's doin' is tirin' himself out tryin' to swim back to us.

I slide farther down the bank, one foot in the water.

"Don't you try to go in there, Marty," Mr. Ellison shouts.

I claw my way back up the bank, eyes stretched wide, thinkin' how I can make better time up on the road, maybe get myself down to the place where the creek narrows, and Shiloh might be close enough I can reach out to him somehow.

David's running beside me. I know I'm cryin' but I don't care. One foot squishes every time my shoe hits the pavement. Run as fast as we can.

And then I see this pickup comin' up the road from Friendly, and I'm like to get myself run over.

Judd Travers stops and leans out the window. "You want to get yourself killed?" he calls, right angry. And then, "What's the matter, Marty?" Sees Mr. Ellison comin' up the road behind me, thinks he's chasin' me, maybe. He gets out of the truck.

I'm gasping. Point to the creek.

"Shiloh! He's in the water, and we can't reach him!"

"Marty, that dog will have to get himself out!" Mrs. Ellison calls from far behind us. "Don't you try to go after him, now."

But Judd crashes through the trees and brush, half sliding down the muddy bank, and I point to the head of my beagle back upstream, out there bobbing around in the current. Once, it looks like he goes under. Now David's cryin', too, squeaky little gasps.

Judd don't say a word. He's scramblin' up the bank again and grabs that rope in his pickup. Hobbles down the road, fast as his two bum legs will carry him, goin' even farther downstream, me and David at his heels. Then he ties one end of that rope to a tree at the edge of the water, the other end around his waist, taking his time to make a proper square knot, and I'm thinkin', Don't worry about knots, Judd—just go!

He's plunging into that cold water—all but his boots, which he leaves by the tree. I see now why he went so far downstream, 'cause if we were back closer to the bridge, Shiloh would have gone past us by now.

Another car stops up on the road. I hear voices.

"What happened?"

"Who's out there?"

And Mr. Ellison's giving the answers: "Judd Travers is going after Marty Preston's dog."

Mrs. Ellison and the girls have reached the spot now. Dara Lynn is dripping water, but she won't hear of going home. Every muscle in my body is straining to keep me as close to the water as I can get, my eyes trained on that muddy yellow surface, looking for Shiloh. Maybe this was a mistake. Maybe I should have stayed back where we saw him last, kept my eye on where he went. What if he's pulled under? What if his strength just gave out, and he can't paddle no more?

David gives a shout. We can see Shiloh now. Looks for a time like he's found something to crawl up on out there in that water, a tree limb or something, but while we watch, he's swept away again.

Judd's treading water out in the center of Middle Island Creek, fighting the current himself, and Shiloh's about twenty feet upstream from him. But then—as I stare—I see him turning away from Judd! I wonder if my dog knows how much danger he's in. Wonder if he figures that between the water and Judd Travers, he'll take the water.

"Here, Shiloh! Come here, boy!" Judd calls, his hair all matted down over his eyes.

Shiloh seems spooked. He's lookin' straight ahead, neither to the right nor left. I see his eyes close again, the way he looks lyin' by the stove at night when he's about to fall asleep.

Judd's working his way out farther and farther, trying to get out in the middle of the creek before Shiloh goes by. He's got his head down now, his arms slicing through the water, but it seems like for every three strokes he takes forward, the creek carries him one stroke sideways.

"Don't give up, Shiloh!" I breathe. And then I begin yelling his name. "Come on, Shiloh! Go to Judd. Come on, boy! Come on!"

I wonder if Judd can make it in time. What if Shiloh's too far out and sails on by? What if the rope's not long enough for Judd to reach him? My breath's coming out all shaky.

Judd's out now about as far as he can go, and that rope is stretched taut. One hand is reaching way out, but seems like Shiloh's still trying to paddle away.

"No, Shiloh!" I plead.

Just then Judd gives this whistle. I know that when Shiloh was his, he was taught to come when Judd whistled. Come or else.

I see my dog start to turn. I see Judd's hand go out, and I hear Judd sayin', "Come on, boy. Come on, Shiloh. Ain't going to hurt you none."

And then . . . then my dog's in his arms, and Judd's shoulders go easy. He is just letting that current swing him on downstream and back to the bank. The rope is holding, and Judd don't have to work much—just let the creek do all the carrying.

I slosh along the bank down to where I can see Judd is headed. The Ellisons are going there, too, and a couple of men up on the road.

"Anybody got a blanket?" I hear someone say.

"I got one in my trunk," a man answers.

Arms are reaching out, hands ready. Somebody puts an old blanket around Judd's shoulders soon as he climbs out.

And now Shiloh's against my chest, his rough tongue licking me up one side of my face and down the other, his little body shaking. With Shiloh in one arm, I reach out and put my other around Judd.

"Thanks," I say, my voice all husky. "Thank you, Judd." I'd say more if I could, but I'm all choked up. I just give him a hug with my one free arm, and strangest of all, Judd hugs me back. It's a sort of jerky, awkward hug, like he hadn't had much practice, but it's a start.

I won't repeat what-all my folks said to us later. Dad does the yelling, Ma the crying, and David's got to sit and listen to the whole thing. That me and David went down to that swollen creek in the first place! That we left the girls alone! That Dara Lynn was reckless enough to climb up on that bridge railing. . . .

"Isn't it enough I have the worst toothache of my life without having to come home and find one of my daughters almost drowned?" weeps Ma.

I keep sayin', "I'm sorry"—David, too—but Dad tells us "sorry" wouldn't bring a dead girl back to life. Neither of 'em says anything about Shiloh. That ain't their worry right now.

Dara Lynn hangs her head like the starch has been knocked out of her. Just sits all quiet by the potbellied stove, arms wrapped around her middle. Becky's on the couch, suckin' her thumb. We are the sorriest-looking family right now, but my dog's safe in my arms, and I can't ask for more. Every time he wriggles to get down, I just hold him tighter, and finally he gives up and lays still, knowin' my arms'll get tired by and by.

Next day, though, after Mr. Howard comes for David, my folks are quiet. Seem like every time they walk by one of us, they squeeze a shoulder or pat a head or stroke somebody's hair.

That night after Becky's had her bath and has gone around givin' everyone her butterfly kiss, battin' her lashes against their cheeks, I go out in the kitchen where Dara Lynn's having her graham crackers and milk, and say, "Well, pretty soon you're goin' to have to be sharing that milk with someone else, you know."

She looks at me suspicious-like. "Why?" she says.

"'Cause we're gettin' another member of the family, that's why."

Dara Lynn's eyes open wide. "Ma's having another baby?"

I laugh. "Not this kind of baby, she ain't. It's gonna be your birthday present from me, Dara Lynn. Somebody brought in a litter of kittens to Doc Collins. You want to come with me some Saturday and pick one out, it's yours."

Dara Lynn leaps off her chair and, with graham cracker crumbs on her fingers, hugs me hard. I hug back—a little jerky and awkward, but it's a start.

Everybody's talkin' about Judd Travers. Michael Sholt thought he was going to have the best story of all—that Halloween dummy he and his cousin dumped in the creek to fool us—but it's Judd everyone wants to hear about.

After David told his dad what had happened, Mr. Howard drove up to Judd's a few days later to write a story about him for the paper. But then, everyone from here to Friendly could tell it—how Dara Lynn fell in the creek, how Shiloh jumped in to save her, and Judd went in for Shiloh.

Asked what he was thinking about out there in that rushing water, Judd said, "Well, I guess I was worried some but I was more scared of not saving Shiloh, on account of that dog once saved me."

Once that newspaper story come out, someone even asked Judd if he'd like to be a volunteer for the Rescue Squad down in Sistersville. He's thinking on it.

We talk about it some in school—how dangerous a flood can get—and on the way home one afternoon, sittin' there beside David Howard, I say, "If you'd asked me last summer if Judd Travers would be a hero, I would have bet my cowboy hat it couldn't happen."

"I'd have bet my new Nikes," says David.

"Not in a million years," I say.

I eat the snack Ma's put out for me, and then—with Dara Lynn and Becky playin' out on the bag swing—I head over to Judd Travers' place. His pickup's not there—he's still at work—but I got a hammer stickin' out of one pocket, pliers and wire clippers out of the other.

His dogs bark like crazy when they see me comin' around the trailer, but they know me now, and I let them sniff my fingers before I unhook that wire fencing and start to work on the gate. Me and Judd almost had it done. I see how he got one of the hinges around that pole, and I set to work on the other. What'll it be like, I'm wondering, not to have to worry anymore about Judd Travers hurting my beagle? To visit him and not have to worry is he drunk? Pretty nice, I reckon.

Gettin' the gate to swing right ain't—isn't—as easy as it seems. You got to get the hinges on straight up and down, or the gate will hang crooked. I see I got the pin shafts turned to one side so the gate's tipped. Got to loosen the bolts and start all over again. But finally, when I give the gate a push, it opens in and it opens out, just the way Judd needs it to do.

I clip off the extra fencing, put it back behind Judd's shed. And then, makin' sure that gate's latched the way it's supposed to be, I go back up the road to where Shiloh's still waiting for me at the bridge. I scoop him up in my arms and let him wash my face good—beagle breath and all.

I'm thinking that someday, maybe, when I cross that bridge and head down this road to Judd's trailer, Shiloh might come along, sure that he's mine forever and nothing's going to change that.

Don't know if a dog—or a man, either—ever gets to the place where he can forget as well as forgive, but enough miracles have come my way lately to make me think that this could happen, too.

The Shiloh Trilogy

by

PHYLLIS REYNOLDS NAYLOR

Shiloh

Shiloh Season

Saving Shiloh
